André Malraux, Compagnon de la Libération and Officier de la Légion d'Honneur, was born in 1901. He was educated in Paris, where he studied archaeology and orientalism, and made his first Asian visit, to China and Indo-China, in 1923–25. He has held a number of important posts: he was president of the World Committee for the liberation of Dimitroff, responsible for taking protests to Hitler against the trial of the Reichstag offenders, and served with the Spanish Republican Government in 1936. He served in the Second World War. Malraux is a member of the Council of French Museums and of the Sanscrit University of Benares. He is also an Hon. D.C.L. of Oxford and a D.S.O. He has been Minister of State for Cultural Affairs of the Fifth Republic of France since 1960. Translations of his other books into English include, *The Walnut Tree of Attenburg*, *Psychology of Art*, *The Voices of Silence*, *The Human Condition*, *The Metamorphosis of the Gods*, and his most recent work, *Antimemoirs*, is also available in Penguins.

ANDRÉ MALRAUX

DAYS OF HOPE

Translated from the French by

STUART GILBERT
AND ALASTAIR MACDONALD

PENGUIN BOOKS
in association with Hamish Hamilton

Penguin Books Ltd, Harmondsworth, Middlesex, England
Penguin Books Australia Ltd, Ringwood, Victoria, Australia

—

L'Espoir first published in 1938
This translation published in Great Britain by Routledge 1938
Re-issued by Hamish Hamilton 1968
Published in Penguin Books 1970

—

Copyright © André Malraux, 1968

—

Made and printed in Great Britain
by Hazell Watson & Viney Ltd,
Aylesbury, Bucks
Set in Intertype Granjon

Contents

PART ONE

CARELESS RAPTURE

ONE

Careless Rapture

I

ALL Madrid was astir in the warm summer night loud with the rumble of lorries stacked with rifles. For some days the Workers' Organizations had been announcing that a fascist rising might take place at any moment, that the soldiers in the barracks had been 'got at', and that munitions were pouring in. At 1 a.m. the Government had decided to arm the people, and from 3 a.m. the production of a union-card entitled every member to be issued with a rifle. It was high time, for the reports telephoned in from the provinces, which had sounded hopeful between midnight and 2 a.m., were beginning to strike a different note.

The Central Exchange at the Northern Railway Terminus rang up the various stations along the line. Ramos, the Secretary of the Railway Workers' Union, and Manuel were in charge. With the exception of Navarre – the line from which had been cut – the replies had been uniform. Either the Government had the situation well in hand, or a Workers' Committee had taken charge of the city, pending instructions from the central authority. But now a change was coming over the dialogues.

'Is that Huesca?'

'Who's speaking?'

'The Workers' Committee, Madrid.'

'Not for long, you swine! *Arriba España!*'

Fixed to the wall by drawing-pins, the special late edition of the *Claridad* flaunted a caption six columns wide: *Comrades To Arms!*

'Hullo, Avila? How's things at your end? Madrid North speaking.'

'The hell it is, you bastards! *Viva El Cristo Rey!*'

'See you soon. *Salud!*'

An urgent message was put through to Ramos.

The Northern lines linked up with Saragossa, Burgos, and Valladolid.

'Is that Saragossa? Put me through to the Workers' Committee at the station.'

'We've shot them. Your turn next. *Arriba España!*'

'Hullo, Tablada! Madrid North here, Union Delegate.'

'Call the jail, you son of a gun. That's where your friends are. And we'll be coming for you in a day or two; we want to have a word with you.'

'*Bueno!* Let's meet on the Alcalá, second dive on the left. Got it?'

All the telephone operators were staring at Manuel, whose devil-may-care manner, curly hair, and grin gave him the air of a jovial gangster.

'Hullo, is that Burgos?'

'Commandante, Burgos, speaking.'

Ramos hung up.

A telephone-bell rang.

'Hullo, Madrid! Who's there?'

'Railway Workers' Union.'

'Miranda speaking. We hold the station and the town. *Arriba España!*'

'But *we* hold Madrid. *Salud!*'

So there was no counting on help from the North, except by way of Valladolid. There remained the Asturias.

'Is that Oviedo? Yes? Who's speaking?' Ramos was getting wary.

'Workers' Delegate. Railway Station.'

'Ramos here, the Union Secretary. How are things your end?'

'Aranda's loyal to the Government. It's touch and go at Valladolid. We're entraining three thousand armed miners to reinforce our lot.'

'When?' A clash of rifle-butts drowned the answer. Ramos repeated the question.

'At once.'

'*Salud!*'

Ramos turned to Manuel. 'Keep in touch with that train, by telephone.' Then called Valladolid.

'Is that Valladolid?'

'Who's speaking?'

'Station Delegate.'

'How's it going?'

'Our fellows hold the barracks. We're expecting a reinforcement from Oviedo. Do your best to get them here as soon as possible. But don't you worry; here it'll all go well. What about you?'

They were singing outside the station; Ramos could not hear himself speak.

'What?' Valladolid repeated.

'Going well! Going well!'

'Have the troops revolted?'

'Not yet.'

Valladolid hung up.

All reinforcements from the North could be diverted thither. The air was thick with engine-smoke and the reek of hot metal – the door stood open on the summer night – and a faint odour of cardboard files came from the office shelves. Manuel noted down, amongst official messages concerning points and sidings – of which he could make little – the calls coming in from the various Spanish towns. From outside came bursts of song, a clatter of rifle-butts. Time and again he had to have the messages repeated. The fascists merely rang off. He noted down the various positions, on the railway map. Navarre was cut off; all the east of the Bay of Biscay – Bilbao, Santander, and San Sebastian – was loyal; communications were cut at Miranda. The Asturias and Valladolid, however, were with the government. The telephone rang ceaselessly.

'Hullo! Segovia! speaking. Who are you?'

'Representative of the Union.' Manuel looked at Ramos doubtfully; after all, what was his real position here?

'We're coming along to bite 'em off you.'

'We shan't notice it. *Salud!*'

Now it was the turn of the fascist stations to start ringing up: Sarracin, Lerma, Aranda del Duero, Sepulveda, Burgos again. From Burgos to the Sierra, threats came pouring in faster than the reinforcement trains.

*

13

'Ministry of the Interior speaking. Is that the North Station Exchange? Inform all stations that the Civil Guard and the Assault Guard are with the Government.'

✳

'Madrid South speaking. Is that Ramos? How's it going in the North?'

'They seem to be holding Miranda and a good many places further south. Three thousand miners are going to Valladolid. That district looks pretty good for us. How's things your way?'

'They've occupied the stations at Seville and Granada. The rest's holding out.'

'Cordova?'

'We don't know. There's fighting going on in the suburbs of the towns where they hold the stations. We're in the hell of a jam at Triana. At Pennaroya, too. Look here, what you say about Valladolid's a bit staggering; sure they haven't taken it?'

Ramos changed over to another telephone.

'Hullo, Valladolid! Who's speaking?'

'The Station Delegate.'

'Oh! . . . We'd heard the fascists were in.'

'You heard wrong. All's well. What about you? Have the troops revolted?'

'No.'

✳

'Hullo, Madrid North. Who's speaking?'

'In charge of transportation.'

'Tablada here. Didn't you ring us up?'

'We heard you were all shot, or in jug, or something of the sort.'

'We made a getaway. It's the fascists who're in jug. *Salud!*'

✳

'Casa del Puelbo speaking. Inform all loyal stations that the Government, supported by the popular militia, is master of Barcelona, Murcia, Valencia, and Malaga, all Estremadura and the Mediterranean coast.'

✳

'Hullo! Tordesillas here. Who's speaking?'

'Workers' Council, Madrid.'

'Ah! Bastards of your sort are shot! *Arriba España!*'

Medina del Campo; same dialogue. The Valladolid line was the only main line of communication with the South still open.

'Hullo, Leon! Who's speaking?'

'Union delegate, *Salud*!'

'Madrid North here. Has the miners' train from Oviedo passed?'

'Yes.'

'Do you know where it is?'

'Somewhere near Mayorga, I guess.'

Outside in the Madrid streets all was songs and the clash of rifle-butts.

'Is that Mayorga? Madrid this end. Who's speaking?'

'Who are you?'

'Workers' Council, Madrid.'

The receiver clicked dead. What had become of the train?

'Is that Valladolid? Are you sure of holding till the miners arrive?'

'Dead sure.'

'Mayorga doesn't answer.'

'That don't matter.'

*

'Hullo, Madrid? Oviedo speaking. Aranda's just revolted. Fighting going on.'

'Where's the miners' train?'

'Between Leon and Mayorga.'

'Hold on a moment!' Manuel rang up, Ramos beside him. 'That Mayorga? Madrid here.'

'Who's that?'

'Workers' Council. Who are you?'

'Company Commander, Spanish Falangists. Your train's gone by. you fools. We hold all the stations up to Valladolid. We're waiting for your miners with machine-guns. Aranda's been cleaned up. See you soon!'

'The sooner the better!'

Manuel rang up all the stations between Mayorga and Valladolid, one after the other.

'That Sepulveda? Madrid North this end; Workers' Committee.'

'Yes, your train's gone through, you god-damned fools. And we're coming this week to cut your . . . off, you silly bitches.'

'Sounds like you'd got your genders mixed, my lad. Still . . . *Salud!*'

The calls continued.

'Hullo, Madrid! Is that Madrid? Navalperal de Pinares here. Railway Station. We've rushed the town again. Yes, we disarmed the fascists; they're in clink. Pass the good news along. Their people telephone us every few minutes to know if the town is still theirs. Hullo! Hullo!'

*

'We must send false news out everywhere,' Ramos said.

'They'll check up on it.'

'Still, it'll always give them something to scratch their heads over.'

*

'Hullo, Madrid North? U.G.T. here. Who's speaking?'

'Ramos.'

'We're told a train-load of fascists is on its way, with up-to-date armament. Coming from Burgos, they say. Have you any news of it?'

'We should know about it here; all the stations up to the Sierra are in our hands. Still we'd better take precautions. Hold the line a moment.'

'Manuel, call the Sierra.'

Manuel called one station after another, sawing the air with a ruler as if he were beating time. The whole Sierra was loyal. He called up the General Post Office Exchange. Had the same answer. Obviously, on the near side of the Sierra, either the fascists were lying low, or they'd been crushed.

Still, they were holding half the North. In Navarre, Mola, the former Chief of Police at Madrid, was in command; three quarters of the regular army, as usual, were against the Government. On the Government side were the populace, the Assault Guard, and possibly the Civil Guard as well.

'The U.G.T. here. Is that Ramos?'

'Yes.'

'What about that train?'

Ramos passed on the news. 'And how's things generally?' he asked.

'*Bueno!* Excellent. Except at the War Ministry. At six they said that all was over bar the shouting. We told them they were barking up the wrong tree. But they claim that the militia's sure to scuttle. Anyhow, we don't give a damn for their opinion. ...The men here are making such a shindy singing, I can hardly hear you.'

In the receiver Ramos could hear the songs across the noises of the railway station.

Though the attack had obviously been launched almost everywhere at the same moment, it seemed as if an army on the march were sweeping down; the railway stations held by the fascists were getting nearer and nearer Madrid. And yet there had been such tension in the air for several weeks, the dread of an attack which they might have to face, unarmed, had weighed so heavily on all the populace that tonight's warfare came as an immense relief.

*

'Got your "winter-sports bus" handy?' Ramos asked Manuel.

'Yes.'

He deputed one of the railway officials to take over the Central Exchange. Some months before, Manuel had bought a second-hand car for his ski-ing expeditions in the Sierra. Every Sunday Ramos used it for propaganda work. That night Manuel had put it once again at the disposal of the Communist Party. The party was overwhelmed with work, and Manuel had chosen to cooperate once again with his old friend, Ramos.

'We mustn't have 1934 all over again!' Ramos said. 'Buzz off to Tetuan de las Victorias, will you?'

'Where's that?'

'Cuatro Caminos.'

When they had gone three hundred yards, they were challenged by the first sentry picket.

'Your papers, *Compañeros*.'

'Your papers,' meant his union-card. Manuel rarely had with him his Communist Party card. He earned his living in the film industry as a sound-man, and a vaguely Montparnassian style of dressing enabled him to fancy that he had escaped, anyhow sartorially speaking, from the influence of the bourgeoisie. In the dark, rather thick-set features, only the bushy eyebrows struck in any way a proletarian note. But no sooner had the milicianos glanced in his direction than they saw and recognized the jovial, solid-looking jowl of their friend, Ramos, and his shock of curly hair. So the car moved off again amid frenzied back-slappings, a brandish of fists, and cries of *Salud!;* and the darkness was all fraternity.

And yet the conflict between right-, and left-, wing Socialists – Caballero's antagonism to any idea of a Prieto cabinet – had been violent enough during these last few weeks ...

At the second picket some F.A.I. men were handing over a suspect to a group of U.G.T. workers, their former adversaries. Good work! thought Ramos. The issue of arms was still going on.

A lorry, piled with rifles, had just gone up.

'They look like shoe-soles, don't they?' Ramos said. All that could be seen of the stacked rifles was the steel socket at the bottom of each butt.

'That's so,' Manuel said. 'Like tholes.'

'What the hell are you lisping for?'

'Broke a tooth at breakfast. That's all my tongue can think about; it doesn't care a hoot for antifascism today.'

'What were you eating?'

'A fork.'

In the dim light shadowy forms were embracing the rifles that had just been given them, greeted by the envious curses of the others, who stood packed like matches in a box, waiting for their turn. Women went by, with baskets full of ammunition.

'And none too soon,' someone was grumbling. 'Considering

all the time we've been expecting them to launch their bloody rising!'

'I quite believed the Government was going to leave us in the lurch.'

'Don't you fret; we'll show 'em mighty soon where they get off, the dirty swine.'

'The people of Madrid's *sereno* right enough tonight.'

Every five hundred yards came another sentry-post; fascist cars were scouring Madrid with machine-guns. And everywhere were the same clenched fists, the same fraternity. Everywhere, too, the quaintly sheepish gestures of sentries handling a rifle for the first time. The first time in a hundred years.

When they arrived, Ramos dropped his cigarette and stamped it out. 'No more smoking,' he said.

He ran off and came back ten minutes later, followed by three of his pals, each carrying parcels wrapped in newspaper and tied up with string.

Manuel had placidly lit another cigarette.

'Better not smoke,' Ramos smiled. 'It's dynamite.'

The three men stowed away the parcels, half in front and half in the back of the car, and decamped. Manuel had left his seat to tread out his cigarette on the ground. When he looked up at Ramos, there was consternation in his face.

'Good Lord! What's come over you?' Ramos exclaimed.

'You're a god-damned nuisance, Ramos!' Manuel retorted.

'You bet!... Now let's get a move on.'

'Look here! Couldn't we find some other bus? I could drive another one, you know.'

'Listen! We're going to blow up bridges, Avila bridge to start with. We're bringing the dynamite; it'll be sent off right away where it's wanted, see? To Peguerinos, and so forth. You don't want us to lose two hours, do you? This car runs all right anyhow – we know that much.'

'All right,' Manuel gloomily agreed.

It was not so much to his bus that he clung as to the wonderful gadgets it was fitted with. They set out again with Manuel at the wheel and Ramos behind, holding on his lap a bundle of hand-grenades.

Quite suddenly, Manuel discovered he had lost all interest in his car. It had ceased to be: nothing remained but this memorable night, fraught with a vague and boundless hope, this crowded night when every man had his appointed task on earth. And Ramos heard, like the beating of his heart, a distant drum.

Every five minutes the car was held up by a picket.

The milicianos, many of whom could not read, patted the occupants of the car on the shoulder as soon as they recognized Ramos. No sooner did they hear him shout, 'Stop smoking, damn you!' and see the parcels in the car than they began capering with delight. Dynamite it was – the good old romantic weapon of the Asturianos!

At the Alcalá Manuel stepped on the gas. From his right an F.A.I. lorry, packed with armed workers, suddenly slewed to the left. All vehicles that night were doing a good fifty miles an hour. Manuel tried to dodge the lorry, felt his light car lifted clear off the ground, and thought to himself: 'This is the end!'

Suddenly he found himself lying on his belly amongst packets of dynamite rolling over and over like chestnuts – on the pavement, as luck would have it. Under his eyes lay a small black patch; a pool of his own blood glistening in the light of a street-lamp. He felt little or no pain, but his bleeding nose gave him the semblance of a wounded hero. What was Ramos bellowing over there? 'Don't smoke, comrades!' He yelled the same, swung round and saw his friend, his legs crossed, still nursing the bundle of hand-grenades, while armed civilians swarmed round him, fussing around the packages they did not dare to touch. Plumb in the middle a cigarette butt – Ramos had taken advantage of the fact he was in the back of the car to light yet another cigarette – smouldered in solitary state. Manuel crushed it out. His friend began to stack the packages along the wall. As for the little sports car, the less said about it the better.

Somewhere a loud-speaker bawled: *The insurgent troops are marching on the centre of Barcelona. The Government has the situation well in hand.*

Manuel helped to stack the dynamite. Ramos, usually so active, did not move.

'Why the devil don't you lend a hand?'

The insurgent troops are marching on the centre of Barcelona.

'Haven't got over the shock. Can't move my arm. But it'll come back. Let's stop the first empty car that comes by, and get on with it.'

II

The first faint light of a summer dawn was rising over Barcelona, silvering the cool, newly-watered streets. The little tavern looking out on the huge, deserted Avenida had remained open all night, and in it Sils, known as 'the Negus', a member of the Iberian Anarchist Association and the Railway Workers' Union, was handing out revolvers to his pals.

The insurgent troops were entering the suburbs of the city.

Everyone was talking at the same time.

'What are the troops here going to do?'

'To do us in, you can bet your boots on that.'

'But yesterday the officers took the oath of allegiance to Companys.'

'Allegiance be – ! Listen to the radio !'

The little wireless set at the back of the narrow room was crooning away every five minutes: *The insurgent troops are advancing on the centre.*

'Has the Government handed out rifles?'

'No.'

'Yesterday two of my pals from the F.A.I. were jugged for going armed. We couldn't get them out till Durruti and Oliver lent a hand.'

'That's bad.'

'What do they think at the *Tranquillidad* café? Will they be given guns or not?'

'More likely not.'

'How about revolvers?'

The Negus went on doling out his stock. 'Those worthy gentlemen, the fascist officers, were kind enough to place these little fellows at my disposal. My beard inspired confidence, I guess.'

With two friends and some accomplices he had rifled the

21

armouries on two warships that night. He was still wearing the workman's suit of blue overalls which he had put on to get himself admitted on board the ships.

'And now,' he said, as he handed out the last revolver, 'let's pool our cash. We have to buy ammunition at the first gunsmith's shop that opens. We've only twenty-five rounds each, and that's not enough.'

The insurgent troops are advancing on the centre.

'The gunsmiths won't be open today. It's Sunday.'

'Don't worry. We'll have them open all right. Now each of you's got to go and collect his pals, and bring 'em along.'

Six men remained behind. The others went off at once.

The insurgent troops ...

The Negus was in command. Not in virtue of his position in the Union, but because he had done five years in prison, and because one night when the Barcelona tramways, after a strike, had dismissed four hundred of their men, the Negus with a dozen friends had set fire to the trams in the Tibidabo depôt and launched them down the hill, brakeless and in flames, amid panic-stricken hootings from the cars along the road, into the heart of Barcelona. And, after that, his campaign of less spectacular sabotage had prospered for two years.

As they stepped out into the mist-blue radiance of daybreak, each of them was wondering what the next dawn would bring. The men who had been the first to leave the tavern had done their work well, and the friends they had enlisted were gathering in groups at every street corner. When they reached the Diagonal, they saw the troops advancing towards them, from the sunrise. The regiments from the Pedralbes Barracks, headed by their officers, were moving up the long straight avenue, the largest street in Barcelona, towards the centre of the city.

The tramp of marching feet stopped suddenly and a volley raked the boulevard.

The anarchists took cover in the nearest by-street; the Negus and two of his companions went back to the Avenue. This was not the first time they set eyes on those officers; they were the very men who had rounded up the thirty thousand captives in the Asturias, the men who played a ruthless part in 1935 at Saragossa, who had connived at the repression of the agrarian

22

revolt; thanks to whom the confiscation of the Jesuits' wealth, enacted for the sixth time in a century, had remained a dead letter. And these were the men who had dispossessed the Negus's parents. According to Catalonian law a winegrower is evicted when the vineyard he is working becomes fallow. During the phylloxera epidemic all infected areas were declared fallow, and the growers were evicted from vineyards they had planted and been cultivating for thirty to fifty years. The men who took their places, having no claim on the vineyards, were paid lower wages by the owners – amongst whom were, perhaps, those very officers.

The main body moving along the centre of the avenue was preceded by an advance-guard patrolling the pavement on each side. Whenever they came to a side-street, the patrols halted, and scoured it with a volley before continuing on their way. The street-lamps had not yet been switched off; sky-signs wove traceries of light more vivid than the dawn. The Negus went back to his friends.

'They must have spotted us. We'd better cut round and have a whack at 'em higher up.'

They ran noiselessly – almost all were wearing canvas shoes – and took cover in the doorways of a street at right angles to the Diagonal. A street of rich folks' houses with wide, deep porticos. The trees along the boulevard were alive with birds. Each man saw in front of him, across the way, a comrade, revolver in hand, motionless as a statue.

Little by little the empty street began to echo with the tramp of the advancing troops. And now the column was only fifty yards away. An anarchist fell; someone had shot him from a window. Each doorway was in full view of the windows across the street. In the porches of the deserted avenue, that throbbed to the measured footfalls of the column, the anarchists stood motionless, waiting to be mowed down, like tin rabbits in a shooting gallery.

The patrol fired a volley. Bullets zipped past like a swarm of dragon-flies. The patrol moved on. As the main body crossed the end of the street, from every doorway a revolver barked. ... The Spanish anarchist is a good marksman.

The officers shouted 'Forward!', and led their men not up

23

the side-street, but towards the centre of the city; each thing in its due time. Through the intricate stonework of the portico under which he was sheltering, the Negus had only a partial view of the soldiers, from the belt down. He could not see the rifles, shoulder high, aiming along the side-street. But he noticed a good many civilian trousers under the tunics; the fascist fighting wing had joined the troops. The rearguard marched by, the sound of marching feet receded. The Negus assembled his men, took them down another street, and halted. What they were doing now was mere waste of time. Obviously the real fight would take place in the Plaza de Cataluña. Their best plan was to take the enemy in the rear – but how?

A detachment of soldiers had been left behind at the first square – rather rashly, perhaps; but the soldiers had a sub-machine-gun with them.

A worker ran past, revolver in hand.

'They're giving out arms to the people.'

'To us as well?' the Negus asked.

'I tell you, they're arming everybody.'

'Including the anarchists?'

The man did not stop to answer.

Entering a café, the Negus telephoned to the anarchist news-paper. Yes, arms were being issued to the people, but so far all the anarchists had got was sixty revolvers. 'Simpler to go and help oneself to them on the warships,' he grinned.

A factory whistle shrilled through the morning air. As on the days when only trivial destinies are in the making; as on the workdays when the Negus and his friends had heard the hooters calling and hurried to their work, by the long grey and yellow walls, walls without end; in the same flush of dawn, with the same street-lamps still alight, seeming to dangle from the trolley-wires. . . . Another siren hooted. Ten, twenty sirens.

A hundred !

All stopped dead in the middle of the road, struck dumb with wonder. Never had any of them heard more than five hooters going at once. As in old Spanish cities all the belfries jangled a summons to the townsfolk in the hour of peril, so now at Barcelona the proletariat answered the volleys with the tocsin of their factory whistles.

'Puig is at the Plaza de Cataluña.' The man who spoke was running towards the centre, followed by two other men armed with rifles.

'I thought he was still in hospital,' one of the Negus's companions remarked.

Shrilling all together, the sirens had no longer the funereal accent of a liner putting out to sea; rather they seemed to voice the jubilation of a revolting fleet.

'Rifles!' the Negus exclaimed, staring at the detachment with the submachine-gun. 'We'll fix that up ourselves!'

His lips set in a hard smile, his teeth protruding slightly between the black beard and heavy moustache. From all the factories occupied by workers the stridence of the hooters throbbed in longdrawn howls or short, staccato blasts, through streets and houses, over the bay up to the sunlit hills.

The troops in the Park Barracks, like the others, were marching on the centre of the city. Puig, a short, squat figure in a black sweater, had occupied a square with three hundred men. All were not anarchists; more than a hundred of them had been furnished with arms by the government. Some, who had little experience with rifles, were being taught how to handle them. 'No question of private ownership today,' Puig grinned, as he transferred the rifles to the best marksmen, amid general approval.

The soldiers were coming up the main avenue. Puig posted his men at various points in the streets at right-angles to it. The Negus had just arrived with his men and the submachine-gun, which only the Negus knew how to operate. There was not a sound; the milicianos moved noiselessly on their canvas shoes, the trams were silent, and the soldiers were still too far off to be audible. And now that the factory whistles, too, had fallen silent, an ominous tranquillity pervaded Barcelona.

The troops moved forward, rifle in hand, under the huge publicity posters of an hotel and a scent manufacturer. All the anarchists brought their rifles up to their shoulders.

The front rank of the column – they were in civilian trousers – fired down a side-street and deployed under a rising cloud of pigeons, several of which dropped back into the street. The second rank fired down another street, and also scattered. Puig's companions opened fire from concealed firing-points; not as the men with the Negus had done, merely across a section of the street, but sweeping all the square from different angles.

The front rank of soldiers broke into a run, came against the Negus's submachine-gun, and streamed back into the avenue under a hail of bullets, leaving behind them a straggling line of bodies, fallen full-length or huddled, like jetsam flung by a wave along the foreshore.

Some foreign sportsmen, visiting Barcelona for the Olympic Games, appeared at the windows of their hotel, in their shirt-sleeves, and started applauding – whether the soldiery or the anarchists there was no knowing. Again a factory hooter bayed like a fog-bound ship. The workers darted forward, at the soldiers' heels.

'Back to your posts!' Puig bellowed, waving his stumpy arms. No one heard him.

In less than a minute a third of the pursuers had fallen; and now the troops had taken cover in the porticos along the avenue, and the tables had been turned upon the workers. At the far end of the square lay dead and wounded men in khaki, in the foreground, dead or wounded in blue or black; and, between the two groups, lay the dead pigeons. Again the mingled blasts of twenty hooters jarred the sunlit air. More and more workers were flocking up and, despite their losses in the square, Puig's men were plugging away at the enemy. Across the dying fall of the sirens ripped the brisk rounds of rifle-fire. The soldiers were retiring at the double. Otherwise the forces of the Popular Front might have run round the side-streets parallel to the avenue, attacked them under cover of a barricade, and cut off their retreat.

The Barrack doors clanged to ...

'Where's Puig?'

'I'm Puig. What you want?'

New helpers were steadily pouring in. As the Civil Police and Assault Guard were engaged in the centre of the city and communists were few in Barcelona, the command automatically devolved on the anarchist leaders. Puig was relatively little known; he did not contribute to the workers' newspapers. But it was common knowledge that he had organized the evacuation of the children from Saragossa, and non-anarchists preferred to deal with him rather than with the leaders of the F.A.I. In the spring of 1934, for five weeks, the workers at Saragossa, led by Durruti, had put through the biggest strike that Spain had so far known. They had turned down all financial aid, and all they had asked of the proletariat was to show their sympathy by doing their utmost for the children. Over half a million persons had contributed money and provisions to the *Solidaridad*. Puig had seen to their distribution, and got together a fleet of lorries which had conveyed the children of the Saragossa workers to Barcelona. As the anarchists paid no contributions to a common fund, Puig, like Durruti and all the group of 'Solidarists', had on occasion attacked and captured vans carrying gold to the Bank of Spain. The proceeds were used to assist strikers and the 'Anarchist Library'. Those who had heard of his romantic career were always taken aback when they set eyes on this dwarf-like but sturdy little man, with the predatory face, hook nose, and twinkling eyes. The only thing that fitted in with his reputation was the black sweater. ... All that eventful morning the little man had never ceased grinning.

He left on the spot a third of his rapidly increasing force, and the submachine-gun, which one of the newcomers knew how to handle. The men he set to work building barricades. A number of soldiers who had come over to the People's Front swelled their ranks; they were in their shirt-sleeves, to prevent mistakes, but had kept their helmets on. Each man had been issued with two tots of rum that morning, so they said, and told he was wanted to put down a communist rising.

Puig went with the others to the Plaza de Cataluña. The first thing was to crush the rebels in the heart of the city; after that, they could deal with the barracks.

They approached it by the Paseo de Cataluña. Opposite them the Colon Hotel with its pineapple tower and nests of machine-guns loomed above the square. Troops from the Pedralbes Barracks in separate detachments occupied the three main buildings on the Square: the hotel at the far end, on the left the Eldorado, on the right the Central Telephone Exchange. The troops were doing little in the way of fighting, but the machine-guns enabled the officers, the fascists disguised as regulars from the waist up, and those who had 'turned soldier' during the past fortnight to keep command of the square.

Some thirty workers made a rush across the central portion of the square, which stands above the level of the roadway, taking what cover they could behind the trees that border it. The machine-guns chattered, and they fell in bunches. Shadows of the pigeons wheeling above at no great height glided across the fallen bodies, over a man who still was staggering, waving his gun at arm's length above his head.

Round Puig were grouped the leaders of all left-wing parties; thousands of men behind them. For the first time, Liberals, members of the U.G.T. and C.N.T., anarchists, Republicans, Trade-Unionists, and socialists joined in an attack on their common foe and his machine-guns. For the first time the anarchists had voted, so as to ensure the liberation of the prisoners in the Asturias. Mingling at last today, all the various strains of the Asturian blood had brought about the unity of Barcelona, quickening Puig's hope that now at length he would see unfurled and triumphant the red-and-black banner which had hitherto rarely known the light of day.

'The troops from the Park have gone back to their barracks!' shouted a bearded man who was running past, a cock under his arm.

'Goded's just landed from the Balearic Islands.' (Goded was one of the best fascist generals.)

A car sped by, with 'U.G.T.' in white paint on the bonnet, '*Our* shop-sign,' Puig smiled to himself, remembering the posters on the little square.

Other attacking parties were trying to slip by along the walls, under what little cover they could get from porches and balconies. But always they were under fire from at least two machine-guns. Watching the men drop one after the other, Puig felt his throat grow parched and hot as if he had just smoked three packets of cigarettes.

They were acting thus, he knew, because frontal attacks were in the revolutionary tradition. Once held up in front of the hotel, on the sunlit pavement cluttered with round café tables, they would be shot down from the windows. Heroism, which is but a replica of bygone heroisms, leads nowhere. Puig had a liking for hard-bitten men, he liked the men who now were falling – and he was appalled. A brush with the Civil Guard in a successful raid on Government gold was a different matter from storming the Colon Hotel, but however scanty, his experience told him uncoordinated tactics such as he now was watching were doomed from the outset.

Over the smooth asphalt of the wide boulevard around the square, bullets were capering like crickets. ... And what a number of windows! Counting those of the hotel – over a hundred – he saw, or seemed to see, a machine-gun peering through each big 'o' of the huge sky-sign, COLON.

'I say, Puig!'

'What?'

He answered the little bald man with the grey moustache who had accosted him, almost vindictively. They were going to ask him for orders. And all that lay deepest in his heart forbade him to give orders.

'Say, Comrade, shall we have a shot at it?'

'Wait a bit!'

Small bodies of men were still trying to get across the Plaza. Well, Puig had told his men to wait a bit; they had trusted him and waited. ... What was happening now?

Another wave of attackers had swept forward – white-collar workers, some with hats on. They started at the double from the Calle de Cortes; only to crumple up at the corner of the Paseo de Gracia, mowed down by the machine-guns posted in the Eldorado and in the Colon Tower. ... More bodies, more blood, calm in the calm sunshine.

Puig heard the boom of the first cannon. If the artillery was in the workers' hands, the hotel was good as taken. But if the troops were marching up from the barracks with field-guns supporting them, things would go with the people just as in '33, in '34.

Puig ran to a telephone. There were only two guns, and the fascists had them.

He collected his men, rushed the first garage on their way, piled his men into two lorries, and started out. Along the road sparrows flew up from all the sunlit trees.

Two eighteen-pounders were in position on either side of a

wide avenue, sweeping it from end to end. In front of them was a group of soldiers, all in mufti trousers, with rifles and a machine-gun. Behind them were about a hundred more, without machine-guns, so far as Puig could make out. The avenue ended two hundred yards away, where another avenue crossed it at right-angles. In the centre of the 'T' was a portico, from which a light mountain gun was firing.

Puig sent a small party of his men to reconnoitre the defences of the gunners in the cross-bars of the 'T', and posted the rest in a side-street leading off the avenue.

Suddenly, with a syncopated stridence of horns and klaxons two Cadillacs tore up the road behind them, wildly zigzagging like cars in gangster films. The driver of the front car, the bald man with the small moustache, drove headlong through a barrage from rifles and machine-guns, under shells which hurtled harmlessly above him. Like a snow-plough, the car scattered the soldiers on either side, and raced between the two eighteen-pounders, crashing against the wall just beside the mountain gun, which presumably had been its objective. Black, blood-spattered wreckage; a squashed fly on a wall.

The gunners went on firing at the second car. With its klaxon in full blast, it screamed past the eighteen-pounders and dived into the portico at seventy miles an hour.

The mountain gun ceased fire. From all the side-streets, workers were staring at the black maw of the portico; the klaxon was silent, all was silent. Waiting for the men in the car to reappear. None of them reappeared.

Again the hooters blared across the silence. It was as if the roar of the klaxons had swelled prodigiously, soaring up into the high air, till the whole city echoed with a dirge for the first glorious victims of the revolution. A cloud of pigeons, used to the daily hubbub of the city, circled above the avenue. Puig felt envious of his dead comrades' fate, yet at the same time eager to see the days that were at hand; for today Barcelona was pregnant with his whole life's dreams.

'No need to make a song about it,' said the Negus smoothly. 'A smart piece of work – but there's more important jobs to hand.'

The men Puig had sent on reconnaissance came back. 'Over

there, on the right, there are ten or a dozen fellows just behind the guns.'

Obviously the fascists had not enough men to cover all the streets around them; Barcelona is laid out like a chess-board.

'Take command,' said Puig to the Negus. 'I'll try to get round the other way and nab them from behind. Bring your men up as close as you can to the eighteen-pounders, and try to rush 'em once we've got through.'

He hurried off with five of his mates. The Negus and his companions advanced.

Barely ten minutes had elapsed. Taken by surprise, the soldiers turned their heads; the gunners tried to swing their guns round. Puig's car had broken through the little picket, was charging down on the gunners, the muzzle of his submachine-gun peering between the panels of the windscreen, while the butt jerked from side to side like a pendulum gone mad. Puig watched the gun crews, unsheltered by their bullet-shields, looming large and larger, like close-ups on a screen. A machine-gun opened fire, enlarged in nearness. Four bullet holes in the triplex glass. Handicapped by the shortness of his legs, Puig leant well forward and stamped with all his might on the accelerator – as if he were trying to break his way through the floor-boards so as to reach his mates on the far side of the gun. Two more holes starred the triplex. A cramp in his left foot, his fingers knotted on the wheel, rifle barrels jabbing the wind-screen, the submachine-gun roaring down his ears – houses and trees turned a somersault – veering, the pigeons all changed colour – the Negus shouted something . . .

He recovered consciousness to find the Revolution in full swing, the eighteen-pounders captured. When the car turned turtle his neck had had a nasty jar, nothing worse. Two of the men with him were dead. The Negus was bandaging his wound.

'There's a turban for you, Puig. You look fine as an Arab.'

At the far end of the street some Civil and Assault Guards were marching past. Officers and fascist volunteers in tunics and civilian trousers were being escorted to Police Headquarters, and the disarmed soldiers to the barracks. The latter chatted with the workmen who had taken over their rifles and were

31

now accompanying them. Everyone else was moving up towards the Plaza de Cataluña.

There the position was unchanged, except that more corpses were strewn about the square. This time Puig entered it from the Paseo de Gracia, at the corner of which street is the Colon Hotel. A loud-speaker was announcing: *The 'Prat' airmen have joined the defenders of the people's freedom.* So far, so good. ... But where were they?

Once again there was a general rush forward, from all the streets facing the hotel – anarchists, socialists, some bourgeois in starched collars, and a few groups of peasants – for, as the morning wore on, the peasants were beginning to flock into the city. Puig halted his men. The assaulting wave, caught by the three nests of machine-guns, receded, leaving behind its driftsam of the dead.

Like a flight of pigeons, the papers of a fascist league, flung from the windows, fluttered slowly down, or settled on the trees.

For the first time, Puig had an impression that he was witnessing, not a hopeless struggle like that of '34 – like every other he had seen so far – but quite possibly a victory in the making. Though he had studied Bakunin – perhaps he was the only member of the group who had read that author between the lines – he had always looked on the Spanish revolution as another *Jacquerie*. Since he saw no hope for the world, exemplary revolts were the utmost he could hope from anarchism. And so for him every political crisis resolved itself into a test of character and courage.

He remembered Lenin dancing in the snow the day when the duration of the Soviet State had outlasted that of the Paris Commune by twenty-four hours. Today the task for him and for his friends was not to give examples, but to achieve a victory. If his men rushed blindly forward like those others, they would fall like them, and the hotel would not be captured. Along the two boulevards which converge across the square in a large inverted 'V' pointing towards the Colon, and the Calle de Cortes which runs along the frontage of the hotel, three brigades of the Civil Guard came into view at exactly the same moment. Puig watched the cocked hats of his traditional enemies glinting in the sunlight. The loud cheers which greeted their approach showed they were on the Government side. Such was the hush which fell upon the square that the flapping of the pigeons' wings was clearly audible.

Even the fascists withheld their fire, in the shock of finding the police standing by the Government. And, as they knew, the Barcelona Civil Police are all crack shots.

Colonel Ximenes limped up the steps, on to the central precinct of the square, and walked straight towards the hotel. He was unarmed. Till he was a third of the way across no one fired. Then on three sides machine-gun fire broke out. Puig ran up to the second floor of the nearest house. Of all their enemies, it was the police whom the anarchists detested most. And today they were actually fighting side by side, allied in an incredible fraternity!

Ximenes was carrying the bâton of his rank, as Chief of the Civil Guard. He turned and raised it, and the men in the cocked hats began to charge up the three streets. Ximenes was walking on with a curious waddling gait – Puig remembered that his men called Ximenes 'Old Quack-Quack' – alone in the midst of the enormous square under a hail of bullets. The police on the left were now advancing alongside the Telephone Building, the defenders of which could not fire down vertically on them; the posse on the right, along the Eldorado. The gunners in the latter building should have fired at the men approaching from the left. But, now they were up against the civil police, each fascist group fought only for itself, without troubling about the others.

The machine-guns in the Colon were hard put to it, having to aim right and left alternately. The police were advancing not on a long front but in a thin column of attack, skilfully taking advantage of the cover afforded by the trees. Anarchists came swarming out of all the streets, and followed them. Then, with a rapid thud of heavy boots, the detachment from the Calle de Cortes doubled past under Puig's eyes. The fascists had ceased firing at them. In the centre of the square the Colonel limped on, straight ahead.

Ten minutes later the Colon Hotel had been captured.

*

The Civil Police were occupying the Plaza de Cataluña. All that night Barcelona resounded with shouts and songs and gun-shots. Armed civilians, workers and members of the middle class, soldiers and Assault Guards streamed under the lights of the great beer-house on the Plaza, where police-officers sat drinking at all the tables.

Colonel Ximenes, too, was drinking in a little room on the second floor, taken over for his Staff Headquarters. He was in charge of the whole district, and for the last few hours the heads of the local organizations had been coming to get instructions from him.

Puig entered. Wearing a leather windbreaker and carrying an enormous revolver, he cut a romantic figure under the grimy, blood-stained turban.

'Where can we be of the most use?' he asked. 'I've a thousand men.'

'Nowhere; all's well for the moment. But they'll be trying to get out of the barracks – from Atarazana anyhow. You'd better stay around for half an hour; your men may come in very handy any moment. It seems they've got the upper hand at Seville, Burgos, Segovia, and Palma – not to mention Morocco. But we'll beat them here.'

'What are you doing with the captured soldiers?'

They might have been fighting side by side for a month, judging by the free-and-easy manner of the anarchist, whose attitude conveyed discreetly that he had come here for sugges-tions, not for orders. Ximenes had often studied his dossier in the police records but, familiar though he was with the man's appearance, he now was struck by his extreme shortness and sturdiness. 'A pocket pirate,' he smiled to himself. Though Puig was not one of the 'big shots', he interested Ximenes more than the others because of the part he had played in rescuing the Saragossa children.

'The Government has given orders that the soldiers are to be disarmed and set at liberty,' the Colonel replied. 'The officers will be court-martialled. By the way, you were in that Cadillac, weren't you? The one to which we owe the capture of the guns?'

'Yes.' Puig remembered having noticed the cocked hats of the

Civil Guard flash past the end of the street, at the critical moment.

'A good piece of work. If they'd brought those guns up here, things might have been very different.'

'You had luck, too, when you crossed the Plaza.'

Fanatic in his cult of his beloved country, the Colonel was grateful to the anarchist, not for the compliment, but for a form of speech so characteristically Spanish; for speaking as might have spoken one of Charles the Fifth's captains. For it was obvious that by 'luck' he had meant 'courage'.

'I was scared,' Puig said, 'scared stiff, of not being able to get up to that gun. Living or dead, I *had* to get there. . . . And what were *you* thinking of?'

Ximenes smiled. His head was bare, and his white, close-cropped hair, like the down on a duckling's neck, suited the nickname his beady eyes and shovel nose had helped to earn him.

'At such times my legs say: "Stop it, you blinking idiot! What are you up to?" Especially my game leg.' Shutting one eye, he raised a monitory finger. 'But my heart says: "Go on!" Never before had I seen bullets bouncing along like hailstones. Of course, firing from above, one mistakes a man's shadow for his body, and it's hard to aim correctly.'

'That attack was well carried out.' There was a note of envy in Puig's voice.

'Yes. Your men are good in a scrap, but they're no soldiers.'

Below them on the pavement, stretchers were being carried by, empty but blood-stained.

'Yes they're good fighters,' Puig agreed.

Flower-sellers had strewn carnations on the stretchers; white flowers lay on the straps beside the blood-stains.

'When I was in prison,' Puig said, 'I never dreamt that such fraternity was possible.'

The word 'prison' reminded Ximenes that he, a colonel commanding the Barcelona civil police, was now hob-nobbing with one of the anarchist leaders; and he smiled again. All the leaders of the extremist groups had shown courage; many had fallen, or been wounded. For Ximenes, as for Puig, courage was a second fatherland. Anarchist militants went past, their unshaven cheeks showing black under the restaurant lamps. There had been no time to shave before the fighting started. Another stretcher passed, with a lily hung on one of the slings.

A ruddy glow spread up the sky beyond the square; another kindled in the distance on a hillside. Then, on every hand, wisps of bright red fire began to flicker above the house-tops. That morning Barcelona had summoned all and sundry with the stridence of her sirens, now by night she was sending her churches up in flame. Through the windows, open on the summer night, came a reek of burning. Ximenes watched the lurid smoke-clouds, lit from below, billowing above the Plaza de Cataluña. Rising, he made the sign of the Cross. Not overtly, as though wishing to advertise his faith; but for himself, as if alone.

'Ever studied theosophy?' Puig inquired.

In front of the hotel some foreign journalists were chattering excitedly about the neutrality of the Spanish clergy, about the monks of Saragossa who laid out Napoleon's veterans with cruci-fixes. The speakers were out of sight, but their voices rang clear across the darkness, across the thudding explosions and the shouting in the distance.

'No,' Ximenes muttered, watching the smoke-clouds rolling overhead. 'God should not be dragged into man's family squabbles, like a communion-cup looted by a thief.'

'What chance have the Barcelona workers had of learning about God? Through the lips of those men who in his name declared the treatment meted out to the Asturians was just and proper – eh?'

'No, but they could have learnt about Him through those few things that *tell* in a man's life – childhood and death and courage. Not from the lips of preachers. Let's assume the Church in Spain has fallen short of its duty to our countrymen. But why should the ruffians who set up to share your views – and heaven knows there's any number of them! – why need they prevent you from carrying out yours? It's a mistake ap-praising men by what is lowest in them.'

'When you condemn folk to low living, you can't expect high thinking of them. During the last four centuries who's had the "cure of souls" as you would call it? If they'd not been taught

36

so well to hate, perhaps they could learn better how to love – eh, Colonel?'

Ximenes gazed out at the distant flames.

'Have you ever noticed something about the portraits of men who've championed the noblest causes? They should look cheerful, shouldn't they? Or, anyhow, serene. Well, the first thing you notice is their sadness ...'

'Priests are one thing, the heart's another; that's sure. But I can't explain to you how I feel about it. I'm used to speaking and I'm not an ignoramus – I'm a printer. But there's always something. ... It's just the same when I talk to writers at my press. I can talk to you about priests, and you'll speak of Saint Teresa. I can talk to you about the catechism, and you'll quote – what's his name? – Thomas Aquinas.'

'The catechism's more important to me than Saint Thomas.'

'Your catechism's not the same as mine; our lives are too different. I read the catechism again when I was twenty-five; I picked it up near here in a gutter – sounds like the beginning of a moral tale, don't it? It's no use telling folk who've been having their cheeks smacked for the last two thousand years to "turn the other cheek".'

Puig was a puzzle to Ximenes; in his personality intelligence and stupidity were compounded otherwise than in the men the Colonel was accustomed to.

The last men to be released from cellars, garrets, closets, and store-rooms where the fascists had interned them, were coming out into the open – bewildered faces lit up by the ruddy glow from the burning buildings. The smoke-clouds were steadily thickening and the smell of burning was as pungent as if the hotel itself were on fire.

'About the clergy. ... Listen! For one thing, I don't care for folk who talk a lot and do damn-all. I belong to another species. But the trouble is I'm of their species, too; that's what makes me hate them. To teach poor people, workers, to accept what happened in the Asturias – why, it can't be done! And to do so in the name of a "God of Love" – I ask you! – could anything be lousier? Some of my mates say we're acting like fools, we'd do better to burn down the banks. I tell them: "No! Leave that to the bourgeois, it's in their line. The priests, that's another mat-

37

ter. Those churches where they've gloated over having thirty thousand men arrested and tortured, and the rest of it – let 'em all burn, and a damn' good thing too !'' '

'And ... Christ?'

'An anarchist who brought it off. The only one. Oh, and, speaking about priests, I'll tell you something – only very likely you won't tumble to it, as you've never been poor. It's this. I hate a man who says that he forgives me for doing the best thing I've ever done. *I don't want to be forgiven.*'

A radio blared across the darkness. *The troops of Madrid are still undecided. The Government has the situation in hand. All is quiet in Spain. General Franco has been arrested in Seville. At Barcelona the victory of the people over the fascists and the army is now complete.*

Waving his arms, the Negus burst in. He shouted to Puig: 'The soldiers have come out again. They've built a barricade.'

Puig turned to Ximenes. '*Salud!*'

'*Au revoir*,' the Colonel replied.

In a peremptorily chartered car Puig and the Negus drove top-speed across the glowing darkness of the clamorous night. In the Caracoles quarter, from the windows of the brothels, milicianos were tossing down mattresses into lorries waiting below, which made off at once for the barricades. Everywhere in the city barricades were springing up, built with mattresses, paving-stones, and furniture. One of the oddest was made of confessionals; another, in front of which a number of horses had fallen, showed in the fleeting radiance of the headlamps like a fresco of dead horses' heads.

Puig could not make out the purpose of the barricade set up by the fascists, for they were now fighting a lone hand, the soldiers having turned against them. They were firing from under cover of a shapeless mound of debris bristling with the legs of chairs, in almost complete darkness, for the street-lamps had been extinguished by rifle-shots. No sooner was Puig's turban recognized than the street echoed with gleeful shouts. The people were getting a taste for leaders, as always happens when a struggle lasts long. With the Negus at his sides, Puig entered the first garage they came to and commandeered a lorry.

In the flame-lit night the trees flanking the avenue showed as patches of dark blue. The fascists, who had a machine-gun – always and everywhere the fascists had machine-guns – were invisible.

Puig changed into top speed, and, as he had done in the morning, pressed with all his might on the accelerator. As the rattle of the changing gears died out, between two bursts of firing, the Negus heard a single shot. Suddenly Puig straightened up, his fists flattened on the steering-wheel as if it were a table; from his mouth came the rattling gasp of a man whose teeth have just been shattered by a bullet.

A mirror-wardrobe flashed up into the headlamps, crashed upon them like a fisticuff. Raked by the shrill tattoo of the Negus's sub-machine-gun, the mound of furniture burst open like a stove-in door.

The milicianos poured in through the breach, past the lorry jammed amongst the wreckage. The fascists fled to the nearest barracks. Still firing, the Negus glanced round at Puig. His face was hidden by the turban; he lay crumpled up across the steering-wheel, dead.

III

20th July

Amongst men in their shirt-sleeves or naked from the waist up, amongst women no sooner ordered off than hurrying back, the Civil Police and the Assault Guard were vainly trying to impart order to the crowd. Scattered in front, it formed a solid mass behind, loud with the deep incessant hum of voices. An officer was taking to a café a soldier who had just escaped from the Montaña Barracks. Jaime Alvear had noticed them on their way and entered the café just in front of them. Like heart-beats of the serried crowd, there came at regular intervals the boom of cannon, drowning the thin patter of shots from doors and windows, reverberating through the tumult of voices and the heavy fumes of heated stone and tar pouring up from Madrid.

The heads of all the people in the café gathered like flies around the soldier.

'The Colonel, he told us,' he panted: '"You got to save ... to save the Republic."'

'The Republic?'

'Sure! Seein' as it was being ... being done in by the bolshies ... by Jews and anarchists and what not.'

'What had the soldiers to say to that?'

' "Bravo!" they said.'

' "Bravo"?'

'Sure! They didn't give a damn one way or the other. Of course, they were mostly rookies, the ones who said it. For the last week, the whole place was stiff with rookies.'

'What about the left-wingers?' someone asked.

In the motionless glasses the brandy and manzanilla quivered in rhythm with the gun-fire. The soldier took a drink. Gradually he was getting his breath back.

'The only ones left are the men they didn't know about. All the others were shifted – a fortnight ago. Must have been about fifty left behind, all told. But they didn't show up; they've been stowed away in some corner, so I heard.'

The rebels had never dreamt the Government would give arms to the people. They had been waiting for the Madrid fascists, who so far had made no move.

Suddenly all fell silent. The loud-speaker was beginning an announcement. As newspapers came out only once a day, it was the wireless that made known the destinies of Spain.

The Barcelona Barracks are continuing to surrender. The Atarazanas Barracks have been taken by the trade-unionists, led by Ascaso and Durruti. Ascaso fell in an attack on the Barracks. Fort Montjuich has surrendered to the people without a fight.

Cries of jubilation filled the café. Even in the Asturias no name had more sinister associations than that of Montjuich.

The garrison refused to obey their officers, when informed by wireless, in the name of the lawful government of Spain, that they were under no duty to obey the insurgent officers.

'Who are keeping up the fight at your barracks?' the officer inquired.

'Only the officers and rookies. Our mates are beating it as fast as they can. But the cellars must be crawling with them. Once your big guns started in, we saw how the land lay, and we weren't taking any, not us! We knew the anars and bolshies

40

hadn't any artillery. "That speech of the Colonel's," says I, "that was just another piece of fascist ballyhoo." Nothing doing, when he wanted us to fire on the people. Not me! So I hopped it over to you.'

The man's shoulders still heaved uncontrollably. The punctual boom of cannon continued, followed like an echo by the shell-burst. Jaime had seen the gun that was in action. It was manned by a captain from the Assault Guard who had so far only discovered how to fire it; training it was beyond him. Lopez, a sculptor and *comandante* in the socialist militia, to which Jaime belonged, was helping the captain, strenuously if ineffectively. The lie of the land was such that they could not level the gun directly at the gate, so the captain was firing haphazardly at the walls. The first shell went high and burst somewhere in the suburbs; the second exploded in a cloud of yellow dust on the brick wall. The gun, not being fixed in any way, recoiled savagely at every shot, and Lopez' men, their arms straining on the spokes – like the gunners in old prints of the French Revolution – trundled it back into position as best they could. One shell went through a window and burst inside the building.

You'll take care, won't you, when you're inside?' the soldier said. 'Seeing as how the mates, they haven't fired a shot at you. On purpose, they didn't.'

How can we tell which are the new recruits?'

'Right away like that? Well I can't hardly say. But later on it'll be simple enough. They haven't any families.'

What he meant was that the fascists who had lately joined the army to facilitate the rising kept their wives out of the way – they were too obviously 'ladies'; whereas the neighbouring streets were full of soldiers' wives, waiting in suspense, the only silent members of the excited crowd.

Suddenly the rattle of rifle-fire intensified, accompanied by a rumble of heavy vehicles. Another detachment of the Assault Guard was coming into action. One of the armoured cars was already in position. The cannon was still firing, making the wine in the glasses tremble at each round. Men with rifles under their arms were drifting in, bringing the latest news, like the film actors who go into a studio bar, in costume, between two takes. But here on the white-tiled floor were tracks of blood-stained shoes.

'There's another battering-ram.'

A gigantic beam was gliding forwards, flanked by men in parallel lines on either side – like some strange geometrical monster. The men were straining forward like boat-haulers; some wore collars, some not; each had a rifle across his back. It moved across the wreckage on the roadway, the debris of railings, and rubble of bricks and plaster, hit the barracks entrance with the clang of a tremendous gong, and recoiled. Full as it was of shouts and swirling smoke and gun-fire, the whole place rang hollow like a convent, and quaked behind the massive door. Three of the men carrying the battering-ram fell, hit by shots from the defenders. Jaime stepped into the place of one. Just as the ram was starting forward again, a tall man with shaggy eyebrows – one of the Trade-Unionists – suddenly clasped his head between his hands as if to shut his ears, and slumped across the moving beam, arms dangling on one side, legs on the other. Few of his companions noticed him; the battering-ram continued lumbering slowly forward, with the dead body riding it. Jaime was twenty-six and, for him, the 'Popular Front' meant emotions such as this: fraternity in life and death. The hope he set on the workers' organizations was intensified by his despair of all the folk who had ruled the destinies of Spain during the last few centuries. Those he knew best in left-wing groups were certain obscure, inveterate die-hards, always out to tackle any job, embodiments of the spirit of devotion in modern Spain. So now he put all his heart into the fight, as he helped them to push the massive beam, straddled by their dead comrade, towards the doorway, under the brilliant sunlight and the fascist bullets. Again the battering-ram clanged on the door; the corpse astride it lunged forward. The two men beside him, one of whom was Ramos, caught it and began carrying it away. The beam swung back more slowly. Five more men fell. The track the ram had followed, flanked on each side by dead and wounded, once more shone white and empty.

The July morning was warming up; faces were beginning to glisten with sweat. Listening to the boom of the gun and the crashes of the ram that dinned their rhythm on all the other sounds of conflict, a crowd of employees, workers, and small shopkeepers stood waiting for the final rush, along the sloping streets and at the foot of the flights of steps leading up to the barracks. All were staring up at the great door, rifle in hand – the Government had omitted to issue slings, and loops of cord were dangling from each weapon – their cartridge-pouches hung across their chests on straps that were too short.

The battering-ram slowed down; the guns ceased firing. Even the fascists held their fire. The deep drone of a plane was throbbing overhead.

'What's up?'

Eyes squinted in Jaime's direction. All his comrades in the socialist militia knew that the big fellow, like a redskin, with the tousled black hair, was an engineer in the Hispano factory. The machine, Jaime said, was one of the old Spanish Army Bréguets – but there were fascists in the air force, too. Over the dense silence of the crowd the machine planed down in a wide sweep. Two bombs exploded in the barrack square, and some pamphlets fluttered slowly down, like confetti, lingering in the sky above the cheering crowds.

Up flights of steps, from all the neighbouring streets, there was a general rush towards the barracks. Once more the ram clanged against the door; it was greeted by a half-hearted burst of firing. As it recoiled, a sheet fluttered out from a window, loosely knotted at one end to make it easier to launch. Not noticing the signal, the battering-ram team once more charged the gate; it gave way at once, the fascists had just unbolted it.

The inner square was absolutely empty. Beyond the empty space, behind the windows, beyond the closed doors of the patio, the prisoners began.

The soldiers came out first, waving their union-cards; many were half-naked. One of the men in front was staggering; as the crowd pressed him with questions, he flung himself on all fours and began lapping the water in the gutter. The officers came next, their arms uplifted. Some were unconcerned or trying to appear so, one man hid his face in his forage cap, another was smiling as if the whole performance struck him as a farce. Holding his hands only shoulder high, he looked as if he were going up to the milicianos to embrace them.

Above them, the last remaining shutter at one of the central windows, which a shell had grazed, came clattering down. Suddenly a young man burst through the opening on to the balcony, half of which had been blown away; he was roaring with laughter, he had three rifles across his back and was trailing two others behind him by the barrels, like dogs on a leash. Crying 'Salud!' he flung them all down into the street.

The wives of the soldiers, of the battering-ram team, and Civil Police, rushed forward into the barracks. Their voices echoed down the long, monastic corridors on which, now that the firing had ceased, an eerie silence had descended. Shouldering their rifles, Jaime and his friend climbed to the second storey. Other milicianos had entered through a breach in the wall. A merry company of townsfolk in their workaday clothes – collars and ready-made suits – with cartridge-pouches dangling on their chests, crowded round the officers who were coming out.

Obviously the breach was a wide one, for the milicianos were pouring in by hundreds. A roar of cheers from the huge massed crowd outside crashed against the walls. Jaime looked out of the window; a thousand bare arms, a thousand clenched fists shot up all together from the seething mass, like a concerted movement at an athletic tournament. The distribution of the captured rifles was beginning.

The wall, in front of which the ceremonial swords and modern rifles were being stacked, hid from the crowd a large courtyard into which Jaime could see. At the back of the yard was a cycle shop. While the milicianos were fighting, looters had been at work; the yard was littered with sheets of packing-paper, wheels, and handlebars. And suddenly Jaime remembered the crumpled body sagging across the battering-ram.

In the first room he entered, an officer was seated, his head propped on his hand, above a pool of blood, his own, still spreading over the table. Two other officers lay on the ground, each with a revolver just beside his hand.

In the next room, which was rather dark, some soldiers were lying on the floor, yelling 'Salud! Hey! Salud!' They did not move; they were tied hand and foot. These were men the fascists had suspected of loyalty to the Republic, or sympathy with the workers' movement. Their bonds did not prevent them from tapping their heels in jubilation. Jaime and his companions, as they set them free, embraced the prisoners in characteristic Spanish style.

'There's some more of the mates down there,' one of them remarked. They ran down an inner staircase, and, in a still darker room, found another batch of comrades shackled in the same way; them, too, Jaime and his companions kissed. They had been shot the day before.

IV

'Hello there!' Rising from his seat at the Granja café, Slade held out a friendly hand to a black cat; it eyed him suspiciously, hesitated, then ran back into the crowd. 'Since the revolution,' Slade observed, 'the cats, too, are free; but they're still down on me. I'm always one of the down-trodden.'

'Oh, come back to your chair, you owl,' Lopez said. 'Cats — they're unfriendly little brutes; fascists, for all I know. And dogs and horses are sappy; a sculptor can't make anything of them. The only animal that's the friend of man is ... the Pyrenean eagle. During my 'birds-of-prey' period I used to keep one. The only food they eat is snakes, and snakes cost a lot of money. I'd thought of scrounging 'em from the Zoo, but nothing doing. So I bought hunks of meat and cut them into strips. I shook them in front of my eagle, and, like the nice chap he was, he pretended to be fooled and gulped them down.'

Radio Barcelona here, the loud-speaker blared. *The guns captured by the People are trained on the Capitania where the rebel leaders have taken refuge.*

As he watched the Alcalá, the American was jotting down his notes for next day's article. It flashed on him how — the shock of hair and blubber lip notwithstanding — the sculptor's Bourbon nose recalled a portrait of George Washington. But, above all, the head of a macaw. All the more so that just then Lopez was flapping his arms like wings.

'Hi there! On the set, everyone!' he yelled. 'We're shooting.'

Bathed in the bright glare of its street-lamps, gay with the motley of the revolution, Madrid looked like an enormous film

45

studio. Suddenly Lopez calmed down; some milicianos were coming up to shake hands with him. His popularity with the artists who forgathered at the Granja café was due less to his exploit with the field-gun – in the best sixteenth-century manner – during the previous day's attack on the Montaña Barracks, or even to his talent, than to a famous retort he once had made. One day an embassy attaché had asked him to make a bust of the Duchess of Alba. 'Certainly,' he had replied with a smile, 'but only if she'll sit for me as the female hip-po-po-ta-mus.' He spent all his time at the Zoo, and was on still friendlier terms with all the animals than ever was Saint Francis. He declared that the hippopotamus came up when he whistled, held the pose quietly, and trotted off when no longer wanted. The Duchess, in point of fact, was well out of her rash project. Lopez carved in diorite and his model, after hearing his hammer clanging like a blacksmith's for hours on end, was apt to find that the bust had progressed by a mere quarter-inch.

Soldiers were passing, in their shirt-sleeves, greeted by cheers and followed by swarms of children. They were the troops from Alcalá de Henares who had turned against their insurgent officers and gone over to the People's Front.

'Look at all those kids going by,' Slade remarked. 'They're crazy with pride. And I must say I like the way the men here are just like kids. There's always a touch of the child, more or less, in everything I like. You look at a man, somehow you get a glimpse of the child in him, and you fall for him! Do the same thing with a woman, and you're sunk! Yes, look at them! They usually try to disguise their childishness – now it's coming out. The boys here are revelling in a perfect orgy of toothpicks, while out there on the Sierra their pals are dying; and it's all the same thing. In America they see the revolution as an outburst of blind fury – whereas what hits you in the eye here is the good humour of it all.'

'Good humour's not all there is to it.'

Only when he was discoursing about art did Lopez' wits work nimbly; now he could not find the words he wanted.

'Listen!' was all he said.

Cars were racing past in both directions, placarded with huge white inscriptions indicating one or another of the various

Unicns, or the U.H.P. The men in them waved their fists by way of greeting, shouting *'Salud!'* and the roar of acclamation swelled in a never-ending chorus, the strident triumph of fraternal unity. Slade closed his eyes.

'There's a spark of poetry,' he said, 'in every man, and one day he has to come out with it.'

'Guernico said the driving force of revolution is – hope.'

'Garcia said the same thing. Guernico's a bore; all Christians bore me stiff. . . . Go on !'

The American journalist was rather like a Breton curé; that, Lopez reflected, might, in the last analysis, explain his hatred of the Church.

'But it's true, you owl ! Look at me, for instance. What have I been crying for these last fifteen years? A renewal of art. See? Everything here is ready for it. That wall over there, for instance. All those saps go trotting their shadows over it, and never give it a look. Well, we've here right now a mob of painters, they sprout between the paving-stones; why, I ran up against one the other day in an attic in the Escorial – asleep he was You've got to give them walls to work on. You can always find one when you need it; white, yellow, or burnt Sienna. Well, you just rub it down with whitewash, and make it over to a painter.'

Smoking his clay pipe with the elegance of an Indian chief, Slade was listening attentively; he knew that just now Lopez was in earnest. The madman apes the artist, and the artist resembles the madman.

Slade mistrusted the theorizing about art which is the bane of every revolution, but he knew the work of the Mexican artists, and the huge, barbaric frescoes, so typically Spanish, bristling with claws and horns, that Lopez painted – vivid symbols of the spirit of man engaged in mortal conflict.

'Yes, sir, we'll give our painters bare white walls. "Get to work ! Draw ! Paint ! The folks who're going to pass this way want you to *tell* them something – see? You can't fake up an art that means something to the masses when you've nothing to say to them. But we're all fighting the same fight, to build up a new world, so we've plenty to say to each other. The cathedrals helped in the fight, all for all, against the devil – who, by

47

the way, has rather Franco's mug. Well, we, too, must help ... !" '

'Oh, cut out the cathedrals! They make me sick. There's more "brotherhood of man" right here in this street, than in any old cathedral on the other side. . . . Sorry! Go on!'

'Art isn't a matter of the themes it treats. There's no great revolutionary art, and why? Because they're always wrangling about what it should be, instead of about what it is. So we've got to say to our artists: "Have you anything to tell the man at the front? (It's got to be something definite, not a vague abstraction like 'the masses'.) No? Well then, do something else. Yes? Then, there's your wall. That wall's yours to play with, old chap. Two thousand people will go past it every day. You know them. You want to speak to them, don't you? Fix it up your own way; you're free to use it and you want to use it. O.K." We may not turn out masterpieces, masterpieces aren't made to order; but we'll create a *style*.'

Looming on high across the shadows, the Spanish palaces – occupied nowadays by banks and by insurance companies – and, a little lower down, the Government offices with their exotic pomp and splendour – seemed putting forth into the darkness upon the tide of time, with all their pageantry of gorgeous hearses, the glow and glitter of clubs, the chandeliers, and the banners of old-world galleons drooping in the Admiralty court-yard, still in the still night air.

An old man who was leaving the café stopped to listen. He laid his hand on Lopez' shoulder.

'I'll paint a picture of an old man toddling off and a young fellow having a bath. The nincompoop who bathes, and goes in for sports, who can't keep quiet for a moment – that's a fascist.'

Lopez looked up; the man who spoke was an excellent Spanish painter. Obviously he had half a mind to add: 'Or else, a communist.'

'. . . as I say, a fascist. And the old chap toddling off, he's – Old Spain. Now, my dear Lopez, I'll wish you a good evening.'

As he hobbled away a sound of cheering surged across the darkness; the Assault Guard and the loyal regiments who had defeated the insurgents at Alcalá were re-entering Madrid. Clenched fists shot up at every table, along the crowded pavements. And the Assault Guard marching past brandished their clenched fists in answer.

'It's unthinkable,' Lopez broke out, 'that, given people who have something to say and people who are out to listen, we won't create a style. Just give them a free hand, give 'em all the air-brushes and spray-guns, all the modern contraptions they can want and, after that, a chunk of modelling clay – and then you will see!'

'What pleases me in your idea,' Slade murmured pensively, fingering the ends of his bow tie, 'is that you're such a born idiot. The only people I like are saps – innocents, as they used to be called. Most people have the big head, and they can't do a thing with it. But all those folks there are saps – like us.'

Above the stridences of changing gears the street was shrill with voices, snatches of the 'International' rising above the din of tramping feet. A woman walked past the café with a sewing-machine in her arms, hugging it to her breast, like a sick animal. Slade flicked back his little soft hat with the upturned brim, and sat unmoving, grasping the stem of his pipe. An officer with a brass star on his blue one-piece uniform came by; he shook hands with Lopez.

'How are things going in the Sierra?' Lopez asked.

'They won't get through. The milicianos are pouring in.'

'Good!' said Lopez as the officer went on his way. 'One day that new style of ours will catch on in the whole of Spain, just as the cathedral style spread over Europe, and their painters have given Mexico a revolutionary fresco style.'

'O.K. for your new style – if you'll kindly undertake to shut your trap about those damn' cathedrals.'

All the cars in the city, commandeered for the war or for the service of a dream, were roaring down the streets amid fraternal shouts. The photographs taken at the Montaña Barracks by photographers formerly employed by the fascist press – which had been nationalized that morning – were passing from hand to hand along the café tables. Milicianos were examining them eagerly. 'That's us!' 'That's me!'

Slade felt inclined to devote that night's article to Lopez' scheme, to the glamour of the Granja, to the hope that triumphed in the street. Why not to all these things? Behind him an American woman was waving her arms; she had the Stars-and-Stripes, 18 inches wide, pinned across her chest – the reason being, so he had just learned, that she was deaf and dumb. Yes, a style might well spring up from all these empty walls, and the men who walked by them; the very men who just now were streaming past him, exulting in their carnival of liberty. They shared with their painters in the dark, underground communion that Christianity had once provided, that today the Revolution gave them; they had chosen the same way of life, and were dying the same deaths . . .

'Either it's a loony idea,' Slade observed, 'or it's something that should be taken in hand by you, or by the Government, or by the League of Revolutionary Artists, or – how about the Worshipful Company of Eagles and Hippos?'

Some of the people going by were carrying bundles of linen or neatly folded squares of sheets, like lawyers' portfolios, under their arms. A man who looked like a small shopkeeper was pressing to his chest a quilt – scarlet in the bright glow from the tavern – just as the woman who had just gone past had hugged her sewing-machine. Some passers-by carried chairs piled upside-down upon their heads.

'It'll be done,' Lopez said. 'Not by me, anyhow at present. My company's ordered off to the Sierra. But we shall bring it off, don't you worry!'

Slade blew into thin air a little cloud of pipe-smoke. 'Jesus, Lopez, if you only knew how sick to death I am of all the race! . . .'

'It's hardly the right moment . . . !'

'Wait! Day before yesterday I was at Burgos, don't forget. And it was just the same as here. Absolutely. The poor fools are fraternizing with the troops.'

'Well, and here, you owl, it's the other way round. The troops are fraternizing with the poor fools.'

'And in the swell hotels I saw bare-backed countesses chumming up with royalist peasants in berets and woollen blankets.'

'And the peasants getting themselves shot for the said countesses, who certainly weren't getting themselves shot for the peasants. But, of course, that's as it should be!'

'When such words as "Republic" or "Trade-Union" were

spoken, they spat, the poor fatheads! I saw a priest with a rifle; he obviously thought he was defending his Faith, and in another quarter of the town I came across a blind man with a brand new bandage over his eyes. On it was written in violet ink: *Viva El Christo Rey!* I'll bet he thought he was a volunteer like the rest of them.'

'He was blind ...'

Once more, as always happened, when the loud-speakers belly-bawled '*Hullo!*', a deep hush followed.

Radio Barcelona speaking. General Goded is about to address you.

No one present but knew that Goded was the fascist leader at Barcelona, and the officer commanding the rebellion there. Silence seemed spreading like a tide up to the furthest limits of Madrid.

The voice sounded listless, apathetic, but not without dignity. *General Goded is speaking. I want to let everybody know that the day has gone against me, I am a prisoner. I make this known so that those who do not wish to keep up the struggle may understand they are absolved from any obligation towards me.*

It was the same declaration as that which Companys had made in 1934. A wave of cheering broke across the nightbound city.

'That bears out what I was just going to say,' Lopez went on, tossing off the contents of his glass at a gulp in token of his joy. 'When I was making those bas-reliefs which you call my "Scythian dinguses", I hadn't any stone to work with. Good stone costs a heap, you know; but the cemeteries are stiff with it, that's all you find in 'em. So I looted the graveyards, nights, and all the stuff I turned out in those days was carved off R.I.Ps. That's how I came to give up using diorite. Now we're going to do things on a bigger scale. Spain's a graveyard full of tombstones, and we're going to turn them into works of art — got it, you owl?'

Men and women were passing, laden with bundles wrapped in black sateen. One old woman had a clock; a child carried a handbag; another, a pair of shoes. All were singing. A little behind them a man was dragging a hand-cart loaded, it seemed, with the stock-in-trade of a curiosity-shop; he was singing, too, but lagging a beat or two behind the others. An agitated young man started waving his arms to stop them. It was a newspaperman who wanted to take a snapshot by the light of his flash-bulb.

'Is this moving day, or what's the big idea?' Slade jerked his little hat back over his forehead. 'Afraid of a bombardment?'

Lopez raised his eyes. For the first time their gaze was simple and sincere.

'You know the whole country's lousy with pawn-shops, don't you? This afternoon the government ordered them to open up and hand back all the pledges right off. All the down-and-outs in Madrid rolled up, you bet. They took their time, they didn't hurry. (I guess they didn't quite believe the news.) Now they're on their way home with their quilts and watch-chains and sewing-machines and what-not. It's the poor folk's night out, tonight!'

Slade was fifty. He had travelled a good deal and life had given him some nasty knocks — amongst others, a taste of utter destitution in the States, and the lingering, incurable illness of a woman he had loved. And the only things to which he accorded any importance were things he called 'idiotic' or 'brutish': elemental things like pain and love, humiliation, innocence.

People were moving down the avenue in groups, some behind wheelbarrows bristling with chairlegs, others carrying wall-clocks. The picture of the Madrid pawn-shops kept open all the night for the benefit of the under-dog — top-dog for once — and the sight of the crowd scattering across the city to the slums with their rescued pledges gave Slade his first notion of what that word, 'Revolution', can mean for men.

Above the rumble of petrol-waggons requisitioned to combat the fascist cars that were scouring the darker streets with sub-machine-guns, sounded incessantly the cries of *Salud!* failing and roaring up again, rapped out in measured beats, dying away; and through them, men and darkness seemed united in a fraternal pact — all the tougher for the fight that was impending. The fascists were entering the Sierra.

2

1

WITH the exception of the men in workmen's overalls with zippers – the garment known as the *mono* and adopted as the militia uniform – all the volunteers in the International Air Force were in cheerful mood. The sun was hot, their shirts were open at the neck; they might have just come home from a morning rabbit-shoot or a bathing party. Only the professional pilots and the machine-gunners from China or Morocco were at the moment in action; but the turn of the others, the new recruits daily arriving, for their baptism of fire would come in the course of the day.

In the centre of the aerodrome a sleek, bright form of aluminium shone in the sun; it was a three-engined Junker whose pilot, hearing the Seville wireless announce the capture of Madrid, had trustingly come down.

At least twenty cigarettes lit up at once. Camuccini, the squadron clerk had just remarked:

'Two and a quarter hours all in, for the "B".'

In other words, the large warplane lettered 'B' had fuel for that time and no longer. And everyone – from Leclerc squatting monkey-wise on the bar-counter to the more serious spirits poring over their machine-gun manuals – everyone knew that the plane manned by their comrades, that had left for a flight over the Sierra, had been away just two hours and five minutes.

The cigarette smoke ascended, not in long, lazy spirals, but in quick short puffs. All eyes were focused, parallel, across the panes upon the crest-line of the hills.

Now or tomorrow, anyhow quite soon, one of the planes would fail to return. And each man knew that his own death would mean, for those awaiting him in vain, just those quick puffs of smoke from nervously lit cigarettes, in which hope seemed gasping to survive, like a man who is being throttled.

Polsky (known as 'Pol') and Gardet walked out of the mess, without once taking their eyes off the hills.

'The boss is in the "B" you know.'

'Sure about it?'

'Oh, don't play the idiot! You saw him start.'

The 'Boss' was liked by all – and he was in the missing plane.

'Two hours, ten minutes.'

'Wait a bit! Your watch is out of order, isn't it? It was barely one when they took off; that makes only five minutes over the two hours.'

'No, Raymond, old chap, there's no getting out of it. It's ten good minutes over the two hours. Look at little Scali up there – see how he's hanging on to his phone!'

'That chap Scali, what is he exactly? An Italian?'

'I believe so.'

'He might be Spanish.'

'Look at his mug!'

Scali's face had the somewhat mulatto cast characteristic of the peoples of the western Mediterranean.

'You've only got to see the state he's in!'

'Things are looking grim – there's no getting round it.'

The conversation went on in undertones, as if both men were fearing death might overhear them.

The Ministry had just advised Scali that two Spanish pursuit planes and two adapted bombing planes of the International Flight had been knocked out by a squadron of seven Fiats. One of the bombers had crashed behind the Republican lines; the other was only slightly damaged and trying to return. Scali raced downstairs to Sembrano's office, his fuzzy hair blowing in all directions.

Magnin, 'the boss', was in command of the International Air Force. Sembrano was in charge of the civil aerodrome and the airline machines converted into war-planes. He had a look of Voltaire – but a younger, more amiable edition of the sage. Reinforced by old army planes from the Madrid aerodromes, the new Douglases bought by the Government from the Spanish airlines could, if necessary, tackle the Italian war-planes. For the present, anyhow ...

Suddenly the hum of conversation ceased abruptly. No siren could be heard, nor the droning of an engine, but all the 'Pelicans' were pointing at some object in the distance. One of the bombing planes, both engines shut off, was skimming a hill-top, coming down to the landing-ground. In the harsh light of early afternoon the sallow-coloured expanse looked lifeless as the surface of a dead planet; close above it the cockpit, with its freight of dead and living comrades, was gliding silent as a dream.

'The ridge!' Sembrano shouted. 'The ridge!'

'Darras is an air-line pilot,' Scali replied, cocking his nose-tip with his forefinger.

'The ridge!' Sembrano cried again.

But the plane had just bucked over it, like a horse, and was beginning to circle the field. Down in the mess, everyone held his breath, listening for a shout; not a scrap of ice tinkled in the wine-glasses.

'Look, his tyres are cut to shreds!' Scali exclaimed. 'He'll turn turtle.' He was waving his stumpy arms, as if trying to help the plane to land. Then it touched earth, tilted, scraped a wing-tip, and halted at a slant, but without turning over.

All the Pelicans rushed up, shouting, round the hermetically closed cockpit.

Pol, a lump of toffee sticking in his throat, stared at the hatch, which showed no sign of rising. Behind it, in the cabin, were six of his mates. Gardet, his cropped hair bristling forward, was vainly tugging at the handle. All eyes were riveted on the hand battling so furiously with the hatch, which obviously had jammed. At last it rose half open. Some feet showed in the opening; then the trouser-legs of a blood-stained suit of overalls. The slowness of the man's movements made it clear that he was wounded. As Pol stared, half suffocated by the lump of toffee, at the blood – whose was it? – and the limb feeling its way gingerly out of the cabin, it struck him that here was an ocular demonstration of the word 'fraternity'; none of them here but felt it in his bones.

Little by little the pilot worked his leg out of the doorway; drops of blood, scarlet in the dazzling sunlight, were dripping from it. At last his head emerged – the blotched face of an old wine-grower from the Loire, crowned by a gardener's wide-brimmed hat, his mascot.

'So you brought the bus back after all!' Sembrano's timid voice was loud with admiration.

'What about Magnin?' Scali cried.

'Safe and sound,' Darras replied, as he tried to get a purchase on the door to wriggle out.

As Sembrano rushed forward and kissed him, the hats of both men fell to the ground. Darras' hair was white. The Pelicans giggled nervously.

Once Darras had got clear, Magnin sprang out. He was in flying-kit; his drooping, greyish-yellowish moustache and the crash-helmet gave him the look of a bewildered Viking – the bewilderment being imparted by his horn-rimmed glasses.

'And the "S"?' he shouted to Scali.

'In our lines. Damaged. The crew's only slightly hurt.'

'Look after the wounded men. I'm off to the telephone to make my report.'

The men who were uninjured jumped out, greeted their pals excitedly, then tried to climb back into the cabin to help the wounded out. Gardet and Pol had already entered it.

Amongst red splashes and the prints of blood-stained shoe-soles, a very young man was lying. His name was Rouse, 'Captain Rouse'. He had not yet been given a one-piece uniform. He had been gunner in the lower turret, and this, his first flight, had brought him five bullets in his legs. He spoke only English – and perhaps one or two dead languages. A little copy of Plato, in Greek, scrounged that morning from Scali (who had raised hell about it!) jutted from the blood-stained pocket of his red and blue blazer. Propped against the observer's seat, the bomber, who had two bullets in his thigh, sat waiting. Some time a Breton sailor, he had enlisted as a bomber in the Morocco air force, and set up to be a 'tough guy'. He was gritting his teeth, but, despite his wounds, his rubicund, bloated face kept its normal jovial expression, while Gardet cautiously extracted him from the cockpit.

'Steady on mates!' Pol cried officiously, his eyes bulging like marbles. 'I'll go and fetch a stretcher. That's the only way to fix it without mucking the poor chap up worse nor he is.' Leaning on the arm of Seruzier, his chum (known as the 'Flying Wonder' on account of his constant air of puzzlement), Leclerc, a lean, monkey-like little scallawag in overalls and an incongruous grey hat, launched out on the tall tale of one of his exploits.

'Got to wait a bit, old boy, before they ship you for the torture truck. To pass the time away. I'm going to spin you a yarn. My last brush with the petty bourjoys in gay Paree. It all happened 'long of a chum. Like this. His concierge, the silly old bastard what opens the door o' nights, couldn't bear the sight of him. Always licking the boots of the tenants with the moneybags, and treating us poor bloody proletarians like so much dirt. That's the sort of swine he was One night when my pal came home, the concierge fairly tore the poor bloke up for arsepaper just because he'd forgotten to sing out his name when he was passing the concierge's cubby-hole. "O.K.," says I. "Just you wait a bit." So one night at two in the morning, I unharness an old hack that's standing in the street. And I lead him just inside the hallway in front of the concierge's door and I bawl out in a sort of hollow voice: *"Monsieur le Horse!"* Then, by your leave, I make a getaway quite quiet . . .'

The bomber stared at Leclerc and Seruzier without moving a muscle; then, casting a lordly look on the young Pelicans, commanded:

'Get me a copy of *The Worker*.'

And relapsed into silence till the stretcher came.

II

A puff of smoke drifted up from the crest of the Sierra. The glasses shivered, the tinkle of the tea-spoons in them followed the crash of the explosion by the tenth of a second. The first shell had fallen, at the far end of the street. A tile came slithering down the roof on to a table, the glasses tumbled off, a pit-a-pat of running feet drummed on the bright air of noon. Evidently the second shell had landed half-way down the street. All the peasants crowded into the café rifle in hand, chattering volubly, but with steady, watchful eyes.

At the third shell — only ten yards away — all the window-panes caved in, volleying splintered glass at the faces of the men in bandoliers who were lining the back wall, incapable of movement.

A sliver of glass impaled the cinema poster spattered with tiny wine-drops.

Another crash. Then, another, much farther off, on the left

57

this time. Now everyone in the village seemed to be shouting at once. Manuel had a walnut in his hand; held it up above his head, between two fingers. Another bomb exploded, nearer.

'Thanks,' Manuel said, and exhibited his walnut, broken in pieces. (He had cracked it with his fingers.)

A peasant asked in a low tone: 'Eh, but what may a man do to keep them shells from coming this way?'

No one replied. Ramos was with the armoured train. All stayed on, sometimes moving away from the wall, but always coming back to it, waiting for the next shell.

'There ain't no sense in what we're doin' here.' Old Barca's jerky voice broke the silence. 'If we stay in here, we'll all go dippy. Better go and have a whack at them, says I.'

Manuel looked at him intently, wondering if the man were in earnest.

'Well, there's lorries on the square,' he said.

'Know how to drive 'em?'

'Yes.'

'Big lorries?'

'Yes.'

'Oh, boys!' Barca yelled.

Such was the shock of the explosion that all the peasants flung themselves on the floor. When they rose, the house in front had lost its front wall, and the rafters were tumbling down belatedly, like spilt matches. Forlornly, a telephone was tinkling above the void.

'There's lorries yonder,' Barca continued. 'Let's climb in and have a whack at the bastards.'

All began speaking at once. 'Good for you!' 'Nay, we'll get our heads blown off.' 'We ain't got no orders.' 'Put a jerk into it, you sons of bitches!' 'Want orders, do you? Well the order is: "Shut your traps and get into them blinkin' lorries."'

Manuel and Barca had run outside. Most of the others followed them. Anything was better than staying where they were. More shells were falling. A little behind them were the laggards – the look-before-you-leap men.

Thirty peasants clambered into a lorry. Shells were falling thick all round the village. It struck Barca that while of course the fascist artillery could see the village, they could not see what was going on in it. For the moment, no planes were up. Laden with villagers singing the 'International' and brandishing their rifles above the racket of the changing gears, the lorry gathered speed.

Since Ramos' propaganda campaign in the Sierras, the peasants had come to feel a certain, if somewhat diffident, regard for him. It had steadily intensified as he grew more and more ill-shaven, and the face with the pale green eyes under the jet-black lashes, which brought to mind that of a rather heavy-jowled Roman emperor, became more and more like a Mediterranean fisherman's.

Shells were sweeping overhead through the bright air, with a rustling swish like the sound of pigeons' wings, and dropping in the village. With Manuel at the wheel, the lorry forged ahead along the hill road. His nerves were strung up and he was singing at the top of his voice the song from *Manon*.

Adieu, notre peti-te table . . .

Equally excited, the others were breaking in with the 'International'. They stared at two dead men, past whom the car was speeding, with the uneasy thrill of comradeship that men going up into the line feel for the first to fall. Barca was wondering exactly where the field-guns were stationed. 'The smoke, that ain't enough to tell you.'

'Hi! One of the boys has fallen off.'

'Stop!'

'No!' yelled Barca. 'No stopping! Let's get at those muckin' guns!'

The other men gave in. Barca had taken charge of the situation. Changing gear, the lorry emitted a harsh screech that shrilled above the crash of the shell-bursts. More dead men were lying on the roadside.

'There's three more lorries just behind!'

Everyone, even Manuel at the wheel, looked round, shouting 'Hurrah!'

All began to sing in Spanish, stamping their feet, in unison with Manuel.

Adieu, notre peti-te table . . .

*

59

At the opening of a tunnel from which a long, inquisitive snout – the locomotive of the armoured train – protruded, Ramos was gazing down on the lorries across four hundred yards of pine-clad slopes.

'It's a ten to one chance, my boy,' he said, to Salazar, 'against their bringing it off.'

Ramos had replaced the commander of the armoured train, who had gone over to the fascists – or was it merely for a 'binge' in Madrid?

Against the vastness of the mountain-side the lorries looked absurdly small. But their bonnets were catching the sunlight, and the fascists could hardly help seeing them.

'Why not give them a hand?' Salazar suggested, stroking his handsome moustache up the wrong way. He had served as a sergeant in Morocco.

'Our orders were not to fire. There's no getting them changed. Your home-made telephone is working like a good 'un; only there's no one at the other end of the line.'

Three milicianos in *monos* were setting out two chasubles and a priest's stole on the permanent way some yards in front of the locomotive. But their eyes were fixed on the lorries moving along the pale blue ribbon of road across which two dead bodies lay.

'Shall we get a move on?' one of them shouted.

'No,' Ramos replied. 'The orders are to stay here.'

The lorries were still advancing; the hum of their engines was clearly audible between the anvil-clangs of gun-fire. A miliciano, one of those Castilian peasants whose elongated faces give them a family likeness with their horses, climbed down from the tender, picked up the chasubles, and began folding them. Ramos went up to him.

'What are you up to, Ricardo?'

'We been talking it over, me and the mates,' he muttered.

He unrolled a short length of the stole, with a puzzled air; the brocade glittered in the sunlight.

The lorries were still climbing. The engine-driver's head, peering out of the cab, showed bright against the dark mouth of the tunnel. He was grinning.

'It's like this,' Ricardo said. 'We got to be mighty careful.

How can we tell these lousy contraptions won't bring bad luck to our mates in the lorries, or heave the old locomotive off the rails. I don't trust 'em, that's sure.'

'Give them to your wife,' Ramos suggested. 'She'll find some use for them.'

The big, good-humoured young man with the curly hair inspired the peasants with confidence. But, just now – how could they be sure he wasn't joking?

'My wife wear that there thing?' Disgustedly the peasant flung the glittering roll of fabric into the ravine.

The enemy machine-guns opened fire, in punctual, measured cadence.

The lorry in front skidded, swung round and toppled over, spilling its human freight like apples from a basket. Such as were not killed or wounded took cover behind it and began firing. All that the men in the armoured train could make out of Ramos was his curly hair and bulky field-glasses. On their radio, someone was singing an Andalusian song. A coffin-like scent of resin from the uprooted pines filled the warm air, which throbbed as if it were being churned up by the machine-guns.

There were olive-trees on each side of the wrecked lorries. Some milicianos ran out from behind it towards the trees; they fell one after the other. The road being blocked, the lorries behind halted.

'If only the boys would lie down!' Salazar exclaimed. 'There's cover if they knew how to use it.'

'To hell with orders! Get back to the train and open fire.'

Salazar ran back, a martial figure, somewhat hampered by his gorgeous riding boots.

As the milicianos could no longer advance, Ramos ran the risk of firing on them. But he had only once chance in a hundred of hitting the enemy machine-guns, for he had no idea of their location.

On a siding were some goods trucks still bearing the inscription: *Good Luck to the Strikers*.

The armoured train crept out of the tunnel, menacing but blind. Once again Ramos was conscious that all an armoured train amounts to is one field-gun and a few machine-guns.

The men behind the lorry were aiming at the place from

which the noise of firing came. They were learning that the most important and hardest thing in warfare is not so much tackling the enemy as getting him 'taped'; that it's a matter not so much of man-to-man attack as of cold-blooded slaughter.

Just now it was they who were being slaughtered.

'Hold your fire,' Barca shouted, 'until you see something. Else we'll have used up all our ammunition when the bastards attack.'

Nothing would have suited them better than an attack from the fascists; a straight fight rather than this sick suspense – like the ordeal of a doctor's waiting-room.

A man ran forward towards the batteries; at his seventh step he was shot down, as the man who had tried to run to cover behind the olive-trees had been shot down.

'If they turn their field-guns on us ...' Manuel remarked to Barca.

Obviously for some reason, this was impracticable otherwise they'd have done it already.

'Comrades ... !' A woman's voice!

Almost everyone looked round in amazement. A girl in the militia uniform stood behind them.

'You've no business here.' Barca spoke without severity; all were grateful to the girl for having come to join them.

She carried a fat, squat handbag, bulging with tinned provisions.

'Say,' Barca asked, 'how did 'ee get here?'

Her parents, it seemed, were peasants, living in the village; she knew all the footpaths about the hills. Barca's eyes followed the pointing finger; forty yards without cover.

'Well? Can we get round that way?' a miliciano asked.

'Sure,' said the girl. In her 'teens, a good-looker.

'No,' Barca said. 'See that open patch we'd have to cross? They'd mow us down.'

'She came that way. Why shouldn't we ... ?'

'Steady on! Ain't it possible they let her through o' purpose? We're in a tight corner sure enough no need to make it worse.'

'Seems to me, we might get through to the village.'

'You're not thinking of turning back?' the girl exclaimed, in

62

a shocked tone. 'The people's army never retreats from its position; the radio said it again, only an hour ago.'

Her voice had the theatrical intonation which comes so readily to Spanish women, but, quite unconsciously, she was wringing her hands. 'We'll bring you anything you want.' She sounded like a kind lady offering toys to a group of children, to get them to behave.

Barca was pondering. 'Comrades,' he said at last, 'that ain't the point. That kid says ...'

'I'm not a kid!'

'Very well. Our comrade says we can get away, but it's up to us to stay here. What I say is: It's up to us to clear, but we can't do it nohow. Got to get things straight, ain't we?'

'You've pretty hair,' Manuel whispered to the militia girl. 'Do give me – just one hair.'

'Comrade, I haven't come here for – for silliness.'

'All right, stick to it, you mean thing.'

While chatting with the girl – without much real interest – he had been keeping his ears open. Now he cried:

'Listen! What's that?'

They listened. Only the vast, birdless silence. And the distant machine-guns reeling off band after band. One out of action? No, only jammed; off again at once. But no more shots were coming near the lorry.

Suddenly someone shouted, 'Look there!'

'Keep your head down, you bloody fool!'

He lowered his head. In the direction where the man was pointing, tiny blue-clad forms were moving up towards the fascist batteries along a line parallel to the road, taking advantage of the cover of the wood. It was the Assault Guard.

'That's the stuff!' Barca exclaimed. 'If we'd gone about it that way ...'

'Good work!' a miliciano exclaimed. 'Say, boys, shall we lend a hand?'

'Wait a bit!' Manuel said. 'Mustn't muck it up again this time. Number off by tens, all of you ... got it? Right! The first man of each section is in command. You'll advance by sections ten yards apart – four sections. You've got to get there, all of you, at the same moment. The leading section will be ahead, but that won't make much odds as they've got to spread out wider than the others. Got it?'

'No, I ain't got it,' said Barca. 'Sounds sort of muddled up to me.'

Yet everyone had listened as closely as if it were a lecture on first aid to the wounded.

'Now then ! Number off by tens.'

They did so. The section leaders came up to Manuel. From the hill-top the guns were still pounding the village with shells, but the machine-guns firing only at the Assault Guard, which continued its advance. Manuel was used to handling men of his Party, but unfortunately there were few of them here.

'You take command of the first group of ten. We'll deploy on the right of the road, all of us; no use getting cut in two if those swine come down the road in an armoured car or something of the sort. And it will bring us nearer the Assault Guard. ... Ten comrades, over a hundred yards. Now, number one, get a move on with your ten mates. When you've gone three hundred yards, leave one man behind every ten yards. When you see the section on your left advancing, you'll advance. If anything goes wrong, hand over the command to the next man, and run back. You'll find, behind you ...' Whom would he find? Manuel had thought of sending Barca himself, things being as they were, it was up to him to be in the front line. No, there was nothing for it. '... you'll find Barca.'

Someone else could be sent to the men in the other lorries.

'When I whistle, everyone falls back on Barca. Got it?'

'Yes.'

'No, say it again.'

All was going well.

'Look, boys – the armoured train !'

All felt like kissing each other, for sheer joy. The train was firing at the presumed emplacements of the batteries and machine-guns – firing blind. But the milicianos, now they heard their guns answering the fascist guns, had no longer the impression of being cornered. They greeted the second boom with an ovation.

Manuel dispatched a communist to Ramos to tell him how things were; a U.G.T. man to the Assault Guard; and the oldest of the anarchists to inform the men in the lorries of his plan of campaign.

'Take something to eat with you,' said the militia girl. 'You never can tell!'

'Jump to it, lads!'

'Well, I'll bring you your grub, later on,' she said determinedly.

While the others went ahead, Barca ran back to the lorries.

The enemy was still plugging away at them, but now with rifles only. The second section started off, the third, and then the last, with Manuel in command.

There was nothing to impede the view along the vistas between the olive-trees. Up one of the spacious, tranquil avenues, Barca saw a miliciano advancing, then ten men, then a long file. He could not see beyond five hundred yards, and the long procession covered all his field of view; the whole grove seemed full of men advancing to the thunderous rhythm of the guns. The Assault Guard were firing on the adjoining hillside, but, now that he was amongst the trees, Barca could see them no longer. Evidently they had a sub-machine-gun, for a mechanical purring linked the ragged rifle-shots and merged with the incessant stutter of the fascist machine-guns. The line of milicianos kept on advancing, under a rather ineffective rifle-fire from the fascists. Manuel broke into a double, and all the line followed suit, like a cable dragged along a river-bed. Now Barca, too, was galloping uphill carried along by the confused fervour of an ideal which he called 'The People', a ferment of emotions worked up by the chaos and confusion of the day, the bombardment of the village, the wreckage of the lorry, the gun-shots from the armoured train – and now embodied in the little band that like one man was charging up against the fascists.

As they ran they trampled fallen branches underfoot; before the advance of the Assault Guards the machine-guns had been trained across the olive grove. Here the tang of resin gave place to the warm fumes of sun-baked soil. On branches grazed by bullets the foliage drooped and faltered, falling leaf by leaf as in an autumn wind. And, to the incessant rhythm of the guns, the little group raced upward, upward, showed up and disappeared, now flashing through tracts of sunlight, now all but invisible in shadows of the grove. The firing from the armoured train and the submachine-gun sounded in Barca's ears the promise of a new world; never again would the vineyards be wrested from the men who planted them.

They had twenty yards of open ground to cross. The moment they came out of the olive grove, the fascists turned one of their machine-guns on them. Round Barca the air was alive with bullets zzz-ing like angry wasps; he ran towards the rifles through the shrill steely swarm – invulnerable! Suddenly his legs crumpled up, he rolled over. Despite the searing pain, he went on looking straight ahead. Half his men had fallen, and lay where they fell; the other half had got through. Beside him lay the village grocer, dead, the shadow of a butterfly flickering on his face. The front line of the men from the other lorries stood hesitating on the edge of the olive grove. A distant drone of aeroplanes came to Barca's ears. Whose? Theirs or ours? he wondered. Then, from beside the place where the submachine-gun was firing, a rocket soared up into the sunlit air. The armoured train ceased fire.

Salazar turned to Ramos. 'Have the Assault Guard reached the field-guns?'

They had sent a runner to the train to say they would loose off a rocket when they reached the battery. They must be very near it now. So Ramos had ceased fire.

'Looks like it,' he said.

'How are our men getting on?'

'They're out of sight. They can't have got through as the heavies and machine-guns are still firing.'

'Shall I go and have a look?'

'Manuel seems to be putting up a damned good show, with Barca's help. He's just sent a message through to me.'

The field-glasses gave Ramos a close-up view of all the false serenity of rocks and pines and olives, festering now with wounds. But it was impossible to make out what was happening. He could only listen.

'What's so sickening,' he said, 'is that it's always the enemy who put up the real show, not our folk.'

The fascists began by a bombardment, cleaned up an area,

then marched their men into it. The people, leaderless, and all but unarmed, could merely fight . . .

'By the look of things just now, those poor chaps below must be getting butchered like sheep. Still, as they've risked an attack, there's always the chance the Assault Guard may rush the battery.' Ramos' voice was tremulous with excitement, his sensual lips were thin and anguished, his smile was gone; even his wayward hair looked like a wig.

'Anyhow the fascists won't get through.'

'The battery on the left has ceased fire.'

The foreheads of both men were tingling with the strain of listening to each sound.

A plane approached, gold-glinting on the sunbright sky; a light, fairly speedy machine. It dropped a bomb five hundred yards from the train. Probably it had no bomb-sights, and not being fitted for dropping bombs, had launched it through a window. Ramos had given instructions to the engine-driver, who now took his train quietly under cover of the nearby tunnel. After dropping all its bombs into the pine-wood, the plane went off, satisfied. The smell of resin grew still more pungent.

From the armoured train, they could see nothing. Between the thuds of clanging steel that shook the train from end to end, Pepe, an Asturian, naked from the waist, was explaining to his mates how the train had been fixed up.

'We used cement instead of steel plate. It ain't much to look at, but it's tough, you can bet your boots on that. This train looks like it was built of cardboard, but it'll stand up against 'most anything. In 'thirty-four, in the Asturias, we armoured the trains real fine — a good job of work that was, my lads. But this time, seems as if everyone was absent-minded — that's how the revolution is. The boys forgot all about the locomotive! What do you make of that — an armoured train charging full steam through the Tercio lines with an ordinary, unarmoured engine pulling it? Thirty miles out, you couldn't count the bullets that had gone through her guts — and through the driver's too. Riddled like a sieve. Well, we managed to slip past at night with another train and engine — armoured this time — and we had the boys entrained before the Tercio had time to bring their guns up.'

'Say, Pepe!'

'What?'

'That battery's still not firing.'

Ramos had come out of the tunnel to see how things were going with the rebels; he was switching his field-glasses in all directions, like a blind man groping for something with his hands.

'Our men are beating it for the village,' he said at last.

The milicianos were falling back, firing – rather ineffectively – as they did so. They vanished into a cutting. The fascists following them had three hundred yards of open ground to cross.

Ramos leapt into the engine-cab, brought the train forward to a point where it had the treeless patch in range – though it could not be seen from the fascist batteries which were still pounding away.

After the helter-skelter of the militia, the advancing fascists seemed moving like automata.

Now the machine-guns on the train spoke for the first time.

From left to right the fascists began falling, limply, their arms in air or fists clenched upon their bellies. The second wave hesitated at the edge of the clearing, took heart, dashed forward at the double; the hail of bullets mowed them down from right to left. The gunners in the train might be poor soldiers, but they were good shots. For the first time that day Ramos saw, again and again, that curious caper of a man who is shot while he is running – one arm upraised and his legs doubled under him, as if he were jumping to catch death on the wing. The fascists who had not been hit ran back into the wood, from which such as had escaped the machine-guns on the train had opened fire.

Shots rang out on the right, where a group of milicianos were posted. The fascists retreated through the wood, firing as they fell back.

'They have officers, and equipment,' Ramos murmured, running his fingers through his curls, 'but I'm damned if they'll get through. No, they won't get through.'

Under the tranquil summer sky pilots were still being put through their trial flights.

A volunteer, wearing a sweater despite the heat, came up to Magnin.

He gave his name: 'Captain Schreiner.' A vulpine little man with steely eyes and a pointed nose, some time the second-in-command of Richthofen's famous 'circus'. From above his large moustache Magnin peered benevolently down on the little man.

'How long since you last flew a plane?'

'I haven't been up since the War.'

'Ah, the devil! And how long would it take to get your hand in?'

'A few hours, I suppose.'

Magnin looked at him without replying.

Schreiner repeated: 'Yes, an hour or two should do.'

'Had a job in aviation?'

'No, I've been working in the Alès mines.' Schreiner did not look at Magnin as he answered; his eyes were intent on the whirling propeller-blades of the practice plane. The fingers of his right hand were twitching.

'The money-order came too late,' he said. 'I had to lorry-jump it as far as Toulouse.'

Closing his narrow eyes, he listened to the engine, while his fingers, still twitching, plucked at the creases of his sweater. Magnin's own keenness for aviation was such that the sight of the fingers plucking the rough fabric warmed his heart towards the German. Without opening his eyes, Schreiner was sniffing eagerly the vibrant air. 'Like a prisoner,' Magnin thought, 'who's just been set free.' Yes, that chap might make a useful officer. Magnin was short of subalterns, and Schreiner's voice had the crisp intonation common to professional soldiers and many communist leaders.

Towards them, across the shimmering sunlight, came Sibirsky, the chief instructor. Another instructor called up Schreiner, who walked off to the practice plane unhurrying but with his fingers still twitching.

Standing in the airways mess or on the tarmac, all the pilots were watching. Several of them had served in the Great War, and Magnin felt a little ill at ease. Yet, as regards this man, who had brought down twenty-two Allied machines, the only sentiment felt by all, even the mercenaries, was that of purely professional rivalry.

Near the bar, Scali, Marcelino, and Jaime Alvear were taking turns with the field-glasses. Jaime Alvear, who had spent his student years in France, had been appointed Combatant Interpreter to the International Air Force. He was a tall, swarthy young man with the look of a Red Indian chief; a rugged face and black hair always flapping on his forehead. Beside him stood another 'redskin', a smaller man with wine-red cheeks; Vegas – to his pals, 'Saint Anthony' – who, in the name of the U.G.T., showered cigarettes and gramophone records on his friends, the Pelicans. Scali's black basset, 'Raplati', was poking his long nose between the two men. Raplati was by way of being the squadron mascot. Jaime's father was, like Scali, an art-historian.

Some gusts of firing came from the far end of the landing-ground where Karlitch was putting the machine-gunners through their paces. Schreiner's machine took off, fairly well.

'Those volunteers will be a bit of a problem,' Sibirsky said to Magnin. Magnin, too, was conscious that it might be troublesome getting the mercenaries to work under the orders of volunteers, when the latter were, professionally speaking, well below their standards. 'I'm grateful for the confidence you've shown in me, Monsieur Magnin, by appointing me Instructor,' Sibirsky continued.

They took some steps side by side, without looking at each other; both were gazing up at the plane, now in full flight.

'Know anything about me?' Sibirsky asked abruptly.

'Why, of course.' As he spoke, chewing his long moustache, Magnin reflected that really he knew nothing about the man. He liked Sibirsky; for all his rather foppish looks – golden curls, a diminutive moustache – the sadness in his voice suggested, if not intelligence, at least experience. All Magnin really knew of him was his value as a technician; there was no questioning that.

'I want to tell you, Monsieur Magnin. Here they all think I'm a Red. That has its uses, I suppose. It's just as well. But I'd like you to know I'm not a White, either. They don't know much about life, these airmen of yours, even those who are getting on in years.' Uncomfortably, Sibirsky stared at his shoes. Then, raising his eyes, he watched the plane in flight for nearly a minute. 'Well, he can fly it – but that's the most one can say.' There was no irony in his voice. Schreiner was one of their oldest pilots; he was forty-six and had spent the last ten years in a factory; not one of the airmen present but was dreading to see what havoc age may work on a great pilot.

'We'll need at least five machines tomorrow, for the Sierra.' Magnin sounded anxious.

'I hated the life I was leading with my uncle in Siberia. People talked of nothing but fighting. Then I went away to college. When the Whites came, I joined them. Afterwards, I went to Paris. I was a chauffeur for a bit, then a mechanic; then I took to flying again. I'm a lieutenant in the French army.'

'I know. You'd like to go back to Russia, eh?'

Many Russians who had been 'White' were now serving in Spain, hoping thus to prove their loyalty and be permitted to return to Russia.

Another burst of machine-gun fire rattled across the sunlight from the far end of the flying-ground.

'Yes. But not as a communist. As a partyless man. I'm here on a contract; but even for twice the money I wouldn't have joined the others. I'm what you call a liberal. Karlitch, now, believed in 'order'; he used to be a white. Now that order reigns in Russia – and there's force behind it – he's gone red. Personally, I'm all for democracy – the States, France, England. ... Only – Russia's my country.'

He looked up at the plane again; this time to avoid meeting Magnin's eyes.

'There's just one thing,' he said, 'I hope you'll let me ask you. I don't want to have to bomb objectives within a city – not under any circumstances. I expect I'm rather too old for pursuit work. But for reconnaissance or bombing at the front ...'

'The Spanish Government doesn't countenance bombing open towns.'

'You see, I was detailed once to bomb the enemy's G.H.Q. The bombs fell on a school.'

Magnin did not dare to ask whether the headquarters and the school had been German or bolshevik. Schreiner's machine was getting into position to land.

'Undershooting,' Magnin grunted, steadying his binoculars.

'Perhaps he'll give her the gun.'

As Sibirsky expected, the pilot opened his throttle again. Both men had halted and were following every movement of the plane. There was any amount of room and the pilot had no excuse for muffing a first landing like that. Magnin was familiar with practice flights; he had been a chief pilot in one of the French airlines.

The plane returned, landed a trifle short. The pilot pulled his stick back and the machine leapt like a stone skipping off a ripple, then plumped down with a rending crash. It's lucky, Magnin thought, that machine has no military value.

Sibirsky, who had run towards the damaged plane, came back, followed by Schreiner and the assistant instructor.

'Forgive me,' Schreiner said, in such a tone that Magnin dared not look him in the face. 'I told you I needed two hours. Two days wouldn't be enough. It's all those years spent in the mines; I've lost my reflexes.'

Sibirsky and his assistant moved away.

'We'll talk about that later,' Magnin said.

'No use. But, thank you. I never want to see a plane again. I'm through with flying. Put me down for the militia, please.'

To the clatter of machine-guns, drumming nearer and nearer, the milicianos were dragging another machine across the tarmac; a sporting plane once the pride of some young *señorito*.

Schreiner walked off the grounds, with unseeing eyes, staring into emptiness. Like men shrinking from the sight of a child's agony, or of a disaster where all human words are futile, the pilots moved aside to let him pass. The war assimilated mercenaries and volunteers alike in a romantic venture; but aviation united them as childbirth makes all women one. Even those incorrigible gossips, Leclerc and Seruzier, had for once dried up; each man knew that the experience he had just witnessed would be his own one day. No one dared meet the German's gaze – which shrank from that of all.

But one pair of eyes was fixed on Magnin; the eyes of the pilot whose turn came after Schreiner's: Marcelino.

'Five machines are needed for the Sierra tomorrow,' Magnin repeated mechanically.

The machine-gun rapped out five shots, ten shots, and stopped. When Karlitch, the machine-gun instructor, saw Magnin coming, he went up to him, saluted, and drew him aside. Without saying anything, he produced three cartridges from his pocket; the caps had been dinted by the striker, but the bullets had not gone off.

'Made in Toledo,' Karlitch said, tapping the inscription with his finger-nail.

'Sabotage?'

'No, bad workmanship. And if a gun stalls while we're up, in the middle of a fight, and we've got to start it going again, you know what that means.'

Karlitch had gone to England, a broken man, and the privations he then endured had shattered what he had taken hitherto for his convictions. After some desultory years the former champion machine-gunner of Wrangel's army had joined the 'Back-to-Russia' movement which was developing amongst the émigrés. He was perhaps the only volunteer who hated the enemy simply because he was the enemy.

'What about the ground guns?' Magnin asked. 'We need some for the Sierra right away.'

The milicianos had no experience in handling any kind of machine-gun whatever, still less in restarting it when it jammed. Magnin had converted his best machine-gunners into instructors, under Karlitch's control. The ground force machine-gunners were being given a course in air gunnery and a group of picked milicianos was being trained in the use and upkeep of field machine-guns.

'Those men in the militia,' Karlitch said, 'are A1. They've been well picked. They're disciplined, they take pains, and they listen. So far, so good. But that fellow, Wurtz, Comrade Magnin – he's a wash-out. Always at Party meetings, never on his job. The only help I get is from Gardet. Our men have learnt all about handling machine-guns in the air, but I can't say how they'll do when they're actually up. I've nothing to test them with; no towed targets, no camera guns, no doped petrol, precious little ammunition, and bad at that. They know how to work their turrets. At the after-guns I'll post only men with air experience – we can't have 'em putting bullets through the tail! For training, I guess, they'll have to practise on the enemy!'

Karlitch gave a high-pitched cackle of delight, his cockscomb hair and eyebrows lifting, his nose-wings fluttering with glee. He had harked back to his beloved machine-guns, as Schreiner to his planes. And it struck Scali, who had just come up for the end of their conversation, that war has its physiological side as well.

*

All the revolutionary pilots who, on pacifist grounds, had dropped their spells of military training, had now to be put through a course of instruction, or written off the strength. But there was no question of waiting till next year to tackle Franco. And for the moment, the only men Magnin could count on were the professional civil pilots and those who had kept up their annual refresher courses.

He had cashiered several pilots from Morocco, used to old-fashioned aircraft and bombing a defenceless foe. The sight of their first casualties had stirred them to noble sentiments. 'After all, those chaps haven't done us any wrong. Why'd we want to start scrapping with 'em?' And so forth. But without definitely giving up their contracts. To France with the whole useless lot of them!

A Frenchman called Dugay was the first of the volunteers who had asked for a private interview with him. He was fifty years old; his grey moustache was paler than his cheeks.

'Comrade Magnin,' he began, 'this idea of packing me off to France – it ain't fair, you shouldn't do it. I served as an instructor in the War. Seems I'm too old to go up again – O.K. to that. But just give me a scrap of cotton waste and a job as a mechanic's mate. With a bus to look after – any old bus will do me proud.'

74

Sembrano dashed up, waving his arms.

'Listen, Magnin. We want a machine for San Benito right away. They're marching on Benito.'

'Ah ... yes, of course. But all the fighters are in the air, you know. And without fighters, what can we do?'

'Just got the orders. We're to send three machines; I've only two Douglases left.'

'Very well! What is it? A motor column?'

'Yes.'

'Right.'

He went to the telephone. Sembrano hurried off, his underlip protruding.

'Well, Comrade Magnin' – Dugay's voice again – 'what about me?'

'What? ... Oh, all right, you can stay. Now what – wait a bit! What am I forgetting?'

He was forgetting nothing; but that flustered air – like the phrase he had just used – had become a mannerism with him. In point of fact his actions were always cool and calculating.

No sooner was Dugay gone than he was pestered by a group of newcomers. 'We've all got our tickets for light planes, and we're quite willing to learn.' Next a meaner group, men who were out merely for the pay, and would 'swing the lead' at the least pretext. Magnin shipped the whole lot back, 'unserviceable goods', to the far side of the Pyrenees.

Jaime came in, Raplati trotting between his legs. Magnin was not expecting him.

'Comrade Magnin, I wanted to tell you. ... I know you don't need me as interpreter just now, but – well, it's like this. Marcelino's got to go through his trial flight, of course. Only I thought, Comrade Magnin, in case you haven't heard about it, you ought to know that Marcelino's been two years in prison, under the fascist régime.'

Listening, Magnin felt drawn to the tall young Spaniard in the tight-fitting overalls, with the prominent chin and brow and aquiline nose. Friendship, it seemed, could get no purchase on those rugged, strongly-moulded features, and showed only in the changed expression of his eyes.

'He used to be a professional hydroplane pilot. Then, after

Lauro de Bosis' death, he dropped pamphlets on Milan. Balbo's flight brought him down, of course; he was in a light plane. He was sentenced to six years' imprisonment, but he managed to escape from the Lipari Islands. He hasn't flown any sort of plane since the trial. Or a fighter since he left the Italian army. He's ... a broken man. What I mean to say, Comrade Magnin, not that I want to bias your decision in any way, and of course there's no question of giving him a pilot's job – I'd like to suggest that something should be done for him; the Spanish comrades who're here would be awfully glad if you could ...'

'I'll be glad, too,' Magnin replied. Jaime went away. Captain Mercery came up. He, too, was nearly fifty. A grey moustache straddled his upper lip; he had the hard-bitten look of an old pirate chief – a look which he deliberately accentuated – and he wore cavalry boots outside civilian trousers.

'See here, Monsieur Magnin, it's all a question of technical knowledge, there's no getting behind that. It's experience that tells ...'

'Are you going back to France?'

Mercery raised his arms excitedly. 'Monsieur Magnin, my wife was in Spain on the sixteenth. For the Stamp Collectors' Congress, you know. Well, on the twentieth, she writes to me: "What's happening here is too foul for words. No man would submit to it." A woman, mind you; a woman wrote that. But I'd started off already! I'm at the service of Spain. In any capacity – but serving Spain. We've got to smash fascism. As I said to the reactionary folk back there in Noisy-le-Sec, "No, gentlemen, it's not the mummies that keep Egypt going, it's Egypt keeps the mummies."'

'Just so. Exactly. You're a captain. Would you like me to place you at the disposal of the Ministry of War?'

'Yes. Well I mean ... I'm a captain, as you just said. I might be in the Reserve of Officers, only I've always refused to do my periods of service, on account of my convictions.'

Magnin had been told that Mercery served in the War as Company Sergeant-Major, and that he was 'captain' of – a fire-brigade! Then, he had taken it for a joke.

'Why ... yes ... of course.'

'Wait a bit. I know what a trench looks like. I went through the War.'

For all his rodomontade, obviously the man meant well; and, thought Magnin, a competent sergeant-major can be quite as useful to us as a captain.

It was Marcelino's turn. Wearing a loose, beltless flying-suit, he was staring at his boots with a woebegone air. He raised his eyes and said gloomily: 'Prison life, you know ... doesn't do the reflexes any good.'

A gust of gunfire cut him short; Karlitch was on his job at the far end of the ground.

'Still I used to be quite a hand at bombing,' Marcelino went on, 'and I expect I'm all right still.'

A fortnight earlier, while Magnin, in the intervals of recruiting volunteers and hiring mercenaries, was trying to buy for the Spanish Government all the aircraft available on the market, he had found one morning, when he came home, a young man with a drooping moustache, misted eye-glasses, and hat set well back on his head, waiting on the landing between the two doors of his flat. When they entered, all the telephones were buzzing and several visitors, strangers to each other, were pacing up and down the various rooms. He had installed Marcelino on his little boy's bed, with his back to an open cupboard, and clean forgotten about him. Returning at about two in the afternoon, he had found the Italian pilot still seated on the bed, surrounded by a number of dolls which he had unearthed from the cupboard, and telling stories to himself about them.

'If you send me up as a bomber, I might be able to do a bit of dual control as well. I'm sure I'd get my hand in pretty quickly.'

Magnin looked hard at the spare figure in the flapping overalls, the head with its sleek curls like the head on a Venetian medal. 'We'll give you a bombing test tomorrow, with cement bombs.'

Sembrano's Douglases and one of Magnin's transport planes were being brought to the far end of the landing-ground.

After the events in Algeria, when the Italian war-planes flying in battle formation had crashed, several governments had put their older war planes out of commission and sold them off. The machines which were now being brought on to the tarmac

77

would have short shrift against the new Savoias, if the Italian pilots put up a good fight.

Looking round, Magnin noticed that Schreiner had stepped into Marcelino's place. The German's silence contrasted both with the young Italian's timid insistence and Dugay's blundering assertiveness; it was an animal dumbness.

At last he spoke. 'Kamerad Magnin, I've been thinking. I said I was through with flying, and that's so – I am no longer goot for it. But I am still a goot marksman. Yes, my eye's always in for shoooting. I know it; haven't I practised at the village fairs, and with my revolver?'

His face was expressionless, but his voice was vibrant with an undertone of hatred. His slotted eyes were fixed on Magnin, his predatory head sunken between his shoulders like a vulture's. Magnin was watching an anarchist car moving past the hangars; it was the first time he had set eyes on the black flag.

'Seems the planes don't want me any longer,' Schreiner said. 'Right. Give me an anti-aircraft job.' Again, two or three gusts of gunfire. 'Please to have that kindness.'

Is there a 'style' common to revolutions? The figures of the volunteers passing in the dusk behind the Le Corbusier buildings on the aerodrome brought equally to mind the men of the Mexican revolutions and those of the Paris Commune. All the planes had been tethered for the night. Magnin, Sembrano, and his friend Vallado, were drinking tepid beer. Since the war, ice was no longer forthcoming at the airport.

'Things are in a bad way at the military aerodrome,' Sembrano remarked. 'The army of the revolution wants organizing from A to Z. Otherwise Franco'll fill the graveyards with the victims of *his* law and order. How do you think they managed it in Russia?' Seen in profile against the lights in the mess, with his protruding underlip, he looked still more like Voltaire – an amiable Voltaire in a white flying-suit.

'*They* had rifles. *Plus* four years' discipline and active service. And the communists, as you know, stood for discipline.'

'Tell me, Magnin, why are you a revolutionary?' Vallado asked.

'I wonder! Well, I've run several factories; people like us, men who've always been interested in our work, can hardly

78

realize what it means to spend one's whole life – wasting eight hours a day. ... But I want men to know *why* they're working.'

Sembrano's view was that as a rule the owners of industrial concerns were incapable of running them, and left them to be run by experts; as an expert, he preferred to work for the collectivity, rather than for a private owner of the business. His view was shared by Jaime Alvear and most of the leftist technicians.

Vallado saw things from another angle; what he wanted was a Spanish renaissance and he saw no hope of it from the Right Wing. Vallado belonged to the upper middle class; it was he who had dropped the pamphlets on the Montaña Barracks. But for the absence of the small moustache, which he had shaved off at the outbreak of the rebellion, his was a typical señorito's face.

Magnin was struck by the arguments these men were using to rationalize their instinctive feelings.

'Personally, I rather think,' he said, 'I'm Left because ... that's the way I'm built. And there are all sorts of links, and loyalties, between me and the leftists. I've seen what they are aiming at, I've helped them to achieve it, and I've been drawn nearer and nearer them each time there's been another effort to hold them up.'

'When one's merely wedded to a political belief,' Sembrano smiled, 'that's no great matter. But when one has children by it ...'

'By the way, what used you to be? A communist?'

'No a right-wing socialist. Were you a communist?'

'No,' Magnin said, pulling his moustache with little febrile tugs. 'I, too, was a socialist. But on the revolutionary left-wing.'

'Personally' – and now Sembrano's smile was dimed with a regret that seemed in keeping with the gathering darkness – 'I was above all, a pacifist.'

'One changes one's ideas,' Vallado remarked.

'The people for whom I'm fighting haven't changed. And that's the only thing that matters.'

In the warm shadows of the summer nightfall mosquitoes circled droning round them. And as they talked on, the advancing night flooded the flying-field with the grave, unfathomable gloom of all great open spaces.

Twenty milicianos in *monos* were coming down from the Sierra, for lunch. No officers were amongst them; presumably, as there was no depending on the outposts in the mountain passes staying on duty at meal-times, the officers had thought it better to assume that task themselves. Fortunately, Manuel reflected, things were much the same with the enemy.

Five of the young men wore women's hats, saucer-shaped, in sentimental shades of green and blue – in the 1935 fashion – above a three days' growth of beard. Wild roses, the summer's last on the Sierra, were stuck into the crowns.

'From now on,' Manuel said, 'only the comrades detailed for that duty by the workers' and peasants' unions will be authorized to doll up as mannequins. Preferably, elderly men with written references from at least two unions. Get that into your thick heads, my lads!'

'The sun was in our eyes when we attacked, and we couldn't see a darned thing. There was a hat-shop near by – closed, of course, but we helped ourselves. Afterwards, we hung on to the hats.'

Their headquarters that day (it was also the base of the armoured train) was a village some six hundred yards distant. The market square was surrounded by a wooden balcony, like the courtyard of a farmhouse; there were some shops painted red and orange – one of them adorned with an enormous mirror – for the benefit of summer visitors, and a sugar-loaf tower in the Escurial style.

'They don't suit us too bad,' a young man grinned. 'We look hotsy-totsy all right.'

They sat down at the café tables, their rifles slung across their backs, the flowered hats still on their heads. Behind them, on the slopes of the Sierra that stretched away for fifteen miles and more, last patches of the bluebells, which two months earlier had clothed the hillsides, were turning brown and sere, above the yellow cornfields of the plain. The hum of a car driven full speed came nearer and suddenly a brown Ford loomed across the portico and three arms shot up parallel, in the fascist salute. Below the raised arms were the Napoleonic cocked hats and the green, yellow-braided uniform of the Civil Guard. They had not noticed the milicianos, who were having their meal on the left of the portico, and evidently imagined they were in a fascist village. The armed peasants in another, adjoining café rose slowly from their seats.

'Friends!' shouted the newcomers, stopping the car with a jerk. 'We are on your side!'

The peasants brought their rifles up. The milicianos had opened fire already. Though many members of the Civil Guard had come in from the enemy lines, none so far had given the fascist salute. At least thirty shots were fired. Across the rifle-shots Manuel heard the duller explosions of bursting tyres. Most of the peasants had aimed at the car. One of the guards, however, was wounded. A gust of wind filled the little square with the perfume of sun-scorched flowers.

Manuel had the guards disarmed and searched, and dispatched them to the mayor's office under an escort of milicianos – the peasants had a particular animosity towards the Civil Guard – and telephoned to Colonel Mangada's headquarters.

'Is it urgent?' an orderly officer inquired. 'Any special danger?'

'No.'

'Then, no "summary justice", please. We'll send an officer for the court-martial. They'll be tried in an hour's time.'

'Right. There's something else. Their coming like this shows that we're within reach of a fascist locality. I've posted a sentry at the entrance of the village and another man in the road. But that's not enough ...'

The court-martial took place at the mayor's office. In the large, whitewashed room, behind the accused men, stood the peasants in their black and grey smocks, and the milicianos. In the front row were the wives of peasants who had been killed by the fascists. Each man and woman watched in silence, with the grim aloofness of an Islamic warrior.

Two of the prisoners made statements. Yes, they had given the fascist salute; that was because they believed the village to be fascist, they had been passing through it on their way to the

Republican lines. A story as pitiful in the hearing as in the telling – like all obvious falsehoods. They seemed floundering in a morass of lies, gasping for breath in their stiff trappings, like men in uniform being slowly strangled by it. A peasant woman went up to the presiding officer. The fascists had occupied her village, a neighbouring village that the Republicans had recaptured. She had seen the guards drive up in their car.

'When they bade me come, 'long of my son, I thought as 'twas to bury him. No, that weren't it – seems they wanted to question me, the filthy scum!' She moved back a pace, as though to have a better view. 'That fellow there, he was one of 'em. If 'twas his son had been killed, what'ld he have to say about it, eh? What'ld *you* say, you brute, you?'

It was the wounded man she was accusing. He tried to defend himself, puffing and blowing like a fish out of its element. Quite likely, Manuel thought, the man was innocent. The woman's son had been shot before she was questioned, and she was seeing his murderers everywhere. Now the accused was speaking of his loyalty to the Republic. Beads of sweat were forming on the shaved cheeks of the man beside him, trickling down on both sides of his waxed moustache. It was as if fear had turned his blood to water and his very life were ebbing away in the stillness of the courtroom.

'You say you came here to join us,' the presiding officer observed. 'How is it you have no information to give us?'

He turned to the third prisoner, who had said nothing so far. The man looked him straight in the eyes, making it clear that he was addressing the president alone.

'Listen. You are an officer – though you've gone over to these people. I've heard quite enough talk from those two fellows. I have my identity card with me, No. 17 in the Segovia Falangists. It's your duty to have me shot. Well and good. I suppose you'll have it done today. Only, before I die, I'd like to have the satisfaction of seeing those two filthy renegades shot first. Their cards are Nos. 6 and 11. They make me vomit! Now, as soldier to soldier, will you oblige me by making them shut up, or else, put me outside the courtroom.'

'Ain't he putting on airs!' the old woman muttered. 'Ain't he proud of hisself, the baby-killer!'

'I'm on your side!' the wounded man screamed to the tribunal.

The presiding judge was looking at the officer who had been speaking. With his very flat nose, thick lips, curly hair, and short moustache, he might have stepped out of a Mexican film. For a moment he seemed about to strike the wounded man; but nothing happened. His hands were not a policeman's hands. Had the fascists disseminated agents in the Civil Guard, as they had done in the Montaña Barracks?

'When did you join the Civil Guard?'

The man made no reply; the proceedings had ceased to interest him.

'I'm on your side! On your side, I tell you!' For the first time, there was a note of sincerity in the wounded man's voice. 'I'm on your side!'

*

Manuel did not enter the square until the volley had been fired. The three men had been shot in a neighbouring street; they had fallen forward on to their faces, their heads in sunlight, feet in shadow. A very small kitten was sniffing the warm blood of the flat-nosed man. A boy came up, pushed the cat away, dipped his forefinger in the blood, and began scrawling on the wall. Manuel watched the moving finger with a tightening of his throat. *Death to the Fascists*. Rolling up his sleeves, the youngster went to the fountain and began washing his hands.

Manuel stared at the dead body and the cocked hat in the dust beside it; then looked up at the writing on the wall, which still was almost crimson, and the peasant bending over the fountain. 'When we are building the new Spain,' he thought, 'we shall have both alike to contend against. And one will be no easier to handle than the other.'

Ruthlessly sunlight clanged on the yellow walls.

v

Ramos and Manuel were walking on the embankment, and the evening was like any summer evening without sounds of guns. Fragrant with the scents of pines and rock-plants, and bathed in a grey-green twilight like the backgrounds of old equestrian portraits, the Sierra rolled its decorative foothills down the great plain of Madrid. In the tide of darkness flooding the plain, only one thing looked new or strange, the armoured train crouching in its tunnel; and it, too, seemed like the relic of some bygone war that had receded with the failing light.

'I've just been having the hell of a hoo-ha with our men,' said Ramos. 'Half an hour ago! Ten of them wanted to go home to dinner; one man actually wanted to trot back to Madrid!'

'It's the hunting season now; they can't tell the difference. And how did your "hoo-ha" pan out?'

'Five are staying, seven leaving. If they were communists, every man would stay.'

Some desultory gun-shots and a distant boom of cannon made the great silence of the mountains deeper still.

'What made you become a communist, Ramos?'

Ramos pondered for a while, then said:

'Growing old, I think. Oh, I know at forty-two one's not so very ancient. But in my anarchist days I was much fonder of mankind in general. Anarchism, for me, meant the "Syndicate" – but above all, human relations, human contacts. The political shaping of a worker is, to start with, a matter of outside influences; it only becomes a personal affair later on.' He glanced up at the sky; the night promised to be fine. 'There's one thing, Manuel, I do wish you'd explain to me – if you can make any sense of it. There, over against us, is the Spanish Army. Oh, I grant you it's mostly the officers. Well, in the Philippines, they took it in the neck didn't they. In Cuba, too. Because they were up against the Americans? Let's say that was it; superior equipment, *plus* first-class organization. In Morocco, too, they took a nasty knock – but Abd-el-Krim wasn't the Americans, not by a long chalk. Why should our little gentlemen with the tooth-brush moustaches cut and run before the Krim, and not now? A "comic-opera army", that's what we always called them. Why the hell don't they skedaddle now, like they did in Melilla?'

The relations between Manuel and Ramos were changing. Till now they had been such as an experienced trade-unionist might have with a thirty-year-old man who, for all his frivolous air, was fundamentally serious and applied himself to analysing the world on which he had set his hope and drawing a clear line between romantic fancies and verified realities – but lacking political experience. Now he was beginning to acquire that experience, and Ramos knew that Manuel's knowledge covered a much wider field than his own. As on that first night at the telephone exchange Manuel had kept on waving a ruler, so tonight he had a pine-branch in his hand – with its tuft of pine needles still on it – which he kept on waving like a feather-duster. He could not bear to feel his right hand empty.

'No, Ramos, old chap, there aren't any comic-opera armies – only comic operas about the army. What they call a comic-opera army is an army suited for a civil war. Why, in ours – the Spanish Army – there's an officer for every half a dozen men. Do you think, in the innocence of your heart, that the army budget is meant to pay for war? Not a bit of it; it's to pay the officers – who belong to the owning class or serve its interests – and to buy automatic arms quite inadequate for actual warfare (too much goes in graft) but adequate to police the country. Our machine-guns, for instance, are of the 1913 type, our planes are over ten years old: worthless in real war, but good enough to crush a rising. Our armament's not up to the standard of a colonial war, let alone an international one. No one ever hears of the Spanish Army except in connexion with defeats or rackets. And repressions. It's not a comic-opera army, it's a poor imitation of the Reichswehr.'

Sounds of distant gunshots drifted up from the valleys. Some wounded men were carried past on sheets held at the four corners.

'Every day,' Manuel said, gazing towards the hill-tops behind which were the fascists coming from Segovia, 'the people saves Madrid.'

'Yes, and after that it goes to bed!'

'But starts again next day.'

'You're shaping well, Manuel. I'm glad of it. You led your men damned well in that attack on the battery.'

'Perhaps something's changed in me, for as long as I live. But it doesn't date from that "do" with the battery the day before yesterday. No, the change came today when I saw that fellow writing on the wall with the blood of the shot fascist. I hadn't any more sense of responsibility then, when I was giving orders in the olive-grove than when I drove the lorry or, in the old days, when I used to drive my "winter-sports bus".'

' "In the old days!" ' Ramos sounded amused. The 'old days' were – a month before!

'The past isn't a matter of mere time. But when I saw that writing on the wall – well, I realized a duty lay on us. Yes, Ramos, old chap, I was blooded to responsibility.'

Within the region under Government control, distant tongues of flame were leaping, a shepherd's or a peasant's fire; and on the flames the night mist seemed converging, rolling up swathe on swathe. The world of day was fading out, and nothing glimmered on the darkening hillside but the firelight; the spirit of peace, hounded down from the mountains and driven to earth, like the armoured train within the tunnel, seemed leaping joyfully to life amid the dancing flames. Another fire lit up, much farther away on the right.

'Who's looking after the wounded?' Manuel asked.

'The head physician of the Sanatorium. A very painstaking fellow.'

'A Republican leftist?'

'Right-wing socialist, I think. The militia girls are very helpful too.'

Manuel told him about the young girl who had so unexpectedly turned up behind the lorries.

Running his fingers through his curls, Ramos smiled. 'What's your impression of the militia girls, Manuel?'

'In an offensive, useless; all they're good for is to rattle the men's nerves. In a defensive action, excellent. Their courage works by fits and starts (so does a good many men's, for that matter), but they're magnificent at times.'

'Do you know, there's one thing pleases me in this war. In every village Franco takes, everybody gets more servile than ever; not only our people – that's inevitable – but even the children, who're sent back to the padre, like the women to their kitchens. That's why all the underdogs, in every walk of life, have joined our side.'

There is a curious potency in fire, and the flames rising and falling with the cadence of a forge seemed beaconing the bodies of the fallen and quieting the frenzies of the living with night's anodyne.

Ramos felt the smile dying from his lips. He watched the second fire a while. Then put up his field-glasses again. Those were not shepherds' fires, but signals.

Was he, like the milicianos, getting to see spies everywhere? But such fire signals were nothing new; moreover – he had been counting – yes, those swine were using Morse, but unluckily the message was in code.

The other fire, too, was flashing a message; the fascists had made their preparations well. How many similar fires were lighting up tonight behind the republican lines? On all those hillsides, as far as eye could reach, comrades in arms were lying, sleeping. All was silent but for the faint hum of cicadas. Those who had fallen in the day's fighting, stretched full length on asphalt roads or sprawling in the brushwood of the hillside, were entering now on their first night of death. Under the tranquil afterglow brooding above the Sierra, only the soundless speech of treachery floated up from the rising tide of darkness.

3

1

Manuel began to realize that the whole duty of the soldier is to do his best to riddle enemy flesh with shreds of iron.

Agonizing screams – they might have been either a man's or a woman's, for at the extremest pitch of pain there is no difference – echoed down the ward of the San Carlos Hospital, and died away.

It was a high room, lit from above by small round airholes almost entirely blocked by luxuriant foliage, through which the rays of the high summer sun were filtering. The greenish light and vast, blank walls in which no window was to be seen except high overhead, the twisted bodies in pyjamas hobbling to and fro on crutches in the uneasy silence of the hospital, and the spectral forms, like masquers in a carnival, shrouded in their bandages – all gave an impression that pain had set up its kingdom here for all eternity, beyond time and change.

Next to this cavern of sea-green gloom was the ward for serious cases, whence the screams originated; a room of normal height, with proper windows and eight beds. All that Manuel saw as he went in was a line of box-shaped mosquito-nets, and a nurse sitting by the door. In the full light of day the ward looked strangely empty, Manuel thought, comparing this sunny room with the dim torture-chamber haunted with white-swathed ghosts, which he had just left. But the sounds he heard were enough to dispel any illusions as to the nature of the place.

From a bed in the centre of the room came moans of pain, pain so intense as to transcend all human speech, the suffering that wrings from the sufferer those cries of speechless agony which are common to both man and beast; that succession of hoarse screams, rising and falling with the breath, which gives the impression that they can only end when the breath itself gives out. And now, when at last they did stop, they were followed by a grinding of the teeth, for the sufferer a relief, like the shrieks of a woman in childbirth, but appalling to listen to.

Manuel felt convinced the screams would start again once the man got back his breath.

'What's the matter with him?' he whispered to the nurse.

'A flying accident. He was brought down with all his bombs. They exploded when they hit the ground. Five machine-gun bullets, twenty-seven splinters.'

The muslin of the mosquito-net bulged, as if the wounded man were sitting up on the edge of his bed.

'It's his mother,' said the nurse. 'He's twenty-two.'

'Of course you're used to this sort of thing.' There was sadness in his voice.

'We haven't enough nurses. I'm a surgeon, really.'

The screams began again, even shriller than before, as though the man were trying to intensify his agony to the point of swooning; then stopped abruptly. And now Manuel could not hear even the grinding of teeth. But he dared not approach the bed.

An almost imperceptible sound made him aware that the

wounded man's fingers were plucking at the bed-sheets. Then he heard another sound, so soft at first that he was puzzled what it could be; at last it grew distinct ... a sound of fluttering lips. When the whole body is a quivering mass of pain, what use are words? In this brief respite, his mother was doing the only thing she could; kissing him.

Manuel could hear her smothering her son with kisses, in feverish haste as though, knowing the pain was on the point of coming back, she hoped to stave it off with her caresses.

A hand seized the mosquito-net and wrung it convulsively; Manuel felt as if the agony he seemed to see poised in empty air were throbbing in his own arm. Suddenly the clenched fist opened and the screams began again.

'How long has ... has this been going on?' Manuel asked.

'Since the day before yesterday.'

Now for the first time he took stock of the nurse. She was small, very young. She was not wearing a veil, her hair was black and glossy. 'We nurses ...' she began. 'Well, one gets used to hearing the patients' screams; but when their people start shrieking, it's different. We simply have to send them away or we could never do an operation.'

'Is Barca still here?' asked Manuel, between two spasms of cries. It seemed to him that never more in this room could there be a respite from those sounds.

'No, next door.'

Manuel was relieved; he was sensitive to the suffering of others, but incapable of expressing the sympathy he felt. Only too aware of his awkwardness in such cases as this, he resented it bitterly.

Barca's ward was just beyond and communicated with the green-lit cavern which he had passed through first. Manuel opened the door, then hesitated a moment, feeling that to close it behind him would have been too much like shutting down the lid of a coffin upon the wounded man. Finally he left it ajar.

Barca was sitting up in bed. Yes, he had everything he wanted. He had plenty of oranges and picture papers. And lots of pals to see him. Only – those god-awful fools refused to give him morphia. If they were afraid of him turning drug-fiend at his time of life, he'd never heard such bloody nonsense.

As it was, they'd put a great weight on the end of his leg – it was broken in two different places – and the result was he couldn't sleep. If only they could get him to sleep, 'twouldn't be too bad.

'You could manage to sleep with all that –?'

Manuel was thinking of the screams from the adjoining ward, which reached him, only slightly muffled, through the half-open door.

'Well, I couldn't bear it in the same room. It ain't easy to explain, but that's the way it is. In another room, I can manage. O' course, they ought to put the quiet ones together. Shut the door; we're a quiet lot in this ward, anyhow.'

'What was he, that chap?' Manuel felt as though by speaking of the man he were somehow reopening the door he had just closed on him.

'A mechanic. He was in the militia first; then in the air force. Bomber.'

'Was he a militant?'

'Not him !'

'Then why was he on our side?'

'Which side would you expect him to be on – him, a mechanic? With the fascists?'

'Well, he might have stood out.'

'Stood out? Hm ...'

Barca knitted his brows and raised his head, as a fresh twinge shot up his leg. Then he rested his head on the pillow, and once more the pain he was enduring showed in the worn old face, deepening the hollows of his eyes and giving his features that strange fluidity, that grave, disconsolate air of a sick child, which we so often see when suffering brings forth the nobility latent in a face. Already, at the Sierra, Manuel had been struck by Barca's eyes. His cheeks were weathered still duskier than his hair, the small grey moustache seemed darker than the limpid eyes. The whole expression of his face, commonplace enough in its main features, came from the thick eyelids, weary with all the bitterness of a long life resentfully endured. Covered with a network of tiny wrinkles, like a piece of crackle china, they gave his face its air of rustic humour; whenever the eyes closed, you fancied he was smiling.

'How's the armoured train getting on?'

'Pretty well, I think,' Manuel replied. 'But I don't really know; I'm not on it any longer. I've been appointed company commander in the Fifth Regiment.'

'Like it?'

'I've lots to learn.'

Across the closed door they heard again the sound of groans.

'That young 'un was with us because — well, that's how he was.'

'What about you, Barca?'

'There's a heap of reasons . . .'

His face twitched, he tried to move, then turned towards Manuel, as though waiting for him to explain himself.

'You weren't really bound to join up,' Manuel remarked.

'I was a trade-unionist, mind you.'

'Yes. But not a militant; you weren't really in any immediate danger.'

'See here, lad, I'd like to know how you'd have taken it, that phylloxera racket.'

Barca had used to be a tenant wine-grower in Catalonia, as his father and grandfather had been before him. The phylloxera epidemic had given his landlord a pretext for robbing him of the fruits of over half a century's toil.

'But you'd made a fresh start, you had enough to live on.'

From the tone of his voice Barca realized that Manuel was out to get to the bottom of his motives, not to question them.

'You mean to say: Why wasn't I neutral?'

'Yes.'

Barca smiled and to his smile it seemed that pain had lent a curious depth of experience.

'There's folk that never can stay neutral. When was I ever neutral, I'd like to know?'

Manuel had a glimpse of men on crutches in the glaucous twilight of the next room gliding past the open doorway, one following the other.

'All the same it ain't no laughing matter,' Barca went on. 'It's a mighty serious business. Yes, there's one thing worser than the worsest fascist — and that's being dead!' He closed his eyes.

'And I tell you this bloody leg of mine hurts more than owt a fascist could put upon me.' He tried to raise his hand, but weakness cut short the gesture. 'No, that ain't so. No, come to that, I'd do the same thing all over again. Well then?'

Another burst of screaming came from the next room. Would *that* man do the same thing over again? That question was no doubt in Barca's mind.

'Mind you, what you asked just now,' he went on, 'that ain't no new idea with me. That day in the pine-wood, when I reckoned like as not my number was up, well, I thought it all over. Like any man thinks things over now and then. Not like you do, perhaps. In my own way. When I don't know something, I can pick it up, often enough, when I set my mind to it. But as far as understanding what I am. . . . It's the words that get me down. See what I mean?'

'Quite.'

'That's because you've got the brains. Well, the long and the short of it is this: I won't have folk look down on me. Listen, lad.' He did not raise his voice, only he spoke more slowly, in the sort of tone he might have used had he been sitting with others at a table and raised a monitory finger. 'That's how it is. All the rest's beside the mark. You're right about the money; I could have fixed it up with them maybe. But those folk want to be looked up to, and I'm darned if I'll look up to them. They ain't worth it. There's some as I can respect, but not them. I can respect a man of learning like Professor Garcia, sure! Not them.'

Garcia was one of the leading Spanish ethnologists. He used to spend his summers in San Rafael, and Manuel had been struck by the regard in which he was held by the militants in that part of the Sierra.

'And there's summut else,' Barca continued. 'I'm going to tell you a thing I once heard. Perhaps there ain't nothing in it, perhaps there is. When I used to be a peasant – before I went to Perpignan – the Marquis he came once to have a look at us. I heard him talking to the folk who'd come with him – talking about *us*, he was. This is what he said – I remember it word for word. "Did you ever see such people!" says he. "Why, they think more about humanity at large than their own kith and kin!" His voice was scornful like. I couldn't have said nowt against it right off, but it set me thinking. Yes, that time too, I thought it over. And this is how I see things: when we, our people I mean, try to do something for humanity we're working for our own kith and kin as well. But them others, they pick and choose – see what I mean? They sort folk out.' After a moment's silence, he continued. 'Señor Garcia came and saw me here the other day. We've known each other quite a while. He's a man who's always interested in things, is Señor Garcia. Now that he's in the Intelligence, as they call it, he wants to know what's happening in the villages. "What about 'equality?'" he asks me. See here. Manuel, there's summut very important you don't know, neither you nor him. That's because you and him are ... oh, let's say things always went too easy for you. The likes of Garcia, he don't hardly know what it means to be ... badgered. And let me tell you, the opposite of that – humiliation, as he calls it – it ain't equality. You know that bellyaching motto the Frenchies put up on all their buildings, *Liberté, Egalité, Fraternité*. Well, those chaps weren't such fools as you'd think. Seeing that's just what "Fraternity" means: the opposite of being badgered.'

In the main ward, beyond the open door, men could be seen walking about with their arms set in plaster, swathed in cocoons of bandages. Sometimes an arm held by the splints in an unnatural position far from the body or at right angles to it gave its owner the look of a strolling fiddler in the act of playing on his violin. There was something particularly eerie in the scene; those monstrous, rigid arms paralysed in never-ending gestures, and the soundless violinists sgliding like waxwork figures trundled to and fro in the green twilight, in a spectral silence murmurous with the low, incessant drone of flies.

II

On the aerodrome six machines of the latest type had lined up for the start, and even the sweltering heat could not abate the general enthusiasm. A column of Moors engaged in the Estremadura offensive was marching from Merida on Medellin. A strong motorized force, it was believed to contain the pick of the fascist army. Staff Headquarters had just sent through a telephone message to Sembrano and Magnin, informing them that Franco in person was commanding the column.

Unarmed and officerless, the militia in the Estremadura was putting up a more or less forlorn resistance. A scratch force of field labourers, potboys, innkeepers, saddlers, and the like, some thousands of the most downtrodden folk in Spain were sallying forth from Medellin with shot-guns to face the submachine-guns of the African brigade.

Three Douglases and three multi-seaters armed with 1913 machine-guns occupied half the width of the aerodrome. (There were no fighters, all had been sent to the Sierra.) Round them stood Sembrano and his friend Vallado; the Spanish Air Line pilots Magnin, Sibirsky, Darras, Karlitch, Gardet, Jaime, and Scali and some novices. In front of the hangars were old Dugay and all the mechanics – with them, Jaime's dog, Raplati. The whole ground staff had turned out in force for the occasion. Jaime was singing a Flamenco folksong.

The squadron took off and soared south-west in two V-shaped groups.

Though up in the planes the air was cool enough, the world below was blanketed in a heat-haze like the quivering air above a furnace. Here and there a peasant in a wide-brimmed straw hat showed up against the corn. From the Toledo mountains to the hills of Estremadura, up to the limit of the battle area, the harvest-coloured earth drowsed in its afternoon siesta, wrapped in peace from one horizon to the other. Dust-clouds welling up across the light made spurs and foothills flat as shallow stencils patterning the plain. Badajoz, Merida (taken by the fascists on the 8th) and Medellin were still almost invisible – tiny specks upon the vastness of the shimmering fields.

Gradually the countryside became more rugged, and at last Badajoz, with its Alcazar and deserted bull-rings, hove into view, gaunt as the land of treeless crags around them, with their roofs of weathered tiles grey in the sunlight – like Berber skeletons stretched on an African desert. The pilots studied their maps, bombers glanced down their bomb-sights, machine-gunners trained their foresights, tiny whirligigs that fluttered in the rushing air outside the cockpit. Now below them lay the time-scarred Spanish city with its dusky women at the windows, olives and aniseed put out to cool in buckets of well-water, children strumming the piano with one finger, and lean cats listening for each note to trickle out and die upon the heat-mist. Everything looked so parched and desiccated that one fancied tiles and stones, houses and streets would crumble into dust at the first bomb, in a brittle din of bones and rubble. Above the central square Karlitch and Jaime waved their handkerchiefs in greeting, and the Spanish bombers let fall scarves dyed in the Republican colours. Next came a fascist town; the observers identified the ancient theatre and ruins of Merida — though it might as well have been Badajoz, or any other country town in Estremadura. At last they made Medellin.

Their task was to locate the road along which the column was advancing; but all the treeless road shone yellow under the sun, only a little paler than the countryside, and all alike were empty as far as the eye could reach.

The squadron flew over the open square, ringed round with houses, of Medellin, and began following up the road that led towards the enemy lines but also towards the sun. Against the blinding glare they saw the road as little more than a ribbon of incandescent light. The two Douglases accompanying Sembrano's plane began to slow down, then moved behind in line; the enemy column was approaching.

Darras, who had just handed back the controls to the first pilot, leant sideways, his whole body slewed across the cockpit in a pose of tense expectancy. During the World War his quarry had been merely this or that German flight. But now his quarry was that against which he had been fighting for so many active. years — in his mayoralty, in workers' organizations laboriously built up, defeated, resurrected — the enemy he fought today was fascism. After Russia, Italy, German, and China, now it was Spain's turn; hardly had the hope which Darras was fostering in the world been given a chance, than here in Spain was fascism once more — almost under his wings. Yet the only indication of its presence for the moment was the movement of his squadron taking up its battle formation.

To get into position again, the machine in which he was (Magnin's, the leader of the Internationals) began to turn, and now Darras could see the road in front studded with little red dots at regular intervals. Then, as the plane took the straight again, the sun came back and all he saw was an empty white road.

The road swerved round, the sun slipped to one side, and the red dots reappeared. They were too small to be cars, yet moving too mechanically to be men. It looked as if the roadway itself was in motion. Suddenly Darras understood. It was as if he had just acquired a gift of second sight: seeing things in his mind, not through his eyes. The road was a solid mass of lorries covered with drab tarpaulins, yellow with dust, and the red dots were the bonnets painted in red oxide; there had been no attempt at camouflage. Spanned by the silence of the far horizons round the three cities, the land lay bathed in tranquil light, threaded with roads that forked out like the imprint of some huge bird's talons. And amongst all those quiet ways, one road there was that throbbed and thundered – the road of fascism.

On both sides of the roadway bombs were exploding; twenty-pounders that spurted spear-heads of red flame and veiled the fields in smoke. There was nothing to show that the fascist column had put on speed, except that the road was throbbing still more violently. Lorries and planes were advancing on each other. Against the sunlight Darras could not discern the falling bombs; he could only see them as they burst – in bunches now, but still along the fields. His wounded foot was beginning to hurt again. One of the Douglases, he knew, was not equipped with bomb-dropping apparatus; the latrine vent had been enlarged to take its place. Suddenly one section of the road stopped vibrating. The column had halted. Unnoticed by Darras, a bomb had hit one of the lorries, slewing it across the road.

Like the head of a cut worm crawling off by itself, about a third of the column, its vanguard, pressed steadily on towards Medellin, while the rain of bombs continued to sweep the road. Darras' plane came just above the moving segment. But a second pilot cannot see the ground below.

Meanwhile Scali, the bomber on the second international machine, had been watching the bombs falling nearer and nearer the road. He had a thorough training in the Italian Army behind him, and, till he left his country, had put in a yearly 'refresher course' with the reserves. Three raids on the Sierra had got his eye in again. During the fifteen seconds while Sibirsky, his pilot, had been directly above the road, he had been watching the explosions draw nearer and nearer the lorries. It was too late to aim at the leading section. The lorries behind were trying to squeeze round on either side of a vehicle lying across the road, which had, it seemed, been stove-in by a bomb. Seen from the plane, the lorries seemed stuck to the road like flies on a strip of flypaper.

From his vantage-point above, Scali saw them in imagination, buzzing up into the air, or darting aside across the fields. But most probably the road was flanked by embankments. The compact line of a few minutes past was trying to spread out round the obstacle, like a torrent flowing round a rock. Scali could distinctly make out the white tips of the Moors' turbans. In a flash of memory he pictured the poor devils at Medellin with their shot-guns and, just as the swarm of lorries glided across his bomb-sights, he loosed off his two racks of light bombs. Then leaning above the opening in the floor, he waited for the bombs to strike; nine fateful seconds intervened between him and victims. Two, three ... impossible, looking through the trap, to see back far enough. He ran back and looked through the machine-gun slit in the tail. Down below people were running, their arms above their heads, scuttling for dear life over the berm. Five, six. ... A battery of machine-guns below was opening fire upon the planes. Seven, eight. ... 'See how they run!' Nine ... under twenty simultaneous bursts of scarlet flame they all stopped running. The plane sailed on, as if all that were none of its concern.

The squadron circled, to launch another attack. Magnin's machine came over the road just after Scali's bombs had burst, and Darras had a glimpse of a welter of lorries sprawling bottom upmost under the thinning smoke clouds. Only at the actual moment when the bombs flared red did death seem to play any part in the picture. Darras saw only, flying for their lives, little specks of khaki dotted with the white turbans, like panicked ants carrying away their eggs.

Sembrano had the clearest view of what was happening, for the leader of the Douglases came back behind the Internationals, closing the circle. Sembrano realized, far better than Scali, the plight of the Estremadura militia – that they were helpless, and only the air force could save them. He circled the road again for luck; if any light bombs were left, they might knock out some more lorries. Motor transport, as he knew, was the fascists' trump card. But now the great thing was to catch up the vanguard of the column on its way to Medellin, before the enemy aviation came to its rescue.

More lorries were slithering down into the fields, their wheels in air. Now they were no longer head-on to the sun, massive shadows trailed behind them, cast by the declining rays; like dead fish rising to the surface of a dynamited pool, they became visible only when derelict. The pilots had had time to adjust their course exactly above the road, and shadows of the disabled lorries began to pile up in front of the column and behind it, like barricades.

'A pretty kettle of fish for Franco!' Sembrano chuckled to himself. Then, falling in line, he flew towards Medellin.

Now as ever, pacifist at heart, Sembrano was, however, a far more competent bomber than any Spanish pilot; only, to salve his conscience, whenever he flew solo he came down very low to drop his bombs. Somehow the sense of danger, the risks he was going out of his way to run, solved, for him, the ethical problem. Like Marcelino, like most diffident men, he was brave by nature. And now he was saying to himself: 'Either the lorries are inside the town, in which case we've got to bomb them all to hell; or else they're outside it and, if we're to save the militia from being butchered, well, in that case also we must bomb them all to hell.' So now he set his course towards Medellin at a hundred and seventy miles an hour.

The lorries which had formed the head of the column were massed in the shadows of the city square. As the populace was hostile they had not dared to scatter. Sembrano came down as low as he could, followed by the five other machines.

The afternoon sun had lined the streets with shadows yet from a thousand feet up they could just distinguish the various colours of the houses – salmon pink, pale blue, pistachio green – and the outlines of the lorries.

Some of the vehicles were hidden away in by-streets. Instead of following him, a Douglas was heading towards Sembrano; the pilot, he supposed, had fallen out of formation.

The planes began to circle at a tangent to the square. His first air-raid came back to Sembrano's mind, the one he had taken part in with Vargas, now director of field-operations, and he remembered how the workers at Pennarova, hemmed in by the fascists, had hung at windows and in courtyards their gaudiest possessions – curtains and counterpanes – to greet the Republican airmen.

The falling bombs flickered across a belt of sunlight, vanished, and sped on with the free movement of torpedoes. The square began to fill with smoke, and bursts of sudden flame exploding everywhere like mines. Upon the highest flame, in a swirl of dense brown smoke, a plume of white shot up; then, suddenly, above it, a tiny black lorry turned a fantastic somersault and fell back into the murk below. As he waited for the smoke-cloud to clear off, Sembrano glanced ahead and saw once again the Douglas that had fallen out of line, and two more with it. Now only two Douglases, including his own machine, were taking part in the attack; how account for that mysterious third? He waggled his plane to indicate that the squadron was to take up its fighting formation.

So preoccupied had he been with what was going on below, that he had failed to to notice anything else. But now he knew; those unaccountable machines were not Douglases, but Junkers.

Just at that moment Scali had come to the conclusion that military aviation was a disgusting business. Indeed, from the moment he had seen the Moors running to cover, he had been wanting to quit. But this did not prevent him now from keeping his eyes fixed on the bomb-sights, like a cat at a mouse-hole, waiting for the square to flash across them (he had still two hundred-pounders left). Machine-guns were firing up at him from below, but he paid no heed; he felt as if he were at once a justiciary and a murderer – and of the two roles the former struck him as by far the fouler. Those six Junkers, three facing him (the ones Sembrano had seen) and three below, swept his mind clear of introspection.

Yet now the sole resource was flight; with its one wretched

machine-gun placed beside the pilot, it was folly for a Douglas to engage a German war-plane with three emplacements and its modern machine-guns. Sembrano had always looked on speed as the best means of defence for bombing machines. So now the Douglases swerved at full throttle away, while the large international machines plunged down on the three Junkers below them. They were three against six Junkers in all; but luckily the latter had no fighter escort. Now the Douglases had attained their object, there was no question of fighting; only of getting away. Magnin decided to attack the lower group; in a moment they would show up against the sky whereas Magnin's machines, thanks to their camouflage, would be almost invisible against the fields at this hour of the evening. So he, too, flicked his throttle full open.

Hermetically closed like submarines, their 'dust-bins' dangling like pendulums between the spats on their undercarriage wheels, the Junkers from below approached. One of them was still banking and the Internationals could clearly see its aerial, and the form of the rear gunner showing above the fuselage. Gardet stood waiting in the forward turret, a rifle slung across his back. Too far to make himself heard by the crew, he was pointing towards the enemy planes, gesturing frantically with his left arm. Standing beside Darras, Magnin watched the Junkers looming large and larger as if air were being pumped into them. Suddenly all on board realized that a plane can crash. Gardet spun round his turret and the planes swept past each other with a fantastically accelerated rattle, all their machine-guns drumming in the cockpits. Few shots – only those fired by the under-turret machine-guns – had touched the Internationals. The Junkers fell away behind; one of them began to come down, without, however, crashing. Steadily the distance was increasing, when of a sudden a dozen shots zipped through the cockpit of Magnin's machine. Under fire from the rear guns of the Internationals the five Junkers turned back to their lines, while the sixth went floundering down across the fields.

Back at the landing-ground, Magnin telephoned his report; then asked for Gardet.

'He's in the Junker, the one that landed here under the impression that Madrid had fallen!' Camuccini said.

'All the more reason for me to see him.'

To his surprise, Magnin found a man from the Secret Service Bureau awaiting him.

'Comrade Magnin,' the man said after casting a shrewd, exploring glance round the white-painted office, 'the Chief of Police has asked me to inform you that three of your German volunteers' – he took a piece of paper from his pocket – 'Krefeld. Wurtz and er ... Schrei ... Schreiner, that's it, Schreiner, are Hitlerian spies.'

Magnin's first reaction was to answer: 'He's mistaken'; then he remembered that in such cases one's first idea is always that. As a matter of fact Karlitch had warned him that Krefeld was always taking photographs (but would a spy take photographs?), and Magnin had been surprised one day to hear him mention the name of an official in the French Intelligence Department.

'Right, Krefeld ... you're sure, eh? Well, that's your pigeon, of course. Still, I must say I'm very much surprised about Schreiner. Wurtz and Schreiner are communists – have been communists for quite a while, I believe. And their Party vouches for them.'

'Parties are like people, Comrade Magnin, they trust their friends. *We* trust our information.'

'What does your Chief want of me?'

'He wants you to see that those three men don't set foot again on an aerodrome.'

'And what then?'

'He'll see to that himself.'

Tugging at his moustache, Magnin thought it over. 'This business about Schreiner – I can't stomach it somehow. And ... well, the long and the short of it is, I don't believe he is guilty. Can't you have further inquiries made?'

'Oh, there's no violent hurry. The Chief will ring you up presently; but only to confirm what I've just said.'

Presently Gardet arrived. His little rifle had been stowed away with his equipment; his unkempt hair lurched over his forehead, there was a twinkle in his eye.

The police-officer left the room. Gardet's unruly mane and pointed cheek-bones brought to mind the head of a tiny kitten;

but when he smiled the little teeth, set well apart, gave their triangular face a look of keen alertness.

'What the hell have you been up to in that machine?' Magnin asked. 'Sampling the gunners' seats?'

'I know a thing or two,' Gardet grinned. 'I'd been round one of 'em before, of course, but it struck me there was something I hadn't quite tumbled to. Well, I got it straight this time, and it's not so dusty! Now they've fired at us. I know just how things are with them; those buses are good as blind in front. That's why they couldn't hit us once with the first round, but got us fair and square when we were on their tails.'

'I suspected as much,' Magnin said. He had studied their structure in the technical magazines. The third engine on the Junker takes the place of the forward turret in two-engined machines, and Magnin had suspected that a submachine-gunner posted low down in the cockpit, firing between the wheels, and another at the tail, would be inadequate to defend the forepart of a plane against attack. That was why he had launched a frontal attack, single-handed, on the two enemy planes.

'Say, Magnin, do you think they were going all out when they came after us?'

'I'm sure of it.'

'Then – Christ, how those Fritzes must have been laughing up their sleeves these last two years! ... A good twenty m.p.h. less than we make with our old buses! So that's all there is to it – Goering's god-almighty air force.' He paused, then added ruefully : 'Still there's no two ways about it, their machine-guns can knock spots off ours, the home-made Spanish brand. Didn't jam a single instant, did they? I was listening. ... Ah, if only the Russians or those lousy fellow-countrymen of ours would get a move on with some new ones!'

As Magnin went off to General Headquarters, something was on his mind. Yes, he must visit the hospital first.

*

His features drawn with pain, the bomber was arguing apathetically with his neighbour, a Spanish anarchist; his bed was strewn with copies of *The Worker* and Courteline's stories. Rouse, however had a room to himself – an ominous privilege.

When Magnin opened the door Rouse saluted him smilingly with a clenched fist – but his eyes were unsmiling. Raised thus, horizontally, his fist seemed as childishly pathetic as his smile.

'How are you getting on?' Magnin asked.

'How can I tell? Nobody here knows English.'

The Captain's answer was given less to his friend's inquiry than to his own obsession. What he couldn't tell was whether or not he would have to be amputated.

With his incipient moustache, a mere smudge of yellow under the pointed nose, Rouse looked like a schoolboy tucked up in his dormitory bed. That clenched fist had been irrelevant, a heedless gesture. Surely far truer to the youngster's personality were the hands that now lay docile on the sheets, or that face which, in some far-away cottage, a Mrs Rouse was picturing most likely just as it looked now, at rest on a white pillow. But there was another truth, of which the good lady had certainly no idea; the two legs with five bullets in them under the tight-drawn sheets. And, the lad's not twenty-five yet! Magnin mused. What can I say? Words are so futile, when a boy's got to have his legs off.

'Well ... er ... is that so?' Magnin stammered. 'Wait a bit, I've got some oranges for you downstairs.'

He went out. To Magnin infirmity seemed more horrible than death; he hated lies, and had not known what to say. Well, the great thing now was to *know*. He went upstairs to the M.O.'s office.

'No,' the doctor told him. 'That English pilot was lucky; no bones were touched. There isn't the least necessity for an amputation.'

As Magnin dashed down the stairs a silvery chime of spoons came tinkling up them, and seemed to echo in his heart.

'No bones were touched,' he exclaimed as he entered the room; his story about the oranges had gone clean out of his head.

Rouse raised his fist again. As no one in the hospital knew English, he had got into the way of making the gesture automatically; he had no other way of conveying friendliness or gratitude.

'There's not the slightest question of – er – an amputation.'

Magnin stumbled over the words, embarrassed at having to repeat in English what the doctor had just said in Spanish.

Torn between hope and apprehension of a charitable lie, Rouse stared down at the sheets. Then, mastering his breath again, he asked point-blank:

'When'll I be able to walk?'

'I'll go and ask the M.O. right away.'

As Magnin once again dashed up the white-enamelled staircase, he was thinking: That doctor'll take me for an awful idiot!

'Excuse me,' he said. 'The young Englishman wants to know when he'll be able to walk again. . . . I'd hate to lie to him.'

'In a couple of months.'

Magnin returned to the bedroom. No sooner had he uttered the words 'two months' than he grew conscious of a resistless tide of joy surging up from the bed, the joy of a prisoner set free, mysterious in its immobility. For there was no need for Rouse to move a limb; his arms lay motionless on the sheets, his head upon the pillow. Only his fingers twitched and his rather prominent Adam's apple rose and fell convulsively – outward signs of a vast delight, oddly identical with those of terror.

*

In the suburbs of Madrid, fewer milicianos were visible brandishing rifles in fewer cars, and the cars flaunted fewer placards. Now the young men were practising foot-drill near the Toledo gate. . . . Magnin thought of France. Till this war the Junkers had constituted the bulk of Germany's air force. They were commercial machines converted into war planes, and such had been the general belief in German efficiency that they had been regarded as a formidable weapon of offence. But their armament though good, was inadequate, and ordinary American commercial planes, such as the Douglases, could show them a clean pair of heels. True, they were more than a match for the ramshackle buses Magnin had bought on various European markets; but they could not have held their own against the modern types of French machines, or against the Russian air force. But now all that would be changed; the army manoeuvres of the western world had tragically opened here. For two years Europe had quailed before the constant menace of a war which Hitler was not equipped for waging.

When Magnin entered the Ministry he found Vargas, the Officer Commanding Field Operations, listening to Garcia, who was reading out a report.

'Evening, Magnin!'

Vargas rose, but remained where he was at the edge of the sofa. His *mono*, slipped off from the waist upon account of the heat, but still clinging to his legs – was it mere laziness or to be readier for an emergency? – hampered his movements. (Magnin was amused to find himself recalling the skinned rabbits sold in France with their pelts clinging to their legs.) Vargas sat down again, stretching out his long legs cased in the close-fitting trousers, a glow of friendliness on his thin, bony face – the face of a beardless Don Quixote. He was one of the officers with whom Magnin had collaborated in reorganizing the Spanish air lines, before the rebellion; it was with his aid and Sembrano's that Magnin had blown up the line between Seville and Cordova. After introducing Garcia and Magnin to each other, he called for drinks and cigarettes.

'Good work!' Garcia said to Magnin. 'You've pulled off our first victory in the war.'

'Really? I'm glad to hear you say so. I'll pass on your congratulations. Sembrano was our Squadron-Leader.'

The two men exchanged a look of cordial scrutiny; this was Magnin's first direct contact with a chief of the Spanish Intelligence Service. Garcia, of course, had heard Magnin's name mentioned every day.

Garcia was far from being as Magnin had imagined him. His corpulence and big tip-tilted nose came as a surprise, as did the general likeness with some great landowner of Northern France or England. Nor had Magnin expected this eminent 'intellectual' to have that genial, humorous air, any more than those pointed ears; nor that the ethnologist who had spent arduous years in Peru and the Philippines should seem so physically robust. And somehow he had always pictured Garcia as wearing glasses.

'It wasn't a big show, of course,' Magnin continued, '– more like a frontier raid. Six machines. Still we managed to do in some of their lorries on the road.'

'It wasn't the bombs you dropped on the road that did them the most damage, but the ones in Medellin itself. Several heavies landed plumb in the market square. Don't forget it's the first taste the Moors have had of what a serious air-attack can mean. The column had gone back to its base. Our first victory. ... Unfortunately, Badajoz has fallen. Which means that Franco's army has joined up with Mola's.'

Magnin looked up at him questioningly. Garcia's attitude, too, was a surprise to him. Where he had expected reticence was expansiveness, almost exuberance.

'And Badajoz adjoins the Portuguese frontier,' Garcia continued.

'On the sixth,' Vargas said, 'the Montesarmiento brought fourteen German machines and a hundred and fifty trained men to Lisbon. On the eighth, eighteen bombing planes left Italy. The day before yesterday twenty arrived at Seville.'

'Savoias?'

'That I can't say. And twenty more Italian machines are on their way.'

'Including the eighteen you mentioned?'

'No. Within a fortnight we'll have a hundred up-to-date machines against us.'

The Junkers might be inefficient, but the Savoias were in another class. For bombing purposes they were far superior to any aircraft at the Republicans' disposal.

Through an open window the Republican anthem floated in, diffused from twenty radios, and with it a smell of sun-burnt leaves.

'I'll go on reading,' Garcia said, picking up his report again. 'This morning's news from Badajoz,' he added, for Magnin's benefit.

5 a.m. The Moors have just entered Fort San Cristobal, which has been practically wiped out by bombardment.

7 a.m. The enemy artillery, posted in Fort San Cristobal, is bombarding the town continuously. The militia are holding out. The

dispensary at the Provincial Hospital has been demolished by an air-atack.

9 a.m. The ramparts on the east are wrecked. On the south the barracks are in flames. We have only two machine-guns left. The guns in San Cristobal are still firing. The militia are still holding out.

11 a.m. Enemy tanks are arriving.

He let fall a page of typescript and picked up another.

12 noon. The tanks have reached the Cathedral, followed by the infantry. We have repulsed it.

'How ever did they manage that?' he mused aloud. 'With only four machine-guns all told at Badajoz!'

4 p.m. The enemy troops are entering the town.
4 30 p.m. House-to-house fighting in progress.

'At four?' Magnin sounded surprised. 'But we were told at five that we were still holding Badajoz!'

'The news has just come in.'

A picture rose before Magnin's eyes of the tranquil city of the crags aglow in the long rays of the evening sun. He had served in the artillery at the beginning of the World War. Then he had always been conscious that he knew nothing of the battle in progress, for the good reason that he saw nothing of it. But that little town, which at this very moment was all too literally a shambles, never had he ceased to picture it calm and companionable. Well, he had seen it from too high up – like God! *The tanks have reached the Cathedral* ... the old Cathedral with long shadows flowing from it, the narrow streets, the arenas ...

'When did the fighting end?' he asked.

'An hour before you passed over it,' Vargas replied. 'Except for the hand-to-hand fighting in the houses.'

'Here's the latest news,' Garcia said. 'Timed about eight o'clock. Perhaps earlier. Despatched from our lines – if so be that we have any left!'

The fascist prisoners have been released, safe and sound. All milicianos and doubtful characters are being court-martialled and shot. Twelve hundred have been dealt with so far. The charge is: 'armed resistance'. Two milicianos shot in the Cathedral, on the high-altar

107

steps. The Moors are wearing scapulars and emblems of the Sacred Heart. Firing squads have been busy all the afternoon. We can still hear the volleys.

Magnin called to mind the handkerchiefs that Karlitch and Jaime had waved in friendly greeting to the men who were now being shot.

Once more the nightlong rumour of Madrid, the anthem welling up from all the radios, snatches of song and cries of *Salud!*, shrill in nearness or low-pitched in the distance, like careless notes jangled across a keyboard – sounds of hope and exultation spanned once more the silence.

'It's good for them to sing,' Vargas nodded approvingly; then, in a lower voice, 'This is going to be a long war.' After a pause, he continued. 'Yes, the man in the street's an optimist. So are the political leaders. Major Garcia and I, for all we should be temperamentally inclined that way ...' His eyebrows flickered. The little movement gave him an air of curious naïvety; for a moment he looked quite boyish. And it struck Magnin that he had never thought of Don Quixote as having been young. 'Just think what happened today, Magnin. You held up that column with six machines – in what you likened to a frontier skirmish. The column turned its machine-guns on the militia and Badajoz has fallen. And, mark you, they were anything but cowards, our militia. Yes, this war's going to be a war of mechanized equipment – and we're running it as if noble emotions were all that mattered!'

'Still, you can't deny it was the people's army that held the Sierra.'

Garcia looked attentively at Magnin. Like Vargas he was convinced that this would be a technicians' war, and did not believe that foremen become experts merely by the grace of God. And the destinies of the Popular Front, he suspected, lay to a great extent with its experts. Everything about Magnin struck him as significant: his lack of ease in company, his seeming absent-mindedness, his 'jumpy' mannerisms, his look of a superior works-overseer (in point of fact he had taken an Engineering Degree at the *Ecole Centrale*), and, above all, the energy, disciplined but unmistakable, that shone out behind his round, puzzled-looking eye-glasses. Perhaps it was his moustache that gave Magnin something of the look of an old-school Parisian cabinet-maker; artist and artisan at once. But there was also something in his drooping lips – they brought to mind a seal's – which betrayed his age; as, in his eyes (when he removed his glasses), as in his smile and gestures, one glimpsed the subtle hall-mark of the intellectual. Magnin, he knew, had been director of one of the leading French Airlines, but Garcia, who made a point of stripping men of the glamour of their functions, was trying to see down into the nature of the man himself.

'The people is magnificent,' Vargas exclaimed. 'Absolutely magnificent – but helpless!'

'Let's get things straight,' Garcia said, aiming his pipe-stem at Magnin. 'I was in the Sierra. Well, it took the fascists by surprise. The positions were particularly suited for guerrilla warfare, of course. The people has a striking power that can be terrific – only it doesn't last.

'My dear Monsieur Magnin,' he continued, 'we're aided but no less handicapped by two or three rather pernicious superstitions. The French superstition, to begin with; the People – with a capital "P" – brought off the French Revolution, I grant you that. But the fact that a hundred pikes can knock out some inefficient muskets doesn't prove that a hundred shot-guns can beat the modern war-plane. Then the Russian Revolution – it's made confusion worse confounded. Politically speaking, it's the first revolution of the twentieth century; but don't forget that, militarily speaking, it was the last of the nineteenth. The Czarists had neither tanks nor planes; the revolutionaries used barricades. What was the idea behind these barricades? To resist the Imperial cavalry, for the people never has horses. To-day Spain is littered with barricades – to resist Franco's war-planes.

'No sooner had his cabinet fallen than that fine fellow, our President, dashed off to Sierra, gun in hand. Perhaps, Monsieur Magnin, you don't know Spain quite well enough. Gil, the one competent aircraft manufacturer we had, has been killed at the front, fighting in the ranks.'

'But surely . . . the revolution –'

'We are not the "revolution". Ask Vargas there what he

thinks about it! We stand for the masses, I grant, but not for the revolution – though we used to talk of nothing else. By "revolution" I mean the change of system that follows a revolt, a change that's organized by political and expert groups formed during the conflict and capable of promptly replacing the régime that they've destroyed.'

'And, above all, Magnin,' Vargas said, hitching up his *mono*, 'don't forget it isn't we who started the present conflict. We haven't any organization. Franco hasn't any either, except the army *cadres*, but he has with him the two nations you know of. No militia will ever defeat a modern army. Wrangel & Co. were beaten by the red army, not by enthusiastic amateurs.'

'From now on no social change, still less a revolution, can make good without war; and no war without organization on the technical side.' Garcia emphasized each point with a jab of his pipe-stem.

Vargas agreed, nodding in rhythm with the movement of the pipe.

'Organization, discipline – I don't see men giving their lives for that!' Magnin exclaimed.

'In times like the present,' Garcia said, 'I'm less interested in the reasons men may have for giving up their lives than in the means they have for killing off their enemies. And make no mistake: when I speak of "discipline" I don't mean that cast-iron authoritarianism we hear too much of nowadays. Anything but that. What I mean is an organization of the factors which give an army in the field its maximum efficiency.' (Garcia's taste for Johnsonian definition was notorious.) 'It's just a method like any other. Needless to say I don't care a hoot about the military salute and so forth.'

'You hear those sounds coming in through the window? Well, to me they're something real, concrete. Something which – you know it as well as I do – we're far from using to the best advantage. You say, we're not the revolution. Well, I say: let's be it! And don't you think it likely the democratic nations may come to your aid?'

'Don't be too sure about that, Magnin,' Vargas said.

Garcia pointed his pipe-stem like a revolver, at each man in turn.

'I've seen the democracies come in against pretty well everything – except fascism. Apart from Mexico, the only country which might help us is Russia. And Russia's too far away ... As to those sounds coming in through the window, Monsieur Magnin – I might define them as an Apocalypse of fraternity. They work on your emotions, I can well understand it; they stand for one of the most moving things on earth, and one of the rarest. But all of that's got to be transformed – or perish !'

'Well, you may be right. Only, mind you, for my part I don't acknowledge, and I won't acknowledge, any conflict between all that revolutionary discipline stands for, and those who still are blind to its necessity. Even the wildest dreams of absolute liberty, of power given to the worthiest and the rest of it – all these things, as I see them, are part of what I'm here to implement. I want each individual man to have a life that isn't classified in terms of what he can exact from others. See what I mean?'

'I'm afraid you don't quite grasp the actual position. We have to deal with two separate, but simultaneous *coups d'état*. The first is nothing more or less than our old friend, the *pronunciamento* of the 'families'. Burgos, Valladolid, Pampeluna, the Sierra. On the first day the fascists had all the garrisons in Spain with them. Now, they've only a third of them. In a word, that famous *pronunciamento* is beaten, knocked out by the Apocalypse.

'But the fascist states, who are no fools, allowed for that possibility in their plans. Hence what I may call the problem of the South. And that, mind you, is of a quite different order. To get things clear, let's drop that blessed word : fascism. Franco doesn't give a damn for fascism; he's a playboy dictator on South American lines. Secondly, Mussolini doesn't personally give a damn if fascism is set up in Spain or not. Ethical problems are one thing, foreign policy's another. What Mussolini wants here is a government which he can have in his pocket. That's why he is using Morocco as the base of his campaign. An up-to-date army with modern armaments has been sent out from that base. As they can't depend on the Spanish troops – they've seen what's happened to Madrid and Barcelona – they're relying on a small, but highly efficient army composed of the Foreign Legion, the Moors and ...'

'But Garcia,' Vargas broke in, 'there are only twelve thousand Moors in Morocco.'

'Let me set you right there, Vargas. Forty thousand. No one over here has devoted the least study to the relations between the spiritual chiefs of Islam and Mussolini. But wait a bit! France and England will have some nasty jars. If the Moors can't see it through, there'll be Italians sent over here.'

'What do you think Italy's after?' Magnin asked.

'Impossible to be sure. But I suspect their idea is to get a hold on Gibraltar; in other words, to be able to convert, automatically, an Anglo-Italian war into a European war, by forcing England to operate across the territory of a European ally. While the British were more or less disarmed Mussolini would have preferred to tackle them single-handed; now that they're rearming, Italian policy has to make a fresh start ... But all that's mere guess-work – pressmen's gossip. We are up against one solid fact: that Franco's army, backed by the two fascist states, firmly supported by Portugal, and equipped with motor transport, submachine-guns, Italo-German aircraft and organization, is going to have a shot at taking Madrid. To protect his rear, Franco will have to practise large-scale terrorization; he's begun it at Badajoz. The question is: how are we going to tackle this new phase of the war, which had nothing whatever to do with what's been happening in the Sierra?' Garcia rose from his chair and moved towards Magnin; his peaked ears showed sharply up against the glow of an electric lamp standing on the desk.

'For me, Monsieur Magnin, the whole problem consists in this: a popular movement, or a revolution, or even a rebellion, can hold on to its victory only by methods directly opposed to those which gave it victory. Sometimes opposed even to the sentiments from which it started out. Just think it over – in the light of your own experience. For I doubt if you expect to keep your flight up to the mark on a basis of mere fraternity.

'The apocalyptic mood clamours for everything right away. Tenacity of purpose wins through bit by bit; slowly, laboriously. That Apocalyptic fervour is ingrained in every one of us; and there's the danger. For that fervour spells certain defeat, after a relatively short period, and for a very simple reason: it's in the very nature of an Apocalypse to have no future ... Even when it professes to have one.'

Putting his pipe back in his pocket, he added sadly: 'Our humble task, Monsieur Magnin, is to *organize* the Apocalypse.'

TWO

Prelude to Apocalypse

I

THE staff headquarters at Toledo into which Garcia was just turning, his long nose and pipe well to the fore as usual, had been a modest boot-shop in happier days. On the right of the door was posted a large photograph, cut from a picture magazine, showing the hostages who had been interned by the fascists in the Alcazar and were to be spared when the Republican army stormed the subterranean vaults. Under each likeness was a name. As if the storming party, in the heat of battle, were likely to remember all – or any – of those faces! After the garish sunlight of the street with its bare torsos and Mexican sombreros, Garcia had an impression that the room was in complete darkness.

'That battery's got us taped!' a voice was shouting.

'What battery, Negus?'

'Our own!'

'I rang them up and told them they were firing short. What d'you think the officer replied? "I've had enough of firing on my pals. So we're plonking you for a change." '

'It's an outrage on the highest principles of civilization.' A shrill, affected voice, with a strong French accent.

'So another traitor's shown his hand!' A lower voice, languid but charged with bitterness. The Captain, whose face Garcia was just beginning to make out in the faint light, had spoken. To a subaltern he added: 'Take twenty men and a machine-gun and rout them out.' And to a clerk: 'Inform the C.O. about it.'

'As to that man at the battery –,' the Negus said, 'I've sent three mates to settle his hash.'

'I'd cashiered him once, damn it! If the F.A.I. hadn't gone and reinstated him ...'

Garcia could not hear the end of the sentence. Still, as compared with the din outside, it was fairly quiet in the room. Sporadic explosions, like thunder underfoot, punctuated the Valkyries' Ride that was blaring from the wireless in the Square. Now that Garcia's eyes were used to the dimness, he recognized Captain Hernandez. Hernandez resembled the Spanish kings of the well-known royal portraits – all of which resemble Charles the Fifth as a young man. The gilt stars on his *mono* glimmered palely in the gloom. Behind him, on the wall, a series of oval patches disposed in formal patterns was slowly growing visible, framing his body as a fringe of rays surrounding the bodies of certain Spanish saints – the cobblers' lasts and soles, which had been left behind when the little shop was taken over. Beside the Captain was Sils, a leading anarchist from Barcelona.

At last Hernandez' eyes fell on Garcia, who was smiling, his pipe stuck in a corner of the smile.

'Major Garcia, isn't it? Intelligence has just rung me up.' He shook hands with Garcia and led him out into the street.

'What can I do for you, Major?'

'I should like to spend a few hours in your company, having a look round ...'

'Just now I'm off to Santa Cruz. We're going to try using dynamite against the Military Government Buildings.'

'Right. Let's go there.'

The Negus, behind them, was appraising Garcia with a friendly eye; for once in the way, Madrid had sent them someone who 'looked the goods'. Funny ears, a hefty bloke, with not too much of the bloody bourgeois about him. (Garcia was wearing a leather windbreaker.) Beside the Negus another man, in an alpaca coat, riding breeches and boots, was waving his arms excitedly; a man who seemed all bones and sinews, with grey hair curling broadside on. It was Captain Mercery who had been sent by Magnin to the War Ministry and was now posted to Toledo staff-headquarters.

'Comrade Hernandez,' a voice cried from within the shop, 'Lieutenant Larreta's just phoned up to say the officer in charge of the battery has hopped it.'

'Get someone to take his place.' Hernandez shrugged his shoulders disgustedly, and stepped over a sewing-machine lying on the road. An escort was following them.

'Who's in command here?' There was only a shade of irony in Garcia's voice.

'Whom would you expect to be in command? Anybody and everybody, of course. Ah, you're smiling . . .'

'I'm always smiling. It's a habit — a cheerful one anyhow. Who gives orders here?'

'Officers, lunatics, delegates of political groups, and God knows how many more.' Hernandez spoke without bitterness; only a flicker of the black moustache on his thin upper lip suggested his profound discouragement.

'How do your professional officers get on with the political groups?' Garcia inquired.

Hernandez looked at him in silence, as though no words could possibly express how appallingly bad things were in that respect. Cocks were crowing in the bright sunlight.

'And why?' Garcia continued. 'Because every god-damned fool sets up to have authority. All revolutions begin like that, of course — with a host of jacks-in-office, political racketeers!'

'That's one thing. And then, confound it, we're up against the colossal ignorance of all the people who come and start telling us how to run the war. An army of two thousand men who really knew their job could wipe out our militia. Why, even the *real* leaders seem to believe in the "people" as an effective military force.'

'*I* don't. Not for the present anyhow. Well, what's to be done?'

In the streets, bathed equally in light and shade, life was going on as usual. But rifles were lying across the baskets of tomatoes. A Flamenco folk-song rose across the tumult of the Valkyries. Guttural, throbbing with emotion, it had at once the accent of a dirge and the desolate clamour of a caravan lost in the desert. Tentacles of sound seemed tightening around the city and the stench of horses, as dead men's fingers clench the dust.

'Well, Major, for one thing, when a man wants to join the socialist or communist parties, or any of the liberal organizations, he has to produce a modicum of guarantees; but anyone at all can join the C.N.T., no questions asked! Of course it's no

116

news to you; but for us it's a damned serious matter, confound it! Every time we nab a Falangist he's got a C.N.T. card on him. There's some anarchists who are dependable – the comrade behind us, for example. But so long as the policy of the "open" door is persisted in, it's the door open to every sort of disaster. That trouble with the officer commanding the battery, for instance.'

'The regular army officers who are on our side – what were their motives for joining us, do you think?'

'Some of them think that as Franco hasn't pulled it off right away he'll be beaten in the end. Some are attached to one or other of the senior officers who are on bad terms with Franco, Mola, Queipo, or some other leader of the revolt. Then there are the officers who haven't budged because they couldn't make up their minds or hadn't the guts to take a line; they chanced to be with us, and they've stayed with us. But, now that the political committees have taken to cursing them up hill and down dale, they wish they hadn't!'

In the Sierra, Garcia had come across officers professing to be Republican, who approved of the silliest things done by the milicianos, then spat when they were out of sight. And he had seen the staff officers at a military aerodrome moving away the chairs and tables in their mess when badly dressed foreign volunteers turned up. And other regular officers correcting the milicianos' mistakes with unvarying patience, teaching them their duties, training them. And he had been told of the tragedy of the Republican officer commanding the XIIIth Lancers, one of the regiments which had revolted at Valencia. He had gone to the barracks to take up his command fully knowing the risk he was running. The door had closed behind him and a volley had been heard.

'Can't *any* of your officers get on with anarchists?'

'Yes. The worst get on very well with them. The only man whose orders the anarchists – or, rather, those who profess to be anarchists – obey to any extent is that French captain. They don't take him very seriously, but they like him.' Garcia gestured a question with his pipe. 'He gives me the most ridiculous advice about how to run the War – and very sound advice on practical matters.'

All the streets converged on the city square, the no-man's land between the Alcazar and its besiegers. Being unable to cross it, Garcia and Hernandez made a circuit round it, Hernandez' footsteps dragging, Garcia's ringing on the ancient cobblestones. At the far end of each street spanned by a barricade of mattresses, and at the end of every alley, beyond a perilously low line of sandbags, they caught sight of it again. The men were firing lying down, in badly placed groups, and offered an easy target for the enemy marksmen.

'What do you think of this barricade?' Garcia watched his companion from the corner of an eye.

'I think as you do. And now I'm going to show you something ...'

Hernandez went up to the man apparently in charge of the barricade. He had the jovial face of an old-time cabby, a swashbuckling moustache, a knock-out Mexican hat, and was lavishly tattooed. Strapped to his left arm was a death's head in aluminium.

'You should raise that barricade eighteen inches, spread out your men, and post some at the windows on both flanks.'

'Py ... pers,' growled the 'Mexican' amid a series of detonations fairly close at hand.

'What?'

'Yer pypers, blast you, yer id-entity pypers!'

'I'm Captain Hernandez in charge of the Zocodover sector.'

'Then you don't belong to the C.N.T., and my barricade ain't none of your bloody business. See?'

The man's gorgeous headgear fascinated Garcia; round the crown was a garland of paper roses, and below it a ribbon inscribed: THE TERROR OF PANCHO VILLA.

'What's that mean?' he asked. '– "The Terror of Pancho Villa"?'

'It's plain enough, ain't it?'

'I suppose so,' Garcia smiled.

Hernandez looked at him without speaking. The two men moved on. On the wireless the marvellous Flamenco song had ceased. Down a side-street, in front of a dairy, was a row of milk-jugs on each of which rested a card with a name written on it. As the women disliked waiting in a queue, they had left their jugs there; the milkman filled them and they came to fetch them later – unless ...

The firing died down. For a moment, there was no sound besides the footfalls of the escort drumming on the silence. Then Garcia heard a voice. 'As Mrs Mercery wrote to me, and she's a very brainy woman, comrades: *They're greatly mistaken if they think they'll wash out their defeats in Africa with the workers' blood!*' From a back street came the tinkle of a child's scooter.

Rifle-fire again. More streets, sheltered from the guns of the Alcazar and, like the others, halved by light and shade. Along the shady side people were chatting on their doorsteps; some seated, others standing, leaning on their shot-guns. At the corner of a by-street they had a back view of a man standing by himself, in a soft hat, and, though the day was hot, with his coat on. Firing shot after shot.

The little street abutted on a lofty wall, the back of one of the Alcazar outbuildings. No loopholes or windows, not an enemy in sight. Surrounded by a swarm of flies, the man was deliberately firing again and again at the blank wall. When one cartridge-clip was empty, he slammed in another. Hearing steps behind him, he turned. He was a man in the forties, with a serious face.

'I'm shooting.'

'At the wall?'

'At anything I can hit.' Darkly he looked at Garcia. 'You don't happen to have a child inside there, do you?' Garcia returned his gaze, but said nothing. 'Then you can't understand.'

The man swung round and started firing again at the huge blocks of stone.

They went on.

'Why don't we take the Alcazar?' Garcia emphasized the question with a brisk tap of his pipe on the back of his left hand.

'How should we take it?' After they had walked a few paces Hernandez continued: 'Firing at the windows of a fortress has never led to its capture. We're besieging it, yes; but not attacking it. So what do you expect?' Both men gazed up at the towers.

'Have you noticed how the air smells, Major?' Hernandez asked. 'There's been a curious change. It doesn't smell of the enemy any longer. This Alcazar business is – just play-acting! We used to get this smell at first, but nowadays – not a whiff, confound it! In fact, if we took drastic steps just now, we'd feel like murderers. Ever been on the Saragossa front?'

'Not yet. But I know Huesca.'

'When you fly over Saragossa, you see the country all around pitted with shell-holes. The strategic points – barracks and so forth – are hit ten times less than the open country. Why? It isn't just bad aiming or cowardice. But it's quicker work getting a civil war afoot than getting men to hate each other all the time. Duty is duty, I grant you, and those shell-craters round Saragossa don't give me any pleasure to see. Only ... I'm Spanish – and I can understand.'

His explanations were cut short by loud bursts of cheering that died away upon the sunlight. They were passing a rather squalid music-hall gaudy with posters. Once again Hernandez shrugged his shoulders; then went on in a slower voice.

'It's not only the Toledo militia who're attacking the Alcazar; many of the ordinary townsfolk are taking part, and the youngsters the fascists have with them in the Alcazar are the Toledo milicianos' children.'

'How many hostages are there?'

'Haven't a notion. Trying to make inquiries here is – beating the wind, confound it! There must be a good many, with quite a large proportion of women and children. They made as big a haul as they could in these first days. What holds us up isn't so much the hostages. Quite likely there aren't so many of them as we fear ...'

'So it's impossible to get any definite figures?'

Like the Captain, Garcia had seen at the Jefatura the photographs of the women and children who were definitely known to have been taken as hostages; with beside them, other photographs – of empty rooms, abandoned toys ...

'We've tried four times.'

They were half blinded by the dust of a cavalcade of mounted peasants, who looked like a tribe of Mongul nomads, entering Santa Cruz. Beyond it were enemy windows, those of the Military Government Building; the Alcazar frowned above it.

'Is this where you propose to try dynamite?'

'Yes.'

They walked across a chaos of scorched gardens, cool halls, and flights of steps, to the Museum. The windows were barricaded with sandbags and broken statuary. In the atmosphere of a stokehold, streaming with sweat, milicianos were firing through the loopholes, their naked torsos mottled like pantherskins with flecks of sunlight. Enemy rifle-fire had riddled the brickwork of the upper portions of the wall till it was like a sieve. Behind Garcia, on the outstretched arm of an Apostle, machine-gun loading-belts were hung out to dry like washing. He hooked his leather waistcoat on the pointing finger-tip.

For the first time, Mercery approached. 'I'd have you know, sir,' he said, bringing his heels together, 'that the best statues here have been stored in a safe place.'

Let's hope so, Garcia thought, clasping a saint's hand in his.

After passing through a series of passages and dim-lit rooms, they came out on a roof. Sunlight drained the colour from the roof-tiles, but beyond them the Castilian harvest fields glowed to the pale horizon in a motley of sunburnt flowers. The vibrant frenzy of the air throbbed in Garcia's body; the intense glare and heat almost turned his stomach. Then, as his eyes fell on the graveyard, suddenly, strangely, he was humbled; it was as if those stones and monuments, dead white against the yellow-brown expanse of fields, made all human conflict seem a vain and tawdry thing. Bullets sped past them with a wasp-like drone and hit the splintered tiles with a harsh, brittle crack.

Hernandez moved forward, stooping, revolver in hand; Garcia, Mercery, and the men with the dynamite followed him. They felt the sunlight blistering their backs and the heat accumulated in the roof roasting their bellies. The fascists were firing at ten yards' range. A miliciano flung a dynamite cartridge; as it burst on a roof, splinters of slate rattled on the wall behind which Garcia, Hernandez, and the rest were crouching. A stream of bullets flowed diagonally above them.

'Bad work,' Mercery remarked.

A machine-gun joined in. Should a bomb land in all that

dynamite —! Garcia left the thought unfinished. Mercery stood up, half his body above the wall. Now that he was visible from the waist up, the fascists started plugging away at the grotesque figure in the alpaca coat and red tie, ears plugged with wadding, that was launching a charge of dynamite with the gesture of a discobolus.

The whole roof burst in fragments with a terrific crash; tiles flew high into the air, and rained down upon the watchers, who were shouting with excitement. Mercery squatted down behind the wall, beside Hernandez.

'That's the way!' he shouted to the men who, dynamite in hand, were taking cover behind the wall. His face was a foot away from the Captain's.

'What was the Great War like?' Hernandez asked.

'Living — not living — waiting — carrying on — getting the wind up!'

Just now Mercery felt he was 'getting the wind up' because he wasn't doing anything. He grasped his revolver, aimed and fired, his whole head visible above the wall. Now he was doing something, fear had left him. The third charge of dynamite exploded.

The tassel of Hernandez' cap was just in front of a crack in the wall. A rush of air flicked it violently aside; the cap dropped. Hernandez was bald. He replaced the cap, and became a younger man.

Some shots tore across the wall, and whizzed through a loop-hole, almost under Garcia's nose. At last he brought himself to tap out his pipe and stow it in his pocket. The frontage of the fascist stronghold blew out, as if a mine had been touched off behind it. A man on Garcia's right sank to the ground, blood spurting from his head, his arms still lifted in the gesture he had made to fling the dynamite. Across the space where his neck, now smeared with blood, had been, Garcia saw on a terrace of the Alcazar in front of the graveyard, a motor-car drawn up full in the line of fire. In the harsh light it looked undamaged; five people were seated in it, motionless, two in front and three behind. Ten yards below a woman lay on the slope, one arm extended and the other clasping her head; he could clearly see the crisp, dark curls. She might have been asleep (but her head was pointing towards the bottom of the valley), were not the body under the flimsy dress flatter than any living woman's, and welded to the soil by the peculiar earthward impulse of the dead. And all those phantoms of the flaming light seemed corpses only by their odour.

'You don't happen to know of any experts in explosives, at Madrid?' Hernandez asked.

'No.'

Garcia's eyes were still fixed on the graveyard; in all those cypresses and stones was something unnerving, an intimation of eternity, which gripped his bowels. The stench of rotting flesh seemed to be flooding his senses wave on wave, and throbbing with the beating of his heart under the dazzling effulgence that merged living and dead together in a holocaust of light. The last charge of dynamite burst in the last surviving fragment of the fascist building.

In the hall of the Museum the heat was intense as ever, so was the din. The dynamite-throwers exchanged congratulations with the men on duty in the vaults and, above ground, in the Museum. As Garcia slipped his waistcoat off the saintly finger, the lining stuck, the saint refused to let it go. Some milicianos, naked from the waist up, emerged from a flight of steps leading down to a cellar. They carried chasubles in bundles, glimmering rolls of pale pink silk and greenish gold; another man, with a sixteenth-century cap set on the back of his head, and a bare tattooed arm, noted them down in a register.

'What's the point of what we've just been doing?' Garcia asked.

'By blowing up those buildings we'll render it impossible for the rebels to make a sortie. No more than that; but it's the least silly thing to do, confound it! Till now we used bombs containing petrol and vitriol, with an outer case of wadding steeped in potassium chlorate and sugar. Poor stuff it was.'

'Do the Cadets still try to sally out?'

Mercery, who was beside him, raised both arms in protest. 'It's all a ramp, the biggest fake in history!' Seeing Garcia's puzzled look, he continued; 'I will submit a full report to you, sir, if you desire it.'

But Hernandez had laid his hand on Garcia's arm and, in

123

deference to his superior officer, Mercery drew back. On Hernandez' face was the 'it's-beyond-everything' look he had worn when describing the relations between the anarchist organizations and the officers – with some astonishment thrown in. An aeroplane droned overhead.

'You too !' he exclaimed. 'The Intelligence Department !'

Garcia waited, nose in air, his squirrel eye alert and twinkling.

'The cadets of the Alcazar,' Hernandez said, 'are just a myth; but a marvellous piece of propaganda. There aren't twenty cadets in the place; all the students of the Military Academy were on holiday when the rising occurred. The Alcazar is being defended by the Civil Guard, under the command of the officers of the Military Academy, Moscardo and the rest.'

A group of milicianos ran up, the Negus amongst them.

'They're out again – with a flame-thrower !'

Through dark, narrow staircases Hernandez, Garcia, the Negus, Mercery, and the milicianos rushed down into a high-roofed cellar. It was full of smoke, echoing with gun-shots. Before them loomed a large, tunnel-like corridor in which the smoke glowed red. Milicianos ran by with buckets of water held by the handle or hugged between their arms. The din of the battle going on outside was hardly audible here and the fumes of burning petrol had effectively dispelled the stench of carrion. The fascists were in the corridor.

The nozzle of the flame-thrower, glinting in the darkness, roved to and fro, spraying roof, floor, and the wall opposite. the slowness of its movements suggested that the man behind it had to cope with an unwieldly length of hose. Hampered by the narrow doorway, the jet of liquid flame could not reach the walls to right and left of the entrance. Despite the ardour which his men showed in sousing the walls and hissing flames with the water from their buckets, Hernandez felt that all were anxiously awaiting the moment the fascists would burst in, and the way some of them were hugging the walls gave him an impression they did not mean to put up much resistance. It had nothing to do with warfare, this fight against an element of nature. As the spray crept slowly forward, the movements of the milicianos drenching the walls with water grew more and more febrile. The hiss of steam mingled with nerve-wracking coughs from throats rasped by the pungent fumes of petrol and the rancid sweat forming upon the nozzle. Sizzling, the shaft of fire gained foot by foot, and sudden, spluttering bursts of bluish flame chequered the walls with a fantastic rout of dancing shadows as the milicianos turned and twisted in their frantic saraband; it was as though a horde of phantoms were capering with glee around the madness of the living men. And somehow the living forms seemed more spectral than those wildly capering shadows, less palpable than the stifling fog across which solid shapes showed flat as stencils, less real than the angry hiss of fire and water and the weak, whimpering cries of a burnt man.

'I've gone blind!' The cries came from the floor. 'I've lost my sight. Get me out of this!'

Hernandez and Mercery had grasped his shoulders and begun dragging him away, but the man went on shouting. 'Get me out of this, mates! Take me away!'

Now the flame-thrower had reached the threshold. Revolver in hand, the Negus was standing near the door, flattening himself against the wall. As the brass nozzle peeped round the corner, he snatched at it, but let go at once; his skin was peeling off. His flowing silky hair glimmered like a blue aureole in the vivid flamelight; bullets were crackling all around him. the fascist swerved aside so as to bring his projector to bear on the Negus, whose hand was pressing on his chest. The Negus fired. The projector clanged on the stone floor, flung all the shadows up on to the roof. The fascist, an elderly officer, stood tottering above it for a moment, his face lit up from below, bathed in the livid sheen of the dancing flames. Then with the unnatural languor of a slow-motion picture, he fell alongside the Negus, his head bumping against the nozzle, which spluttered and flung it off, like a foot kicking aside an obstacle. The Negus picked up the projector and pointed it in the other direction. At once the room was plunged into darkness, and the tunnel filled with clouds of glowing smoke traversed by flying shadows. The milicianos thronged excitedly into the tunnel, following the blue flames, in a wild hubbub of shouts and gunshots. Suddenly everything went dim. The only lights remaining were an electric torch and a single hurricane-lamp.

'They turned off the gas once they saw we'd got hold of the projector,' a voice called in the darkness. Then, after a moment, added: 'I know what I'm talking about. I was an officer in the fire-brigade.'

'Halt!' Hernandez shouted from the tunnel. 'They've a barricade across the exit.'

'You can't go native to order!' the Negus remarked to Hernandez. (The milicianos were relighting the other hurricane-lamp.) 'It was touch and go,' the Negus went on. 'He had just time enough to turn the jet on me before I fired. But I was looking him in the eyes, you know. It's queer the way men are. Yes, it must be hard to bring yourself to burn a man who's looking at you!'

The corridor by which they returned was in darkness, but for a glimmer of light from the door at the far end. The Negus lit a cigarette; as one man, the others followed his example – a homely symbol of their return to the world of life. Each man's face showed up for a second in the brief, brisk glow of match or lighter; then the gloom closed again.

When they entered the hall of the Museum, they were greeted by shouts. 'There's a plane up there, above the clouds.'

'The hardest thing,' the Negus went on, 'is not to hesitate. It's a question of seconds. Two days ago the Frenchman turned a projector around like that – the same one, as like as not. He didn't get burnt himself, but all the same he didn't do in the other chap. That Frenchie said he knew what it was; when a fellow looks at you, you just can't turn the flame on him. You can't bring yourself to do it.'

II

An officer in the International Air Force reported daily at Staff headquarters; sometimes at the Special Police Bureau as well. It was Scali, as a rule, whom Magnin detailed for this duty; thanks to his culture he got on excellently with the air force general staff, composed for the most part of regular army officers (Sembrano and his pilots formed a group apart.) Scali was a thick-set man, who would certainly run to fat as he grew older; his tact and cordiality made a good impression on everyone, not excluding the functionaries of the Special Police. He was hail-fellow-well-met with all the other Italians in the Flight, who had elected him as their spokesman, and with nearly all the other airmen. Last but not least, he spoke Spanish fluently. He had just received an urgent summons to police headquarters.

The entrance gates were guarded by machine-guns. The building, before being taken over as an annex of the Special Police Bureau, had been a private mansion, and the furniture had not been changed. Around richly gilt and scalloped chairs, majestic and untenanted, hovered the sorry company of nondescripts that a war always brings to the surface.

'We've something important for you,' the Police clerk said, 'Two fascist airmen, Italians, have crashed behind our lines south of Toledo. One is dead; the other's here. The Intelligence Department wants you to have a look through the papers we got off them.'

Scali flicked the papers over with his stubby little finger – the task rather disgusted him. There were letters, visiting-cards, photographs, and club membership cards found in a pocketbook, as well as maps found in the cockpit. It was the first time Scali met an enemy Italian with an illusion of intimacy; and the man whom he met now was dead. One sheet especially held his attention.

A long rectangle, like a folded air-map, it looked as if it had once been pinned to the pilot's chart. A sort of log-book, judging by its aspect. There were two columns. *Course. From . . . To . . .* with a space for the date of each journey, 16th July (i.e. *before* Franco's rising) *Specia*; then *Melilla, 18th, 19th, 20th July*; then *Seville*, and *Salamanca*. In the margin the purpose of the flight was noted: Spotting, Bombing, Escort, and the like. The last entry – the record of the day before – read: *From Segovia to . . .* The destination, *Death*, was blank.

But below it, written some days earlier with a different pen, were large block letters covering both columns: TOLEDO, with a date, the next day but one. Obviously an important flight over Toledo was impending.

In the next room someone was bawling down the telephone. 'Yes, President, yes, of course, I'm aware our personnel is under strength. But I'd have you know that under no circumstances, none whatever, will I take men for the Assault Guard who aren't vouched for by a political organization.'

'. . .'

'And what about the day when we've got to smash a fascist mutiny with regiments that have been "got at"? As long as I'm responsible, not a man who isn't vouched for! There were quite enough Falangists in the Montaña barracks; I won't have any in the Special Police.'

From the start Scali had recognized the voice as that of the Chief of Special Police.

'His grand-daughter's a prisoner, at Cadiz,' a clerk observed.

A door banged to, and they heard no more. Then the dining-room door opened, and the clerk who had first spoken to Scali came back.

'There are some more papers with the Intelligence Department. Major Garcia says they're important. He wants you to sort out the ones you have there – to separate the dead pilot's papers from the observer's. You're to turn the whole lot over to me and I'll take it to him at once. You'll send in your report to Colonel Magnin.'

'A great many of these things,' Scali observed, 'are printed forms or maps; how can I possibly say to whom they belong?'

'The observer's here; you've only got to question him.'

'Very well.' There was no enthusiasm in Scali's voice. His feelings towards the prisoner were as mixed as those he had had when given the documents. Still his curiosity was aroused. Two days before a German pilot who had crashed in the Sierra near staff headquarters – where two inspecting officers had chanced to be present – had been taken before them to be questioned. When the interpreter told him the names of those confronting him, he was evidently amazed to find himself in the presence of generals; he had imagined that the 'Reds' had no such officers. 'Good God!' the German had exclaimed. 'I never dreamt of it! Why I flew over this shack three times without dropping a single bomb!'

'Wait a bit,' Scali said to the clerk. 'Tell the Major I've just seen something here which may have its importance.'

He had in mind the pilot's log with the dates proving he had left Italy before Franco's rising.

He went to the office where the observer was in custo Sitting at a table, his elbows propped on the green table-cloth, the prisoner had his back to the door by which Scali entered. All Scali could see at first was a hunched-up form clad half in mufti and half in uniform, a leather windbreaker and blue trousers. At the sound of the opening door the fascist airman rose to his feet and glanced towards it; the movements of his legs and long, emaciated arms, and his back, still bent when he was standing, gave the impression of a rather neurotic consumptive.

'Wounded?' Scali inquired.

'No, only bruised a bit.'

Scali laid his revolver and the documents on the table beside him, sat down and signed to the two sentries to leave the room. The fascist sat down opposite him. He had the sparrow face — tiny eyes and a perky nose — which is common amongst airmen; it was accentuated by his shock of hair and prominent cheek-bones. Though he was not like Rouse one could see he came of the same family. Just now why was the man looking so puzzled? Scali glanced round; behind him, under Azaña's portrait, was a yard-high dump of silverware; dishes, plates, tea-pots, ewers, Arab trays, clocks, vases, knives and forks, the harvest of recent house-to-house perquisitions.

'Is that what's puzzling you?'

The prisoner hesitated. 'That? You — you mean ... ?' He pointed to the glittering profusion of an Aladdin's hoard. 'No ... of course not!' he stammered, like a man at bay.

What surprised him most, perhaps, was the man in front of him. Looking at Scali, one thought at once of an American film comedian. This was due less to his face — there was really nothing very odd about it, despite the thick lips and horn-rimmed glasses — than to the disproportionate shortness of his legs, which gave him a 'Charlie-Chaplin' walk, the buckskin waistcoat (so unexpected on a 'Red'), and the pencil tucked behind his ear.

'Look here!' Scali addressed him in Italian. 'I'm not a C.I.D. man. Just an air force volunteer, posted here as technical adviser. I've been told to sort out your papers from those of the ... of your dead companion. Only that.'

'That's all right for me.'

rver fell to sorting out the papers into two heaps.
y glanced at them. His eyes seemed held by the
broken gleams that faceted the pile of silver under the brilliant
ceiling-lights.

'Did your engine conk out,' Scali asked, 'or were you shot
down?'

'We were on a scouting flight, the pilot and I. A Russian
machine downed us.'

Scali shrugged his shoulders. 'Have it your own way! The
pity is – there aren't any Russian machines over here. But let's
hope we'll have some soon.'

The pilot's log, however, showed clearly that they were on a
bombing raid, not scouting. And suddenly Scali was conscious
of that rather nauseous sense of superiority which comes from
knowing that another man is lying. Still he hadn't heard of any
Italian two-seater bombing machines in service on the Spanish
front. Well, that was a problem for the Intelligence, not his
affair. All the same he made a note of it. On the right-hand
pile the observer laid a receipt, some Spanish bank-notes, and a
small photograph. Scali, who was long-sighted, peered through
his glasses at the photograph; it showed a detail of a fresco by
Piero della Francesca.

'Is that yours or his?' he asked.

'You told me : my things on the right.'

'Very well. Carry on.'

Piero della Francesca. Scali glanced at the passport. '*Student.
Florence.*' But for fascism this man might very likely have
been one of his pupils. Till now Scali had imagined that
photograph had belonged to the dead man and felt a vague
fraternity towards him. In the old days he had published a
study of the Piero della Francesca frescoes. During the previous
week a similar examination of a prisoner, conducted by an
airman, not by the police, had wound up in a heated argument
about flying records.

'Did you jump?'

'The machine didn't catch fire. We came down in open
country, that's all.'

'You cracked up?'

'Yes.'

'And then?'

The observer hesitated before replying. Scali glanced through the report. The pilot had climbed out first; the observer – the man whom he was questioning now – had been trapped in the wreckage. A peasant had come up; the pilot had drawn his revolver. The peasant had continued to approach. When he was three paces off, the pilot had taken from his left-hand pocket a wad of notes, large white thousand-peseta notes. The peasant had approached nearer, while the pilot added a handful of dollars, which doubtless he had kept ready for such an emergency – doing all this with his left hand, his right still grasping the revolver. Once the peasant was close up to the pilot, almost touching him, he had levelled his shot-gun at the pilot and shot him dead.

'Why didn't your companion shoot first?'

'I can't say.'

Scali remembered the parallel columns in the log: *Point of Departure; Destination*. That man's destination had been the peasant's gun.

'Right. What did you do then?'

'I waited. A number of peasants gathered round, they took me to the mayor's office first, then brought me here.' He paused, then added: 'Shall I be tried?'

'What for?'

'Without a trial!' the man exclaimed. 'So they'll shoot me out of hand!' An exclamation less of horror than of acquiescence with the long-expected. Obviously, ever since he had crashed, the young man had been convinced that the most he could hope for would be to be shot without a trial. He was standing up, clasping the back of the chair with both hands as if determined not to be wrenched away from it.

Scali pushed back his spectacles and shrugged his shoulders with a gesture of profound hopelessness. That notion, so prevalent amongst the fascists, that their enemies were as a matter of course a lower race, despicable and subhuman – that impulse to disdain, so typical of fools – had not been least among the reasons for which he had left his country.

'There's no question of your being shot,' he replied gruffly, using once more the tone of a school-teacher rating an idle pupil.

But the prisoner did not believe him. And the fact that his disbelief made him suffer gave a bitter satisfaction to Scali's sense of justice.

'One moment,' he said. Opening the door, he called to the clerk. 'Bring me that photo of Captain Vallado, please.'

The clerk handed him a photograph which he passed on to the observer.

'You're an airman, aren't you? so you can tell whether this cabin is in one of your machines or ours.'

Sembrano's friend, after shooting down two Fiats, had been himself brought down in a transport plane on the Sierra. The militia had occupied the village next day and found the airmen still at their places in the cockpit. Their eyes had been torn out. The mutilated bomber was the Assault Guard captain who had never handled such a gun before.

The man stared at the face with the eyes plucked out. His teeth were clenched and his cheeks were quivering.

'I've seen several Red pilots who'd been taken prisoners ... none of them had been tortured.'

'You've yet to learn that neither you nor I know much about this war. We're fighting in it, but that's another story.'

The observer's gaze strayed back to the photograph, as though fascinated by it. In his expression there was something childish, which went with his little gnome-like ears; the faces on the photograph were expressionless.

'What's there to prove,' he asked, 'that the photo isn't – I mean, wasn't sent to you after being faked?'

'Very well, that explains it,' Scali replied despondently. 'We pluck out the eyes of our best pilots just to make these photos! We use professional torturers, Chinese communists you know, for the job!'

Scali himself used to suspect, when shown the photographs entitled 'Anarchist Atrocities', that they were faked. It is always hard for a man to credit the vileness of those beside whom he is fighting.

The observer had gone back to his task with the papers, as if he found in it a refuge from his thoughts.

'Are you so very sure,' Scali asked, 'that if I were placed as you are at this moment, your people ... ?'

He stopped. From the mound of silverware there stole out, like mice, one, two, three, four little silvery chimes. It was as if the treasure-hoard itself were striking; not a clock buried in a jumble of pathetic bric-a-brac. That chiming clock breaking into their conversation (how long, he wondered, before it would run down?') that little clock so far from those who once had owned it, striking now its desultory hour, gave him a feeling of the utter indifference of things, a sense of eternity so poignant that whatever he might say seemed futile; he no longer had any wish to speak. He and the man before him, each had *chosen*.

Scali was glancing absent-mindedly at the dead pilot's map and tracing over with the pencil which he had dislodged from behind his ear some of the criss-cross lines. Beside him, the prisoner had just turned Vallado's photograph face downwards. Suddenly Scali adjusted his glasses, stared first at the observer, then back at the map.

The flying log showed that the pilot had taken off from Caceres, south-west of Toledo. Now the Caceres aerodrome, which was inspected daily by Republican scouting planes, was known to be unused. The map was a Spanish aviation chart; all details were clearly shown and the aerodromes indicated by small rectangular blocks of violet ink. Some twenty-five miles from Caceres was another rectangle, a mere indentation on the map and hardly perceptible; the outlines had been traced in pencil and, as the graphite would not take on the glossy surface, all that could be seen was a faint grooved line. There was a similar rectangle near Salamanca, and there were others south of the Estremadura, in the Sierra. All the secret air-bases of the fascists had been marked thus, including those whence their machines took off for the Toledo front.

Scali's face had grown tense, and he was conscious of the change. His eyes met enemy eyes; each man knew the other had understood. The fascist did not stir, did not say a word. But his head sagged between his shoulders and his cheeks twitched, as when he had been shown Vallado's photograph.

Quietly Scali folded up the map ...

The landing-ground was sweltering under the fires of a Spanish summer afternoon as the battered plane, piloted by Darras, squelched on the turf its flat, shot-scarred tyres. On the road behind the olive-trees, a peasant was singing an Andalusian folk-song.

Magnin, who had just returned from the Ministry, had gathered all his personnel round the bar.

'I want a volunteer crew for the Alcazar.'

There was a longish silence, filled by the hum of flies. Every day now planes were coming back with wounded crews and tanks ablaze; under the blinding sunlight or in the dusk, silently, their engines cut off, they limped home − if they returned at all. The hundred machines whose coming Bargas had predicted had reached the fascists, and many more as well. To fight them, they had not a single pursuit plane and the enemy's pursuit was operating in full strength along the Tagus.

'A volunteer crew for the Alcazar,' Magnin repeated.

III

Marcelino shared Magnin's view that as they had no pursuit planes the best thing they could do was to operate from behind clouds. Often he flew back from an engagement on the south Tagus front, when the sun had almost set and Toledo lay like a gigantic garland flung on the harvest-fields, with the Alcazar looming up at the river's bend. Here and there a ribbon of smoke from a burning house slanted across the pale expanse of yellow stone, trailing off into tenuous wisps sparkling with motes of light like sun-glints in a pool of shadow. In the spacious calm of one of war's 'off hours', under the evening glow, the smoke rose from each smouldering house as placidly as from a cottage chimney. Marcelino, still well enough up in airmanship to foresee each reflex of the pilots on board, had not taken again to flying a machine himself; he was, however, the best bomber in the flight and an excellent commander. And now, he knew, somewhere under the cloudbank, the battle was raging round Toledo, and the enemy planes were not far away.

Above the clouds the air was marvellously clear. An infinite peace brooded upon the white sea of clouds under their wings, and there was as yet no sign of enemy air-patrols moving towards the city. Now, by the pilot's reckoning, they were quite near Toledo. The plane accelerated to its maximum speed. Jaime was singing, the others straining to see ahead, with the fixed stare of absent-mindedness. In the distance some isolated mountain peaks pierced the level whiteness of the cloud-floor, and sometimes through a rift they had a glimpse of cornfields.

By now the machine was presumably above Toledo. But there was no instrument to record the drift due to a wind blowing directly at right-angles to their course. Once the plane came down through the clouds it was almost certain to be spotted from the town and, if they were too far from it, the enemy pursuit planes would be on them before they had had time to drop their bombs. The plane swooped down.

Expecting every moment to catch sight of the earth below, of the Alcazar, the enemy pursuit planes and his lines of defence, Marcelino and the pilot watched the height-gauge more passionately than they had ever scanned a human face. 2,500 ... 1,800 ... 1,200 feet ... But still they were immersed in clouds. There was nothing for it but to climb back, and wait till a hole appeared below them.

They zoomed into the upper air, poised motionless above the clouds that seemed to stream away beneath them, borne round by the earth's movement. The wind was driving the cloudbank from east to west, and here it was pocked with holes. They began to circle, with the immutable precision of a star, in the empty firmament. Jaime, who was in charge of the forward machine-gun, waved his hand to Marcelino.

For the first time both men grew conscious of the earth's rotation. An unheeded atom in the vast cosmic movement, the aeroplane gyrated like a tiny planet, waiting till the old city, the rebel Alcazar and its besiegers hove into view below, rolled round in the incessant rhythm of earthbound things.

But at the first rift in the clouds – too small for observation – the instinct of the bird of prey came uppermost again. Like a circling hawk the plane swung round and round, prospecting for a larger opening, and the gaze of all on board set vigilantly earthwards. It seemed to them that they themselves were stationary and the clouds and peaks were wheeling slowly round them on a far-flung orbit. Suddenly at the fringe of a cloud-hole the earth came into view, and two hundred yards or so away a little puff-ball floated past; the Alcazar had opened fire. The machine swooped again.

The zenith dwindled and the bright air faded out as they dived below the clouds. Here was man's little world. The Alcazar.

Toledo was on the left and, at the angle of their descent, the gorge above the Tagus loomed larger than the city, than the Alcazar itself, which was still firing up at them. The gun-layers were officers in the Artillery School, but the real danger for the crew lay in the enemy's pursuit planes rather than in gunfire from below.

Slanting at first, Toledo was swinging back to the horizontal. Even at this tragic moment it had not lost its quaintly decorative air, and the expanse of roofs was striped with ribbons of smoke from burning houses. The plane began to circle, at a tangent to the Alcazar. This hawk-like circling above their quarry was imperative, as the besieging troops were so close up to the Alcazar; every bomb had to be dropped with absolute accuracy on the target. But each successive circle gave the enemy more time to bring up his pursuit planes. Marcelino's machine had come down to nine hundred feet, and now he saw below him ant-like forms with round white hats, moving in front of the Alcazar.

The first time over, Marcelino opened the trap, took his sight without loosing off the bomb, and checked up on it. The sighting was a good one, as far as he could judge. The Alcazar was a small target and fearing the 'scatter' effect of light bombs, he decided to use heavy ones only. He had withheld the signal and the rest of the crew stood by, waiting. A second time the cockpit telegraph told the pilot to turn. The puff-balls of smoke were coming closer.

'Stand by!' Marcelino shouted.

Standing up in the cabin, his overalls flopping all round him as usual, Marcelino looked a figure of ungainly fun. But he never let the Alcazar out of his ring-sights. Then he pulled the trap-hatch wide open and squatted down. A gust of cold air swept up the cabin and all of them knew the fight was going to begin. It was the first cold snap of the Spanish war.

The Alcazar veered again, approached. Now Marcelino was lying flat on his stomach, his wrist in air, counting up the seconds. The hatted ants flashed past beneath him. Then his arm fell as if he were ripping down a curtain. The Alcazar swept underneath, with a few ill-aimed shells circling it like satellites, spun round and sheered off to the right.

A tenuous puff of smoke showed up in the main courtyard; was it the bomb? The pilot continued to wheel round, taking the Alcazar again at a tangent. Yes, the bomb had fallen plumb in the middle of the courtyard. Followed by bursts of shrapnel, the plane dropped a second bomb, swerved off, returned. Marcelino raised his hand again, but this time did not let it fall. In the courtyard white sheets had just been hastily outspread; the Alcazar was surrendering!

Jaime and Pol fell to shadow-boxing out of sheer high spirits, the crew were capering with glee.

Level with the clouds, the enemy's pursuit came into view.

IV

At the Jefatura, a college now converted into barracks, Lopez with his genial, Bourbon air was concluding his examination of a group of fugitives from the Alcazar; a woman hostage who had been smuggled out under a false permit given her by the chief armourer (who, too, had fled), and ten soldiers who had been incarcerated on the first day, but had managed to escape by jumping down into a ravine.

The woman was a dark, robust, matronly creature in the forties, with a snub nose and keenly alert eyes; but privation had left its mark on her.

'How many were there of you?' Lopez asked.

'That I'm afraid I can't tell you, sir. Seeing as how we weren't all kept together; the prisoners were scattered about here and there in different places. In the cellar where we were there must have been a good twenty-five of us, but that was only one roomful seemingly . . .'

'Had you enough to eat?'

The woman looked Lopez in the eyes. 'More than enough.'

Some peasants walked past the Jefatura with enormous wooden pitchforks shaped like candelabras on their shoulders and a gun tucked under each right arm. Behind them an abundant harvest was entering Toledo, carted by oxen whose horns were wreathed with sprigs of broom. The woman went on speaking.

'There's some folk here who say they've nothing to eat in the Alcazar. Don't you believe it, sir. It's only horseflesh and a poor sort of bread; but starving, that they ain't. I've eyes in my head and I keep an inn, and I guess I know more about cooking than menfolk do. Yes, sir, they've enough to eat.'

One of the escaped soldiers caught her up. 'And what about the planes that drop sardines and ham? Of course the ham's kept for the officers. We didn't get a smell of it, not once in all those cruel weeks. A mean shame, I call it. And to think the Guard is standing by those chaps!'

'What else did you expect the Guard to do, my lad?' the woman asked.

'Why . . . like we done.'

'Oh, that's your idea, my lad, is it?' she said slowly. 'But 'taint the same for you; you haven't killed no one in Toledo, have you?'

The remark confirmed what Lopez had suspected; when the 'Right' was in power the Civil Guard had carried out 'punitive measures' in the Toledo district. So now they were afraid to move, for they apprehended that the terms of their surrender might not be respected, once their faces were recognized.

'What about the fascists' wives?'

'They!' There was scorn in her voice. Her expression, too — respectful, while she had been addressing Lopez — had changed. 'What's come over you men, I'd like to know, that you're so mighty shy of hurting them women? They ain't all your mothers, be they? Those there bitches, why they treated us worse than the men did. Eh, if it's the women you're skeered of, just hand those bombs over to us, lads!'

'You wouldn't know how to throw them.' Lopez was smiling, but somehow he felt ill at ease.

He turned to some journalists who had just strolled up, notebook in hand. 'We've made a proposal that all non-combatants should be evacuated, but the rebels have turned it down. They say their wives wish to stay with them.'

'That's a good 'un!' the woman broke in. 'That woman up there what's just had a baby, does she want to stay? And the one who started firing a revolver at her husband, does *she* want to stay? Or maybe she'd like to have another shot at him! And that other creature who keeps yelling all night – for all that she's screwy, does *she* want to stay?'

'Yes, and you can't help hearing them – all the bloody time!' one of the soldiers said. Then he burst out hysterically, pressing his fists against his ears: 'It gets a man down, that noise of theirs. It wears you out.'

A voice outside made itself heard. 'Comrade Lopez, Madrid wants you on the phone.'

Lopez left the room, his nerves on edge. The picturesque was all very well; human suffering another matter. The thought of all the rancour festering up there in the Alcazar where men were being shot down in courtyards, and children born, was beginning to prey on his mind. One morning he had heard cries in the Alcazar: 'We want to surrender! We want –!' A gun-shot had given them quietus.

Over the telephone he summarized what he had just learned – little enough.

'One thing's sure,' he concluded, 'somehow we've got to save those folk.'

'The fascists have roped in hostages all over Spain.'

Lopez could hardly hear what was being said. Out in the courtyard an officer was strumming on a piano, a phonograph was playing an old rhumba, a loud-speaker bawling raucous lies.

The voice from Madrid grew stronger. 'I quite agree we must do our best for them. But we've got to clean up the Alcazar and shift the militia to the Talavera front. You'd better give those bastards up there another chance. Fix up a parley as soon as you possibly can. We can deal with them ourselves, through the diplomatic corps.'

'They've asked for a priest. You have priests at Madrid, eh?'

'Right – through the Church then. We'll ring up the O.C. at once. Thanks.'

Lopez went back to the room. One of the soldiers was speaking.

'The women are kept underground, because of air-raids. If

they're our women, they're put near the stables — where they had us cooped, you know. Their own women are elsewhere. Round the stables the stench is something awful. There's thirty bodies buried there, in the riding-school, only an inch or two deep, not to speak of the skeletons of horses lying about with bits of skin left on 'em. The stink round there knocks you flat. The bodies — that's the folk who wanted to surrender. So you see how we were — between the devil and the deep sea, as they say; with the stiffs under foot and those chaps upstairs who hung out sheets when the plane came over. That plane of yours gave us the jitters when it was laying eggs on us, but we were mighty glad to see it all the same. That's when they hung out the sheets.'

'Who did that? The Civil Guard?'

'No, the soldiers. The others — well, they let 'em do it. But when the plane had gone, why they got busy with their mangles, blast 'em! The mates began tumbling down all over the shop, like rabbits; on top of their sheets, some of them. When the Guard came and gathered up the sheets, they weren't white no longer. They hauled them away by the corners, like hand-kerchiefs. Well, we put our heads together; looked like we'd be mopped up next. So we took a chance, and jumped ...'

'Know if they killed a chap called Morales, a corporal?' someone asked. 'That's my brother. A bit of a socialist in his way.'

The soldier made no answer.

'Of course,' the woman said resignedly, 'those folks up there kill everyone!'

When Lopez left the Jefatura, children were coming home from school, satchel in hand. As he walked along, his arms swinging loosely, with unseeing eyes, he all but stepped into a black puddle on the road; an anarchist drew him aside, as if he were about to tread on a wounded animal.

'Mind where you step, mate. That's blood.' And added reverently: 'Comrades' blood.'

v

Half the 'Pelicans' lay dozing on the wall-sofas in the airport mess. Only half. The ground staff, however, were all at their posts. About a quarter of the pilots and machine-gunners were away — heaven knew where! Magnin was puzzled how to institute some sort of discipline, without using coercion. For all their unruliness and horse-play, their gasconade and irresponsibility, any Pelican was good to win a 'dog fight', one against seven. The same applied to Sembrano's Spaniards and to the Bréguet crews from Cuatros-Vientos and Gétafé. All had lost more than half their war strength. Several mercenaries, including Sibirsky, had asked to be allowed to serve one month in two without pay; thus making sure of, anyhow, a pittance and — better still — of comradeship. Daily Saint-Antoine came back, with his freight of cigarettes, field-glasses, and gramophone records, in still more melancholy mood. The machines that had set out to cross the Sierra without an escort of pursuit planes (where were they to come from?), hoping that the early hour, their wariness or a fight elsewhere in progress would see them through, as often as not failed to return and, when they did return, had been cut to tatters. The consumption of alcohol at the bar was going up.

The men lying on the wall-sofas rose and began roaming up and down the terrace; they looked like prisoners at exercise. Even if the trolley-man with the bomb-racks had not reminded them of the time, every man would have known that Marcelino's machine was overdue. By now he had only fifteen minutes' fuel left at most.

Enrique, a Commissar attached to the Fifth Regiment (formed by the communists in the early stages of the war as the nucleus of a regular army in the making), who claimed — perhaps with truth — to be a Mexican, was walking with Magnin on the landing-ground. The sunset was behind them and the Pelicans saw Magnin's limp moustache glinting in a last ray above the sharp-cut, totem-like profile of the Commissar.

'Actually, how many machines have you left?' the Commissar asked.

'I'd rather not talk about it. As a regular air force, we're blotted out. And we're still waiting to get decent machine-guns. What the hell are they up to, the Russians?'

'And what are the French up to?'

'Oh, what's the good of talking about it? The point is to

decide what's feasible as things are. Apart from an occasional stroke of luck, I'm going in for night raids – and playing hide-and-seek amongst the clouds. Fortunately, the autumn's coming on.' He raised his eyes; the night promised to be fine. 'It's the look of the weather that interests me most just now. We're no more than a guerrilla air force nowadays. If we don't get some more machines sent us from abroad, all that's left us is to get killed – to the best advantage. ... By the way, what's behind that damn-fool story of Russian planes arriving at Barcelona?'

'I was in Barcelona the day before yesterday. I saw a fine machine in an open hangar; it was covered all over with red stars. There was a hammer-and-sickle on the tail, and inscriptions written on the sides. Oh, and in front a big LENIN. Only the Russian "I" ' – his finger traced it in the air – 'was upside down, like the Spanish "N". Well, I went up close to have a squint at it, and I saw it was your old "Negus" plane.'

Magnin had picked up in the English market the Emperor Haile Selassie's private aeroplane. A fairly fast machine, with capacious tanks, but tricky to handle, it had come to grief and been shipped to Barcelona for repairs.

'Can't be helped! But why was it faked up like that?'

'Some childish nonsense: sympathetic magic, I dare say – to conjure up the real Russian planes or, more likely, just a provocative gesture.'

'Very likely. ... Oh, by the way, how's things your end?'

'Going quite well – but damn' slowly.' Enrique halted, drew from his pocket a Reorganization Plan, and switched his torch on to it, for the night was getting dark. 'Factually speaking, you may take this plan as operative from now on.'

His scheme was practically the same as that of the 'Shock Battalion' organization. Magnin remembered how at Saragossa the militia had gone out to fight without ammunition; how field telephones were non-existent on almost the whole Aragon front; and how at Toledo alcohol and pocket-flasks of iodine did duty as first aid.

'Have you succeeded in restoring discipline?'

'Yes.'

'Had to drub it into them?'

'No.'

'How did you manage?'

'The communists are disciplined already. They obey their group secretaries and military delegates (often, you know, the same men hold both posts). Any number of people who want to take part in the war joined the Party, just because it's decently organized, and that appeals to them. Formerly our lot were disciplined because they were communists; now plenty of people become communists because the Party stands for discipline. In each army unit we have a fair-sized group of communists, who themselves keep discipline and make a point of seeing that the others keep it too. Each group is a solid nucleus round which the new recruits gravitate, so to speak – till these in turn split off into another nucleus. When all's said and done, ten times more men than we can cope with are joining up, men who realize that by joining us they're doing good work against fascism. Oh, and by the way, I'd like to have a word with you about the Germans.'

This was not the first time Magnin had been tackled on the subject, and it was getting on his nerves.

Enrique took his arm; the gesture, coming from the hard-bitten warrior he believed Enrique to be, took Magnin by surprise. He had always divided communist leaders into two categories: the soldierly type and the priestly type. Having to place this fellow, as big and bulky as Garcia himself, a man who had fought in five civil wars, in the second category, disconcerted him. Just then he noticed that, for all their likeness to those of a Mexican idol, Enrique's lips pursed at moments like an Algerian carpet-hawker's.

The Police, he knew, had definitely 'put their foot down'. Never again must the three Germans be allowed on an aerodrome. Magnin regarded Krefeld as a suspicious character, and incompetent into the bargain; he had given himself out as an instructor, but did not know how to handle a machine-gun, and he was always at meetings of the Communist Party just when Karlitch needed him; in fact Karlitch had to do everything single-handed. The Schreiner affair had been most regrettable; the man was certainly innocent. In any case, however, he was best out of the Anti-Aircraft Corps.

'Of course,' he said, 'the whole business is lamentable from the humane point of view, but I can't put forward any valid reason for turning down what the Police are asking for – and have the power to insist on. I'm not a communist, and, under the circumstances, I can't profess to be obeying a mandate of my Party. Good relations between the air force, the police, and the Intelligence Service are too vitally essential for us just now, when we have to play into each other's hands to get things done, for me to risk upsetting them over this affair. They'd simply think I was being pig-headed. You see how I'm placed?'

'They've got to stay,' Enriques said. 'The Party vouches for them. You must see that, if they're compelled to go, all their comrades will take it to mean that they've fallen under suspicion. Really, you can't treat people who have been good militants for years like that.'

The machine-gunner belonged to the Party; Magnin did not.

'Personally,' Magnin said, 'I'm convinced that Schreiner's innocent; but that's not the question. You've had a report on him from the German section of the Party at Paris; you accept it. Well and good; make the Government realize you take full responsibility. For myself, I've no means of making inquiries and I can't decide off-handedly like that an issue which may have very serious consequences. All the more so since, as you know, they're perfect duds as airmen.'

'We might fix up a dinner at which I'd convey to you the welcome of the Spanish comrades, and you could say a word of welcome to the German comrades. I've been told that in the Squadron there's some bad feeling against the Germans – a touch of nationalist prejudice.'

'I haven't the least wish to drink the health of people who have such queer methods of imparting information.' The high esteem in which Magnin held Enrique's work, if not the man himself (he knew him very slightly), merely intensified his annoyance. He had watched the battalions of the Fifth Regiment being knocked into shape; they were the best militia battalions, by and large. The whole army of the Frente Popular might well be organized on the same lines. They, anyhow, had solved the crucial problem, the problem of revolutionary discipline. So Magnin regarded Enrique as one of the ablest organizers of the Spanish popular field force; but he was convinced that the man beside him, who for all his geniality was no less shrewd than conscientious, had he been in his, Magnin's place, would never have assented to such a request as that which he had just now put forward.

'The Party has looked into the question,' Enrique said, 'and considers that the men should be kept.'

It all came back to Magnin, the disgust he used to feel in the days when socialists and communists were perpetually squabbling.

'Sorry; for me the Revolution counts for more than the Communist Party.'

'Comrade Magnin, I'm no fanatic. And I used once to be a "Trotskyite". Nowadays fascism goes in for the export industry. It exports finished articles: armies and aeroplanes. That being so, I maintain that in the fight we're putting up our first line of defence isn't so much the world proletariats, as Soviet Russia and the Communist Party. A hundred Russian planes would help us more than fifty thousand volunteers with no war experience. But if you want the cooperation of the Party, you must take it as it is, without reserve.'

'Very true. But those Russian planes – they aren't here. As for your three ... comrades, if the Communist Party vouches for them let it vouch for them to the police, or take them on its strength. I've nothing against that.'

'So that's your last word. You're determined they shall go.'

'Yes.'

Enrique dropped Magnin's arm.

They were standing now in the glow coming from the airport buildings. Enrique had moved from the shadow into a ray of light and now that he had dropped Magnin's arm and was standing at a certain distance, Magnin had a good view of the man's exotic face. One of Enrique's sayings – he had heard it quoted but it had slipped his memory – came to his mind. 'For me a Party comrade counts for more than all the Garcias and Magnins in the world.'

'Don't forget,' Magnin continued, 'I know what a Party means; I belong to a weak one, the socialist revolutionary left-wing. But when one turns the switch, all the lights have got to go on at once. It can't be helped if some of the bulbs are a bit weak and, anyhow, big bulbs so often light up badly. So — Party first ... !'

'You'll keep them, then?' Enrique spoke with studied tone-lessness, less to feign indifference than to show he was not try-ing to bias his companion.

'No.'

The Commissar was more interested in decisions than in mental processes.

'*Salud!*' he said.

There was nothing to be done about it. True, Magnin had built up the air force, had found the men, had risked his life unsparingly, and had a dozen times engaged the squadrons he directed in adventures which he had no right to authorize. But he was not a member of the Party, and that settled it. His word weighed less than that of a gunner incapable even of taking down a machine-gun; and here was a man whom he esteemed for his worth and work, trying to force on him a fatuous line of conduct, just to gratify the least worthy whim of a Party comrade. Of course all that could be defended. And, there was no denying it, to Enrique's organizing ability they owed the best Spanish troops. After all, hadn't he himself acquiesced in Schreiner's dismissal? Action, he mused, always involved injustice.

Now the aerodrome was in almost complete darkness.

No, it was not in the cause of injustice that he had come to Spain.

Some distant gun-shots rattled across the flying-ground. How trivial all that was compared with the realities: villages going up in flames, the peasants streaming forth into the darkness from their blazing homes !

For the first time he was profoundly conscious of the lone-liness of war, as he trudged across the flying-field, through the dry grass, walking towards the hangar where men were busy patching up old machines – men united in a spirit of fraternity.

Darkness, it seemed, would steal a march on Marcelino's homing plane – and night landings are 'unhealthy' for wounded pilots. The ground staff seemed lost in contemplation of the nightfall; but what they were watching in hushed suspense, under the tranquil menace of the dusk, was the unseen race between the airmen and the advancing night.

Attignies walked up, his eyes fixed on the crest-line of the hills.

'My dear Siegfried,' Magnin said, 'the communists are getting on my nerves.'

The Spaniard and all his friends always referred to handsome, fair-haired young Attignies as 'Siegfried' – but only amongst themselves. It was probably the first time he heard his nickname. He took no notice of it.

'Each time,' he said, 'I hear there's friction between the Party and a man like you – whose aims are ours – it distresses me profoundly.'

Of all the communists in the Flight, Attignies was the one whom Magnin held in highest esteem. He knew that Attignies was against Krefeld and Wurtz. He felt a need to speak out, And he knew that Attignies was fond of Marcelino, and, like himself, was on tenterhooks, waiting for his friend's return.

'I quite admit the Party is taking a wrong line about that matter,' Attignies replied. 'But are you quite sure you aren't a bit in the wrong as well?'

'A man who works on impulse, my son, is always a bit in the wrong.' Magnin's tone was not patronizing but paternal. 'There's something to be said for both sides, of course.' He had no wish to air his grievances, but could not help adding: 'Do you think I'm not aware how the communists have been attacking me ever since Wurtz has been busy on his dirty job of police-dog for the Party?'

'Wurtz isn't a policeman. He has been campaigning in Hitler's Germany and I shouldn't be surprised if the men who are putting up a fight in the Reich just now aren't the best of our bunch! The whole business is absurd, I grant you; but there's no help for it. Look here, as a revolutionary and a man of experience, can't you ... well, can't you take it in your stride!'

Magnin reflected before answering. 'If the men on whose side I'm fighting don't trust me, why go on fighting, my son? I might as well throw up the sponge.'

'If your son is in the wrong, do you cast him off for that?'

It was Magnin's first experience of the deep, almost physical bond between the best communists and their Party.

'Jaime's in the plane, isn't he?' Attignies asked.

'Yes. He's the forward gunner.'

Swiftly the dusk was deepening into night.

'Our personal feelings,' the young man said, 'even our lives, are things of little importance in this war.'

'Quite so. But if your father's in the wrong ...'

'I didn't say, "your father". I said, "your son".'

'Have you a son, Attignies?'

'No. You have, haven't you?'

'Yes.'

They took some steps side by side, watching the horizon. Would Marcelino never come? Magnin felt that his companion was about to speak.

'You know who my father is, Comrade Magnin?'

'Yes. I suppose that's why ...'

All the squadron knew what Attignies – the name was not his real one – fancied a secret: that his father was one of the fascist leaders in his country.

'Friendship,' he said, 'doesn't mean being with one's friends only when they're right, but with them right or wrong.'

Together they went up to Sembrano's quarters.

The beacon was ready and all available cars had been posted round the landing-ground with orders to switch on their head-lamps the moment a signal was given.

'Better light up at once,' Magnin suggested.

Sembrano looked dubious. 'I'd rather wait a bit, if you don't mind. If the fascists come this way, there's no point in having the ground lit up for them. Yes, I'd rather wait.'

Magnin knew that it was merely superstition that made Sembrano prefer not to light up. Nowadays almost all the airmen had grown superstitious.

Every window stood open; this was the hour when, before the war, the Superintendent of the airport used to call for his first prepRandial whisky. From the earth was rising the dark-ness of a late summer night.

Suddenly there was a general cry: 'Lights on!' They had heard the sound of the plane signalling its approach.

Sembrano had turned on the alarm whistle at once, though neither he nor Magnin had yet caught sight of the plane. Judging by the sound it was on the far side of the buildings.

Midway between the short rays of the motor headlights the station beacon laid its long, pale beam across the field. Magnin raced down the stairs, followed by Attignies.

Below, all heads turned in the same direction told him whence the machine was coming. No one had actually observed its approach but now, guided by the sound, all caught sight of it as it turned to make its landing. The slate-grey sky was steadily darkening and the plane glided below it clean-cut as a paper silhouette; framed in a pale blue halo, it stood out like a building seen against the glare of floodlights.

'An outboard engine is on fire,' someone said.

The plane grew larger and, ceasing to turn, began gliding earthwards in their direction. The wings dwindled to straight lines, and merged into the shadows massing upon the surface of the field. But now all eyes were gazing only at the shapeless mass of the fuselage on which the fierce blue flame of a steel-welder's blow-pipe seemed to be battening like some bird of prey. The landing was interminably protracted; planes freighted with the dead are slow to take the earth.

Magnin's fingers were nervously gripping the rims of his glasses. 'The bombs!' he muttered.

Just as the machine touched earth, fuselage and flames interlocked in the last furious round of a struggle to the death. The body of the plane crashed down on to the flames which writhed and flattened out, only to leap up again with a hissing roar. Then the machine turned turtle.

Alert as death itself, the ambulance flashed by. Magnin jumped into it. The moment they saw how the plane would land the Pelicans had started running towards it; the pilots followed, cursing them up hill and down dale. Now they were racing round the huge straight pillar of fire, their shadows veering from them like the spokes of a wheel. Once more the flames had spread out from the body of the plane, swathing it in a pale sheen of throbbing light. The cockpit had snapped in two like a cracked egg. With the deft gestures of a doctor stripping a bandage off a wound, the Pelicans fell to rescuing the men within, peeling them off the wreckage with infinite precaution as if their blood had clamped them to it. Patiently they worked, but in feverish haste, alarmed by the ominous reek of petrol. While extinguishers sprayed the flames, dead and wounded were carried to a safe distance. Their comrades pressed round them in a chequerwork of shadows; under the spectral glare the watchers moved like unquiet corpses guarding the quiet dead.

Three wounded and three dead, amongst them Marcelino: six accounted for. Where was the seventh, Jaime? He emerged long after the others, clawing the air with shaky fingers, a comrade leading him. A tracer bullet had burst before his eyes. Blind.

By the feet and shoulders the airmen carried their dead to the mess. The van would come for them later.

Marcelino had been shot in the nape of his neck and there was little blood on his body. There still was beauty in the face, though the eyes had been left unclosed and a ghastly light was playing on them.

One of the barmaids scanned his features.

'It takes an hour at least for the soul to begin to show,' she said.

Magnin had seen death often enough to know the peace it sets on many faces. With thoughts and cares, wrinkles and crows' feet are smoothed away. Gazing at that face washed clean of life, but to which the open eyes and leather helmet gave yet a look of keen endeavour, Magnin recalled the words he had just overheard, an opinion he had often encountered under many forms in Spain: only an hour after death does a man's true self show up across the mask of life.

I

THE fascists were occupying a group of three farms; yellow roofs and stonefields nestling in a gully of white rocks. The first thing was to drive them out. There was nothing complicated in the task. The rocky nature of the ground along the Tagus, between Toledo and Talavera, enabled the militia to approach them from under cover all the way, provided they went about it methodically and carefully.

During the night Ximenes had indented for hand-grenades. The officer in charge of munitions was a German émigré, and at dawn Ximenes, all admiration for his promptitude, had seen the lorries rolling up, laden with – pomegranates! In German, as in Spanish, the same word serves for pomegranates and for grenades.

A little later, duly re-indented for, the grenades he wanted were forthcoming.

One of Ximenes' companies was composed of milicianos with only a few days' service who had not yet had their baptism of fire. Ximenes had put his best N.C.O.s in charge of them, and today was personally taking them in hand.

He began by putting them through a course of bomb-throwing.

'C' Company – the company to which the new recruits were posted – betrayed its inexperience. One of the men, after lighting his bomb, kept it in his hands. 'Throw it, you fool!' the sergeant yelled. It was just going to explode, blowing the poor devil to smithereens, when Ximenes' fist crashed against his elbow. The bomb exploded in the air and the man fell. Blood streamed down Ximenes' face.

The recruit had had luck; he was wounded in the shoulder only. After he had been bandaged and led off those around began preparing bandages for Ximenes. He waved them away. 'Let's leave the turbans to the Moors. Get me some sticking-plaster.' The effect was far less heroic; his face looked as if it had been patched up with postage-stamps. He took his stand beside the man whose turn for bomb-practice came next. There were no further accidents. Twenty incompetents were weeded out.

Under orders from Ximenes Manuel had been exploring the lie of the land. His Party had been wise enough to attach him to one of the officers from whom he could learn most. The officer had taken a fancy to Manuel, who was amenable to discipline, not because obedience – or its counterpart, authority – appealed to him, but because he was built that way and liked efficiency. Moreover, he was a man of culture, and Ximenes appreciated him as such. The Colonel, whose ideas of communists were mainly based on lurid hearsay, was amazed to discover in the cinema soundman (who was also a gifted musician) a born officer. He had not realized that the duties of a militant communist of the front rank inure him to the use both of strict discipline and of methods of persuasion, and that his experience as organizer, propagandist, and man of action gives him every chance of becoming a first-rate military leader.

The attack on the first farm began. The morning air was still; the leaves hung motionless as stone, save when now and again there came a breath of wind with a slight chilliness, an unexpected presage of the autumn. The milicianos carrying hand-grenades moved ahead in open formation, sheltering behind rocks and covered by their sharpshooters. The fascist position was rapidly becoming untenable. Suddenly a band of thirty milicianos jumped on to the rocks and dashed forward in the open, yelling, with the reckless frenzy of a savage tribe.

'They've done it!' Ximenes crashed his fist down on the window-ledge of his car.

Already twenty men were sprawling on the rocks, huddled up or with their arms spread out. Some had their fists pressed against their faces as if to shield them. A pool of blood beside a fallen man spread slowly, glistening in the sun, over a flat rock that sparkled white and crystalline as a sugar-loaf.

Fortunately the other attacking parties on each side of the farm had already reached the rocks abutting on it. They had not seen their comrades falling. Under a hail of bombs the roof-tiles began spouting up like geysers, and the farm was rushed within a quarter of an hour.

The new recruits had been detailed to attack the second farm. They had seen everything that happened.

Ximenes climbed on to the bonnet of his Ford.

'Listen, my lads,' he said, 'we've taken that farm. The men who disobeyed orders and left cover are dismissed from the column, whether they reached the farm or not. Don't forget that we're under observation; history is watching us, is judging and will judge us, and it calls for the sort of courage that goes in and wins, not the courage that consoles...

'If you follow the line of advance we've shown you, you're in no danger up to two hundred yards' distance from the farmhouse. I'll prove it to you by going that far with you, in this car. We shouldn't have a single casualty before that.

'Then we'll start fighting, boys, and capture the farm. Provid ... er ... luck be with us. May He who watches over everything ... the Spanish people, I mean, see us through, since we're all fighting in a cause that we believe to be just.'

He had selected the best shots in the regiment to accompany and cover the advance of the young bomb-throwers.

Before they reached the farms, they saw the fascists evacuating them.

During the previous week some fascist soldiers had come over to them; fifteen had been posted to Manuel's company. A man named Alba was acting as their leader, though not elected to that post. His courage was undoubted, but he had a way of always finding fault; many suspected him of being a spy. Manuel sent for him.

They started walking amongst the rocks, Manuel leading the way, in the direction of the fascist lines. There were no definite front lines, but the enemy after retreating from the farms was known to have taken up a new position some two miles away.

Manuel asked: 'Have you a revolver?'

'No.'

Alba was lying – the way the man's trousers dragged at the belt was enough to tell Manuel that.

'Then here's one for you.'

He took a revolver from his pocket and handed it to Alba, but kept at his waist his long automatic pistol, in its holster.

'Why don't you join the F.A.I.?'

'Don't want to.'

Manuel scanned his face. The features looked puffed out rather than mature or manly, the nose was rounded and the mouth thick-lipped; there was almost a wave in the long hair clumsily plastered over the low-set forehead. Doubtless a 'mother's darling' in his youth, Manuel surmised.

'You're a great grouser, aren't you?' Manuel said.

'There's lots to grouse about.'

'There's lots to be done — that's truer. If you, or I for that matter, were in Ximenes' shoes, things wouldn't be any better; no, they'd be worse. So we've got to help him at his job. After, we'll see.'

'They might be a deal worse, but at least we wouldn't have one of our class enemies bossing us — and that'ld suit me better.'

'I don't care a damn what a man is; it's what he does that counts with me. Why, Lenin himself wasn't a worker. ... But what I wanted to say was this: you can be very useful, and we must see that you pull your weight. Doing something, and not just grousing. Think it over, and then tell me which of them suits you. The F.A.I., the C.N.T., or the P.O.U.M. — whichever you like. We'll call a meeting of the comrades in your group, and you'll be given a responsible post. We're short of lieutenants. Have you been wounded?'

'No.'

'I have — in a dynamite attack and a damn silly stunt it was. Catch hold, will you? This darned thing makes my hips ache.' He took off his belt. 'Every man has some hobby. Mine is fooling about with a piece of stick.'

He moved to the roadside, snapped off a branch, came back to Alba. Unarmed now. For all he knew, the fascists were almost within earshot. And anyhow Alba was at his side. 'Do you know, I rather doubt if you really belong here. Perhaps you never will. But *I* say: Give every man a chance!'

'Even if he's been excluded from the Party?'

Manuel halted, flabbergasted; he had not thought of that!

'If and when the Party issues formal orders on this point, I'll carry them out to the letter. But till then I say: Even a man excluded from the Party. In these times it's every able-bodied man's duty to fight for the Republic.'

'You won't stay long in it – in the Party.'

Manuel turned to his companion with a smile. 'I shall.' He had a boyish laugh, but when he smiled the corners of his lips went down, giving a look of harshness to his rather heavy under-jaw. 'Do you know what they say about you?' He kept on walking as if to show the question had little importance.

'Maybe ...' Alba was still carrying Manuel's belt, and the holster rapped his calves at every step. And in this stony waste they were utterly alone. 'Tell me' – a faint grin flickered on his lips – 'what's your idea about it, what they're saying about me?'

'It's impossible to command men unless one trusts them.' Manuel walked steadily on, flicking the pebbles from the pathway with his stick. 'Fascists may manage it. We can't. If we can't trust our men, there's no point in what we're doing. The cynical outlook *plus* a taste for action makes a man a fascist, or a potential fascist – unless there's loyalty behind him.'

'The communists always call the people who are against them fascists.'

'I'm a communist.'

'What about it?'

'And I don't hand over my revolver to fascists.'

'Are you so sure?' There was a rather uncomfortable look on Alba's face.

'Yes.'

There was no mistaking the man's embarrassment, and Manuel's conviction that he was in no immediate danger left him. Obviously, he reflected ironically, one *would* feel embarrassed, talking to a man one's just going to shoot. So death was walking at his side, in the form of this self-opinionated youth with the plump, babyish cheeks.

'I've no use for folk who like taking command of others,' Alba said.

'Very likely. But they're no worse than folk who shirk taking it.'

They were returning to the village. Though his every sinew

155

was keyed up, Manuel was conscious of a feeling that was almost trust growing up between him and the man beside him; somehow it reminded him of the sudden gusts of affection or sensuality that came and went between his mistress and himself. 'Must be like this one feels,' he thought, 'when one sleeps with a woman spy.'

'The hatred of all authority as such,' he said, 'is a disease. A legacy from childhood. Something to get over.'

'If that's so, what difference do you see between us and the fascists?'

'Well, for one thing, the ideal of seventy-five per cent of our fascists isn't authority but – having a good time. Then, too, it's a second nature with the fascists to look up to their leaders as beings of a superior race. The Germans don't believe in "Race" because they're fascists; they're fascist because they believe in "Race". A fascist commands by divine right. That's why the question of trust doesn't trouble him as it does us.'

Alba drew the belt tighter round his waist, and said to Manuel, but without looking at him: 'Look here, supposing you found you were all wrong about a fellow ...?'

'Spain's a country where just now dying is all in the day's work.'

Alba's hand dropped on the holster, opened it, half withdrew the revolver – slowly, but without concealment.

'I've landed myself in a damn-fool situation,' Manuel thought. Then, at the same moment: 'Still, it's not such a bad way to die ...' Alba thrust back the revolver.

' "All in the day's work!" You're right.'

It struck Manuel that after all Alba might have drawn the revolver – to shoot *himself*. And, perhaps, there had been a touch of play-acting in the gesture.

'Think it over,' he said. 'I'll give you three days for it. Join up with any group you like. Or else do without Party support and take command of the men who don't belong to any party. I can guarantee you'll find it interesting, but that's your concern ...'

'Why?'

'Because if you want to lead men, all sorts of men, you've got to know exactly what your own beliefs are. I don't know much about mine, but I'm learning. ... Well, as I said, that's your own business. Mine's this: you've assumed a sort of moral responsibility amongst us, and I want to see you make it into a practical responsibility. And, needless to say, I shall check up on you. See?'

Had Alba said 'No,' Manuel would have sent him packing at once. But he said nothing. Did he acquiesce? Not if his look was any guide.

In the village Manuel took back his belt and hitched it round his waist; then laid his hand on Alba's arm and looked him in the eyes. 'Have you understood?'

'Perhaps.' Frowning, he walked away.

*

The sun was setting. The three captured farms had been fortified in a rough-and-ready way, and the milicianos who had broken cover in the first attack sent back to Toledo. Ximenes had issued his orders and, with a neat cross of sticking-plaster adorning his close-cropped temples, was walking with Manuel towards San Isidro, where the column was billeted for the night. Tessellated with loose pebbles, the road had the colour of a stone pavement, and up to the horizon everything was stone; the spiked branches of the prickly shrubs were hardly distinguishable from the yellow-fanged rocks.

Manuel was thinking over what Ximenes had just been saying in his address to the officers of the column. 'In a general way, the personal courage of the leader is all the greater for the qualms he feels about his leadership. And remember it's far more important to get definite results than to set an example.' Manuel walked slowly so as not to outpace the colonel who was trailing his game leg. His waddling gait was another reason for his nickname of 'Old Quack-Quack'.

'The new men did very well, didn't they?' Manuel said.

'Not too badly.'

'Well, the fascists cleared off without putting up a fight.'

'They'll come back.'

Ximenes, who was rather hard of hearing, had a habit of talking, almost to himself, as he walked.

'Yes, my boy, things are as bad as they can be; at Talavera they're using Italian tanks ...

157

'Courage is a thing that has to be *organized*; you've got to keep it in condition, like a rifle. Personal courage is no more than the raw material of the courage of an army. Only one man in twenty is, through and through, a coward. Two men in twenty are naturally brave. One builds up a regiment by getting rid of number one, using the other two to the best advantage and training the remaining seventeen . . .'

Manuel recalled an incident which had become legendary. Standing on the bonnet of his Ford in a village square, Ximenes had given a lecture to his men on the procedure to adopt when attacked from the air. An enemy flight, newly arrived from Italy, had left Talavera for Toledo. 'Think of the rose of a watering-can; that's how a bomb spreads out.' The men were in a terrible state of nerves; seven enemy bombers, escorted by pursuit planes, were taking up formation before flying above the village square. Now, if the colonel was deaf, the regiment could hear the engines only too distinctly. 'I'd have you know that at such moments fear and rashness are equally absurd. Nothing less than a yard above the ground is hit. When a company lies flat, an air bomb wounds only the man directly underneath it.' So that's how it is, his hearers thought, watching the zenith from the corner of an eye and listening to the deep drone of the engines coming every second nearer. Even Ximenes' vast prestige could hardly keep them from dropping on their faces. (All of them knew how he had captured the Colon Hotel.) Then, suddenly, unblushingly, every nose jerked up at once; Manuel, without moving, was pointing skywards with his thumb. 'On your bellies, everyone!' Ximenes roared out. Having already learned the movement, they scattered and were down in a trice, and the leading enemy bomber, now that the group had vanished from its bomb-sights, dropped its 'pills' at random on the village. The others reserved their stock for Toledo. There had been only one casualty. Since that day, Ximenes' men had ceased being scared of air-attacks. . . . The colonel was still talking – almost to himself.

'War's a queer thing. For even the most callous general killing's a problem in economy; he expends the maximum of powder and shot so as to save up his human material as far as possible. But we're short of powder and shot . . .'

Manuel knew that, from the Spanish Infantry Manual – a tissue of incomprehensibilities – to Clausewitz and the technical French reviews, all that he had read had taught him merely the syntax of warfare, whereas Ximenes was its living tongue. Behind the village, camp fires were lighting up. Ximenes gazed at them with an affection that was half bitterness.

'It's sheer waste of time discussing their shortcomings. Once an army has to take the field, something wrong with the troops always means something wrong with the staff-work. I've served in Morocco; when the Moors turn up at the barracks, do you imagine they're so magnificent? I grant you it's far easier to build up an army under military discipline; and I grant you we'll have to impose a republican discipline on our men – or be wiped out, if we fail. But even at this stage – make no mistake about it, my boy – it's our defective staff-work that's at the root of our troubles. Well, our task is harder than our adversary's; that's all there is to it.

'What your worthy friends, the communists – who'd ever have believed a year ago that one day I'd be taking a friendly walk with a Bolshevik? – what your friends are organizing, that Fifth Regiment, even if it isn't up to the Reichswehr standard, is a good job of work. But when they're made into an Army Corps, where will they get their arms from?'

'That Mexican boat has reached Barcelona, I hear.'

'Twenty thousand rifles; and we've hardly any aeroplanes left. Hardly any field-guns. As for machine-guns – you've seen for yourself, on our right wing there's one for every two companies. When they're attacked, they pass it round. The fight isn't between Franco's Moors and our army (we haven't any) but between Franco and the organization of our new army. All the militia, poor chaps, can do just now is to get themselves killed so as to gain time for us. But where's the new army to get rifles, artillery, planes? It's quicker fixing up an army than a factory.'

'Sooner or later' – Manuel spoke with conviction – 'the Soviets will give us help.'

Ximenes nodded, and took some paces without speaking. Russian help – that was something more serious than taking a stroll with a Bolshevik. He had expected everything from

France; now he had lost that hope. But Russia? Were the Russians to be the salvation – or the ruin – of his country? A last ray of sunlight played on his close-cropped hair starred with the sticking-plaster cross. Manuel watched the lines of camp fires spreading out. Slowly night was descending on the world of men, making their never-ending struggles seem infinitely vain, lost in an abyss of darkness, the massive indifference of the earth.

At last the colonel spoke. 'Russia's a long way off.'

The countryside along the road had been lavishly bombed by fascist planes, but many of the bombs were 'duds'. Manuel picked one up, unscrewed the cap and took out a small type-written note. He passed it to Ximenes who read, in Portuguese: *Comrades, this bomb won't burst. That's all for the present.*

It was not the first of its kind.

'Well, that's fine !' Manuel exclaimed.

Ximenes did not care to show his emotions. 'What have you done about Alba?' he asked abruptly.

Manuel described their conversation.

The stony waste seemed sinking back into the abject desolation whence daylight had temporarily rescued it. And whenever a certain aspect of the rocks brought back to Ximenes' mind his childhood, his thoughts harked back to youth. 'Soon,' he said, 'you'll have to start training young officers. They want to be beloved. That's only human. And it's an excellent thing, my boy, provided you get them to grasp this: An officer should be liked for the way he uses his authority – because he's more competent, juster, better than the average – not for his personal charm. Do you see what I mean when I say an officer ought never to "play up" to his men?'

Manuel called to mind the revolutionary leader's task: it struck him that to make oneself loved without courting popularity is one of the finest careers a man can hope for.

They were near the village; the flat, greyish houses seemed clamped upon a hollow in the cliffs, like drawing-pins along a fissure in a tree.

'Yes, it's a most dangerous foible, wanting to be loved.' Ximenes sounded half in earnest, half in his 'quack-quack' mood. The heel of his game leg crunched heavily the pebbles at regular intervals. For a while they walked on in silence; the hum of insects had died out of the air. 'It takes more nobility to be a leader of men,' the colonel added, 'than to be oneself; and it's far harder . . .'

They had reached the village.

'Good day to you, my children,' Ximenes called in answer to the cries of welcome. The troops were encamped east of the village which was practically empty and which they had not occupied. A crenellated château faced the village church.

'Tell me, colonel, why do you call them "my children"?'

'You mean I ought to have called them "comrades". I can't do it. I'm sixty; it's beyond me, I'd feel I was play-acting. So I call them "boys" or "my children"; and it does just as well, you know.'

They were walking past the church. It had been fired; this was the Tagus front. From the open porch came a musty cavernous smell mixed with an odour of dead ashes. The colonel entered. Manuel stared at the façade.

It was one of those Spanish churches, in a style at once baroque and popular, to which the use of stone instead of Italian stucco gives an almost Gothic aspect. The flames had burst forth from the interior and great black tongues of smoke gone writhing up the walls from every lintel, to flatten out under the feet of the topmost statues, charred and tottering above the void.

Manuel went in. The whole interior of the church was black and littered with scraps of twisted iron-work; the shattered pavement was a mass of sooty wreckage. Peeled to a chalky whiteness by the flames, the plaster statues in the aisles loomed tall and pallid at the foot of the smoke-grimed pillars; on the frantic gesturings of the saints hovered the mist-blue evening light that streamed in from the Tagus through the broken porch. Deeply impressed, Manuel felt himself an artist once again. What savage grandeur was in those convulsed statues, that somehow had outlived the holocaust! It was as if the flames had set them dancing in the church and their agony had given birth to a new school of art, the school of fire.

The colonel seemed to have vanished. Manuel's eyes were seeking him too high; he was kneeling amongst the embers, in prayer. Though Manuel knew that Ximenes was a Catholic, he was none the less dumbfounded. He left the church and waited for his friend outside. For a while they walked in silence.

'Will you allow me to ask a question, colonel? How do you come to be with us?'

'You know I was at Barcelona. Well, I got a letter from General Goded summoning me to join in the rebellion. I thought it over for five minutes. True, I'd never taken an oath of loyalty, but I knew that in my heart I'd pledged myself to serve the Government. So I had no trouble in making my decision; still I didn't want to be left with an impression later on of having acted on a sudden impulse. After those five minutes' thought, I went to Companys and said: "President, the XIIIth Tercio and its colonel are at your disposal."'

He gazed once more at the church. In the quiet evening fragrant with the scent of hay it seemed fantastically incongruous, with its torn frontage and charred statues outlined against the sky.

'Why,' he murmured, 'oh why must people always confound the sacred cause of Him who at this moment watches us, with that of his unworthy ministers ... of those amongst his ministers who are unworthy?'

'But, colonel, who but those unworthy ministers you speak of have made Him known to them?'

Silently, with a slow gesture, Ximenes led his eyes towards the peaceful countryside around them.

'Here's a case in point,' Manuel continued. 'Once in my life I fell in love. Head over heels – in dead earnest, I mean. Well, it was as if I were up against a brick wall. I might have been that woman's lover, but it wouldn't have made an atom of difference – there was a barrier between us, the Spanish Church. I loved her, yes, and when I think about it now I feel as if I'd been in love with a madwoman, a sweet and childish cretin! Look, colonel, just look at this country. What has the Church reduced it to? A sort of beastly second childhood! What has the Church taught our women? Two things only: to obey and to procreate ...'

Ximenes stopped short on his wounded leg and, puckering his eyes, gripped Manuel's arm.

'My boy, if you'd made that girl your mistress, very likely she'd have developed brains! ... And, I suppose, the nobler a cause is the more scope it offers to hypocrisy and lies.'

Manuel went up to a group of peasants; gaunt black forms against a wall that glimmered whitely in the twilight.

'Look here, comrades,' – his voice was cordial – 'that schoolhouse of yours isn't much to look at. Why didn't you convert the church into a school as they did in Murcia, instead of burning it?'

The peasants did not answer. In the growing darkness the statues on the church were fading out into nonentity. The two officers saw before them a row of unmoving forms, black smocks and wide-brimmed hats, along the wall; the peasants' faces were invisible.

'The colonel would like to know exactly why you burnt down the church. What precisely have you got against your priests here?'

'Why's them padres all against us?'

'That's not it. Why are *you* against them?' As far as he could judge in the darkness the peasants were feeling, above all, perplexed; could they really trust those two officers? Their questions might have something to do with the protection of works of art.

'There ain't a single comrade here, that's done his bit for the common folk, what hasn't had the padres up against him. That's how it is!'

The peasants blamed the clergy for the way they backed the upper class, for having condoned the punitive measures which had followed the revolt in the Asturias, approved of the spoliation of the Catalonians, and always taught the poor folk a meek submission to injustice; and now the Church was sponsoring a Holy War against them. One of them disliked the priests' voices 'because they don't talk like proper human beings'; many resented the harshness or hypocrisy – according to their rank – of the men the priests employed to bolster up their influence in the villages. All were indignant that, in the conquered villages, the priests had denounced to the fascists such as were 'irreligious', knowing full well that this consigned them to the firing squad. And all reproached the clergy with their wealth.

'Yes, that's so,' one of the peasants muttered. 'That's how they are. Just now you were asking about the church, why not turn it into a school? Well, my kids – they're my kids, ain't they? – and it can be main cold here in winter. But sooner than have my children in that there building, I'd see 'em frozen stiff!'

Manuel handed the man a cigarette, and clicked on his lighter. The speaker was a typical peasant, clean shaven, in the forties. The tiny flame lit up for a moment the face of the man beside him, a face shaped like a kidney-bean, the ill-defined nose and mouth slotted between a projecting chin and forehead. Asked for reasons, they had produced them; but what rang truest was the last speaker's voice.

Another voice came from the darkness, another peasant speaking. 'And I say they're frauds, the whole darned lot of 'em.'

'You mean it's money they're after?' Ximenes asked him.

'Every man's after the main chance. These fellows say they're not, I know ... but that's not it; I mean they're frauds deep down in 'em. It's something you can't explain. Yes, they're humbugs.'

'Them priests! Folk what live in cities don't know the first thing about them!'

Dogs had begun barking in the distance. Another man spoke up, raising his voice a little.

'He was sentenced to death by the fascists, was Gustavo.' His tone implied: And there's no more fooling him! And suggested, too, that all were hoping he would voice an opinion.

'Don't make no mistake.' The new speaker was presumably Gustavo. 'Collado and I, we're Christian folk. But we're agin the priests, there's no denying it. Only, as it so happens – I *believe*.'

'That's the kind he is! He'd splice his daughter to Saint John of Compostella if he could!'

'I'd rather see her on the streets, by God I would!' Then went on in the slow voice of a peasant trying to explain himself:

'Them fascists opened a door, you know. They shoved a poor devil out. He let off a "What!" Then it started all over again. We never heard the firing squad. The padre's bell, we heard that all right. When that bastard started tinkling, we knew what it meant; one of us was for it! Trying to make us confess. Sometimes he came and pi-jawed us, the son of a bitch. To give us absolution, says he. What for, I'd like to know? For defending ourselves against the generals? I heard that bloody bell tinkling away for a bloody fortnight. Then I says to myself: "Those pardons is a racket." I know what I'm talking about. It ain't only a matter of money. Now listen! What does a priest tell you when he's confessing you? He tells you to repent. If so be there's a single priest who got a single one of us to repent of having defended himself – well nothing's too bad for him. Because repentance – it's about the best thing a man has in him. That's the way I see it.'

Ximenes remembered Puig.

'Collado there, he's got something to say.'

'Spit it out!' Gustavo commanded.

The peasant kept silence.

'Come along, man! Out with it!'

'One can't talk like that, to order,' replied the man who had not yet spoken.

'Tell us the same yarn you told us yesterday. Give us a sermon.'

'It ain't a yarn ...'

There was a clatter of rifles in the darkness. Some milicianos were approaching. Now there was no light left.

'All that fuss' – he sounded sarcastic – 'because I told 'em the King had once passed through the Hurdes' country. On a shoot. Those folks are nearly all goitrous, half-witted, sick. And that poor, the King couldn't believe it possible to be so poor. It's made dwarfs of them. So he says: "Let's do something for these poor folk," and his people said, "Yes, sire," as usual. But nary a thing they did as usual. Then, as it was a miserable sort of place, they found a use for it; they put the penitentiary there. As usual. Then ...'

The clear enunciation, the way he spoke, betrayed a man accustomed to speaking in public, despite the sometimes rustic turn of phrase. Though the man hardly raised his voice at all, Ximenes caught every word.

'Then Jesus Christ thought, "That ain't as it should be," and

165

he says to hisself, "I'll go there." The angel looks around for the best of the women hereabouts, and one day he appears to her. She says, "Don't trouble, Lord. The child'ld come before its term, seeing I'd not have had enough to eat. There's only one man on our road has had a bite of meat this last four months; he killed his cat." '

Already the tone of irony had given place to a fierce rancour. Ximenes knew that in some parts of Spain there were *improvisatori* who delivered homilies at the local 'wakes', but he had never come across one till now.

'So the Lord went to another woman. Round the cradle there was only – rats. Nothing much to keep the baby warm, and cold comfort for a friend. So Jesus thinks to hisself: "Things is as bad as ever in Spain." '

From the centre of the village came the sound of lorries and grinding brakes, mingling with distant gun-shots and the barking of dogs. A smell of smoke and stone drifted to them from the gutted church. For a while the rumble of lorries drowned the speaker's voice.

'... and compelled the landlords to lease their farms to peasants. All the cattle-owners let off a howl saying they were being dispossessed by rat-owners. And called in the Roman soldiers. So Our Lord went to Madrid, and, to shut His mouth, the kings of the world began slaughtering the children in Madrid.

'So then He says to hisself: "There's nowt to be done with mankind. They're that foul that even bleeding for them night an day throughout eternity wouldn't suffice to wash them clean." '

The rumble of lorries persisted. They were waiting for Ximenes at the Commissariat. As the man went on speaking, Manuel was at once impressed and irritated.

'The descendants of the Wise Men didn't attend His birth, seeing as they'd all gone a-roaming – or settled down in government jobs. Then, for the first time on earth, from every land, men who lived near by and men who lived thousands of miles away, men from countries where it's hot and men from countries where it freezes – all who were brave and unhappy shouldered their guns and started marching, marching, marching ...'

In the voice there was a note of loneliness so intense that

Ximenes knew, despite the darkness, that the speaker had closed his eyes.

'And they understood in their hearts that Our Lord was living there, amongst the poor and oppressed ones of the earth. And so, from the ends of the world, they marched in, all who knew poverty well enough to die fighting against it; some had guns, and those who hadn't guns had their hands anyhow, and one after the other they came and lay down on the soil of Spain.

'They spoke all languages; why, there were even Chinese shoelace-sellers amongst them.'

The voice sank lower still; the orator was speaking through his teeth, huddled up like a man with a belly-wound in the darkness. A ring of heads – Ximenes' amongst them, with its sticking-plaster cross – clustered round him.

'And when the slaughtering had gone too far and the last company of the poor had set out on the march . . .'

Each word was rapped out with the low-voiced intensity of a sorcerer's incantation.

'. . . a new star rose above them.'

Manuel dared not kindle his lighter. The motor-horns on the lorries were baying in the darkness, with the frenzy of cars wedged in a traffic-jam.

'That ain't the way you told it yesterday,' a voice broke in.

Then Gustavo's voice, louder. 'I haven't no use for suchlike notions; once you start in with them, you don't know what you ought to do. Got to know what one wants, that's the only way.'

'You're wasting your breath.' A slow, resigned voice. 'Those townsfolk don't know nothing about priests, and there's no help for it.'

'They think it's got to do with religion.'

'I tell you – those folk just can't understand.'

'What was his job before the rebellion?' Ximenes asked.

'The man who was speaking?'

For a while there was an embarrassed silence. Then, 'He was a monk,' a voice replied.

Manuel led the Colonel off towards the strident cars.

'Did you see Gustavo's badge when you lit the cigarette?' Ximenes asked as they walked away. 'The F.A.I., I suppose.'

'That or another, it would be all the same. Personally, I'm no anarchist, Colonel. But, like all the rest of us, I was educated by the priests. And, do you know, there's something in me — though, as a communist, I'm against any form of destruction — that understands that man.'

'Better than the other man?'

'Yes.'

'You know Barcelona,' Ximenes said. 'On some churches there, instead of the usual notice, *"Under the People's Management,"* I saw *"Owned by the People's Vengeance"*. And yet ! . . . I remember how on that first day the dead were left lying about in the Plaza de Cataluña. Well, two hours after the firing ceased the pigeons were back in the Square as usual, hopping about the pavements, over the corpses. And one day man's hatred burns itself out.' He added in a slow, meditative tone as if he voiced the afterthought of many thought-tormented years: 'God, anyhow, has time to wait . . .'

Their riding-boots dinned on the hard, dry soil, Ximenes' wounded leg still lagging a little behind Manuel's stride.

'But why,' the Colonel murmured, 'why must His time of waiting mean . . . all this?'

11

Another effort at mediation was impending. A priest was due to reach Toledo during the night and presumably he would enter the Alcazar next morning.

The gas-lamps in the little square were out and the only light came from a hurricane-lantern hung rather low in front of the El Gato tavern. Attracted by the cat on the signboard of the inn, Slade took a seat at a table near the door and whiled away the time playing the shadow of his pipe at different angles on the wall of Toledo Cathedral.

Till 2 a.m. Slade was able to get wires through to his newspaper. Lopez should be back from Madrid well before that hour. It was he who had been deputed to fetch the priest. A first-rate story in prospect, Slade thought. It was not ten yet. The utter solitude gave the square, with its flights of steps and tiny palaces topped by the russet foliage of trees, the glamour of a stage-setting, to which somehow the last gunshots up at the Alcazar added a touch of eerie unreality. A vision rose before his eyes of palaces forlorn in far-off India, with palm-trees sprouting in the rose-red halls, and in the emptiness huge wireless sets bringing the din of distant war only to the ears of apes and peacocks. The stench of corpses in Toledo was like that of an Asiatic swamp. 'Are there radios on the moon?' he wondered. 'Yes, I'd like to think that waves are carrying these vague sounds of battle to the dead stars!' The abandoned Cathedral, still undamaged and at this moment seething, most likely, with milicianos, gratified at once his dislike for the Catholic Church and his love of art.

Voices came to his ear; people talking inside the tavern.

'Our planes gave them a nasty jar today. The fascists got their machine-guns into the bull-ring at Badajoz – that couldn't be helped – but only under the roof, not out in the open as they'd hoped.'

'We'd better be careful about the barracks; they've put the prisoners inside them.'

Another voice joined in, ironical, with a strong English accent.

'After the fight there was some excitement on the Plaza, I can tell you. I could see it – I was only five hundred yards away. Every woman was looking her youngest and prettiest, and guess what they were asking? "Who's that pretty little Scotch boy up there?"'

Slade was still taking notes when at last Lopez turned up; Lopez with his regal mien, arms uplifted, and shock of hair all quivering like a cockscomb. He sat down heavily, lifted his hands again, and dropped them with a resounding smack upon his thighs. The brisk sound jogged the silence, some gun-shots followed up the echo. His little hat pushed back on his head, the American waited for his friend to speak.

'They're asking for priests. Well, they shall have their priests. But, good God ...!'

'Do you mean they're asking you for priests, or is it you who're asking for your hostages?'

Lopez took the air of a man who has been through a trying day and had his fill of it.

'But don't you see it's exactly the same thing, you owl? Like this, it is. They're asking us for priests. That's their look out. But, at the same time, these fourflushers don't want to evacuate the women and children. Neither ours nor theirs. That suits their book, and they know it. ... Well, as it happens, I know some priests, a brace of them. So I phoned to Madrid: "Mobilize those two padres, I'll be along at two o'clock." '

'I suppose they think they're to be found at every corner, priests who haven't cut and run. ... Well, I went to Madrid. To begin with, no damned way of getting in touch with Guernico; he was out with his ambulance corps. At last I got the address of padre number one – a real good scout, by the way. He often used to visit the prison when we were there, in 'thirty-four. I rolled up to his place with four milicianos – we were all in our *monos*. The whole god-damned house was Catholic – Catholic tenants, Catholic *portero*, and the stairs lousy with plaster saints, ugly as sin, at every corner. The motor hadn't died down before they started a racket, yelling on every floor. The fools thought we'd come to shoot them. I tried to explain to the *portero*. No good. He had massacres on the brain, of course. When he saw our car roll up, the padre'd hopped it across the garden. That ticked off number one.'

The pale glamour of the moonlight seemed to have deserted the little square; as usually happened, wherever he might be, Lopez' genial presence filled it to the exclusion of all else.

'Padre number two. I knew he was in touch with the militia general staff. When I got to the mess, the officers were feeding their faces. I called up a pal and told him what I was after. "Right," says he, "I'll have your priest for you at four o'clock." I had the hell of a lot to do, plaguing folk for munitions all over the place, but I got back at four.

' "You know," my pal told me, "the padre was there all the time, having his grub with us, but I wanted to give him fair warning. Looks as if you'd have some trouble getting him; he's backing out, the padre." Backing out, was he? "Those lousy swine, so they won't even do their jobs," says I. Then they explained to me he was a canon at the Cathedral, one of the higher-ups, a big shot in the what-do-you-call-it prelacy. If he'd been a country priest, he wouldn't have made such a fuss, it seems. As a matter of fact, I don't know much about country priests; sculpture isn't in their line, I guess. "Right," says I, have a word with him. If there's any way of getting the kids out of this god-damned war, we've got to find it." I was bone dry, so I hopped down to the beer cellar and no sooner had I turned the door-knob, than what do I see but a guy without a collar, in a filthy shirt and striped trousers, yanking at the beer-taps – and there at last was His Reverence, my priest.'

'A young man? Old?'

'Badly shaved, and the stubble on his chin was white. Fattish. An ugly mug, but looked a good scout in his way. His hands – I'd have liked to draw them. I told him what was up – you know the way I put things. Well, his answer took ten minutes! Here, if a guy takes ten minutes to say what he could say in half a minute, we call him a faker – and he was a faker. I let fire something at him, and he says: "That's the way soldiers talk, I know the style of it." They must have told him I had a rank of sorts, though I was in a *mono* – without a badge of any kind. "An officer like you!" that's what he said to me, to a poor devil of a sculptor! So I said: "Officer or not, when I'm given orders to go to a spot and fight, well, I go. You, you're a priest; there's people over there who need you, and I want to save the kids. Are you coming or aren't you?" He hesitates a bit, then his voice gets serious. "Do you guarantee me a safe conduct?" I'd had my bellyful of him by then. "When I came here two hours ago," I says, "you were packing in the grub with the soldiers; what do you think, do you think they're going to eat you in Toledo for their dinner?" We both were sitting on the table. He stood up and struck a pose with his hand on his waistcoat. "If you think I can save a single life I'll go." "Good," says I. "You look all right to me. Now, if you're going to save lives, you got to do it mighty fast. The car's outside." "Don't you think maybe I'd better put on a coat and collar?" he asks. "Well," says I, "personally I don't give a damn, but the others might like it better if you had your cassock on." "I haven't one with me." I didn't know if it was true or if he had the wind up; most likely it was true. Anyhow he went off and a few minutes later I found him by the car, in a collar, black tie, and alpaca coat. So off we go!'

A long gust of languid wind filled the air with a strong smell of burning; the smoke from the Alcazar was drifting down into the Plaza. And, now that the stench of rotting corpses was obliterated, Toledo seemed another city.

'They kept on stopping the car to check our papers. "I should say it's a hard job getting out of Madrid, these days," he said. Sounded to me as if he'd been thinking it over. All the time we were driving here, he couldn't seem to get away from trying to explain to me the Reds might quite as likely be in the right as the Whites, "perhaps even more so," and to find out just how the interview would be fixed up. "It's a cinch!" I kept on telling him every few minutes. "Just like we went about it with Captain Rojo. We tell them you're here; then we take you to the escort guard. They bandage your eyes and then they bring you to the office of the Commander of the Alcazar, Colonel Moscardo. Once you're there you can shift for yourself." "To Colonel Moscardo's office?" he repeats. "Yes," I says, "Moscardo's office." And so we were all set.

'Me, on my part, I tried to hammer into his head that he must refuse absolutions, baptisms, and all the rest of it, if Moscardo declined to release the women and kids.'

'He's promised to put it through?' Slade asked.

'To hell with his promises! If he feels like doing it, he'll do it. Otherwise his promise isn't worth a busted button! Any way I tried to rub it into him, but I expect I bitched it up. We reached Toledo. We went to the battery and I shouted to the captain. "Cojones!" he bawls out, jumping on the running-board before I could get a word in. "Where are the bloody shells? They promised to send them today – tomorrow night we'll have run out of ammunition." I wigwagged like a semaphore for him to shut up. No matter how little a priest knows here, it's that much too much! No luck! At last the fool of a captain tumbled to it. I introduced them. "The padre – a comrade," The captain points at the Alcazar tower, all shot to pieces and standing on its last legs, and smacks his thighs. "Looks pretty sick, old Moscardo's office, don't it?" There was a big triangular hole in it. "Really, my dear Major," says my padre – yes, we'd got that intimate – with the mulish look on his mug that kids have when they've plotted to play hookey, "do you really expect me to have my interview with Colonel Moscardo in a place like that? For one thing, how on earth am I to get there?" "That's your funeral!" yammered the captain. "But I know God him-self would have a tough time getting through that muck!"'

'Well, it was getting better and better, but I finally made him understand we'd be able to fix it up somehow with Moscardo. The padre's snatching a nap just now. I've got three sentries guarding him.'

'Tell me,' Slade asked. 'Will he go, or will he back out?'

'Tomorrow at nine. There's a truce till noon.'

'Any news about the kids?'

'Not a word. Well, it's up to the big shots and the would-be big shots to explain it all to my little padre. I hope they don't scare the pants off him! There's one tattooed guy amongst the anarchists – he's a nightmare!'

'Let's go and see what's happening up there.'

Silently they trudged up to the Zocodover Square, pausing on the way to admire the Terror of Pancho Villa, whose hat looked even handsomer by night. The higher they climbed, the fuller was the street. On the top storeys of some houses rifles and machine-guns were keeping up an intermittent fire. Slade had been here three months earlier; here at this same hour at night he then had heard the clatter of an unseen donkey's clogs and a party on their way back from a serenade merrily thrumming the 'International' on their guitars. Lit by the searchlights, the Alcazar loomed up between two roofs.

'Let's go up to the square,' he said. 'I'll get my writing done inside the tank.' The newspaper men had got into the habit of taking refuge in an old tank, which was rarely used, bringing a candle with them and writing by its light.

At last they reached the barricade. On the left some milicianos were firing their rifles; others, on the right lying on mattresses, were playing cards. Others were grouped round a wireless set, taking it easy in wicker arm-chairs and listening to an Andalu-sian folk-song. Over their heads, from the second floor of a neighbouring house, sounded the pit-a-pat of a machine-gun. Slade walked up to the barricade and, peeping through a chink, had a clear view of the square.

Completely empty, flooded by the rays of a powerful arc-lamp, the city square, where in days of old kings of Castile on horseback fought with bulls, looked even eerier than the cathedral precinct. The reek of burning, mingled grotesquely with the dewy fragrance of the night, brought to mind the atmosphere of some dead planet rather than any spot on earth. The fierce light of a film studio played on ruins like the wreckage of a temple of the East, on a gaunt archway, on derelict, bullet-scored shop-fronts. On one side lay, singly or linked in skeins of metal ribs, the chairs of an abandoned restaurant. Above the houses flared an immense Vermouth poster, bristling with Z's; in coigns of shadow glimmered the rooms where look-out men kept vigil. Immediately in front, searchlights bathed the narrow streets, converging on the hill-top, in a vivid, theatrical effulgence, and at the end of each street, more brightly floodlit than ever it had been for the tourists' benefit, smouldered the Alcazar, extraordinarily squat against the dark immensity of the sky.

Now and then a fascist fired a shot and Slade's eyes wandered from the card-players to those who fired back at the enemy. Some of them, he supposed, had wives and children up there in the Alcazar. At nightfall the peasants had brought out their brown, country-made rugs; striped like the mattresses on the barricades, they patterned the whole city in a curious, piebald symmetry.

A mule came out into the main street. ('At midnight,' Slade thought, 'they'll exchange the mules and zebras, to carry on the pattern.') In front of the antiquated tank, the turrets of armoured cars, lit up within, fretted the shadows with little squares of light. The window of a milliner's shop near by was almost as bright as if its lamps were on, and an old woman in a feathered bonnet was gazing in rapture at the display of hats, in the best provincial style, lit up by reflections of the searchlights raking the Alcazar.

Now and then an enemy bullet rapped the shield of a machine-gun. Lopez started back to staff headquarters. When Slade entered the tank, the gunner made room for him. No sooner had he taken out his notebook than the gunner opened fire and, simultaneously with him, the armoured cars and marksmen. A machine-gun firing in a turret can make an infernal racket and suddenly all the people in the street seemed to go frantic with excitement. What was happening? Slade jumped down from the tank. Was it a counter-attack from the Alcazar?

The fascists had just sent up a Very light, and every marksman in Toledo was blazing away at it.

III

The priest had been in the Alcazar for half an hour. Journalists and various local 'officials' were strolling slowly behind the barricade waiting for the appearance of the enemy representative in pursuance of the truce. In his shirt-sleeves, his hat well back on his head, Slade was walking with Pradas, a communist official, Golovkin, a Russian journalist, and a Japanese pressman. Every few steps he threw a rapid glance through the openings in the barricade. But nothing except the upended café chairs was to be seen in the square, as yet. The stench of death and that of burning came in alternate gusts as the wind veered about.

A fascist officer appeared at the corner of one of the little alleys issuing from the Alcazar. He went back, and once more the square lay empty. But now the emptiness was not oppressive as in the floodlit nights. The place seemed to have been deserted only for the moment; daylight had given it back to life, the life that had been only waiting, like the fascists and milicianos, at each street corner, to re-enter it.

The truce had begun. But, having been so long a zone no combatant could cross without attracting enemy fire, the square had a bad name. At last, however, three milicianos took heart to enter it. Some parts of the Alcazar had been captured, and in them had been found, so rumour said, mattresses under archways and packs of cards, exactly like those used by the militia manning the barricade. None the less the Alcazar, if only because it was the enemy, had kept its mystery intact. The militia knew they would not be able to enter it during the truce, but they wanted anyhow to approach it. Still the little group, walking across the square, was careful to keep in touch with the barricade.

'Both sides are itching to be at each other's throats,' Slade thought as he peeped through a gap between the sandbags; the sacking on which his forehead rested was already warming up, his hat was further back than ever. 'Rather like cats, they are!'

A group of fascist officers had just come out opposite him, at

175

the place where the first had disappeared. Confronted by the empty square, they hesitated. Milicianos and fascists stared at each other, unmoving. Some more milicianos crossed the barricade. Slade adjusted his field-glasses.

He had expected to see anger on the faces of the fascists; but all he could make out (he could not see their faces at all clearly) was a look of embarrassment, accentuated by the stiffness of their gait and, above all, the movements of their arms, which the close-fitting uniforms made particularly noticeable. The milicianos approached them.

Slade turned to a man who was peeping through the next loop-hole. 'What do you make of it?'

'Our fellows can't bring themselves to speak.'

When men have been trying to slaughter each other for two months, it is not easy for them to start talking to each other. What made them keep their distance, what caused some to slink beside the pillars and the others along the barricade was less the mutual taboo of no-man's-land, than the idea that if they approached each other they would have to speak.

More fascists came out of the Alcazar, more milicianos left the cover of the barricade.

'Four-fifths of the garrison are Civil Guards, aren't they?' Golovkin asked.

'Yes,' Slade replied.

'Notice how they're dressed? They're only letting officers come out.'

As if to prove him wrong, just then some members of the Guard appeared in yellow-braided uniforms, cocked hats – and incongruous white canvas shoes.

'The militia seem to have killed off boots,' Slade observed.

Meanwhile conversations had sprung up in the square, though the groups took care to stand at least ten yards apart. Slade lit his pipe between two sandbags and walked towards them, followed by Golovkin and Pradas.

The two groups were slinging insults at each other.

The sight was all the quainter because each gesticulating group kept its distance, as if the intervening space were forbidden ground, and volleyed repartee without moving a step forward.

'. . . because we, anyhow, are fighting for an ideal, you bastards!' they heard a fascist shouting as they came up.

'What about us? I suppose we're fighting for our money-bags, you son of a bitch? Your ideal, eh? Ours is a finer one than yours, seeing it's for everybody on earth.'

'To hell with an ideal that's for everyone! It's only the *highest* ideal that counts, don't you know that much, you ignoramus?'

They had been sniping at each other for the last two months; now they kept up a war of words, for lack of an alternative.

'Say, call that an ideal, dropping gas on the Abyssinians? And shutting the German workers in concentration camps? And paying farm labourers a peseta a day? Do you call the massacre at Badajoz an ideal, you bloody butcher's boy?'

'Russia – call that an ideal?'

'What about it?'

'For folk who haven't been there, perhaps. The workers' republic! A hell of a lot it cares for the workers!'

'Yes, I suppose that's why your bosses hate it! If you've a scrap of honesty, you can't deny that everything that's rotten in the world is on your side. And everything that's out for justice is on ours, even the women. Show us your militia girls if you can. You're a policeman, not a god-damned prince. Say, why are the women on our side?'

'The women! They'd better keep their mouths shut, eh, you pimp! That's a good joke, when folk who burn down churches start talking of ideals.'

'If there weren't so many, we wouldn't have to burn them.'

'Too many churches lined with gold, and too many villages with no food.'

Slade, who was near the milicianos, felt vexed at being reminded of the futile altercations of Paris taximen and Italian cab-drivers.

A man beside him asked: 'Who's that fellow?' pointing to Golovkin. Slade had been seen about with Lopez on the previous evening and so was looked on as a 'mate'.

'Correspondent of a Soviet newspaper.'

Golovkin had the prominent cheek-bones and gnarled face of the peasants one sees on Gothic carvings. When Slade had visited Moscow on an assignment, he had been struck by the likeness between the Russians, so near their peasant origin, and the Western Europeans of the Middle Ages. 'I look like a Red Indian,' he thought; 'that Russian like a field-labourer, and those Spaniards — like horses!'

The three milicianos who first had left the barricade had halted side by side without moving across the square. The others were still swapping 'ideals'.

'Anyhow,' one of the fascist officers shouted, 'it's all very well talking about an ideal when one dosses every night at home as you do; what about us who have to live in a damned dungeon? You're living on the fat of the land. We haven't even got a fag to smoke.'

'What's that?'

A miliciano crossed the forbidden zone; a C.NT. man, with one sleeve rolled up on an arm blue with tattooings. Almost vertical, the sun cast round his feet the shadow of his huge sombrero, and he seemed gliding forward on a black pedestal. A packet of cigarettes in his hand, he marched towards the fascists, as if he meant to strike them. Slade, who knew that Spanish etiquette forbids a man to proffer a packet of cigarettes, waited to see what he would do. He took the cigarettes, one by one and handed them round, still looking black as thunder. The cigarettes seemed tokens of an attitude — as if he had said to the fascists: 'You're in your right to be sick about our cigarettes. If you bastards haven't any, that's the fault of the war. You're a lot of bloody swine but we got nothing against your cigarettes.' He seemed to be calling the windows to bear witness as he doled out the cigarettes; when his packet was empty, the other milicianos who had joined him continued the distribution.

'What do you make of this damn-fool behaviour?' Pradas asked. Pradas brought to mind a Mazarin who had trimmed his beard to catch a look of Lenin.

'At one of the most heated sessions of the Belgian parliament I saw all the parties join up like one man to throw out a tax on carrier-pigeons. Eighty per cent of members were pigeon-fanciers. Here there's a freemasonry of smokers.'

'Ah, but it goes deeper than that you know.'

One of the fascists had shouted: 'Well, anyhow you get your

morning shaves!' What made the remark still odder was that few of the militia were clean-shaven.

One of them, again an anarchist, started running back towards the town. The two journalists followed him with their eyes; he stopped to speak to a miliciano standing beside the barricade. The latter fired his revolver in the direction of the fascists, then started gesticulating with it as if he were indulging in a furious tirade. The anarchist went on his way, still running.

'Was it like that in Russia?' Slade asked Golovkin.

'We'll discuss that later. . . . It's beyond me!'

The miliciano came back with a box of Gillette blades, opening it as he ran. There were at least a dozen fascist officers. Suddenly he halted, obviously perplexed; there weren't enough blades to go round. He made as if to throw them, as one throws sweets to a group of children, then hesitated; finally he handed the box, with an angry look, to the nearest officer. The other officers crowded round the man who held the box; but when the milicianos began laughing, one of them rapped out an order and they separated. Just then another fascist came from the Alcazar, and from the far side of the square, the man who had fired his revolver when the anarchist was passing came up and joined the group.

'That's all very fine and large,' he began, staring at each fascist in turn. Then he paused. The others waited for his silence to end. 'But what about the hostages? My sister's up there, I'd have you know.' There was a world of hatred in his voice; no question now of bandying 'ideals'.

'A Spanish officer has no right to question the decisions of his superior officers,' one of the fascists answered. But the reply failed to take effect, for just then the last-come fascist spoke.

'I want to see the commanding officer, on behalf of Colonel Moscardo.'

'Come along,' said a miliciano.

The officer followed him. Slade and Pradas also followed, looking absurdly small beside the huge bulk of Golovkin. The crowd was growing denser, and by the way they moved might well have been the usual throng of idlers of a Sunday afternoon – had not all eyes been riveted on the Alcazar.

Hernandez was coming out of the bootshop, followed by the

179

Negus, Mercery, and two lieutenants, as the fascist officer reached the door. The latter saluted and held out some letters.

'From Colonel Moscardo, for his wife.'

Suddenly Slade had a feeling that all he had been seeing during the last twenty-four hours at Toledo and before that, at Madrid had found its ultimate expression in those two men eyeing each other with languid hatred amid the reek of burning and the smoke pouring down from the Alcazar in trailing shreds like wisps of tattered flags. The cigarettes, the razor-blades had led up to those letters; so, too, had the hostages, the comic-opera barricades, the storming-parties and retreats and, when the fume of burning lifted for a moment, the stench of dead horses that seemed here the normal odour of the soil.

Hernandez shrugged his right shoulder – a familiar gesture – and handed the letters to a subaltern, conveying to him where to go with a jerk of his long chin.

'Of all the bloody fatheads!' the Negus exclaimed, but his tone was cordial.

Hernandez shrugged both shoulders for a change but always with the same languid air, and signed again to the subaltern to go.

Pradas steadied his glasses on his nose. 'Is Moscardo's wife at Toledo?' he asked.

'No,' Hernandez replied. 'In Madrid.'

'At liberty?' Slade's voice conveyed his amazement.

'In a nursing home.'

This time the Negus shrugged, but ragefully.

As Hernandez went back to his bootshop-headquarters, Slade could hear a busy typewriter within fretting the silence of the truce. Startled by the sudden lull in the gunfire, dogs were beginning to venture forth into the steep-pitched streets. Audible again as once in peace-time, a cheerful sound of steps and chattering voices filled the town. Pradas caught up the captain and took a few paces by his side.

'What's the idea of sending on those letters?' he asked, tugging his little pointed beard. 'Just courtesy?'

His brows were knitted and he sounded baffled rather than sarcastic. The Spanish officer seemed lost in contemplation of the shadows of the broad-brimmed hats stippling, like huge confetti, the cobbled roadway.

At last Hernandez answered him: 'Generosity.' And turned on his heel.

'Know that captain fellow well?' Pradas asked Slade. His eyebrows had not yet straightened out.

'Hernandez? No.'

'What on earth prompted him to do that?'

'What should prompt him – to do otherwise?' Slade replied.

'That!' Golovkin pointed to a more or less armoured car that was passing by. On the roof lay the corpse of a miliciano; judging by the way it was disposed, the body of a friend whom the men in the car were bringing home. The journalist tugged at the ends of his bow tie; a sign with him, of uncertainty.

'Does that often happen?' Golovkin asked.

'Fairly often, I believe. The officer commanding here has sent on other letters of the kind.'

'A regular officer, eh?'

'Yes. So's Hernandez.'

'What's the dame like?' Pradas asked.

'That's your nasty mind!' Slade grinned. 'I've never seen her, but I understand she's no chicken.'

'Then why on earth? ... Or is it just Spanish solidarity?'

'Do you get any satisfaction out of big words like that? I suggest you go to Santa Cruz, where he's lunching. You can wangle an invite easy enough, and talk with him about it. You'll find some communists there too.'

Noticing the Terror of Pancho Villa strolling amongst the crowd, Slade realized that Toledo was a small town in wartime as in peace; that now he would come across the same odd characters at every moment whom in the past he used to see day after day; the self-same guides and pensioners.

'On the fascist side,' he said, 'a push is never made between two and four, because of the siesta. ... Don't draw any hasty conclusions about what's happening here.'

Almost intact on the side towards the city, the barricade of sandbags and striped mattresses was pocked like worm-holed timber on the side facing the Alcazar. Smoke-clouds were spreading everywhere a pall of shadow, and the houses burning their hearts out tranquilly as ever. And in the furtive lull of war another house caught fire close by the Alcazar.

Two tables at right-angles occupied a corner of the mess-room at Santa Cruz Museum. Some jovial spirits were larking about in the semi-darkness. Sunbeams squeezing through holes in the brickwork flashed on the rifles slung across their backs, and glinted on the sweating faces. Round them were heaps of fruit and branches, and the air reeked with the characteristic Spanish odour of crude olive-oil. Squatting, the Terror of Pancho Villa was repairing rifles.

Hernandez' attitude was all the simpler as his bent back hardly lent itself to soldierly postures, but the men of his escort, at the other table, were self-consciously martial. None of the wounded men had changed his bandage. 'Blood-proud,' Pradas remarked. Golovkin and Pradas had planted themselves opposite Hernandez, who was talking to another officer. With one fleck of light upon his forehead, and a second on his undershot jaw – which gave him the look of one of Cortez' *compañeros* – Hernandez did not seem so much of another nationality than the Russians, as of another epoch. All the milicianos were dappled with specks of light.

'Comrade Pradas here belongs to the technical committee of the Party,' Manuel said by way of introduction.

'I know.'

'Look here, do tell us exactly why you sent on that letter,' Manuel said, continuing the previous conversation.

'Why did the men hand round those cigarettes?'

'That's just what interests me,' Pradas grunted. A pinhead of light glinted on his beard; he had just put a hand behind his ear.

Did the curious gesture mean that he was hard of hearing? But the hand was not steady; he began stroking the back of his ear with it, like a cat washing itself. Hernandez answered Manuel with an indifferent flick of his long fingers. Fitful waves of sound from radios blaring outside under the blazing sun seeped through the bullet-holes, and seemed to swirl round Pancho Villa, who had fallen asleep amongst his rifles under the fantastic hat.

'The Soviet comrade' – Pradas capped his head with his hand – 'says this: "In my country Moscardo's wife would have been arrested out of hand. I want to know why you don't take the same line."'

Golovkin knew French, and could understand Spanish a little.

'You been in prison?' the Negus asked.

Hernandez made no remark.

'In Czarist days I was too young.'

'Fight in the civil war?'

'In the Service Corps.'

'Got any kids?'

'No.'

'Say, Negus,' Slade broke in, 'have you any kids yourself?'

'I . . . used to.'

Slade dropped the subject. Pompous, Mercery oracled : 'Generosity does honour to great revolutions.'

'But,' Pradas insisted, 'our comrades' children are in the Alcazar.'

A miliciano served up a superb ham garnished with tomatoes and cooked in olive-oil – Slade's pet aversion. The Negus, too, declined it.

'What !' Questions of *cuisine* always interested Slade. 'You, a Spaniard, don't like *aceite*?'

'I never eat meat.'

Slade picked up his fork; it was stamped with the arms of the archbishopric. Everyone was eating. In the ultra-modern showcases of the museum – glass, chromium steel, and aluminium – all the exhibits were in perfect order, except certain small objects that bullets had reduced to dust; in front of each of these was a neat round puncture in the glass.

The Negus turned to Pradas. 'Listen to me ! When a man comes out of prison, nine times out of ten his gaze doesn't . . . doesn't *settle;* see what I mean? He's lost the way of looking at people like a man. In the proletariat, too, there's lots of folk can't look at people steadily. That's all got to be changed, to begin with – see?'

The words were meant for Golovkin as much as for Pradas, but he did not relish having Pradas translate them.

'Yes,' Slade murmured with satisfaction. 'I always knew that guy anyhow hadn't the "big head".'

One of the militia came up to him with a cardinal's hat in his hand. 'We've just found this contraption. As it ain't no use to the community at large, we thought we'd make you a present of it.'

'That's nice of you,' Slade smiled. 'I've noticed that good scouts – shaggy dogs and children and what they call extremists – usually like me … but not cats, woe's me! Thanks.' He put the hat on his head, stroked the pompoms and went on eating his ham. 'They remind me of the ball-fringe at my old grandmother's out in Iowa City. Around the bottom of the arm-chairs. Thanks.'

The Negus pointed his stubby forefinger at a Crucifixion in the Bonnet manner, glimmering against the pitch-black background. It had been exposed to the enemy's gunfire for several days. A cluster of bullet-holes almost severed the right arm; the left, protected by the stonework of the wall, had only a few punctures. A burst of machine-gun fire had flayed the body from shoulder to hip, forming a sort of bandolier, neatly picked out like a seam made by a sewing-machine.

'Even if we're beaten here and at Madrid,' the Negus said, 'at least the men will have given their hearts a few days' run. See what I mean? In spite of hatred. They're free today. They've never been that before. I'm not thinking of political freedom, but another kind. See what I mean?'

'Quite,' Mercery put in. 'That's what Madame Mercery always says: It's only the heart that counts.'

'At Madrid things don't look so cheerful.' Slade's voice was calm under the big red hat. 'Still, you're right. In revolution-time life takes a holiday. My today's article will be called, "A Day Off".'

Pradas slid his hand up to the summit of his pear-shaped head. There had been a noise of chairs drawn aside, and he had missed Slade's last remark. They were making room for Garcia who had just come smiling in, a pipe stuck in the corner of his smile.

' 'Tisn't so easy for men to hit it off together,' the Negus went on. 'That's sure. But there's not a great deal of courage knocking around; and it's courage gets things done. Cut the crap! When men are ready to give up their lives for something, they

184

sort of stick out from the rest. But we've no use for "dialectics" or red tape; delegates are all right, but bureaucrats! ... Or an army to defeat the army, or inequality to stamp out inequality, or playing the bourgeois' game. What we are out for is to live the way men ought to live, right now and here; or else to damn-well die. If we fail, there's an end of it. No return tickets for me!'

Garcia's keen, squirrel-like eyes began to twinkle. 'My dear old Negus,' he said in a cordial tone, 'when one wants to make the revolution a way of living, for the mere fun of it, it usually becomes a way of dying. And in that case, old fellow, one ends up by being as satisfied with martyrdom as with victory.'

The Negus raised his right hand; the gesture of Christ addressing his disciples. 'A man who's afraid of dying has an uneasy conscience,' he said.

'And meanwhile,' Manuel remarked, lifting his fork reprovingly, 'the fascists are in Talavera. And, the way things are going, you'll lose Toledo.'

'In the last analysis,' Pradas announced pedantically, 'you are Christians. And while ...'

(There, thought Garcia, he missed a good opportunity to keep his mouth shut.)

'Down with the bloody priests!' The Negus sounded exasperated. 'But there's something in theosophy.'

'No,' Slade put in, toying with the pompoms on his hat. 'But go on!'

'We're not Christians, no bloody fear! But your lot are turning into a priesthood. I don't say communism's become a religion; but I do say that communists are turning priests. For you, being a revolutionary means just – being cleverer than the next fellow. It wasn't like that with Bakunin or Kropotkin – not by a long chalk! You're soaked in the Party, in discipline, in plotting and scheming. If a man don't belong to your little lot, you won't give him a square deal, you've not a scrap of decency towards him. You've lost even your loyalty. Look at us now! We've put up seven strikes since 1934, just out of solidarity; not because we stood to gain a cent by them.'

Anger had loosened the Negus's tongue, set him gesticulating and his hands fluttering around his fluffy crown. Golovkin had lost the thread of his harangue, but a phrase caught here and there alarmed him. Garcia said a few words to him in Russian.

'Factually speaking, it's better to be disloyal than incompetent,' said Pradas.

The Negus took out his revolver and laid it on the table.

Garcia laid down his pipe in the same position.

The room looked like a gigantic still-life, with the myriad pin-point rays piercing the shot-scarred wall caught by the plates and limbeck-necked carafes, making them sparkle like fireflies in the gloom. Fruit gleamed along the branches, and a bluish sheen hovered on the squat, sleek barrels of revolvers.

'All arms are needed for the firing line,' Manuel quoted.

'When soldiers were needed,' Pradas said, 'we were soldiers. Then, when organizers were needed, we were organizers. Yes, we've had to be all things in turn; engineers, factory managers, and the rest of it. If, in the last analysis, we've got to be priests, well – damn it! – we'll be priests. But, mind you, we've built up a revolutionary state, and now we intend to build up an Army. Factually. With our qualities and our defects. And it's the army that will save the republic and the proletariat.'

'And me,' Slade said suavely, both hands grasping the pompoms round his hat. 'I say Boloney! ... But what you do, all of you, is much more to the point than what you say. You guys are all too intellectual, that's how it is. And that's the trouble with your country, Golovkin, everybody's brainy, top-heavy with brains. That's why I'm not a communist. The old Negus, now, may be a little cock-eyed, but I like him.'

The tension in the air relaxed. Hernandez glanced at his watch again, then smiled. His teeth, like his face and hands, were remarkably long.

'It's the same thing in every revolution,' said Pradas, fingering his beard. 'In '19 Steinberg, a revolutionary socialist and commissar of the courts of justice, asked that the Peter-and-Paul fortress should be permanently closed. Thereupon Lenin got his majority to vote that the white prisoners should be confined there; we had enough enemies of that sort behind the lines. In the last analysis, nobility is a luxury no movement can indulge in – in its early phase.'

'But the sooner it does, the better,' Mercery said emphatically.

The Negus spoke again. 'Tomorrow there'll be free shaves

all round, eh? ... Cut the crap! Parties are made for men, not men for Parties. We don't want to build up a State or a Church or an army. Just men.'

'And I'd have them start behaving decently whenever the occasion arises,' Hernandez said, clasping his long fingers in front of his chin. 'We've enough ruffians and murderers who set up to belong with us.'

'See here, comrades!' Mercery said. 'Look at it fair and square, says I. You can't have it both ways. If we win, History will reckon up against the men we're fighting that business of the hostages, and honour us for Madame Moscardo's liberty. Whatever happens, Hernandez, you've given a fine, a noble example. In the name of the League of Peace and Justice to which I have the honour to belong, I take off my ... my *képi* to you.'

Since the day of the flame-thrower attack when they first had met, Garcia had been puzzled by Mercery's personality. Must idealism, he wondered, always involve play-acting? Yet he discerned in Mercery an underlying sincerity; an authentic asset for the cause of antifascism.

The Negus was on the warpath again. 'And don't go about pretending to take the anars for a gang of lunatics. Spanish syndicalism has done some first-rate work during the last few years. Without paltering with principles, what's more. We haven't a hundred and seventy million men behind us, like you; but, if the worth of an idea is to be judged by the number of its supporters – well, there are more vegetarians in the world than communists, counting in the Russians. What about the General Strike? It works, don't it? *You* were against it for years. Read your Engels again, that'll learn you. The General Strike, that's Bakunin. I once saw a communist play with some "Anars" in it. Know what they looked like? Like the bourgeois idea of the communists.'

From their shadowy background, the statues of the saints seemed to be egging him on with their ecstatic gesturings.

'It's wisest to go slow with generalizations,' Manuel said. 'The Negus may have had some – er – unfortunate experiences. Every communist isn't perfect. Except for our Russian comrade – I've forgotten his name. Sorry! – except him and Pradas, I believe I'm the only member of the Party sitting at this table.

187

Look here, Hernandez, do you take *me* for a padre? Do you, Negus?'

'No. You're a good egg! And you don't mind fighting. There's plenty good eggs in your lot. But there's the other sort as well.'

'Another thing. You talk as if you'd a monopoly of honesty; and if anyone doesn't see eye to eye with you, you call him a bureaucrat. But you know as well as I do that Dimitroff's no bureaucrat. There's Dimitroff and there's Durruti; one theory of what's right against another – not a gang of racketeers against all decent folk. We're comrades; let's be honest with each other.'

'Wasn't it that Durruti of yours who wrote : "We're ready to relinquish everything but victory?"' Pradas asked the Negus.

'Yes,' the Negus snapped at him with his prominent teeth. 'Yes. But if Durruti came your way, he'd give you a good kick in the arse !'

'I'm afraid you'll very soon discover,' Pradas observed, 'that, factually speaking, that moral code of yours had no utility for practical politics.'

'No more has any other moral code,' a voice put in.

'And yet the trouble about the Revolution,' Garcia said, 'perhaps its tragedy, is that it can't get on without one.'

Hernandez raised his head. On Manuel's knife a tiny spot of light was dancing; he was eating sunlight.

'There's one thing to the credit of the capitalists,' the Negus went on. 'A mighty good thing too. In fact, what beats me is how they hit on it. I guess it's up to us to fix something of the sort for each of the unions here, when the war's over. Yes, I take off my hat to them for that : the way they use the "unknown". The "Unknown Soldier", that was their stunt. We can go one better. On the Aragon front I've seen lots of graves with a plain S.A.I. or C.N.T. on a stone or a bit of wood. No name. I felt . . . well I guess that was O.K. at Barcelona when the columns going up to the front marched past Ascaso's grave, they all kept silent; that was O.K. too. Better than shooting out one's neck.'

A miliciano came to fetch Hernandez.

'Christians !' Pradas mumbled in his beard.

Manuel stood up. 'Has the priest come out?'

'Not yet. The commanding officer's sent for me.'

Hernandez went out, followed by Mercery and the Negus. The latter picked up his cap – not the Mexican sombrero of the previous day but the red-and-black *képi* of the anarchists. There was a brief silence, broken only by the desultory noises that accompany the ending of a barrack-room meal.

'Can you tell me why he sent on that letter?' Golovkin put the question to Garcia who, he felt, was the most looked up to by all, including even the Negus. Moreover, he spoke Russian.

'Let's take it point by point. Point one: he didn't care to refuse; parental authority sent him into the army, for many years he's been a Republican officer – out of liberalism – and he's more or less an intellectual. Point two: don't forget he's a regular army officer (there are others here) and that tells, whatever his political feelings are about the other side. Point three: we're at Toledo. You know how every revolution is inclined to melodrama, at its early stages. Spain just now is . . . a Mexican colony.'

'And what about the other side?'

'The telephone wire between our headquarters and the Alcazar hasn't been cut and both sides have been using it since the siege began. During the recent parley, it was understood that Major Rojo should be our spokesman. Rojo had been an Alcazar cadet. He was led in blindfolded. When the bandage was removed he found himself at the door of Moscardo's office. You've seen what the left-hand wall looks like from outside? Just one great hole. There was no ceiling to the office. Moscardo in full uniform sat in his desk-chair; Rojo in the chair he used to sit in. On the back wall, which was undamaged, just above Moscardo's head, hung – would you believe it? – Azaña's portrait; they'd forgotten to take it down.'

'What about the *morale* of the troops?' Golovkin asked in a lower voice.

'You better ask someone who's been in closer contact with them than I have. Just now the Assault Guard is our most dependable formation. Manuel!' He translated Golovkin's question into Spanish. Manuel squeezed his underlip with his fingers.

'Mass courage in the field,' he said, 'can't stand up against planes and machine-guns. The truth is that, well-trained and armed, the militia is brave enough; otherwise they cut and run. With enough milicianos and enough columns we can build up an army. To give it courage is a question of organization. The question is: Which men and how many will consent to being "organized"?'

'Now that captain,' Pradas said, 'don't you think, that as a regular officer, he may feel some ... attachment for the cadets?'

'We had it out together. He tells me there aren't fifty cadets all told in the Alcazar. That's true; it's garrisoned by the Civil Guard and by officers. The "young heroes defending their ideal against an infuriated populace" are mainly — Spanish policemen. So be it!'

'Tell me, Garcia, how do you explain what happened in the square?' Manuel asked.

'I think that the fellow who doled out the fags and the josser who fetched the razor-blades, and the others who followed suit, and Hernandez when he took the letter — I think all of them were yielding, without knowing it, to the same impulse: the wish to prove to the men up there that they've no right to despise them. I dare say that sounds rather like a joke; but I'm in earnest. What separates the Right and Left wings in Spain is the taste for, or the horror of, humiliation. The Frente Popular stands, amongst other things, for a combination of all the people with a horror of it. For instance, let's take the case of two impecunious *petits bourgeois* in a village before the rising; well, the one on our side was all for cordiality; the other for stand-offishness. The desire for fraternity on the one hand and, on the other, the cult of hierarchy are very definitely up against each other in this country — and in some others too, perhaps.'

Manuel distrusted the psychologist's views on such subjects, but he remembered the words of old Barca: 'The opposite of humiliation, my lad, it ain't equality; it's fraternity.'

'When I'm factually informed,' Pradas put in, 'that under the Republic, wages have been tripled and, as a result, the peasants have at last been able to buy themselves shirts; and when I hear that the fascist government has put back the old wages and, as a result, thousands of newly opened shops where they sold shirts have had to close — then I understand why the lower middle class in Spain is with the proletariat, heart and soul. "Humiliation" wouldn't bring even two hundred enlistments.'

Garcia was getting to recognize the pet expressions of the various parties; thus 'factually' was a communist speciality. He also knew the mistrust that Pradas, and even Manuel, felt towards psychology. His personal view was that the outlook of the anti-fascist movement should be guided by economic considerations; and he also considered that, economically speaking, there was no difference between the anarchists (and their friends), the socialist masses and the communist groups.

'I quite agree, my friend. Still, it isn't from the Estremadura backwoods where people live on acorns that we get our best soldiers or the most recruits. But, for goodness' sake, don't ask me to work out a theory of humiliation as a stimulus of revolution. I am trying to understand what happened this morning, not the general situation in Spain. Factually (as you'd put it), Hernandez isn't a shirt-merchant — even in a figurative sense.

'No, Captain Hernandez is a plain, straightforward man for whom the revolution means a way of realizing his moral aspirations. For him the dramatic times in which we live are a personal Apocalypse. What's most dangerous about these semi-Christians is their angle on self-sacrifice: they'll indulge in the worst follies provided they pay for them with their lives.'

To one section of his audience Garcia seemed all the more intelligent because they often had to guess what he was driving at.

'Obviously,' he continued, 'the Negus isn't a Hernandez. But between the liberal and the libertarian the difference is only one of terminology and temperament. The Negus told us his people were always ready to give up their lives. That's true of the best of them. Note that I say, "of the *best* of them". They're carried away by a fraternity which they know quite well is bound to take a different form one day. And they're quite willing to die after some crowded hours of ecstasy . . . or of revenge, in certain cases; dramatic hours in which their dreams come true. Don't forget what he said about their "hearts" being in it. And, for them, a death like that justifies everything.'

'I haven't much use for the sort of man who has himself

photographed with a revolver pointing at the camera,' Pradas remarked.

'Yet he's often the same man who, on the 18th July, scared the rich folk into handing over their arms, by sticking his fist in his pocket to look like a revolver.'

'The anarchists . . .' Pradas began.

' "Anarchists," ' Manuel took him up; 'that's only a label, and usually a damned misleading one. The Negus is a member of the F.A.I., I grant you. But when all is said and done, what matters isn't what his "mates" think; what matters is that millions of men – yes, millions – who aren't anarchists think as they do.'

'Think as they think about the communists, you mean?' Pradas grinned.

'No, my friend,' Garcia protested. 'Not that. Think as they think about our efforts . . . about life. Ideas they have in common with, let's say, our French friend, the captain. And, mark you, I found just the same spirit in Russia, in 1917; and, less than six months ago, in France. It's the first stirrings of revolution. Yes, it's high time for everyone to realize that the masses are one thing, and "parties" are another – a fact that's been apparent ever since the 18th July.' He raised his pipe-stem to emphasize the words. 'Nothing is harder than to make people think about what they're going to *do*.'

'Yet that's the only thing that counts,' Pradas said.

' "Doomed to change . . . or to perish," ' Golovkin quoted in a sombre tone.

Garcia fell into a brown study. For him the hybrid term 'anarcho-syndicalism' consisted of two opposed elements. The positive element was the 'syndicalist' activity of the anarchists; the negative element, their ideology. Once the 'glamour' was ruled out, anarchist theory fell absolutely into line with syndicalism; the more enlightened anarchists took their stand on Sorel's teachings, not on theosophy. Yet today's argument, from beginning to end, seemed to have been based on the assumption that anarchists were a race apart; that anarchism was to be defined in terms of *character*; that Garcia should have studied them in his capacity of an ethnologist, and not as a political thinker.

'And to think that throughout Spain,' he mused, 'at this very hour exactly the same things are being said, most likely, at every luncheon table! How much better they'd employ their time hunting for some basis of cooperation, so as to implement the orders of the government by joint action between the various groups, communist, C.N.T., F.A.I., and U.G.T.! It's odd the weakness people have for arguing about anything and everything rather than the practical line of action to be followed, even at a moment when their lives hang on the line they choose. Well, I suppose I'll have to tackle each of those fellows separately and see what can be done.'

A miliciano who had just accosted Manuel came up to him. 'Comrade Garcia, isn't it? You're wanted at the Jefatura. Madrid calling.'

Garcia got in touch with Madrid.

A voice on the phone: 'What about the negotiations?'

'The priest's not back yet. The time given him will be up in ten minutes.'

'Call us as soon as you know anything. What are the prospects?'

'Bad.'

'Very bad?'

'Just bad.'

V

At the Museum Hernandez, who knew that Garcia had been called to the telephone, was waiting for his return.

'One remark of yours particularly struck me. You said that, though a moral code is no concern of practical politics, it can't get on without one. Would *you* have had that letter forwarded?'

'No.'

The click of rifles coming to the half-cock, the flash of 'dixies' in the midday sun, and the smell of corpses, brought so vividly to mind the tumult of the previous day that an ending of hostilities seemed unbelievable. There were less than ten minutes to run before the truce expired, and already peace was getting to seem a romantic memory. Hernandez' long, loping steps glided beside Garcia's brisk, emphatic stride.

'Why?'

'For one thing, they haven't given back the hostages. For another, once you've accepted responsibility, it's up to you to see it through. That's all.'

'But – I had no choice about accepting it. I was an officer and I'm doing my job.'

'I tell you, you accepted it.'

'How on earth could I have refused it? You know how short we are of officers.'

For the first time the city took a siesta unbroken by gunfire, and lay plunged in an uneasy sleep.

'What's the point of the revolution if it isn't to make men better? I'm no proletarian, Major; as a slogan "the proletariat for the proletariat" means as little to me as "the bourgeois for the bourgeois". But, all the same, I put up as good a show as I can – got to, you know!'

'Will the revolution be brought about by the proletariat or by the – the Stoics?'

'Why not by the most humane element of humanity?'

'For the simple reason, my dear fellow, that the most humane people don't stand for revolution. They stand for public libraries and ... cemeteries. More's the pity!'

'A cemetery doesn't prevent an example from being worth the making. Quite the contrary.'

'But meanwhile, we have – Franco!'

Hernandez caught Garcia's arm, with an almost feminine gesture. 'Listen, Garcia. Let's drop the game of trying to put each other in the wrong. You're the only person I can talk to. Manuel's a decent fellow, but nowadays he sees things only from the Party angle. The enemy will be here in a week's time, you know it even better than I. That being so, whether I'm right or you're right ...'

'No!'

Hernandez looked towards the Alcazar; no move had been made as yet.

'And yet,' he said, 'if I'm to die here, I'd have liked ... conditions to have been different. Listen! Last week one of my men – a "comrade" of sorts, who is or sets up to be an anarchist – was accused of having rifled the company cash-chest. He cited me as a witness. I gave evidence in his favour. But it seems that this man had been imposing the collective system on a village which was in his charge, and his mates were beginning to extend that system to neighbouring villages. I quite agree that the whole idea was a bad one, that it's infuriating for a peasant who needs a sickle to have to sign a dozen forms before he gets one. I admit, too, that the communist method of dealing with such matters is the best.

'But ever since I gave that evidence, they have their knife into me. It can't be helped – damn it, I'm not going to have a man who cites me as his witness, and whom I know to be innocent, labelled a thief.'

'The communists – and all who want to get things going properly just now – consider that the fact your friend's an innocent man doesn't prevent him from playing into Franco's hands, if what he does leads to unrest amongst the peasants. The communists, you see, *want to get things done*. Whereas you and the anarchists, for different reasons, want to *be* something. That's the tragedy of a revolution like this one. Our respective ideals are so different; pacifism and the need to fight in self-defence; organization and Christian sentiment; efficiency and justice – nothing but contradictions. We've got to straighten them out, transform our Apocalyptic vision into an army – or be exterminated. That's all.'

'And, I suppose, people who have the same contradictions in their own hearts have got to be exterminated too. That's all, as you say.'

Garcia was thinking of Golovkin's view: 'They've got to change – or die.'

'Many men,' he said, 'hope to find in the Apocalypse a solution of their own problems. But the revolution plays no heed to those innumerable drafts drawn on its future, and carries on.'

'You think I'm under sentence of death, eh?' Hernandez grinned. There was no irony in his grin. 'Anyhow suicide's a restful prospect.' He pointed to the pre-war posters of films and vermouth above their heads and the grin broadened, showing his long teeth, making him look like a dejected horse. 'The good old days!' He paused, then added: 'But – to come back to Moscardo – I, too, used to have a wife.'

'Yes?' Garcia said. 'But we've not been hostages. Moscardo's letters, all you've told me – each of the problems that we're up against is a moral problem. And when one's life is linked up with a moral code, it's always a bit tragic. No less in a revolution than in other circumstances.'

'And to think one believes just the opposite; till the revolution actually happens.'

In the ravaged gardens roses and box-trees seemed to be sharing in the brief lull of truce.

'It's quite likely, Hernandez, that you're on the way to meet your ... destiny. It's never easy to give up what one has loved, all the things one's lived for. I'd like to help you; but the cause you're staking on is doomed from the outset. Because you have to live politically, you have to act in terms of politics; and your duties as an officer bring you every moment into touch with politics. Whereas the cause you have in mind is not political. It is based on the contrast between the world in which you live and the world of your dreams. But action can only be envisaged in terms of action. The business of a political thinker is to compare one set of hard facts with another, one practical proposition with another; our side or Franco's; one system or another system. He is not fighting against a dream, a theory, or another Apocalyptic vision.'

'It is only for a dream's sake that men die.'

'Hernandez, the habit of thinking about what ought to be instead of what can actually be done is a mental poison. For which, as Goya said, there is no antidote. The man who stakes his life on such a cause is bound to lose. It's a fool's game, my dear fellow. Moral "uplift" and magnanimity are matters for the individual, with which the revolution has no direct concern; far from it! I am very much afraid the only link between them, as far as you're concerned, is the prospect you may lay down your life in the cause of both. You know the tag from Virgil: "Neither with you, nor without you ..."'

A dull boom of gunfire, the shrill scream of a shell, an explosion, a tinkle of falling tiles and rubble. A field-gun had opened fire on the Alcazar.

'The priest has failed,' Garcia said.

VI

Yague's army was marching from Talavera on Toledo.

Citizen Leclerc, in a repulsively sloppy white flying-suit, with his grey cloak over his head and his thermos flask under his arm, was approaching the open door of the plane:

'Blast it, what b.f's been mucking about with my *Orion*?' he said in his hoarsest voice, as though it were himself that he was taking to task.

'That's all right, that's all right,' Attignies said calmly as he slipped a jersey on. 'I've fixed up a sight for you.'

'O.K. by me in that case,' Leclerc answered condescendingly. Leclerc disliked Attignies. He disliked his youthful earnestness, and he disliked his manners which, in spite of the young man's cordiality, jarred on him as upper middle-class; he disliked his fund of knowledge (Attignies had been a military cadet), and his austere communism, though Attignies was far from making austerity a rule of life. And while the volunteers felt a debt of gratitude to the technicians, of the mercenaries, like Leclerc, they felt jealous. And Leclerc was obsessed by women.

He started up the engine.

Pelicans and wounded men were moving round the machine; Raplati was trotting after Scali. Jaime still came regularly to the aerodrome, blind though he was, his face straddled by a bandage. Some of the doctors said that he would get his sight back. But he had become unable to bear the presence of a dog near him. Rouse likewise spent the whole of his time at the aerodrome, hobbling on two sticks, imperious, delivering himself of words of wisdom and instruction; he had become intolerable since his wounds had cloaked him with authority. Sibirsky had left Spain.

Ever since the 'Pelican' Squadron had fallen back on night-flights as the only means of continuing their resistance, the atmosphere of the aerodrome had changed. The enemy pursuit planes were ruled out by these tactics; landing at night in the open country is not the easiest sort of joy-ride, but neither is landing on the wrong side of the enemy lines in the daytime. Fatality was now the arbiter, rather than actual engagements in the air. If cavalry troopers feel the limitations of their horses in time of war, at least their horses are neither blind nor threatened daily with paralysis; but for these airmen the enemy was not so much the fascist army as the engines of the planes in which they flew, patched like old trousers. The war had resolved itself into an endless succession of night flights in machines endlessly repaired.

The plane took off; rose through the clouds.

'Say, young feller-me-lad?'

'Well?'

'Take a look at me. I may spend all my time larking around. But I'm a man!'

He did not like Attignies, but every airman on active service respected courage, and Attignies' courage was beyond question.

They went beneath the clouds again.

Listening to the reassuring yet constantly precarious throbbing of the engine, with his grey cloak over his head, Leclerc's feeling of godlike freedom took him back to the Great War, back to China; it was a freedom higher than sleep and war, higher than pains and emotions.

A pause. Then, in the tone of a decision following ripe reflection, Leclerc said:

'You are a man, too.'

Attignies did not want to hurt the pilot's feelings, but this kind of conversation got on his nerves. He grunted by way of answer, without lifting his eyes from the Milky Way etched in lights along the road beneath him; watching it streaming into the darkness in front of them, trembling in a wind they could not feel above, Attignies felt a desperate friendliness for that one sign of human life amid the dark, threatening, hostile solitude. There was no other light; to fall meant death. And as if some instinct more receptive than his conscious mind had forestalled his ears, Attignies suddenly perceived the reason for his feeling of distress: the engine was knocking.

'A valve!' he shouted to Leclerc.

'To hell with it!' the other shouted back. 'We can take a chance.'

Attignies tightened the strap of his crash-helmet; a chance was something he was always ready to take.

Talavera showed up on the horizon, magnified by its isolation amid the darkness. Level with the hills, its lights merged with the stars; they seemed to be coming forward to meet the plane. The stutter of the engine invested the town with an ominous reality. Amid the normal lights of a provincial town and sudden lurid gleams that betokened military activity, the black patch indicating the darkening gas-works had something of the tense repose of a sleeping wild animal. Now the plane was flying over a tarred road, the wet surface of which reflected the light of the gas street-lamps after the recent rain. The mass of lights expanded steadily as the plane approached Talavera, and suddenly Attignies saw them from both windows at once as the old machine dived, like stars round a climbing plane.

He opened the improvised trap-door: the cold night air rushed up into the cabin. On his knees up above the town, he waited, his field of vision limited by the bomb-sight like a horse in blinkers. Heading straight for the square black mass of the gasometer, his ears pricked up, Leclerc was bearing down upon the skeleton of light that was Talavera.

He swept over the black patch and turned round in a fury upon Attignies, of whom he could see nothing except his fair hair, gleaming faintly in the half-light inside the machine.

'What the 'ell are you playin' at !'

'Shut your damned mouth !'

Leclerc tilted the plane sideways; still under the influence of the speed of the plane, the falling bombs were accompanying them, a little below them and a little behind, shining like fish in the moonlight. As pigeons veering in the air narrow into thin silhouettes, the bombs suddenly faded from their sight; their fall was becoming vertical. Close beside the gasometer a row of red explosions sprang into view.

'Missed.'

Leclerc turned sharply and came back over the objective, going still lower. 'Watch the height !' Attignies shouted; the change of height would alter the deflection. He looked at the altimeter, and then through the trap-door again. Seen from the opposite direction now, Talavera had changed in appearance like a man who turns round: the confused light thrown upon the streets from the military staff offices had given place to the lighted rectangles of windows. The outline of the gasometer was less clear. Machine-guns were firing down below, but it was unlikely that the men handling them could see the plane distinctly. Every light in the town went out, leaving the illuminated dashboard and the shadow of Leclerc's cloak upon the dial of the altimeter the sole things visible against the starlit sky.

Its far-flung lights had given the town a vague semblance of life, and the sharply defined lights revealed on the plane's return journey had suggested life in a more precise form; but it was now, in utter darkness, that the town seemed most a living thing. Like sparks struck from a flint, the short flames of the machine-guns appeared and disappeared. The enemy town was on the watch, seeming to move in response to each movement of the returning plane, in which Leclerc was staring fixedly, two wisps of hair protruding from the grey cloak covering his head. Attignies was flat on his stomach, eyes glued to his sight, through which the smallest bend in the river was coming into view, mist-blue in the moonlight: there the gasometer was. He released the second rack of bombs.

They did not see them as they fell, this time. The plane nose-dived to the accompaniment of a stupendous crash, and underneath there was a sudden blast of lightning-coloured fire. To escape the blue flames surging up around them, Leclerc tugged frantically at the stick; the plane zoomed up towards the impassive serenity of the stars; below, there was nothing but a seething mass of red flames – the gasometer had been blown up.

Bullets drove through the fuselage. Perhaps the explosion had disclosed the position of the plane; a machine-gun was following its outline as it entered the halo around the moon. Leclerc began to zigzag. Turning round, Attignies saw a network of red flames spreading out below. The string of bombs had also hit the barracks close beside the gasometer.

A cloudbank hid the ground from them.

Leclerc picked up the thermos flask beside him, then stopped in amazement, holding the cup in the air, and signed to Attignies; the whole plane was phosphorescent, glowing with a bluish light. Attignies pointed to the sky. Till then they had been looking at the ground, engrossed in their raid, and had not noticed the plane itself; above and behind them the moon, which they could not see, was lighting up the aluminium of the wings. Leclerc put the thermos down; what human gesture would not have seemed trivial and inadequate? Taking them far away from their instrument-board – the only visible light in all the wilderness of air around them – that sense of well-being which follows on all physical conflict was merging into an almost geological tranquillity, incorporating them in that mystic union of moonlight and pale metal gleaming as precious stones have gleamed for countless ages on the extinct stars. The shadow of the plane moved steadily over the cloud beneath them. Leclerc raised his forefinger, grimaced in approbation, and shouted gravely: 'Something to remember, eh?' Picking up the thermos again, he noticed that the engine was still knocking.

At last they were clear of the cloud. The roads, which now they could see again below them, seemed to be moving in places. Attignies knew the meaning of that dim nocturnal motion of the roads; a column of fascist lorries was advancing on Toledo.

VII

Till nightfall Manuel had been acting as interpreter; Heinrich, the general commanding one of the international brigades then being formed at Madrid, was inspecting the Tagus front – if 'front' it could be called. From Talavera to Toledo, except in Ximenes' sector and a few others, there were no listening posts, no observers, no organized reserves, no proper defences. Machine-guns were badly placed and of poor quality.

In uniform, Field Service cap in hand, with the sweat pouring off his bald skull (close-cropped to conceal his white hairs), his field-boots crunching on the brittle soil baked by the last fires of summer, Heinrich had been straightening things out indefatigably, with the dauntless optimism characteristic of the communists.

Manuel had learned from Ximenes how to lead men; now he was learning how an army is commanded. During the past two months he had fancied he was acquiring the art of war; what actually he had learned was prudence, method, obstinacy, and strictness. Above all he was learning to exercise these qualities instead of thinking about them. And as he walked through the darkness towards the mass of leaping flame, shimmering like a huge luminous jelly-fish, that was the Alcazar, he was beginning to realize, after eleven hours' observation of the modifications made by Heinrich, what were the functions of an army division in the field. He felt them in his aching bones, and in his exhausted brain there faintly echoed through the rumble of the guns, phrases of the great generals of the past: 'Courage admits no hypocrisy'; 'You listen to what you hear, you copy what you see'; the first remark, Napoleon's, the second, Quiroga's. Ximenes had introduced him to Clausewitz, and his memory harked back to the library at the Military School, not a bad library as it happened. The furnace of the Alcazar was reflected in the lowering clouds, like a ship on fire mirrored in the waves. Every two minutes a 'heavy' crashed into the flames.

Heinrich's scheme was identical with that of the more enterprising elements of the Spanish High Command. He wished to reserve the Assault Guard for use as shock-troops, and, pending the time when the internationals could be moved up into the line, to expand the Fifth Regiment as much as possible. Once its units were sufficiently reinforced, he proposed to transfer them to the regular army, where they would constitute a nucleus capable of leavening the whole army with the 'communist discipline', in the same way as, in the early days of the war, communist elements had disciplined the Fifth Regiment. Enrique's battalions were being made into an army corps. Manuel had begun with a motor transport unit, then he had commanded a battalion under Ximenes' orders, now he was transferred to Madrid to the command of a regiment. But it was not so much he who was 'rising in the world', as the Spanish army.

A sprig of fennel in his hand, he walked up against a blustering wind towards Santa Cruz, to see how the mine was getting on. The short angry flames bursting from the Alcazar cast a red glow on his face. In the city Heinrich, his close-shaved German nape puckering like a fretful forehead, was waiting for a call from Madrid.

In each lull, when the sounds of rifle- and gun-fire died down with the wind, another sound made itself heard, faint but curiously dramatic: the sizzling of flames on the roof of the Alcazar. And somehow that faint sound was congruous with the smell that made the booming guns, the distant shouts and all the vagrant sounds of human warfare seem strangely futile; the mingled reek of fire and corpses was so dense and pungent that it seemed the Alcazar alone could not account for it – it must surely be an elemental tang of wind and darkness.

It was urgently necessary to launch the Toledo militia into the battle of the Tagus. The Alcazar, with the exception of its subterranean vaults, was due to be blown up that night, and the town was being evacuated. An endless stream of peasants with their pigs and goats was passing, silently moving through the lurid darkness, lit not by the Alcazar but by the flaming clouds.

Manuel found one of the officers from Toledo in the mess-room at Santa Cruz; he was a man of forty, and wore his forage-cap well on the back of his head. His hands in his pockets, he had accosted Manuel with gruff, rather paternal good humour.

'Hello, me lad! What's the trouble now?'

'When will the mine be ready?' Manuel asked.

The officer stared at him. 'When they're through with it. Tomorrow.' His manner implied: 'With bloody fools like that, how can one tell?' There was a twinkle in his eye, as if the whole business rather tickled him. If Manuel felt a certain sympathy with Hernandez' melancholy, this fellow's careless, patronizing humour got on his nerves. And, since his accident with Ramos, he had come to look on dynamite as a romantic and, as such, uncertain weapon of attack.

During a brief respite in the noise of battle he heard a rhythmic beat of dull, metallic thuds issuing, it seemed, from the floor and walls.

'Is that the mine?' Manuel asked.

The milicianos nodded. It struck Manuel that the fascists in the Alcazar must be hearing it too, in much the same way.

The leader of the sapping party came in.

'When do you expect to have it ready?'

'Between three and four.'

'Sure?'

The sapper scratched his head. 'Aye, for sure.'

'What will it blow up exactly?'

'Ah, that ain't so easy to say.'

'Well, what's your opinion?'

'All the front part will go up.'

'No more than that?'

The miner scratched his head again. 'Well, the others say there'll be more. But I don't think so. The vaults ain't one upon the other, they're spread-out like, following the lie of the rock.'

'Thanks.'

The man went off. Shifting the sprig of fennel to his left hand, Manuel took the officer's arm. 'If there's an engagement tomorrow, comrade, you'd better see to your defences. Your nests of machine-guns are too low down. And none of them is camouflaged; why, they're visible even in the light of the fire.'

He went out into the glowing darkness, into the reek of corpses and white-hot stone. A gust of wind blew it momentarily away, then once more it settled thickly down upon the garden.

After inspecting the various sectors one by one, he came to the Alcazar outbuildings which had been captured by the Republicans. There, things were very different; well-trained milicianos, detachments of the Assault Guard and the Civil Guard. But he still felt uneasy; the attack which was to be launched immediately after the explosion had not been planned by a military expert.

Between crashes of the field-guns, he still could hear the noises of the mine, welling up from the ground under his feet; in their vaults the enemy must hear those sounds still better.

At the telephone Heinrich was waiting for a reply concerning the defence of Madrid. He wanted to defend Toledo, but, whether Toledo held out or fell, he asked that the system of small isolated units should be abandoned and large reserves built up, with the Fifth Regiment as a nucleus. Franco was expecting great things of a fascist rising in Madrid and was actually beginning to commandeer white horses for a triumphal entry; his troops were advancing with alarming rapidity.

*

The day's work finished, Hernandez was sitting at a table with his friend, Moreno, at the Militia Headquarters, the only place at Toledo where one could still get beer – tepid, at that. On the day of the rising Moreno had been imprisoned by the fascists and sentenced to death. He had made a lucky getaway while being transferred from one prison to another, and had come back to Madrid three days before. He had just been called on to furnish some information; like Hernandez, he had been a cadet at the Toledo Military School. Through the wide-open window they could see a crowd of milicianos, pulsing like the core of vivid blue from which the flames of the vast furnace were racing skywards.

'A pack of lunatics!' Moreno's thick black hair, parted in the middle, straggled over his forehead and all but hid his face. Hernandez looked at him questioningly. They had known each other fairly intimately for fifteen years; but their friendship was half-hearted, made up of sentimental memories and secrets shared.

'I've given up believing in all I once believed in,' Moreno said. 'I believe in nothing now. Yet I'm going into the line tomorrow night.'

He pushed back his hair. He had been famous at Toledo for his good looks; the conventional good looks of Latin countries – very large eyes and an aquiline nose. He had had his hair trimmed but left unusually long, as though to keep in his appearance some reminder of the prison whence he had escaped. He was badly shaved and the stubble on his chin was grey.

A row of houses hid the Alcazar, but the clouds above were glowing with an ever-changing sheen of red and violet and purple, like ripe grapes, and the milicianos streaming by cast flickering shadows on the pavements. And always, punctually, throbbed the muffled thunder of the guns.

'Tell me, while you were in prison, what taxed your endurance most?'

'Learning to ... to go to pieces.'

For some time Hernandez had suspected Moreno of a perverse fondness for the tragic view of life. But now his distress, though his friend could not judge its motive, was obviously sincere.

For a moment they were silent, waiting for the next boom of the guns. The night was loud with creaking axles; the exodus from Toledo had begun.

'It wasn't being in prison that mattered so much, old chap; it was the death sentence. Then something snapped in me. I used to fancy I took some interest in men. I used to be a Marxist, the first Marxist officer in the army, quite likely. It's not so much that I've changed my ideas; I haven't any ideas left.'

Hernandez felt no desire to embark on a discussion of Marxism. With a clatter of rifles some milicianos ran by.

'Listen!' Moreno went on. 'When I was sentenced to death, I was allowed to go down into the patio. All the men there had been sentenced for their political ideas. But nobody mentioned politics. Nobody. If anyone had done so, he'd have found himself pretty soon in Coventry!'

A militia girl, a hunchback, handed a letter to Hernandez. Moreno burst into rather hysterical laughter.

'From the point of view of the revolution,' he asked, 'what's your real opinion of all this play-acting?'

'It's more than play-acting.'

Hernandez' eyes followed the humped, receding figure of the girl; but, unlike Moreno, all he saw was her fine zest, and he felt amiably disposed towards her. So, as far as he could discern across the livid darkness, did the milicianos. She, who till now most likely had been condemned to loneliness, was at last playing an active part in the world. The Captain's short-sighted eyes settled on Moreno; he was beginning to mistrust his friend.

'So you're off for the front, tomorrow?'

Moreno hesitated, knocked his glass over, but took no notice of it. He kept his eyes fixed on Hernandez.

'I'm leaving for France tonight.'

Hernandez said nothing. A foreign miliciano, unaware that he had not to pay, rapped his glass with a coin. Moreno took a copper from his pocket, and threw it up in the air as if he were playing pitch and toss. When it fell he covered it with his hand, without looking to see which side it had fallen. There was a rather wistful smile on his lips; emotion gave the smooth, regular features a youthful, almost childish look.

'For a while, old chap, we weren't in a prison; they transferred us to an old convent. The change was made on purpose, obviously. In the prison we could see nothing, hear nothing – which was so much for the good. At the convent we were more favoured; we heard everything. Firing parties at work all night ...' The troubled eyes settled on his friend's face. In the childish features was a certain innocence, but grimness too. 'Do you think the firing squads used searchlights?' he added.

Without awaiting the reply he burst out. 'Imagine being shot with a spotlight on you! ... Yes, we heard the volleys, and another sound as well. They'd taken all our silver, but left us the small change. And almost everyone was playing pitch and toss. Heads – I shall be sent for a walk in the patio tomorrow; tails – I'm for the firing squad. They didn't chance it on one throw, but on ten or twenty. The noise of the volleys was muffled by the walls and the air cushion between. And all night on every side, I could hear the chink, chink, of little copper coins. Yes, old chap, I could judge the size of the prison by the differences between the sounds – if they were near or distant.'

'What were your warders like?'

'One night a warder heard the noise; he flung open the door of my cell, yelled "Tails! You lose!" and slammed it to again. Some of my warders were swine. Real swine. But not in that prison. ... Listen! You hear those forks tinkling on the plates? Well, it was nearly as loud as that. Most likely we got to hear noises that didn't really exist; that sort of thing wrecks one's nerves, you know. Sometimes I felt positively crushed by all those little jingling noises, as if I was buried in a snowdrift. The other fellows hadn't been arrested, as I was, on the first day; they'd been in the line. It was damn' silly, and damn' pathetic! Playing pitch and toss with death. Like heroes! But where did the heroism come in, that's what I'd like to know?'

He picked up the coin again, tossed it.

'Heads!' He sounded surprised.

He put the coin back in his pocket. Hernandez had seen Moreno in the fighting-line during the war with Abd-el-Krim, and knew him to be brave. The guns were still battering the Alcazar; the strident creak of cart-axles mingled with the hiss of flames.

'Listen, old fellow! A hero can't make good without an

audience; you get to know that once you're really alone. They say that blindness makes its own world; so does loneliness, take my word for it. Once you're in it, you discover that all the ideas you had about yourself belonged to the other world, the world you've left. The damn'-fools paradise. Of course, in your private world you can think about yourself, but it only makes you feel as if you were off your head. Remember Bakunin's confession? That explains it. The two worlds simply don't communicate. In one, men die side by side, singing, or clenching their teeth, or any way they fancy; and beyond it there's that other world, that convent where –'

He took the copper from his pocket again, rang it on the table, shivered, and picked it up, without looking to see which side was uppermost. His eyes had never left the street.

'Look at 'em! Look at them, damn it! All those fellows sniggering at each other: "I'm a thinker, I'm making history." Kisses. Slapping each other on the back. But put 'em in a cell ... and what then? Pennies tossed in the air. ... Oh well, I suppose there'll still be lands without fascists on the earth, before I die. When I escaped I was crazy over getting back; I reported at once for duty. Now I know better. No one on earth can escape what's coming to him, *his truth*; and it isn't death, no, it isn't even suffering ... It's the spin of a coin, of a penny.'

'I'd like to know why, for a sceptic like you, the moment of death should be more significant – more important, if you like – than any other.'

'A man can put up with everything; can even go to sleep knowing it wastes some hours of life before he's shot at dawn; can tear up the photographs of those he loves because he's had enough of sapping his nerve by poring over them; can note with pleasure that he's still jumping in the air like a fox-terrier for another futile peep through the loop-hole up in the wall – and all the rest of it. With everything, I say. What he can't bear is to feel certain that, after being knocked about and trampled on, he's going to be killed. And that after that there's – nothing!'

The handsome face was tense with emotion. In the changing glow, red-brown and violet, reflected from the unseen flames, for all its screen-star symmetry, it had a real beauty.

'Just try to realize it! At Palma I spent a fortnight in the lock-up. Fourteen days. There was a mouse came every day at the same time; I knew the hour by it. Man being *par excellence* the love-secreting animal, I got to love it. Well, on the four-teenth day they let me out into the patio and I had a talk with some other prisoners. When I went back to my cell, that mouse merely got on my nerves.'

'A man can't go through what you've been through without feeling the effects. Look here! You'd better have a meal, a drink, and a sleep. And *think* as little as possible.'

'Easier said than done. Get it into your head, old fellow, that a man isn't *used* to dying! It's outside all his experience. And, when he's up against it, he remembers that.'

'Without having been sentenced to death, one learns here quite a lot of things which it goes against the grain to learn. For instance, I've hit on a certain truth, oh quite a simple one: one expects everything all at once, from "freedom", but to get man to progress a bare half inch a great many men must die. This street must have looked much like it does now in the days of Charles the Fifth. Yet the world has moved on since then. Because men wanted to move it on, despite the pennies — perhaps even with full awareness that those pennies were wait-ing for them in the background. Nothing could be more dis-couraging than fighting here. And still the only thing in the world as ... as *pregnant* as the experience you've told me of is the help that we can give those fellows who are streaming past us now.'

'That's the sort of thing I used to say to myself in my cell, in the morning. But the evenings were another story. Bloody awful! When one's been walking up and down a room three yards by three all day, and the walls are starting to close in — well, it sharpens one's wits, you know. The graveyards of revolutions are just the same as other graveyards.'

'All seeds begin by rotting, but some of them germinate. A world without hope is ... suffocating. Or else, a purely physical world. That's how a good many officers manage to put up with it so well; almost all of them have always lived on the purely physical plane. But that wasn't true of us. Look here, you'd better put in for a fortnight's sick-leave. And if, after that, you still can see only the comic-opera side of our milicianos, if nothing in you responds to the hope that animates them, well then, go to France, there's nothing for you to do here.'

Behind the groups of silent wayfarers rolled farm-carts bulging with sacks and baskets, in which sometimes there showed the red glint of a wine-bottle. Peasant-women rode past on donkeys; on their nightbound faces was pictured the immemorial grief of a Flight into Egypt. In the reek of fire, to the strong sonorous rhythm of the guns, an endless, fugitive procession was passing through Toledo.

*

From the quiet stars the hills fell steeply to the valley, along which the enemy tanks would presently advance. Groups of men with dynamite were spaced along it, under cover of rocks and clumps of trees and farmhouses.

The Republican front lines in the Toledo sector were a mile and a half behind them. A dozen *dinamiteros* were lying under a clump of olive trees. One of them, his chin propped on his hands, had his eyes fixed on the summit of the hill where the observer had been posted. Most of the others had cigarettes, still unlit, dangling from their lips.

The Sierra was holding out, so was the Aragon front, Cordova, Malaga, the Asturias. But Franco's motorized column was advancing at full speed along the Tagus. And things were looking bad for Toledo. As usual when things looked bad, the *dinamiteros* were beginning to talk of '34, the black year of the Asturias. Pepe was describing Oviedo to the recruits who had come from Catalonia. The Frente Popular had followed on that setback.

'We rushed the arsenal,' he was explaining. 'And then we says to ourselves. "Now everything's all right. We're saved." And then we found we couldn't do a blasted thing with the stuff inside it : cartridge cases with no caps, shells without fuses. Duds. So we used the shells as cannon-balls, there being nothing else to do with them. Anyhow the noise made us feel good; so they weren't wasted.'

Pepe rolled on to his back. Moonlight was sifting down through the olive-trees in a bright mist like the leaves' frail silvery sheen.

'Yes, it gave us confidence – that much confidence it landed us in clink.'

A moonbeam was falling on his face, the face of a good-tempered, friendly horse.

'Think they'll get Toledo?'

'The hell they will!'

'Don't be so darn sure, Pepe, I guess things are in a bad way at Toledo. I'm counting on Madrid.'

'And weren't things in a hell of a bad way in the Asturias?'

'Without that dynamite,' another voice put in, 'we'd have been wiped out in three days. We tried to get a move on at the arsenal, with the mates as said they knew all about priming. Nothing doing. The lads had to go off to the front with five rounds each – what price that! – five lousy rounds per man. Say, Pepe, do you remember those women with the baskets? I seen plenty of gleaners in my day but I never seen 'em gathering empty cartridges before. They was that keen on getting shells, we couldn't fire quick enough to content them. . . . Mercy on us!'

No one had looked round to see who was speaking. Large men have a jovial quality of voice that is unmistakable. But, as they listened, all were straining their ears for a distant rumble of tanks.

'Dynamite!' Pepe said. 'That's the stuff! We did mighty good work with it. Remember old Mercader's catapult?' But it was to the Catalonians he turned, who certainly had never heard of Mercader. 'Mercader was a smart boy; he invented a contraption for throwing big charges of the stuff. Sort of trench-mortar. Like in all the old wars, it worked with ropes and pulleys. And took three men to handle it. Well, it fairly knocked the stuffing out of the Moors the first time we used it on them. Real dynamite cartridges at two hundred yards – they hadn't looked for that. Another invention of his was shields; but they didn't pan out so well. Acted like targets.'

In the distance a machine-gun rattled off a drum, stopped, started again; and in the vastness of the night the sound seemed trivial as the purr of a sewing-machine. But still no sign of tanks.

'Them others, they made airyplanes!' The voice sounded bitter.

In the moonlit valley, watching for the coming of the tanks, they bandied tales of derring-do, heroical and homely. Probably *dinamiteros* are the last body of men who can face the machine on equal terms. The presence of the Catalonians here was, so to speak, accidental; but the Asturians were following up a great tradition. They were the oldest revolutionary group in Spain and now at last an organized body; the only men for whom the golden legend of the revolution was being implemented by experience of actual warfare, instead of being disintegrated by it.

'They say the Moorish cavalry has been given machine-guns.'

'To hell with them !'

'And Seville's stiff with Germans. And they're all trained men.'

'Governors of prisons, too.'

'They say that two Italian divisions are on their way ...'

'Say, don't you think the boys will put up a good show against the tanks?'

'Well, they ain't used to them.'

Once more they countered the menace of the new with reminiscences.

'The craziest thing of all in our show,' Pepe said, 'was the way it ended. The boys did mighty well at the peasants' committee-room. But they'd no help, they were outnumbered. The Moors came up; it took them three hours to close their circle round us. The boys were holding out and they had lots of dynamite, but nothing to put it in. So they fixed up a sort of hand-grenade with bolts and nuts and newspaper. Not a rifle to be had; they'd given out long ago. A mate had gone round to the arsenal the day before, and all he'd brought back was a scrap of newspaper. The man that ran the arsenal had written on it in pencil, saying it was no sort of good sending round for ammunition; not a cartridge left. The last ones had been shared amongst the mates who'd been loading them; five rounds each. And off they'd hopped it to the front. So that was that, and our lot were feeling pretty sick, you can bet your life. They all sat round the table in the committee-room, scratching their heads and scowling at each other. Damn-all else to do ! Lots of the boys was standing around, but they kept their traps shut. Just waiting around. You could hear the brownskins and the bloody machine-guns getting nearer, like now. And just then there came a queer, rumbling noise, sort of muffled, so you couldn't hardly hear it, but all the mugs and knives on the table and the picture on the wall started trembling. What the hell was happening? Then they heard bells, and they tumbled to it. It was the cattle pouring in from the country. The brownskins and their guns pooping off in all directions had scared them, and there they were, herds and herds, stampeding up the street. Then one of the boys, a bright lad he was, had an idea. He jumps up and yells; "Say, mates, let's build a barricade! Hold up those cows and get the bells off them." The bells they had on their necks weren't the thin sort, but fat, heavy ones like the mountain cattle wear. Well, they yanked the bells off those cattle in no time and made 'em into bombs, and that's how they held out three whole hours, time enough to have everything evacuated that needed to be evacuated. ... As for those tanks that's coming up, who gives a hoot in hell, now we've got the stuff and can hit back at 'em!'

The armoured train, too, Pepe hadn't forgotten it. We don't need guns, he thought; we can fight with our hands. And, now that they were trained, they could stop tanks, even without anti-tank guns.

A dog began barking in the distance.

'The donkey, Gonzalez. Tell us that one about the moke!'

'Ain't it queer! When one thinks about this war, it's always the funny bits one remembers . . . Mercy on us!'

Most of the men were silent; they had not the knack of spinning yarns. Pepe, Gonzalez, and one or two others were the professional entertainers and mirth-makers of the group. Presumably the tanks would defer their attack till daylight. Not knowing the country well enough, the drivers would fear being ditched. But day would soon be breaking. Now or never for the 'moke' yarn.

'That was a grand notion, that one about the donkey. We'd loaded him with dynamite, lit the fuse and shoo'd him off towards the Moors. Well, the old beast trots off, pricking up his ears; he's no idea what it's all about, poor fool. Only the others, you see, they start plugging away at him, good and hard. At the first shots he waggles his ears, like there was flies on them. After a bit he stops, puzzled-like. He sure can't make it out, and then he starts ambling back. But we weren't taking any, neither. We start firing at him too. Only, you see, we were old acquaintances so to speak; so, after scratching his head, seeing how things are, he thinks he'd rather come back to our lines . . .'

A terrific concussion, as if somewhere near by the earth had split in two, brought down on their heads a shower of dry twigs and leaves. A vast red flame was spouting up in the direction of Toledo, and as they stared blankly at each other, open-mouthed, their cheeks lit by the livid purplish sheen of flame and moonlight mingled, each saw the face that he would wear in death.

All the cigarettes had dropped.

They were used to explosions. But this was not a mine. Not dynamite. Not a powder magazine.

'An aerial torpedo?'

None of them had noticed anything of the sort. They listened. They fancied they could hear the drone of a plane high up. But it might be the rumble of the Moors' lorries.

'Is there a gas-works at Toledo?' Gonzalez asked.

No one knew. But all were thinking of the Alcazar.

One thing was clear; the fascists had taken a knock somewhere over there. Where the column of fire had just died down, the sky still glowed red. A fire? Or dawn?

Not the dawn. It was breaking on the opposite horizon. And, as the light grew, a coolness and a dewy scent of leaves seemed floating down from the olive trees.

Yarning time was over. Now the *dinamiteros* were on the alert, at their posts. Daybreak; the enemy.

The cigarettes were back in their mouths, but still unlit. A vast silence brooded on the Spanish countryside, as on the day when the first Moors had come; the grey hush of how many peaceful and how many tragic dawns! On the horizon the silver streak of daybreak widened out, while overhead little by little the blackness waned. The air seemed charged with the unutterable sadness of the pale hour preceding the trumpet-call of day. Half-heartedly, forlornly, cocks began crowing in the farms.

Pepe shouted: 'There's Ricardo.'

The observer was racing back to them. And, advancing from the same grey limbo, tilted as if they threatened not the earth but the dim zenith, the leading tanks came peering over the crest.

Gonzalez lit his cigarette; Pepe, then the others, followed suit. From all sides bunches of men began creeping towards the tanks.

The crews of the tanks could not see them, though they may have known that they were there. The *dinamiteros* kept down in the valley bed, crouching or lying flat; the tanks showed up against the sky. On Gonzalez' right was a Catalonian boy who had not opened his mouth so far; on his left was Pepe. In the grey light he hardly saw them, but he was conscious of the swinging, manly strides of the two young men beside him. Somehow at such moments he always pictured his friends as molluscs who had been turned out of their shells; soft, lithe, defenceless creatures. He was acutely conscious of his own bulk and their fragility. The tanks – they, anyhow, had shells – were approaching, the rattle growing to a roar, while the wavering line of *dinamiteros* crept towards them in an uncanny silence.

The tanks were in two columns, but spaced so far apart that the attackers took no account of this; each group was allotted a single tank, as if they had been in Indian file. Some Catalonians had not completely hidden their cigarettes in their hands. 'The bloody fools!' Gonzalez murmured. He was behind them, and his only hope was that those tell-tale specks of red might be less noticeable from in front. Borne forward on the same tide of hard, fraternal exaltation, he advanced with them and, as he kept his eyes fixed on the approaching tanks, he seemed to hear the deeptoned song of the Asturias echoing in his heart. Never again as at this moment was he to know all it can mean to be a man.

Soon he would be in the open. The sun was rising. Pepe had taken cover. Gonzalez dropped back on the ground. 'His' tank must be some four hundred yards away, but the tall grass level with his eyes concealed it. It was the sort of grass he used to play with as a boy, an oat-grass with long halms, the heads of which he used to slip inside his playmates' sleeves, up which

215

they wormed their irritating way. Already, he noticed, some ants and a tiny spider were crawling on it. On the ground, in their grassy forest, other creatures were going their small, warless ways. Then, just behind a pair of ants, loomed up the lurching, roaring bulk of a swiftly moving tank. The ground where Gonzalez lay was uneven and, when launching his dynamite, he might have toppled over; he shifted his position to one side.

The tank would pass on his right. The berm would screen him from the turret till the tank had actually come level with him. It was a question – a question of life and death – who would get his blow in first. Anyhow the gunner would have the sun in his eyes. Gonzalez made sure that there was nothing to hamper his right arm.

Where the hell was that Catalonian? The tank on the right had opened fire. Gonzalez' tank was approaching at full speed, tilted up, just above the ants that looked like monsters at six inches from his eyes. Steadying himself with his left hand, Gonzalez brought all his weight on to his bent knee. Here was the tank! He jerked himself erect, launched his dynamite into the clatter of gunfire and machinery, and in the same movement flung himself on to his face, as if he were diving into the explosion.

There was a patter of falling gravel. He looked up. The tank was standing on its turret, upside down. The only entrance into it was through the top of the turret. One of the caterpillar bands was still turning, glinting in the dawnlight. Gradually it slowed down.

Gonzalez had one bomb left and he was holding his cigarette ready beside it. The machine-gun on the tank was silent. The two men inside were dead or wounded; in any case they were trapped inside the turret with no hope of escaping as the full weight of the machine rested on the man-hole. If the petrol-tank had upset, they'd be ablaze within five minutes. Such is civil war.

The band had stopped revolving. Everything was still. Gonzalez looked round. Not a shot had been fired by the Republican artillery – if Republican artillery there was. He rose to his knees. The valley was scored by the trails of caterpillar bands, like the wakes of passing ships; the tank in front of him and four others had been knocked out. Ditched or bottom upmost, they had a quaintly prehistoric look. (When he saw the first one upside down, he had taken if for some new type of tank.) Two were on fire. Far away, in the bright light that now was flooding all the countryside, the rearguard of the column of tanks was gradually disappearing over a patch of rising ground, on its way to the Republican lines, the last lines before Toledo.

The tanks had got through.

'Where's that Catalonian boy?' Gonzalez asked.

Pepe answered. 'Killed.'

The sun was well up by now, but the dead bodies in the grass could not be seen. Bullets were beginning to whizz round the two men; Pepe gave an imitation of their foolish whistling, then dropped under cover again.

A line of white dots, the Moors' turbans, was advancing over the crest of the hill.

*

Mingling with the dewy freshness of the dawn, the smoke from the explosion, which still enveloped the Alcazar, had clotted into a dank mist imbued with the stench of corpses. The wind had flattened out its surface and the still unfallen walls stood up below it like reefs beneath the surface of a lagoon. When a more violent gust dented the smooth expanse, jagged blocks of stone emerged. Lower down, on the right, it was spreading out towards the town, not in billowy masses, but like a quiet tide, seeping into every hole and crevice. Manuel thought: The Alcazar is leaking like a cistern.

Foot by foot advancing down each shattered street and by-way as if it, too, were an invading foe, the smoke was penetrating the Republican positions. The mine had blown up the advanced posts of the fascists, though not the underground chambers, and the opposing troops were now at a greater distance from each other.

For a moment the sound of firing died away and Manuel heard someone stamping his foot on the rock behind him. It was Heinrich; a ray of sunlight fell on his flabby, furrowed nape.

Manuel spoke first, his sprig of fennel in his hand. 'Madrid?' he asked.

'The answer's: No.' The general spoke without looking at him. His eyes were fixed on the high rocks slowly emerging from the smoke as from an ebbing tide.

'Why?' Manuel asked.

'The answer's: No. We had men in front of the building, eh?'

'They were moved away before the mine went up.'

'It seems there's no way of getting at the part that's been blown up except through the main building, eh?'

He was still watching through his field-glasses the battered headland from which the smoke was clearing. His face, for all his years, had the chubbiness of a Polish peasant woman's. He handed the glasses to Manuel.

'Have we machine-guns on the flanks?'

'No.'

'It wouldn't stop them, but it would hold them up a while.'

Tiny specks were moving on the crest-line of the rock, clinging to it like flowers. The smoke had spread far beyond the old front line which the Assault Guard had evacuated before the explosion. Behind the murk the fascists were approaching. Like a gas barrage it covered their advance.

All the positions occupied during the last ten days had been lost.

'We must see about defending the town,' Heinrich said.

The Jefatura telephone was still silent. Santa Cruz reported that the Moors were only six miles away.

They went to Hernandez' headquarters in the little bootshop.

In one of the streets where the crowd was thick as in the approaches to a station during the summer holiday rush, a miliciano handed Manuel his gun, a Mauser.

'Want a rifle, Major?'

'You'll be needing it soon,' Heinrich said to the man, in German.

'I'm through with it. So you may as well . . .'

Their snowy brows usually gave Heinrich's blue eyes a look of childish wonder. But when, as now, they settled to a stare, the hairless skull and almost invisible eyebrows gave him an expression of utter ruthlessness. ... But by now there were twenty or more people between him and the miliciano.

The rifles dropped in doorways were being picked up by sharpshooters who were firing on the milicianos from the shuttered windows. For the first time Manuel felt in a street the same oppression as that which came over him in closed-in places; he dared not set a foot down without first prodding the ground with his big toe. No previous crowd in Toledo, not even that of the Corpus processions before the war, nor the crowds that gathered in Madrid on great occasions, had ever been so dense as this one. The milicianos were carrying their mexican hats like circus hoops, at arm's length. Twenty thousand men seethed in a frenzied mass. On every doorstep lay discarded rifles.

Hernandez' office was wide open. A man in a red and black *képi* was asking, 'Who's in charge here?'

'I am. I'm Captain Hernandez.'

'See here, "Cap." We was in Number 25, Commercial Street. They got us taped there. We moved on to Number 45; they had us taped there too. I'd like to know if it's you as puts them wise each time we shift, so they can wipe us out more easy, the "Caps." that's on the other side.'

Hernandez eyed the man with distaste. 'Carry on,' he said.

'I'd have you know we've had our bellyful of it. Where's our blasted airyplanes?'

'In the air. Where else should they be?'

The Government had no more than ten up-to-date machines fit to take the air against the Italian and German planes.

'I'd have you know, if our planes don't show up within thirty minutes, we down rifles, see? Think we're out to act as gun-fodder for the bloody bourgeois or for the bloody communists? Not us. We're going to down 'em, Cap. Got it?'

He was staring at Manuel's large red star. The hardness had come back to Heinrich's eyes.

Hernandez took the man by the lapels of his tunic and said in a calm peremptory voice, 'You, down them right away!' and pushed him out of the room. The man had not said another word. Then, turning, Hernandez saluted Heinrich and shook hands with Manuel.

'That man's either a fool or a knave – both, I dare say. Those men have treachery on the brain. Perhaps they're not so far wrong. ... And so long as things are that way, there's nothing to be done.'

'There's always something to be done.'

Manuel's hands were shaky; his sprig of fennel had been lost in the crowd. He translated Heinrich's remark.

Hernandez shrugged his shoulders. 'Very good, sir.'

'If that man has quitted his post, he should be shot.'

'By whom?'

'By you, if necessary. Is there anyone else we can count on?'

'No one. There's nothing to be done here. And yet. ... Look here! Don't let any of the good troops enter the city; it's a hot-bed of deserters. Let's put up a fight, if we can, outside it, and with other troops. What troops have you available?'

'There are thousands of men here,' Heinrich said, 'and thousands of rifles. Surely we can put some of them to use. We've got to make the most of the situation.'

'Not one regular soldier is here. Only three hundred milicianos who'll fight to the death; and a handful of Asturians. The rest are a pack of cowards who try to justify their cowardice by finding fault with everything, confound it! They've dumped their rifles in the doorways, and the fascists are beginning to use them against us. Even the women aren't afraid of shouting abuse at us from the windows.'

'Well, try to gain five or six hours, anyhow.'

'The Visagra Gate could be defended, but they won't stir a finger.'

'It's up to us to defend it,' Heinrich said. 'Let's go there.'

The gate, to reach which they had to make a longish detour through side-streets, looked like a rifle dump.

The sight of all those abandoned rifles rattled Manuel's nerves. Something had to be done to steady them. He found a fairly straight branch to replace his lost sprig of fennel. A dozen milicianos were squatting over a game of cards. As he passed them Heinrich stooped, swept up the cards under the players' noses, and put them in his pocket.

'It's sheer insanity,' he said. 'With all those roofs and terraces we could perfectly well hold out here, anyhow till they brought up their field-guns.'

They went back into the town. The general kept on glancing up at the roofs. '*Ach*, what a nuisance it is not knowing Spanish!'

'I know Spanish,' Manuel said.

With Hernandez's help he began assigning posts to the men available, one by one, sending others to fetch ammunition and dispatching such of the cast-off rifles as were in good condition to the sharpshooters already posted. Three Lewis guns were unearthed. In an hour's time the Gate was in a state of defence.

Heinrich went up to Manuel. 'I dare say, comrade, you'll think I'm a bit cracked, but now I'd like you to get them to sing the "International". As they're all under cover, they can't see each other; so they've got to *feel* their comrades are near by.' The general's remark lost none of its authoritativeness by his use of the word 'comrade'.

'Comrades!' Manuel bellowed.

From every window, at each house-corner, heads popped out. Manuel began singing the 'International', but was worried by the leafy bough in his hand, which kept on wanting to beat time. He had a powerful voice and, as the firing against the Alcazar had practically ceased, everyone could hear him. But the milicianos did not know the words of the 'International'.

Heinrich was amazed. Manuel confined himself to the refrain.

'Well, it's better than nothing.' Heinrich sounded bitter. 'We'll be at Madrid round about four. They'll hold out till then.'

Hernandez smiled sadly.

Manuel appointed section-leaders; then the three officers walked to the Puerta del Sol. In three-quarters of an hour defenders had been posted at that gate as well.

'Let's go back to Visagra,' Heinrich said.

Through half-open windows the fascist townsmen were firing with growing zest and, all down the streets, the officers were greeted with abuse. But the crowd had thinned out, over ten thousand men had left the town; it was being drained of its population as a mortally wounded man is drained of blood.

Their car was locked up in a shed.

'Better get it out right away,' Hernandez suggested. 'If we wait . . .'

A small-moustached officer was standing by the door.

'I hear you're going to Madrid,' he said. 'Can you give me a lift?' He showed them a written order to proceed to Madrid.

They drove to Visagra first, Manuel at the wheel. Abandoned rifles lay on every doorstep. While the car was slowing down for a corner, a door was pushed ajar and a hand reached out from within towards a gun. Heinrich fired; the hand went back.

Toledo was putrefying like a corpse.

'The Spanish people has failed to rise to the occasion,' Heinrich said, and for the third time his eyes had that look of brutal fixity which Manuel had already noticed. 'In such cases,' Heinrich continued, 'it's always the staff work that's at fault.'

Manuel remembered Ximenes, and the milicianos who were to be seen in every Madrid street, learning to march in step as children learn to write.

When they reached Visagra, Manuel shouted to his men. No answer. He called again. Still no answer. He climbed to the top storey of a house whence he had a view over the neighbouring roofs. At each point where he had posted a sharpshooter lay a discarded rifle. Even the three Lewis guns had been abandoned. Visagra was being defended – by guns that had no men behind them !

And, on the Malaga, the Aragon, and the Cordova fronts they were short of guns. Also at Madrid.

On a threshing-floor nearby someone was threshing corn.

At last Manuel flung away his branch and staggered down the stairs; his legs were giving way beneath him. Every door stood open. And on every roof, from behind each chimney-top, a rifle was peeping out, with a little pile of ammunition near it.

*

Manuel told Heinrich what had happened. Hernandez had guessed it already.

'We've got to rush some of the young troops to Toledo,' Heinrich said. 'Let's dash off to Madrid. As things are it will be an easy task evacuating Toledo.'

222

'Too late !' Hernandez replied.

'Let's try anyhow.'

Manuel turned to Hernandez. 'What do you intend to do?'

'What do you expect me to do?' A bitter smile parted his lips, baring his long yellow teeth. 'There are twenty of us here who can make good practice with a machine-gun.' He pointed to the graveyard languidly. 'There or here.'

'No, we'll be back in time.'

Hernandez shrugged his shoulders.

'I tell you,' Manuel repeated almost angrily; 'We shall be back in time.'

Hernandez gazed at him with an almost startled air, and Manuel realized that he had never used such a tone before when speaking to Hernandez. It is impossible to convey orders in an unemphatic voice; for some hours he had been translating for Heinrich, and he had acquired the general's way of speaking. He had picked up the language of command, as one picks up a foreign language by echoing what one hears.

'Well, if you can scrape up twenty men,' he added, 'try anyhow to defend this gate.'

'Have new men posted here at once,' Heinrich said, 'before you leave.'

'Very good, sir,' Hernandez replied with the same forlorn indifference. When the men had been assigned their posts, the officers went back to the bootshop. The firing from the windows and the hostile cries were steadily increasing in volume as they walked down the street.

'Those people,' Manuel remarked, 'would like to see Philip II back on the throne. Look here, Hernandez, will you have all the rifles lying about collected, except the ones on the doorsteps. I'll send a section of the Assault Guard, in lorries, to fetch them.'

'It's easier to get them collected than to get them used.'

The death-throes of Toledo were hastening to their climax.

'Let them hold out during the afternoon. After that the *dinamiteros* will look after the situation. Once the young troops and the Fifth Regiment have come we can hold the town for a week. And in a week lots of things can happen . . .'

Hernandez had discarded his *mono* and was in mufti, like most of the last men holding out at Toledo. Now he pondered for a moment. Judging by the sounds, the Republicans were on his right. What did he really want, was it to be saved? Two hours earlier leaving Toledo would have been as easy as catching a peacetime train. Or was it to fight to the end? Most of all he wanted not to be alone again. Nothing could be worse than that. He had been separated from his men when the Tercio launched their first attack. The great thing now was to rejoin them.

He ran beside the wall of a little-by-street. On his left the Tercio machine-guns were steadily approaching. At last he reached a larger street where shots from the Republicans were flaking the high, pale house-fronts, throwing up small white puffs of plaster. Louder and nearer sounded the tack-a-tack of the machine-guns. The Tercio must have reached the corner Hernandez had just left. He was under fire now from in front and from behind.

Ten yards ahead was a lighted street-lamp. When Hernandez came below it he waved his revolver in the air to make known who he was; a sledge-hammer crashed down on the barrel, knocking it to the ground. He dived into a doorway. Here he was sheltered from the fire of the Tercio by the corners of the street, and from that of the Republicans by the walls on each side of the threshold. Machine-guns were firing spasmodically on his right and left; obviously the men behind them could see little to aim at. Presently a gust of bullets brought the street-lamp down in a melodious tinkle of broken glass. After that the machine-gunners could see nothing at all; could only aim at the sudden bursts of bluish flame flickering at each end of the street.

Hernandez went down on all fours, thrust his head forward below the criss-cross stream of bullets, retrieved his revolver, and crept back to the doorway. He had stayed thus for ten minutes when he gave a sudden start. He had felt the muzzle of a revolver prodding his ribs.

'Hernandez! That you, Hernandez?'

'Er ... yes.'

'Move back to the wall.'

The miliciano – he, too, was in mufti – fired three shots at intervals of a second, and both men dashed out. The Republican machine-gun ceased fire.

As they came up to it, another miliciano ran up behind them.

'The Moors are coming!'

'Run to the bull-ring!' The man who spoke was a machine-gunner; he seemed to be in command of the group.

All made a dash for it along the side-streets, the machine-gunner bristling on all sides with the mountings of the Hotchkiss in his arms.

Hernandez did not wish to die alone.

The gunner halted, turned, set down his Hotchkiss, reeled off a drum of fifty bullets, and started off again. He was a poor shot. After pausing for a moment, the Moors, too, pressed forward again.

A few isolated shots zipped by. Then, from the opposite direction, there came to the ears of the Republicans a sound of music, wafted on the breeze – big drums and trumpets, the brassy din of circuses, and country fairs, and armies. Hernandez was puzzled. Could there be a merry-go-round somewhere about? At last he recognized the fascist anthem; the Tercio band was playing in the Zocodover Square.

The machine-gunner halted and let off another drum. Ten, fifteen seconds passed. Then the man beside him started bawling, 'Get a move on, you bloody fool!' and kicking the gunner's backside with all his might. 'For God's sake, put a jerk into it!' The kicks took more effect than the bullets of the advancing Moors. The gunner picked up his Hotchkiss and started running again.

At last they reached the bull-ring. Some thirty milicianos were there already. Seen from below, the huge, tiered walls looked stately as a fortress – 'a lathe-and-plaster castle,' Hernandez smiled grimly to himself. He went up to a window and looked outside. The Moors were beginning to post sentries round the entrances. 'We're for it once they land a heavy in here,' an artilleryman remarked. He, too, was in civilian clothes.

'The civilian fascists have started wearing white armlets,' a miliciano said.

'They're having a *Te Deum* at the Cathedral. The priest's turned up. Seems he was in hiding here all the time.' So much for our 'mass executions!' Hernandez thought. He was still watching the scene outside; on the left the city was not yet invested.

'There's the African cavalry!' someone shouted.

'You're crazy!' a voice replied.

So he was – or nearly so.

'It's a fool's game staying here,' Hernandez said. 'They'll be pouring up all the time, and you'll be caught like rats in a trap. The coast's still clear on the left. Don't trouble about the entrances. I'll just mop up a street with the machine-gun; you can jump down from the first storey – see you don't break your necks, though! Lay out the Moors who haven't been hit and try to stop you. There won't be many. Then cut round to the left. You've better things to do than just be slaughtered here. If they bring up reinforcements I'll look after them till you've made your getaway.'

He put the machine-gun in position, rattled off two long drums, there-and-back – flaying the street from end to end. The Moors fell, or bolted. The men in the arena jumped down and drove back easily enough the few remaining Moors. Some fascists came up on the right. The machine-gun enfiladed them, forcing them back under cover of the doorways. The last Republicans vanished up the street in a confused mass, treading on each other's heels. His mind void of thoughts, Hernandez pressed his shoulder to the butt of his gun; he was utterly happy, happy without reserve.

No one was left in the bull-ring. At last he, too, jumped down. A glancing blow, like a whiplash, seared his forehead, he felt his eyes growing blurred with blood. Another blow crashed down on his back with a lumbering thud; a rifle-butt most likely. His arms beating the dim air, he collapsed on to his back.

IX

In the courtyard of the Toledo jail a man began shouting at the top of his voice. That was very unusual. The authentic revolutionaries kept their mouths shut – because they were revolutionaries; the others, men who fancied they were revolutionaries because those about them were, and had discovered, faced with death, that all they really clung to was life – life on any terms – kept silent too. Silence is the prisoner's safeguard; thus insects try to be indistinguishable from the leaves on which they live.

And there were those who had lost even the desire to make their voices heard.

'You sons of bitches, you god-damned fools!' the man was yelling. 'I'm a bus conductor.' And, nearly bursting his lungs: 'A bus conductor! That's my job, you fools!'

Through the bars of his cell Hernandez watched for the man, unseen as yet, to come into view. When he appeared, he was slapping an alpaca coat which he held in his left hand, as if to beat the dust out of it. In several towns the fascists had condemned to death workers whose coats were shiny on the shoulders – showing that a rifle had rested there. And the men who had carried cartridge-pouches had similar marks, due to the leather straps.

'I don't care a hoot for your god-damned politics.' After taking a breath, he burst out again. 'Blast it! Just look at my shoulder! A rifle leaves a bruise there, don't it? Well, have I a bruise? I tell you I'm only a bus conductor.'

Two warders led him off. To a cell more likely than to freedom, Hernandez thought. Order must be maintained.

The prisoners walked round and round the yard, hag-ridden each by his own destiny. The cries of newspaper boys drifted in from the city.

There were the newcomers, too. Daily, a batch of them. As usual Hernandez looked at them, and, as usual, they looked away, shrinking from his gaze. It was coming home to Hernandez that men condemned to death are reckoned as contagious.

A sound at the cell door, a bolt drawn back; the crucial sound just now.

He had had enough of it, he was looking forward to being shot. The men with whom he would have wished to live were all marked down for death; with the others he had no wish to live. There was nothing particularly repellent in the prison

227

system here, as prison systems go. His jailers, professionals im-
ported from Seville, knew their job. Prison life was another
matter. Sometimes a batch of twenty or thirty prisoners was led
out, there was a sound of a volley and, after it, a desultory shot
or two, finishing off the wounded. Sometimes, at night, there
came the click of a bolt and a voice – almost invariably the same
word: 'What?' Then the chime of a priest's bell. Nothing more.
But boredom set him thinking, and a condemned man's
thoughts all turn on death.

A warder led Hernandez to the office of the Secret Service
police, and stayed there with him. The officer had not come yet.
Here, too, a window opened on the yard; the same prisoners
going the same round.

The men who had not yet been 'tried' were in the patio, the
condemned men in the death-cells. Hernandez tried to glimpse
the men behind the bars on the far side of the yard, facing the
window. They were too far away. All he could make out was
the portion of each hand clutching the bars on which the light
fell. Behind the bars, nothing; only darkness.

In any case, he did not greatly wish to see them. It was with
life, and not with death, that he wanted to exchange a friendly
glance.

The Chief of the Secret Service entered. He was an officer, a
man of about fifty with an elongated neck, small skull and
moustache – the spit of Queipo de Llano. He had Hernandez'
wallet in his hand.

'Is this your wallet?'

'Yes.'

The officer took out a wad of notes.

'These your notes?'

'I couldn't say for sure. But I remember having had some
notes in my wallet.'

'How many?'

'I really can't tell you.'

The officer rolled his eyes towards the ceiling, as if invoking
heaven to witness the fecklessness of the Reds.

'Seven or eight hundred pesetas,' Hernandez added, after a
short pause.

'Do you recognize this note?'

The officer with the pin-head skull watched Hernandez' face; expecting, presumably, some tell-tale change of expression. Hernandez, utterly bored by proceedings, glanced at the note; a tight smile pursed his lips.

What was puzzling the Secret Service officer was a currency note on which, amongst a jumble of obviously pointless scrawls, a dotted line had been traced in pencil, up and then down, forming an inverted 'V', and looking like some kind of symbol.

Moreno had drawn it. (He had not gone north to France, but to the Tagus front.) What was it he had just been saying? 'In the prison, old boy, they talked about everything on earth — except politics. Never a word of politics. If anyone had started saying, "I've fought for what I thought was right, and now I've lost, I'm willing to pay," he'd have found everyone edging away from him. When a man dies, Hernandez, he dies alone; remember that!'

Were they thinking about politics, he wondered, those men there in the yard; or about rifles pointed at them — or about nothing?

Hernandez had said then, 'I don't attach so much importance to death. To torture, yes.' To which Moreno had replied, 'I asked the fellows in prison, who had been tortured, what they were thinking about, while it was going on. Almost all told me they were thinking: "What next?" Even torture doesn't amount to much, compared with the certainty of death. The principal thing about death is that it makes all that has preceded it irremediable, eternally beyond redress. Torture and brutality *followed by death* — those are the really terrible things. Like this . . .' Then Moreno had begun drawing the pattern on the note. 'Every sensation, however terrible it may be, is like that. But when it's over . . .'

'Do you recognize this note?' the police officer repeated.

'Oh yes, I recognize it.' Hernandez' smile disconcerted his interlocutor. No charge was made for drinks at the Militia Headquarters; Hernandez had laid the note on the table in an absent-minded moment.

'What do those signs mean?'

Hernandez did not answer.

'I'm asking you to tell me what that means.'

Such men, it seemed, took themselves seriously. Hernandez stared at the little head, the long neck which would look still longer when the man was dead. And he'd die the usual sort of death; a nastier one, perhaps, than the quick work of a firing squad. Poor fool!

Prisoners were walking past the window, their eyes averted.

'A fellow on our side,' Hernandez said at last, with the same harsh smile, 'made those "signs". He'd escaped from one of your prisons, where he'd been in cells for over a month, under sentence of death. He was explaining to me how in life everything is always offset by something else; and as he talked he drew those two lines, one of which stands for, let's say, misfortune, the other for its compensation. But, as he said, the tragedy of death is that it halts the process once and for all, irrevocably. After death nothing can be compensated for. That, he said, is what makes the moment of death so terribly important even for an atheist.

'But,' Hernandez added in a lower voice, 'he was mistaken.' He felt as if he were delivering a lecture to a slow-witted audience.

Now it was the police officer's turn to hesitate before replying. Had he understood? If so, it was a wonder! Still, even the stupidest always understand a bit. How living people waste time over futilities! Supposing now the fellow demanded further explanations – the devil of a nuisance!

For, despite his courage there was one word Hernandez would not utter: 'Torture'.

At last the police officer came out of his brown study. 'That depends on how you look at it,' he said.

Once more the prisoners walked past the window.

The police officer spoke again. 'Those were queer opinions for an officer to enounce. He'd have done better to go and see a priest.'

'He wasn't on duty then,' Hernandez said, unsmiling.

'Well, now! What about those dotted lines?'

'They're meaningless. The subject of our discussion had got his nerves on edge. That's all.' There was no provocation in his tone, only complete indifference.

A bell rang and a warder entered.

'Break off!' the officer said.

Hernandez was still thinking about Moreno. One spring morning – how far away it seemed now, far as the romantic epoch of the 'Cid'! – at the selfsame table, in Toledo, he had heard Ramon Gomez de la Serna say, 'Of course man has descended from the monkey; you need only watch him shelling monkey-nuts!' The age of Spanish humour – where was it now? Hernandez saluted and began to move towards the door.

'Halt!' the officer roared in an angry tone. Then added: 'I've been given special orders about you, recommending that you should be treated with leniency, but –'

Lost in a maze of memories, Hernandez had been thrown off his guard by the order 'Break off!' rapped out in a military tone. And automatically he had saluted, as he had been saluting for the last two months at Toledo, with his fist clenched. Were they to engage in another argument – about that gesture.

' "Leniency," ' he said, 'when a man's kept in the death-cell! And, anyhow, why those "special orders"?'

The officer stared at him, puzzled, – or exasperated. 'Why do you think? Because they like your looks?' Then, struck by a sudden idea, he wagged his forefinger, as if to dispel an illusion, as if to say: 'No, there's no need to be on your guard – with me anyhow,' and added with a smile: 'I know all about it.'

'About what?' Hernandez calmly inquired.

'A little touched,' was obviously the fascist's judgement of him. A Red, of course . . .

'Why, obviously because of your conduct towards the officers at the Alcazar.'

A man does not go mad out of disgust. But suddenly Hernandez was conscious of his unkempt four days' growth of beard – keeping him warm. He ceased smiling. His fingers, resting on the table, clenched.

'Let's hope,' he said, looking the officer in the eyes and steadying his clenched fist on the table, 'Let's hope such an opportunity doesn't present itself again.' His shoulders were quivering.

'I do not think that such an opportunity will present itself again – for you.'

'So much the better.'

'That depends how you look at it. .... Why did you keep this note?'

'One usually keeps a note, till one spends it.'

Another officer entered. The police officer handed the note to him. And the warder led Hernandez back to his cell.

x

Once again Hernandez was walking in the Toledo streets. The prisoners were linked two by two. A car passed. Then two little girls walking side by side. An old woman with a pitcher. Another car, carrying fascist officers. Ah yes, Hernandez thought, I'm sentenced to death – for 'mutiny'. Another woman passed with a parcel of groceries, another with a pail. A man, with nothing.

Living people.

Death comes to all. He had seen a friend of his, a woman, die of malignant cancer; her body had turned the colour of her chestnut hair. And she had been a doctor. A miliciano at Toledo had been crushed to death by a tank. And there were lingering deaths – from uraemia, for instance. To all death comes. To all except those Moors escorting the prisoners; killers are beyond life and death.

Just as they set foot on the bridge, the man beside Hernandez whispered : 'Gillette blade. Come close.'

Hernandez squeezed up to him. A family passed. (Yes, there still were families!) A small boy eyed them. 'Why, they're quite old,' he said. Old! Hernandez smiled, surely that's overstating it ! ... Is death giving me a sense of humour? A woman passed, in black, riding on a donkey. She'd do better not to give herself away, he thought, looking us over with such concern. All that Hernandez could feel of his long body was the pressure of the ropes upon his wrists. The blade was sawing through the rope.

'Done it !'

Hernandez gave a gentle tug. Yes, the rope was cut. For the first time he looked round; the man beside him had a small, very bristly beard.

'There's still some of our chaps behind the hill,' the man said. 'At the first cross-roads.'

They had crossed the bridge. Just as they reached the buttress, the man jumped.

Hernandez did not jump.

He was too tired, and tired of life as well. It would mean an effort, another effort. What was beyond the embankment – bushes? Impossible to see. He remembered Moscardo's letters. Some Moors were jumping down after the man, firing. There were not enough of them; they daren't leave the column. Well, he would never know if that bearded man had brought it off. Perhaps he had; the Moors had a surly look as they climbed back on to the road.

The drab procession set off again. There was a slight rise in the ground ahead of them, and in it a longish hollow to the bottom of which he could not see. In front of it stood ten Falangists with arms at the order, and an officer. On the right Hernandez saw some more prisoners; with the newcomers there would be fifty all told. Their civilian clothes made the only dark patch in the brilliant sunlight; the khaki uniforms of the Moors were the exact colour of Toledo.

It had come, the moment which had always haunted him, that moment when a man knows he will die without the least chance of resistance.

Seemingly the prisoners were as indifferent to dying as Falangists and Moors to having to shoot them. The bus conductor was with the rest, precisely like them now. All looked a little dazed, like men who are over-tired; no more than that. The firing-squad, however, showed signs of restlessness, though all they had to do was to await the order to fire already loaded rifles.

'Atten-tion!'

The command was rapped out more peremptorily than usual and the ten members of the squad stiffened up, to act their parts in the comedy of 'honour'. Already far beyond all histrionics, Hernandez and his companions stared into vacancy.

Three fascists had just led off three prisoners and, after posting them on the edge of the ditch, withdrawn.

'Ready!'

The condemned man on the left had a mop of round-cropped hair. The three men were posted on a ridge above the level of the watching group, and stood out, taller than life, against the historic mountain-range beyond the Tagus. But how small a thing is history beside living – still living – flesh and blood!

The three men somersaulted backwards. They were already in the ditch when the squad fired. Absurd! How can they possibly escape? Hernandez thought. The other prisoners giggled nervously.

They would not have to escape. The prisoners had seen the somersault first, but the squad had fired before it. A trick of the nerves.

Three more men were lined up. It was unthinkable, knocking all those fifty men over in threes, like ninepins, into the pit behind; something was bound to happen, had got to happen...

One of the prisoners on the ridge glanced down over his shoulder into the ditch and instinctively began to move away from it. Then, as he brought his eyes round, without raising them, and looked ahead, he saw the feet of the firing squad quite near, pointing in his direction. He stopped. The prisoner on the right began to shout something. Then all three crumpled up, their hands clasping their bellies, and toppled over. This time the squad had aimed lower.

The rest of the prisoners stood by, silent and impassive. From the city came the forlorn braying of a donkey, and the cry of an alcarraza-seller; far-off sounds, dying upon the golden air.

One of the men who had been leading the prisoners to the death-stance on the ridge, bent over the ditch, with his revolver pointing forward. A fisherman's attitude. The sky was quivering with light. Coffins at least, Hernandez thought, are *clean*. Europe may have no love left for most things, but she still has for her dead. The soldier crouching above the ditch was following with his revolver something that moved in it. He fired. It is as painful to picture the *coup de grâce* administered to an unconscious head as to picture it given a dying one. And, at this hour in half the land of Spain, young men were playing their grim part in the same tragic comedy, firing across the same bright morning air; peasants like these were falling sheer or leaping back into a pit. ... It struck Hernandez that he had never seen men turn back-somersaults before except at circuses.

Three men were standing where the others had stood, waiting for the plunge.

If, Hernandez mused, I hadn't had Moscardo's letter sent on, if I hadn't tried to 'behave decently', would those three men be there? Two were standing awkwardly, too far forward and looking to the side; the third seemed wondering whether to turn his back on the rifles or to face them. Like seeing a train off, Hernandez thought, with a touch of hysteria; one never knows how to stand! And, damn it, even if I'd acted otherwise, it would have made no difference! There were plenty of fellows who acted otherwise.

The organizers of the death parade went back to the three blunderers and, taking them by the shoulders (not in the least brutally), set them straight. The prisoners, too, seemed trying to help them out — to grasp what was expected of them and behave accordingly. Like mourners being lined up at a funeral. ... But these men were attending their own.

'Seventeen, eighteen, nineteen, twenty.' The prisoners were in three ranks. The man who was numbering them was counting up the men who would be shot before him. 'No. Seventeen, eighteen, nineteen ...'

He could not get the count right; Hernandez was on the point of telling him the correct number. There were only seventeen men all told; not nineteen, not twenty. Somebody made a remark, about dying, most likely. 'All right! All right!' a voice replied. 'You shut your bloody choke! There's worse than that.'

Let's hope, Hernandez thought, this isn't all a dream. Fancy waking and having to go through it all again!

Would they *never* manage to get the prisoners facing the rifles like a wedding group facing the camera, into the correct pose?

Bright air shimmered on the Tagus hills, and bathed Toledo in a crystal sheen. Hernandez was beginning to learn how history is made. Once more in this land of black-clothed women, as so often in the past, a generation of widows was in the making. When such things are being done, what is the meaning of 'nobility?' Or 'generosity?'

Hernandez felt his eyes yearning towards the fresh-turned earth. Earth, inert, reposeful. ... Only living men are torn by anguish and disgust.

The most appalling thing about the prisoners was their

courage. Obedient they were, but not passive victims. How inept was the symbol of the slaughter-house! Men are not felled like cattle; killing them is an intricate process. Hernandez remembered Pradas, their conversation about generosity. At last the three had taken the right pose; yes, all was ready for the camera. Generosity is the top-dog's virtue.

A volley. Two fell back into the ditch, one on to his face. A minion of death stepped forward. Was he going to push the body over with his foot? No, stooping, he dragged it by an arm and leg – a heavy corpse and the ground sloped up. Tiresome unto death – and after! Into the hole with him! ... But would this business *never* end?

They were getting into the routine; those on the right of killing, those on the left of being killed. Three more lined up on the ridge where the others had stood. The drab expanse of ruined mansions and closed factories was taking on an aspect of eternity, the agelessness of graveyards; as if up to the crack of doom, in never-ending sequence, groups of three men would take their stand there, waiting to be killed.

'You wanted the earth,' a fascist exclaimed. 'Now you have it!'

One of the three men was the bus conductor; the smooth patch on the shoulder of the overcoat which had led to his death-sentence glinted in the sun. He had ceased protesting. He stood there waiting; like the others he had let himself be lined up, calmly, without a murmur. 'I don't give a bloody hoot for your god-damned politics!' He was a puny little man with a complexion the colour of black olives. Simultaneously with the movement of the rifles brought up to the shoulder he raised his fist in the Frente Popular salute.

Hernandez watched the uplifted fist; a moment hence those fingers would be clenched on earth.

The firing-squad hesitated, not because they were impressed, but waiting for the prisoner to be called to order – the conqueror's order, pending that of death. The three men in charge of operations walked up to him. The little man gazed at them, stolid in his innocence as a stake rooted in the soil, and gave them a look of undying, elemental hatred that had already something of the other world in its intensity.

236

Ah, Hernandez thought, if that man could get away now!
... He was not to get away. The officer had just given the order
to fire.

Another batch of prisoners took their places in front of the
trench. Their fists were raised.

'Hands down!' The officer shouted.

Under the clenched fists the prisoners' shoulders lifted in a
brief gesture of disdain. The officer stooped to tie a shoe-lace.
Then, straightening up, he too shrugged his shoulders and gave
the order.

Three more prisoners, including Hernandez, walked up to
the ridge. Fumes of hot steel and fresh-turned soil hung on the
air.

PART TWO

THE MANZANARES

ONE

Action and Reaction

I

THE panic-stricken mob that had fled from Toledo, the un-armed milicianos from the Tagus, and the remnants of peasant battalions from Estremadura, were flocking into Aranjuez station. Like leaves whirled together and then dispersed by the wind, groups that had arrived at the double vanished amongst the red-flowered chestnut trees of the park or, like lunatics in their asylum garden, tramped up and down the avenues of majestic plane-trees.

The draggled remnants of so many dramatically named formations – the Unconquerables, the Red Eagles, the Eagles of Liberty – were moving to and fro excitedly on a carpet of fallen flowers, thick as the dead leaves on a forest path. Their arms hung down, dragging their rifles after them like dogs on a leash; now and then they stopped to listen to the sounds of the approaching guns on the far side of the river. Between the shots, rising up from the ground and deadened by the heavy curtain of decaying chestnut flowers, they could hear the faint sound of an ancient bell.

'A church bell at a time like this!' Manuel exclaimed.

'It sounds more like a gardener's bell to me,' Lopez replied.

'It comes from by the station.'

Other bells, large and small, bicycle bells, motor-horns, and even a clatter of cooking-pots, were mingling now with the deep notes of the bell they first had heard. And, across the violet-leaves as large as a man's hand, there poured out of the recesses of the park the wreckage of the revolutionary dream, like wild tribes rallying to their tom-toms, with their paraphernalia of swords, striped blankets, garments made of curtains, sporting guns, and even the latest Mexican hats.

'And to think that at least half of them are plucky enough!' Manuel said.

'The quaintest thing of all, you owl,' Lopez observed, 'is that they haven't smashed a single bust.'

From end to end of the park, the famous plaster busts, rose-pink now in the reflection of the weathered bricks, remained unharmed under the romantic plane-trees. Manuel did not look at them. Eddying like some aviary brought from the Americas by Spanish princes for their Aranjuez garden, the fantastic rout straggled down towards the station, under the brick arcades bathed in the rosy light of the royal vistas.

As Manuel and Lopez began following the crowd towards the station, one word grew clear, and the word was 'Locomotive'. On no account must they go to Madrid! Manuel thought. Only too easy it was to picture the effects of ten thousand demoralized men arriving there, full of the most hair-raising yarns, immediately after the fall of Toledo, just when Madrid was desperately organizing her defences.

They were now quite near the station. 'Drid-drid-drid-Madrid-drid-drid' sounded on all sides like the chirring of a swarm of frenzied crickets.

'Having cut and run, they'll try to make out the Moors are irresistible,' Lopez said. 'The Moors must be better armed, and all the rest of it – just to account for their running away!'

'They bolted because they weren't officered. Before that they fought as well as we did.'

Manuel remembered Barca and Ramos, his comrades in the armoured train, and the others on the Tagus. And, last of all, an old trade-unionist who had been standard-bearer at a popular demonstration some years before. Held up by a large body of police, the demonstrators had been told they might go ahead provided their flags were furled. 'Furl the flags!' the leaders had shouted. Manuel had a very powerful voice. When impatiently he repeated the order, the old man had stared at him without a word, but his eyes seemed to say: 'As we have to do it, we'll do it – but the slower the better. You've still a lot to learn my lad.' Manuel had never forgotten the incident. It wasn't he reflected, always the same people who behaved badly. The link between Manuel and the proletariat was made up of too many memories, too many loyalties, to be snapped by any passing madness – even a lapse as grave as this.

'It's easy enough,' he said, 'being loyal to one's friends when they're in the right; the hard thing is when they're behaving badly.'

'Well, one can always have a shot at it.'

A man with a beard, rather like the Negus elongated by a distorting mirror, had climbed on to the roof of a limousine in front of the station entrance. Inside, the waiting-rooms and passages were packed with people; on the platform there was no more room for a single child. Above them loomed majestically the tall trees of the square.

'Who knows how to drive an engine?' yelled the bearded man. 'There's a train, there's an engine, there's everything we need!'

Suddenly, silence. Everybody was waiting for someone to come to the rescue.

'. . . set 'er going . . . set 'er going.'

'What?'

'. . . set 'er going . . .'

The speaker, at first invisible, was pushed and pulled amidst a clamorous outburst of enthusiasm until he reached the roof of the car.

'I can set 'er going.' He was a meek, furtive creature, bespectacled and slightly bald. 'I tell you – er – if we go carefully about it, I can drive her.'

The temperature dropped. Step by step Manuel and Lopez were nearing the car.

'Can you slow up?' a voice cried.

'Er – aye – I think so.'

'Eh boys, we can hop on her when she's moving.'

Manuel clambered on to the roof of the car.

'And the wounded?' he called out. 'Are *they* going to hop on too?'

A number of the crowd began trying to climb on to their pals' shoulders. What was his game? To march on Madrid or what? Another bloody officer!

'Comrades, listen to me! I am an . . .'

He was no longer audible. The shouting on all sides drowned his words. He lifted up both arms, got three seconds' silence, and shouted: 'I'm an engineer, and I tell you, you can't hold that engine.'

'It's the man who commanded the motorized column,' someone in the crowd muttered.

'Drive her, you!'

'I don't know how to drive her, but I do know what an engine is that's out of control. The men who risk it will be responsible for the death of two thousand of their comrades. And what about the wounded?'

Fortunately the volunteer driver did not inspire confidence.

'Then what about it?' someone yelled from the crowd.

'Make a suggestion.'

'Spit it out!'

'Do you want us to walk?'

'Supposing we're cut off?'

'Is it true that Navalcarnero's fallen?'

'What about it?'

'Stay here!' Manuel roared at them.

The crowd surged round him in baffled, sullen fury. A hundred hands rose and fluttered like leaves tossed by the wind, then sank down again into the swirling mass.

'It's two days since we ...'

'The Moors are on their way!'

Manuel knew that there were no supplies.

'Who's going to feed us?'

'I am,' he answered.

'And find shelter?'

'I shall.'

A breathing-space, he thought; a breakwater – but there was no knowing whether the waves wouldn't prove the stronger.

'It's easier to fight the Moors than make Madrid in a runaway train.'

Again hands shot up above the crowd – clenched fists, now. But not in comradely salute.

'In a quarter of an hour we'll be shot to bits,' Lopez murmured. He had joined his friend on the roof of the car.

'I don't care. So long as they don't go barging into Madrid.' He remembered a remark of Heinrich's. 'Every situation has at least one positive element; the thing's to find it, and to build on it.' He began shouting again.

'The orders of the Communist Party are strict discipline and obedience to the military authority. Communists, hold up your hands.'

The communists were in no hurry to declare themselves. Manuel noticed that the bald little mechanic beside him wore the Party star.

'Where's your gun?' he asked him. 'A communist never loses his gun.'

The mechanic looked at him and said, without the least humorous intention: 'But he does! You can see it for yourself.'

'Then he dismisses himself from the Party. Give me your badge.'

'Certainly, old boy. You don't need to yell like that. Here it is. What the hell are you going to do with it?'

Seven or eight badges fell on the roof of the car with flimsy, feeble thuds.

'In five minutes there'll be pumping lead into us,' Lopez said.

'No fear! They haven't the guts for it.'

He began again, as loud as ever but more slowly so that the crowd could understand each word.

'We've joined up to fight the fascists. We all knew we might be killed. If any of you had stopped one at Somosierra that would have been all in the day's work, wouldn't it? What has made the difference? Because there has been a bloody muddle. The Party and the Government, they've said it straight: military discipline first. We're two C.O.s here, and we take the responsibility. We're going to clean things up. This evening you'll get your rations, and you won't sleep out. You've got arms and ammunition. We won at Somosierra. We'll win here. Let's fight the same way, that's all that's needed. The river's easy to defend and, the tanks can't cross it.'

'What about planes?' cried a dozen voices.

'We'll be in trenches tomorrow morning. Bombproof dugouts in 'em. And the shelter of the hill-sides. There's no question of fighting at Madrid or Barcelona or the North Pole. Or of giving in to Franco, and shaking in your shoes for the next twenty years for fear you've been given away by your tart, or the busybody next door, or the priest. Think of the Asturias! In a day or two our new flights will be ready. The whole country's

245

with us. We've got to hang on – here and nowhere else. Not drag an army of tramps into Madrid. We've got to stay here with the wounded.'

'Right-oh! Good for you!'

'No! They're kidding you again!' The voice seemed issuing from the rotten leaves underfoot.

'Who is? Let's have a squint at you, my lad, to start with.' The man who had spoken made no sign. Manuel knew that to Spaniards it was the personal guarantee that counted. He went on.

'Who d'you mean, by "they"? Listen! We two, and the comrade beside me, we have been fighting from the very start and it's we who're taking the responsibility. I tell you, you'll get food and shelter. You know it's one of yourselves who's talking. We stood together on the 18th July. Today you're rattled, you're hungry, you're badly armed. But don't forget there's men among you who knocked out the field-guns with light cars, who forced the Montaña barracks with a battering-ram, who did in the Triana fascists with knives, and the Cordova fascists with slings. Tell me, boys, did you do all that only to scuttle like rats today? As man to man, I tell you – for all your grousing I *know* that I can trust you.

'If by tomorrow you haven't had all I promise you, you can shoot me. Until then, do as I tell you.'

'Where d'you live?'

'Aranjuez isn't a big place. And I've no escort.'

'Why doesn't he tell us . . . ?'

'That's enough. I promise to get you organized; you promise to defend the Republic. Who's with me?'

In a flurry of dead leaves swirling up to the tree-tops the crowd surged this side and that, as if groping to find a way out. Bent heads wagged to and fro, shoulders swayed as in an oriental dance, hands fluttered in the air. Lopez realized that, in the last analysis a speaker's influence depends on what lies behind it. When Manuel had said 'I trust you', all of them knew he meant what he said and the better part of all their personalities came to the fore. For they could not doubt that he was bent on helping them; many knew, too, that he was a good organizer.

'Communists, fall in by the lorry. You've no more rights than the others, but you've more duties. Got it? Volunteers, on the left.'

'Let's begin digging trenches now,' a voice cried out of the confusion.

'You'll go into trenches when those in command tell you.'

They were all wanting to be doing something now; they were shoving each other into line as they had shoved each other out of the way in their stampede towards the train.

'Militia and Party section-leaders, empty the waiting-room and occupy it. The other comrades, stay where you are. Each man will be served out with a mattress or bedding.'

He jumped down from the car and Lopez after him.

'It'll start all over again in five minutes, won't it?' Lopez said.

'No. They've got to have something to do until they go to bed. It'll be all right now. You stay here.'

'What the hell can I do?' Lopez had no illusions about his incapacity to command.

'Make 'em number off. That's essential, as I shall have to get them bedding. Each group leader to get together his militia unit, or whatever the formation is, and report to you their number. That'll give me an hour. There must be quite fifteen hundred men there.'

'Sure! Go ahead!'

Lopez was not very efficient, but he was plucky and keen.

*

Quite worn out, Manuel was huddled up on what had been a bishop's chair, in the cell of the Superior of a convent; with almost vacant eyes, he was staring out at the plaster busts in the park, glimmering like moonlit statues in a Persian garden.

Lopez's idea was to take the busts to Madrid and after the victory replace them by 'significant' animals. But Manuel had paid no attention to his friend's remarks. As soon as he had left Lopez, he had rushed off to see the Frente Popular committee. Amongst them he had found an enterprising few who knew the town well. They had spotted this convent for him, and collected six hundred straw pallets, beds, and mattresses. The little orphanage girls had given up half their bedding, and were sleeping two in a bed. Everything available in convents, barracks, and guard-rooms had been commandeered. But there was not enough to go round. Some men would have to do with a shake-down on plain straw or rugs.

When he was half-way through the job a deputation had arrived; it had been elected by the soldiers for liaison between them and their commanding officers. It was ten o'clock and the men were all bedded down. Manuel, after being glued to the telephone for an hour and a quarter in communication with the Communist Party, the Fifth Regiment, and the War Ministry, had extracted a promise of three days' rations. He would use that time to organize his supply system. The bulk of the lorries would not arrive before daybreak, though a few were on their way, with enough food for two hundred men. Manuel had given out that they would eat at eleven. Moreover, the Fifth Regiment was to send him some trained soldiers who could start instructing the men here, and form the nucleus of a new regiment.

There was a knock at the door. The deputation had come back.

'Hello!' said Manuel, his head ringed by a halo of Virgins and Sacred Hearts. 'What's the trouble now?'

'There's no trouble. It's the other way about. You see, you and your mate, you ain't soldiers, though you're in command. There's no getting round that. In one way, that suits us better. What you said to us was sense; we haven't done all we have done just to end up like this. And you've kept your promises. At any rate, up to now. And we know it ain't so easy, not by a long chalk. So we – the deputation, and the other boys – we been putting our heads together. See? We've decided – well, about the train, for instance, you were quite right.'

The spokesman was a cabinet-maker with a drooping grey moustache. Out in the park the famous nightingales were in full-throated song.

'So we thought, see, if we put a picket on the station, what happened today likely wouldn't happen again. We've got the men all right. So we came to suggest this picket.'

Behind the speaker, his comrades in *monos* showed up against the white background of the cell, one in front, three be-

248

hind; that was the formation the workers' delegations used always to adopt. That these four realized they were representing their own men, their lives, their faults, their responsibilities, before one of their own side, was so evident that it was as if the revolution itself, in its simplest, most significant form, stood there personified by them. For the speaker the revolution meant just the right to talk like that. Manuel hugged him in the Spanish way, and said nothing. For the first time he was in the presence of a fraternity that expressed itself in action.

'Now we'll have some grub,' he said to them.

They went down together. As Manuel had hoped, in the dormitories and vaulted halls, at the feet of the blue and gold statues of the saints left standing there, the warrior saints, with red flags on their lances, all the men were plunged in the heavy sleep of soldiers on active service.

'Who wants food?' Manuel asked – but not too loud. The only reply was a series of sleepy snorts and grunts, like the sounds of an exhausted herd of animals. There wouldn't be a hundred men to feed, and the supplies from Madrid would suffice. He went on his way, his boot-heels slapping on the flag-stones with the sound of footfalls in a church. He wanted to laugh, and at the same time felt ashamed.

When the meal was over, he went back to the Frente Popular headquarters. That night he would have to organize his equipment, find soap, and be ready at dawn to set on foot the new formations. 'Who'd have thought,' he smiled to himself, 'that soap was needed to make war!' In the gloom the trees were invisible, but he was vaguely aware of the dense profusion of their leaves above him stirring in the night breeze. A faint perfume came from the rose-gardens, smothered by the bitter tang of boxwood and plane-trees, as if it were being wafted across the river by the muffled clangour of the guns. There was no sign of the lorries as yet. The members of the Committee were on watch too.

When he got back Manuel was challenged at the convent gate.

'What the hell are you playing at?' he asked, after making himself known.

'We're the picket,' was the answer.

How many fascist surprise attacks had succeeded through the lack of pickets! In the dim glow that came from the convent, Manuel saw the glint of three rifle barrels against three dark great-coats; the first self-appointed picket of the Spanish war ...

II

The night of 6th November

Three of the bombers had been repaired. Magnin's plane was flying over the sleeping Balearics (it was known as the *Jaurès* now). For the last hour it had been alone above the sea. Attignies was piloting. All around the badly extinguished lights of Palma, the anti-aircraft guns were spitting up their shells against the invisible plane; the town below was defending itself like a blind man screaming. Magnin was looking for a Nationalist cruiser and the ships loaded with arms in the harbour. Searchlights were stabbing the darkness behind and in front of him, intersecting each other. He thought tensely that it was like using thin wands to catch a fly. Except for the pilot's cabin, the bomber was in complete darkness.

Were they fighting against the enemy or against the cold? It was more than eighteen degrees below freezing point. The gunners detested having to fire with their gloves on, but in the intense cold to touch the metal of the guns meant burns. The bombs threw up spouts of water into the night, lighting them with an orange glow. They would have to find out from the War Ministry whether the ships had been hit.

Every one of them was watching the anti-aircraft shells burst around him. With ice-cold faces and bodies enclosed in the warmth of their fur-lined flying-suits, they were alone in the vast darkness stretching over the sea.

The plane suddenly lit up.

'For Christ's sake, put that out!' Magnin shouted. But the very next moment he saw the shadows of the plane's wings, and realized that the light had come from outside.

The searchlight returned, catching the plane again. Magnin saw Pol's good-humoured face and Gardet's back with the little rifle slung across it. They had carried out the bombing of the ships in complete darkness, broken by the blue lightnings of the anti-aircraft shells they had so far avoided. And now a sense of comradeship in arms pervaded the cabin flooded with menacing light; now for the first time since they began the flight, these men could *see each other*.

One and all were peering down at the searchlight to which that blinding beam linked them — aiming at them. They all knew that ranging itself along the same line there was a gun.

Down below lights were going out, pursuit planes were no doubt taking off — and the darkness stretched away to the horizon. And in the midst of the darkness, with the plane shaking them about like shot in a box as it spun earthwards in an unsuccessful attempt to free itself from the following beam, were those seven men bathed in blue effulgence.

Magnin sprang to the side of Attignies, who was tugging at the stick, his eyes closed to escape from that blinding dazzle. Three seconds more, and the anti-aircraft guns would have opened fire.

The left hand of every occupant of the cabin went to the buckle of his parachute.

Attignies banked, teeth clenched and feet tensed against the controls, wishing with every fibre of his body, from his toes upwards, that he were in a pursuit plane: the bomber was turning with the unwieldiness of a lorry. And the light was still after them.

The first shell — thirty yards away. The plane jolted violently. The anti-aircraft guns would correct the error. Magnin tore aside the ear-flap of Attignies' flying-helmet.

'Corkscrew,' the pilot shouted, indicating the manoeuvre with his hand.

It was the device by which a plane frees itself from a hurricane when the controls no longer function: a downward plunge with all the weight of the machine behind it.

Magnin's moustache registered a frantic protest, visible but inaudible in the white glare and the noise of the engines. The searchlight would follow their dive down. He made another movement indicating a sideslip, followed by a turn.

Attignies went into a skid that seemed like a fall, with a noise of clanking metal and cartridge-clips rolling about the cabin. He fell headlong into an abyss of darkness, turned and made off in a corkscrew curve. Above and below, the searchlight went stabbing through the sky, like a blind man feeling his way with a rapier.

The plane was well clear of the searchlight zone now — lost once more in the protecting night. As if sinking into the repose of sleep, the crew of the plane had regained their posts and were luxuriating in the relief which was the invariable sequel to an engagement; driving through the freezing darkness above a lightless sea. But each of them had vividly before him the picture of the features of his comrades as they had been thrown into relief for that brief moment.

*

After a short halt at Valencia among the orange-groves, Magnin had left the *Jaurès* at Albacete, from where it was going on to Alcalá de Henares. Albacete was the last aerodrome in the possession of the Republicans on that side of Madrid. A section of the squadron had remained at Albacete to test the repaired planes; the remainder was fighting at Alcalá.

At Albacete the International Brigade was in process of formation. In the bright morning air keen with a touch of winter, thousands of men thronged the little pink and yellow town; the market-place, with its promiscuous display of knives, quarter-litre drinking mugs, pants, braces, shoes, combs, and badges, was humming like a country fair. The shoe and hosiery shops could be picked out by the queues of soldiers in front of them. A Chinese pedlar was offering his trumpery wares to a sentry who had his back to him. The sentry turned round and the pedlar made off; they were both Chinese.

When Magnin arrived at Brigade Headquarters, the delegate for whom he was looking was at the training camp, and would not return for another hour. Magnin had had no lunch. He went into the nearest bar.

Amid the throng inside, a drunk was shouting at the top of his voice. In spite of every precaution, an extraordinarily motley collection of recruits was arriving for the various international contingents. Rejected and packed off by the noon train, they made themselves a general nuisance all the morning beforehand. On one occasion the entire down-and-out population of Lyons had been sent off to the Brigade, only to be stopped at the frontier and returned to the station they had started from. The Brigade was made up of men who could fight, not 'extras' from a film studio.

'I'm fed up with it!' the drunk was bawling. 'Fed up! Haven't I flown the Prince of Monaco across the Atlantic, and served with the Legion? You call yourselves revolutionaries! Know what you are? A gang of lousy, yellow bastards!'

He had flung a glass on to the ground and was trampling on the broken pieces.

A socialist rose to his feet, but an equally wild friend of the drunk put out a restraining hand.

'Let him alone, he's a friend of mine. He's easy game when he's like that. I'll fix him.'

The friend went up behind the glass-breaker and rapped out:

'Fall in! 'Shun! Eyes front!'

The drunk immediately went through the correct motions.

'Right – turn! Quick march!'

The drunk made for the door and disappeared through it.

'Good as gold, eh?' the friend grinned, and went back to his cognac.

Magnin was looking round for faces he knew, and failing to find any. He went up to the first floor. Three of the paid air force volunteers were playing knuckle-bones on the floor beneath the portrait of a man with a waxed moustache.

A considerable number of the mechanics had returned to France. This lot had their backs to Magnin, their attention concentrated on their chips. The window was open, letting in the cold morning air. Accompanying the click of the big Spanish bones came a sharper noise like hammering, as distinct as the beat of horses' hoofs, but with the regular rhythm of flails and forges. It was the dull thudding of marching troops. The man who had just thrown the bones still had his hand in the air; his bones went on quivering. The hammer-beat of the boots, right beneath the window, was setting the cobwork houses trembling; the thunderous rhythms of war had invaded even the local pastime.

Magnin went to the window: still in civilian clothes, but shod with military boots, with their dogged communist faces or the pale cast of the 'Intellectual', the Brigade was tramping down the narrow street, resonant as a subway. There were old Poles with walrus moustaches and young ones whose faces recalled Soviet films, Germans with shaved heads, Algerians, Italians looking like Spaniards who had strayed by mistake into the international fold, Englishmen with more colour about them than any of the others, Frenchmen on the lines of Maurice Thorez or Maurice Chevalier; and all alike inspired, not with the young Madrid recruits' earnest desire to learn, but by memories of military service or of actual fighting against each other. They were nearing the barracks, and they started to sing. For the first time in history, the strains of the 'International' were rising from men of every nation united to do battle together.

Magnin turned round. The wage-earners were going on with their game. They were not going to let anyone pull that sort of stuff with them.

He had some hopes now of being able to build up an efficient foreign air force. It had taken him more than a fortnight in Barcelona to organize a repair service, and his absence had increased to no small extent the disorder of the 'Pelicans'. But six reconditioned planes would be able to take the air again within a week.

The delegate whom he had to see was with the men passing beneath the window. Magnin started back towards Brigade Headquarters, his eyebrows knitted pensively, full of his half-formed project.

III

'No, but I mean to say, is this going on for long?'

Wearing overalls and a crash-helmet that endowed him with almost Roman dignity, Leclerc was ranting and gesticulating in front of his plane crew at the Alcalá aeordrome. Thirty yards away, out of hearing, a Squadron-Leader friend of Sembrano, of the name of Carnero, was studying the Madrid sky through field-glasses. Filthy weather.

'Why can't we get a move on? They'd still be Fritzolinis to me, even if they were to rig themselves out like bloody archangels!'

Leclerc classed Germans and Italians indiscriminately as 'Fritzolinis'.

Carnero climbed into his plane, which drew into line, ready to take off. The carburettor of the machine he normally commanded was out of order, and he was in charge of the *Jaurès*, with a Spanish crew. Leclerc and a Spanish bomber followed him. The Republican fighters were already circling over Alcalá – miserable collection. A few planes had arrived from America, but still without up-to-date machine-guns. The Government air force was still fighting with the 1913 Spanish-made Lewis.

Since the breaking up of his *Orion* and his appointment as pilot of the *Pelican I*, pieced together from two other machines, Leclerc had abandoned his grey hat in favour of a leather crash-helmet which he contrived to wear with a stupendously official air.

'What about the thermos?' asked the forward gunner in the *Pelican I*. It was just beside Leclerc's seat, out of his sight.

'Thermos be damned! I'm due today for a Caesarian! Got to do it myself. It's no joking matter, me lad!'

A few minutes later, escorted by their fighters, the three planes were over Madrid. With the exceptions of Barajas, all the aerodromes which the Pelicans had used were now in enemy hands. Every road was packed with jostling traffic: in front of Getafe, a field had been transformed into a lorry-park. Yet the lack of protection everywhere was such that it seemed impossible that it could be enemy territory. From his position on the right, Leclerc was carefully watching the other two planes as they came out of the very low clouds. Above them was their escort of fighters. For one moment the clouds lay so near the gound that they had to go above them. In between two layers of grey, the silhouettes of the planes in battle formation filled the pale void with the black wings of war. As the flight came out of the clouds, the lorry-park lay beneath. The roads on both sides were solid with Franco vehicles. The mechanized column from the Tagus had reached the gates of Madrid.

The fascist pursuit planes swooped down from the upper clouds. Seven Fiats were coming head-on, unmistakable with their W-shaped stays between the wings. The uppermost Republican fighters opened their throttles to the maximum and dashed to meet them.

The enemy barrage began.

German anti-aircraft guns had reached Madrid in large quantities. The shells from the quick-firers were bursting at intervals of fifty yards. Leclerc thought of his plane's wing-spread of twenty-six yards. Even in 1918 he had not seen such a barrage. The German gunners were not aiming at the bombers but some hundreds of yards ahead of them, exactly at their height, so that the latter seemed to be throwing themselves deliberately into the danger-zone. Far beyond, the pursuit planes were engaging each other. Leclerc dived; the shell-bursts followed suit.

'They've got electric fire-directors,' the bomber said.

Leclerc could scarcely follow the battle between the fighters, whose intertwined parabolas gave the impression of crashes and of aerobatics at one and the same time.

The machine-gunners were watching the fight, and the bomber the ground below. Leclerc had his eyes glued on Carnero's plane, which was climbing, diving, side-slipping, still confronted by the bursting shells, which suddenly came closer. Following his leader through the wild confusion like a blind man linked to his guide, with no thought for anything but that he must not diverge from the same course, Leclerc was charging into the barrage with the dogged pertinacity of a tank.

The barrage was only a hundred yards away now.

Shells and planes drew together at the same time. Leclerc's machine bounded ten yards higher; the *Jaurès*, broken right through the middle, hurled its eight occupants into the leaden sky like a handful of seeds broadcast on the air. Leclerc felt suddenly as though the arm on which he was leaning had just been severed. In front of the falling men, black specks grouped round a single parachute, he saw the panic-stricken faces of his bomber and forward gunner. He banked still more sharply and made for Alcalá at top speed.

*

'Never seen anything like that, even in the War,' Leclerc had kept repeating ever since he had shut off his engine before landing.

Grouped round him on the landing-ground, the crew did not answer. With tragic mouth and haunted eyes, Leclerc slouched off towards the aerodrome headquarters.

Vargas was waiting for him, sitting in an armchair with his long legs stretched out, his narrow face turned towards the low clouds drifting past the window. He was in uniform now.

Leclerc began an heroic account of his flight. When he got as far as the fall of Carnero's plane, Vargas cut him short.

'What were your orders?'

'To bomb the Getafe column.'

'Were there already some lorries *in front of* the parking-place, coming up in line?'

'Yes. But getting through was out of the question with that barrage. Carnero proved that!'

On the occasions when Leclerc did not dare to use his slang his speech became stilted rather than natural.

'Was the barrage over the lorry-park?' Vargas repeated.

'Yes.'

'But there were lorries *in front*, nearer you?'

'Well, yes.'

'Tell me why you brought your bombs back.'

It had just dawned on Leclerc that he had run away.

'There were the enemy fighters . . .'

They both knew that the battle between the pursuit planes had taken place more than a mile from there. And even if he had been attacked, Leclerc should have dropped his bombs, parallel to the barrage: it was for the pursuit planes to do the fighting. Magnin had carried out several such bombings in the middle of an engagement.

'You did bring your bombs back, didn't you?'

'Well, there was no point in dropping them just anywhere, on our own men. . . . And besides the engine was knocking.'

Vargas's feeling that Leclerc was far from being a coward as a general rule merely increased the bitterness of hearing him answering now like a schoolboy who had broken bounds.

He sent for the bomber, the chief-machine-gunner, and the mechanic, who had been waiting outside.

'How was the engine?' he asked.

The gunner and Leclerc fixed their eyes on the mechanic.

257

'Well . . . not too good,' he answered.

'What was wrong?'

'Just not running well.'

Vargas got up.

'That's all I wanted, thank you.'

'Bombing was out of the question,' said Leclerc.

'That's all, thank you.'

I V

Wearing a uniform for the first time, on the instructions of the Ministry of War, Scali found himself in command of the aerodrome as a result of Magnin's absence at Albacete. Of those who had a better claim, one was in hospital, and the other, Karlitch, had been summoned urgently to Madrid to organize machine-gun units. The lack of all means of compulsion was as complete in the international air force as in half of the whole Spanish army, and had the same effect of limiting the efficacy of orders to the range of the personal authority of the officer issuing them. Two men were obeyed at the aerodrome: Magnin and the chief pilot, who was little more than a boy, but whom everybody liked and who had brought down four fascist planes. But for the last twenty-four hours his personal authority had had to exercise itself on a bout of fever and an amputated arm.

Scali was chuckling over the discovery that one of the Pelicans had imprinted the rubber stamp of the squadron upon Raplati's pink belly so that he should not get lost – when he was called to the phone.

'I am sending you back one of your pilots.'

It was Sembrano speaking.

The said pilot was evidently well on his way. For a few minutes later Leclerc arrived in a lorry – trussed like a turkey and escorted by four milicianos with fixed bayonets. He was accompanied by the chief gunner and the mechanic from the *Pelican I,* who were less drunk. The escort left the room.

Leclerc had decided to go and get royally drunk after he left Vargas. Taking his two particular pals along with him, he had commandeered one of the aerodrome cars without so much as a word of explanation, and driven off to Barajas, where he knew drinks would be forthcoming. Still keeping silence he had drunk six absinthes.

Then his tongue had begun to wag.

Hence the lorry.

He was slowly sobering up. Holding his dog under his arm, Scali was wondering what he was going to do if Leclerc ran amok. That great ape with the clownlike mop of hair and the overlong arms was certain to be extremely strong. Scali was determined not to call the milicianos back unless there was absolutely no alternative. The other Pelicans were regarding Leclerc somewhat aloofly, with mingled hostility and mirth. Attignies had silently reappeared, after having left them. Scali had no doubt that he had come back in order to lend help if the need arose. At last he put the dog down.

Leclerc had begun a harangue while he was being unbound.

'So I throw my weight about, eh? Let me tell you that's a sure sign of class, the sort of class that really gets things done! And if you don't mind my saying so, I've got no bloody use for little sailor-boys like you, nor for tuppeny-ha'penny retired tin-gods from the town hall, neither! They're a lot of mugs. I'm an old communist, I am not a stripe hunter, or a redtape-merchant. Are you going to come and tell me what it's all about? Or are your yellow guts getting you down?

'I've known what sort of blokes line up with Franco ever since the Wrangel army and all the ex-toffs came and cut in on our taxi business. Knew it long before Franco's time! I'm one of the pre-war communists, I am.'

'Dating from before the big split,' Darras said gently. 'That's all right, old chap, we all know you've nothing to do with the Party. That doesn't stop you from being a real sound fellow, but you've nothing to do with the Party.'

His wounded foot had mended, and on the previous day he had carried out a raid with Scali similar to the one over which Leclerc had just come to grief.

Leclerc looked at them both: Scali with the round spectacles, overlong trousers with ballooning legs, and the appearance of an American comedian taking part in a film about aviation; Darras with his flat red face, white hair, calm smile, and wrestler's chest-muscles. The gunner and mechanic remained silent.

'So it's the "Party" that's biting you boys just now? Did I have to show you my Party card before sending the Talavera gas-works sky-high? A lone wolf, that's me! A communist all on his own. But I want to be left in peace. And that's a warning to all the ruddy crocodiles who'd like to come nuzzling under my ribs where they don't belong, got it? Talavera, are you there? Is that you, Talavera darling?'

'We all know it's you,' Scali said, taking his arm. 'Don't worry: come along to bed.'

Like Magnin, he took the view that Leclerc's turning tail was more in the nature of an accident than due to actual cowardice. And he was touched by the way in which he clung to the memory of Talavera at such a moment as this. But there is always something repellent about anger; especially the variety which accompanies drunkenness. In Leclerc's case distended nostrils and swollen lips had reduced his comic face to an expression of sheer bestiality.

'Come to bed,' Scali said again.

Leclerc squinted sideways at him, beneath wrinkled eyelids. From below the drunken mask, the cunning of some peasant ancestor rose to the surface.

'Think I'm tight, eh?'

He was still looking at him from the corner of an eye.

'You've said it. Let's go to bed.'

Scali gave him his arm. Halfway up the stairs Leclerc turned round.

'You lousy bastards! You can all go and . . . yourselves!'

On the first floor he threw his arms round Scali:

'I ain't a coward, not really. No I ain't!'

He was crying.

'And I ain't just goin' to let it go at that. Just you wait!'

*

Nadal had been sent, under the aegis of the Spanish Embassy in Paris, to do some reporting on the Pelicans, some of whom showed themselves disposed to play up to him, masking their sycophancy with an air of aloofness. The crew of the *Marat* – Darras, Attignies, Gardet, and the others – were drawing up a manifesto. Jaime Alvear, sitting at the far end of the hotel dining-room with Scali, wearing black spectacles instead of his bandage, dismissed any suggestion of an interview as useless. He was seated near a closed window, listening to the wireless. Rouse, however, had dictated three columns.

Nadal was a little, thickset, frizzy-haired youth with eyes that were almost mauve, who might have made a successful gigolo if everything about him had not been too rotund; his face and nose, even the over-elaborate sweep of his gestures, were almost childishly in keeping with his too wavy hair. Leclerc had been announced to him as the most 'colourful' of the Pelicans. But Leclerc's view of journalists was that they were a bad enough joke to make the archangels weep; and if one of them took it upon himself to approach him he would, so he declared, 'push his bloody face in'. Moreover he was in bed.

Attignies came back with the manifesto prepared by the crew of the *Marat*. 'We came here without any thought of adventure. Revolutionaries unattached to any party, socialists or communists resolved to defend Spain, we shall carry on the fight wherever and however we may give the most effective service. Long live the liberty of the Spanish people!'

None of this was of any use to Nadal, who was not really out to investigate the doings of the volunteers. His paper's readers included more than a million members of the proletariat. What was expected of him was to provide his editor with good liberalism, tributes to those gallant airmen (especially the French ones), 'atmosphere' on the mercenaries, sob-stuff on the others, garnished with a heartfelt tear over the dead and the badly wounded. (A pity that man Jaime ... ! Still, after all, he was only a Spaniard.) No communism, and the absolute minimum of political ideology.

He also wanted to pick up one or two anecdotes, preferably of a sexual character, to retail in private. The most picturesque features of a dramatic assignment come out when the reporter is back amongst his friends.

His immediate preoccupation was with the liars. Not that he was taken in by them. But they made good copy. Every half-wit secretes a potential novel, he thought; it is merely a question of choosing. His first choice started off with 'My men' (not too loudly, though) ...

Next came the turn of those who had deserted from the French or English armies in order to go to Spain. Several of them had since got married, and he got them to give him photographs of their wives. 'My paper has a lot of women readers.' Next there were the 'aces' among the paid pilots, those who were officially credited with having brought down more than three fascist planes. They referred to the volunteers as 'the politicals', and to themselves as 'the fighters'; but there was no bluffing about them. They let him see their log-books discreetly.

Then there were a certain number of would-be 'bad lots', and a few skrimshankers who had been allowed to remain. He had given up the volunteers as a distinctly unprofitable field.

He was engaged in taking notes from a log-book, and half the contents of a box of jujubes which he had been unwise enough to disclose had already found its way into Pol's pocket, when a lull in the talk and a feeling of tension in the air made him lift his head.

His face twisted in a leer and his back hunched, Leclerc was coming down the stairs. The grey hood had made its appearance again, with the wisps of black hair protruding from it. His smile was far from reassuring, and his arms seemed longer than ever. Pointing to Nadal, a gunner from the *Pelican I* called to him. 'Here's a writer come to see us. Come and have a drink with your colleague.' Leclerc sat down.

'So you're a writer, too, little smartie! What's your line?'

'Short stories. What's yours?' Nadal asked.

'Oh, saga-novels. Been a poet, too. There's never been another airman poet who sold all his stuff like me. If the wide boys got hold of a mug tourist or one who was tiddly, they'd pick every bean off him. But did I? Not me. But I used to palm off my stuff on them, as there was work had gone into that. Only fifteen francs. Sold out every copy. *Icarus at the Wheel* it was called. Because of the poetry and the flying, see?'

'Are you writing just now?'

'Given it up. But I can make some pretty patterns with a machine-gun.'

'What sort of guns do you use?'

Having signed their statement, Attignies and Darras had

joined Scali and were listening to Jaime's radio. Since he had lost his sight, Jaime spent half his life listening-in. Darras moved away from the radio: Nadal's last question was not at all to his liking.

Still he decided not to interfere. Their conversation was just a comedy of errors. Leclerc knew nothing about pursuit planes; he had never handled a machine-gun since joining up. And Nadal, as he went on talking, chewing at his pipe with the wise look of an expert of long standing, was under the impression that sub-machine-guns with ammunition belts were being used, not knowing that the Spanish government planes were fitted with drum-loading Lewis guns – and failed to understand a word of what Leclerc was talking about.

'You like it here?' he asked, casually.

'Yes. This is the life! What the hell should I be doing if I'd stayed in Paris? Piloting a passenger-bus, as like as not – might as well run a bloomin' baby-carriage! If you're a Red you don't stand a chance, you got to take what comes along. No, thank you! Over here, a man's a man. Look at me now! I was at Tala-vera, I was. Ask anyone about it. The gas-works blazed like Christmas puddings. One in the eye for Franco. Me, Leclerc, I stopped Franco, and I ain't one to brag. Get me? And look at the mates there. Do they look the sort of blokes that'ld go round job-hunting just to get the order of the boot? Not they!'

Round the huge kitchen-stove they had fitted up at one end of the room; under the revolutionary posters, the cook and his family were busy as usual, and some Pelicans were engaged in wheedling 'extras' out of them.

Attignies, too, was listening to the conversation, keeping an ear on the radio at the same time. For the last few minutes he had been watching with interest the way the two men reacted to one another. Leclerc was rolling bread-balls between his fin-gers and flicking them almost into Nadal's face. His voice was by no means as friendly as his words.

'And my bus at Talavera was an "Orion" – you know what that means! This may be the land of fighting bulls; but all we get to shoo round's a bunch of half-grown heifers. But we kept our end up with 'em with our little heifers. Get me?'

A bread-ball landed smack on Nadal's nose. Attignies, more

and more interested, watched the game. Nadal was pretending to laugh; well, he could afford to. He'd get his own back in the reported interview.

'What sort of equipment did you have at Talavera?' he asked.

'Bloody awful! A machine-gun through a window, and the privy-hole made bigger to drop our bombs through.'

'And an aviation Hotchkiss on a tripod,' Gardet put in, in his best expert manner.

'Just what we had at Villacoublay,' Nadal said, with an air of aggrieved indignation. It was an outrage, he clearly implied, to ask any man to fight with arms like that. The Pelicans tittered. That Hotchkiss existed only in Gardet's imagination.

'Stop talking!' Attignies shouted.

The speaker from the rebel station he was listening-in to — perhaps a hook-up from Radio-Seville — had just announced 'Aviation', and Jaime had turned the wireless on louder.

'Our planes have successfully bombed the front lines of the Reds, forcing them back from Carabancel into Madrid.

'The city was bombarded from three o'clock to five, without any Red plane putting in an appearance.

'Five government machines have been brought down behind our lines.

'I have already announced from this station that the plane of the Communist Magnin, the notorious renegade and Russian agent, would soon be disposed of. Today it was brought down within our lines. All the crew perished in the crash. Magnin's body has been identified at Getafe. One scoundrel less. Let the others take warning! Good night, all.'

The Pelicans exchanged glances.

'Don't you worry,' Scali called to them, 'they've made a mistake!'

Nadal began to put questions, but he soon saw that he should not press the matter. On this subject, the Pelicans, even the toughest, were superstitious, and their manner became unfriendly. Most of them believed that the aeroplane referred to was the *Jaurès*, manned by Carnero and his crew. Still, Magnin had come down at Albacete; there was nothing to prevent his having fought that afternoon on the Madrid front.

'What do you know about it, you fathead?' Leclerc grumbled. Scali knew a great deal. Since noon, he had felt things were turning out badly, and he had telephoned to ask Magnin to come to Alcalá that night.

But Magnin had already received fuller information than Scali was able to give him. Sembrano had telephoned directly to him – and in greater detail. Leclerc, dead-drunk, had started blackguarding the Spanish pilots, though he knew quite well that, whatever shirkers might be hiding in Valencia, the Spanish pilots, with their decrepit planes, were daily equalling the Talavera 'stunt' of which he was so proud. He had gone on to prove to the Spanish mechanics flocking round him that the war was good as lost, that their patched-up machines were bound to crash – and so forth. Smarting with a sense of shame, he had given free rein to his malevolence. Scali, too, was well aware that Leclerc, after his return, had gone out and talked on the same lines to the Pelicans, button-holing each in turn. And the worst of it was that he had some influence amongst them; they were attracted by the man's picturesque personality, and by his openhandedness, genuine enough, though due primarily to his craving for being liked. Scali knew, moreover, that the Pelicans of Leclerc's own crew had 'played up' to their loquacious comrade.

He had begun by being surprised at this attitude of Leclerc's mates. Of unfailing insight when dealing with men whose character he understood – with intellectuals – he was all at sea with personalities like Leclerc's. Gardet had drawn his attention to the fact that the crews, the personnel of which was modified each time a man was sent to hospital, tended to crystallize around a certain type of mind. When Leclerc had turned back, his companions had not clearly understood what he was about. There were thick clouds, the visibility was poor. And now they were involved in a tragedy far too intricate for their comprehension. Leclerc could not forgive himself for running away; he now was set on involving all his associates in his own disgrace. To get them all to feel as disgusted as he felt with himself gave him the same sort of gloomy satisfaction as he got out of absinthe.

'Magnin rang us up at seven o'clock,' Scali announced.

But everyone wondered if he was speaking the truth or

merely trying to reassure. The latter was quite possible, considering the prevailing mood.

A longish silence greeted his announcement. Nadal was the first to speak.

"What prompted you to come here?' he asked Leclerc, pencil in hand. 'Was it the revolution?'

Leclerc shot him a vicious glance from the corner of an eye. 'What the hell's that to do with you? ... Anyhow everyone knows what I am; I'm a left-wing mercenary. And if I'm here, its because I've bloody well got guts. And I'm air-minded, as they say. That's a man's job, flying; it ain't no job for lily-livered skunks, or weaklings, or – journalists! Every man to his own taste. Get me?'

Looking more emaciated than ever, his nostrils gaping, his hair all ruffled, chest thrown out, and forehead puckered. Leclerc sat at the table gripping a bottle of *tinto* with long, simian fingers. A thrill of uneasy suspense seemed rippling in the air.

Gardet, who had drawn his chair up to Jaime's, ran his fingers nervously through his close-cropped hair, vaguely smiling.

'Whatever it is,' Attignies said to him, 'weakness or cowardice, if Magnin doesn't squelch them soon, these fellows will infect the whole squadron, like dry rot. What's happening? The wine going to their heads?'

'Whatever it is,' Gardet replied, 'I've had enough of Leclerc and his damn' nonsense. I don't like fighting beside fellows who're all nerves. Watch him now, though, playing the hero, puffing out his chest. It's enough to make a cat laugh.'

'You can see he's sick with Nadal for making him play the part. Look at his face. He could kill Nadal, this minute.'

'But grateful, too, for the chance he's giving him of showing off.'

'Grateful? I'm not so sure. See the look on his ugly mug.'

Nadal realized that things looked like turning nasty, and after ordering drinks all round, slipped out with his notes; a small, foxy figure, with a long pipe aggressively belying the crafty smile upon his lips.

'I ain't tight,' Leclerc was bellowing. 'But as for the revolution, what I say's ...'

266

Obviously he meant to say 'to hell with it!' but dared not. Not because of his comrades, whom he might well have liked to challenge. But beyond the two shutterless windows there was Madrid.

The wireless was near one of the windows. Looking round, Attignies saw the sleepy plaza of Alcalá de Henares, with its monuments and, half-hidden behind the columns of the porticos, rows of diminutive taverns where snails were sold, and where just now, most likely, some Pelicans were sipping real Pernods. And all the little town, with its pillared streets and quiet gardens, churches with pointed towers, and ornate palaces, romantic walls and balconies that seemed to invite guitars and serenades, all that old Castille, which looked like the stage-setting of a Spanish comedy, was chipped and frayed by air-bombs, and slept with one eye open and ears alert for the sounds of war.

'When Magnin comes,' Gardet said to Scali, 'please tell him that with the men from the *Marat*, yourself, and some of the others, we can always fix up crews for an offensive raid.'

'You're going to Madrid tonight?' Jaime asked.

'Yes. Garcia's sent me a special order to see him.'

'I wish you'd look up my father. And bring him here.'

Scali knew that Jaime's father was very old. It was probably a sense of dignity that prevented Jaime from trying to justify his request. He had never made his wound an excuse for special consideration.

'Right. I'll do so.'

'Say, Mr Scali,' Leclerc snarled, 'when's the grub going to be a bit better?'

'Ah! So it gives one an appetite, does it, being shown up?' Gardet retorted, from the far end of the table.

Leclerc stared at Gardet, whose unfriendly smile disclosed small cat-like teeth; but said nothing.

'And what about our contracts?' the bomber of *Pelican I* inquired.

'They're not back yet from the Jefatura,' Scali replied.

'Me, I ain't one to make complaints. But all the same, say I'd been killed today – might have happened, you know – what would have become of my contract?'

The tone was at once aggressive and apologetic. The bomber who spoke had little staring eyes and ineffectual-looking hands, and the lieutenant's stars had been sewn on his pale-blue leather jacket the day following his wedding in Barcelona. 'By artificial light he looks more than ever like a teapot in an animated cartoon,' Gardet murmured to himself.

Scali's view was that these fellows should not be taken too seriously, and his plan usually worked. But today things seemed different.

'Your pay would have been handed over to your wife, of course. Now do leave us in peace.'

'And supposing Franco got to Madrid before it was all fixed up?'

'In that case, I damned well hope Franco'd have you shot,' Gardet said, smoothing his hair. 'And then we'd hear no more of you and your pesetas.'

Usually the dangers shared in common by volunteers and mercenaries brought them together more effectively than the business of the contracts estranged them. But tonight the patience of the volunteers was sorely tried.

'And why don't they send us enough pursuit planes?' asked the mechanic of *Pelican I*.

'I must say, they don't look after the wounded as well as they might do,' put in Rouse.

Rouse would have found he was not sufficiently well treated had the King of England himself come to Madrid to visit him.

'It ain't no cinch, this job,' Leclerc's chief machine-gunner remarked. 'Not enough pursuit planes, not enough bombers, God-awful equipment, lousy machine-guns!'

The Spaniards, however, cheerfully fought the anti-aircraft guns with obsolete Bréguets. And without complaining.

Moving back towards Leclerc's table, Attignies overheard a conversation between some Pelicans.

'That's all very fine and large, but he hasn't been seen since this morning; there's no getting over that.'

'You should have seen those poor devils. Slithering down through the air in bunches.'

'Never saw anything like it, even during the War.'

'Yes, but the worst was the *Jaurès*. It broke right in two.'

'Seems the bastards got Carnero taped with their machine-guns.'

'Was that Carnero, with the parachute?'

'Yes, it was Magnin's parachute, with Carnero hanging on to it.'

'At the start one could stick it out, but against a telemeter barrage, what the hell can you do? I don't call that fighting.'

'What's so bloody awful is when the plane splits in two ...'

'We're short on organization, that's our trouble. No planning. Everyone starts a hoo-ha in the evening about what's to be done next day!'

'By bucketsful, the poor devils, the plane just tipped them out by bucketsful.'

'Of course, Magnin's got a swelled head. But if the bloody fool wants to get himself done in that ain't no reason for us to do the same.'

Attignies was struck by the way, when men are ashamed, a moral rot sets in. Reacting as he did, automatically, to ideas, the whole business seemed to him both trivial and profoundly disturbing. Here were men fussing and fuming about a few dozen mercenaries hired by the Republic; while he was thinking of the thousands and thousands of Italians and Germans, and the interminable lines of Moors sanctified 'for the duration' by their Sacred Hearts. Forty thousand Moors, at so much a day – with a court-martial in the background to help them keep their nerve. But if men were needed who would be faithful unto death, what was the point of calling in these so-called 'experts', who were rotting away, as good as dead already? ... Meanwhile, thank goodness, at Albacete and Madrid, the first international brigades were being formed.

Gardet's voice rose above the muffled hum of conversation.

'Listen to me!' he called out, sitting on the table, his under-jaw thrust forward. 'You've all been bloody well disgusted by the smart boys who come to give us the look-over, putting on airs and sucking at their pipes – blighters who never once go into the line and who trot back to Paris and pick holes in all that Magnin's doing – not to mention what we are doing – without the first idea of what we're up against. Well, tonight, it strikes me that you're backing up those bastards. Everything's wrong here, is it? Let me tell you, my lads, if you were with Franco, your mouths would jolly well have been shut up long ago. Perhaps for ever.'

'And that's why I'm here and not with Franco,' the mechanic said.

Pol jumped up, enormous, fuzzy-haired, purple in the face, furiously wagging his forefinger.

'No you don't, Mister Ikey Mo!' he bawled at Leclerc. 'I ain't fooled that easy! I see your little game; you'd like to do us out of our bonuses. And you, Bertrand, you ain't a bad fellow, but when I hear you crabbing Magnin's work it makes me vomit.'

'Then we haven't the right to express an opinion nowadays? We're just so much dirt, and got to keep our traps shut?'

'Call that expressing an opinion? You're shootin' out your bloody neck – because you got the wind up. And, mind you, I ain't got that against you. Accidents will happen, as they say, and I ain't the one to blame a comrade for a thing like that. It might happen to anyone. Yes, by and large, we all know you done your bit. But what I say now is that you want the whole world to rot because you're fed up with yourself. Well, I ain't going to be fooled by you, and that's straight! Nothing doing by me! You're grousing, are you? Well, who'd you put in instead of Magnin? Name someone. Just name one! And if what the bastard on the radio says is true, well what? That he – that he'll not come back. What then?'

'Bonus for me: ten dollars for good conduct.'

'Moral for you: you boys are acting like a lot of god-damned fools.'

Leclerc came up to Scali and grasped the back of a chair beside him, his eyes aflame with hate. There was a silence as he spoke.

'About the revolution, I told you just now and I say it again: let everyone carry on with it. But as to the way this show is run, I don't care what you say, it's bloody awful. They mobilize us for a fight and then they keep us on ice for two bloody days. Forty-eight hours without a razor! It's lasted long enough. Get me?'

Scali, his eyes black with disgust behind his glasses, made no reply.

'Without a razor? You don't mean to say so!' All were startled to their feet by the voice which rang our from the far end of the room.

Since Jaime had come back from his plane for the last time, he had never spoken to any except isolated comrades round his table, in a corner. Now it was as though he had recovered his singing voice of the old days, that voice which recently had fallen on silence as if something in it had gone blind, too. Not a man present but knew that each time he went up he was threatened with a like fate. Jaime was their comrade, and he was also the living, ominous image of just what might befall each of them. With his large nose jutting out between the black glasses, his hand scrabbling at the tables, on the under side, so that his groping fingers should not be seen, he advanced, moving from empty plate to empty plate, and all the Pelicans shrank back as though horrified by the thought of touching him.

'And the men in the trenches,' Jaime asked, in a lower voice, 'do they shave?'

'Ah, it's you!' Leclerc muttered between his teeth. 'We all know you're a bloody hero of the revolution. But get the hell out of this!'

Scali was standing four or five yards away to the left, near the wall, hitching up his service trousers (which were far too long for him), but his eyes had never left Leclerc. Suddenly Leclerc went towards him, leaving Jaime to his slow, groping progress along the table-edge.

'I'm fed to the teeth with machine-guns that are only fit for the shooting-gallery at a fair,' Leclerc shouted. 'Fed to the teeth. I got hair on my chest, I have, and I'm going to act like a bull, not a god-damned stool-pigeon. Get me?'

Scali, too disheartened for words, made a gesture of disdain.

Leclerc mimicked his gesture. He was wild with anger, his teeth were set with rage.

'You! I say s...to you! Get me? S...to you!'

His face was convulsed with bestial fury.

'The same to you,' Scali stammered lamely. He had no knack of repartee in vulgar brawls, any more than of giving orders. Like a good intellectual, he not only wanted to explain, but to convince. And as for physical violence, he had an aversion from it amounting to disgust. Leclerc, who felt instinctively this disgust, mistook it for fear.

'No, *I* said it first. Not you. Get me?'

Pol remembered the day when they had all waited together for the coming of the first plane filled with wounded.

Then:

'*Salud!*' Magnin called, waving his fist like a handkerchief in the air. Statue-like he stood on the threshold, his moustache on the near side blown down by the wind.

*

He strode forward, amongst looks of hostility, relief, or feigned indifference, and stopped before Leclerc.

'So, you had your thermos with you?'

'It's not true! I hadn't a thing to drink!'

Leclerc screamed the words in a tone of righteous indignation; it delighted him to be unjustly charged with drunkenness now that he wished so urgently the charge of cowardice should likewise seem unjust.

'Nothing? That was unwise,' Magnin said.

He preferred a drunken pilot to a demoralized one.

Leclerc hesitated, puzzled, groping for a way out.

'The *Pelican*'s crew will return to Albacete at once,' Magnin announced. 'The lorry's at the door.'

'A lorry! Cripes! Why not a bloody push-cart? ... I want a proper car!' Once more Leclerc's face was working with insensate rage.

'Can't we even have time to pack our kit?' the bomber grumbled.

A pointless remark. Everyone knew the crew had arrived by plane, without so much as a toothbrush between them. Magnin made a contemptuous gesture.

He looked at Leclerc, then at Leclerc's men, who were now dispersed about the room. Had they died this morning, he mused, we'd remember only what is best in them. And even were they to be killed tomorrow. ... The memory of Marcelino was stronger than Leclerc's presence. He looked at them, volunteers and mercenaries, as if all they were saying, doing, thinking about themselves, were a mere passing madness, a dream from which they must awaken sooner or later, stiff under their flying uniforms, real with the reality of death.

Leclerc marched up to Magnin as he had done to Scali. On his face was an expression of undiluted hatred, terrifying in its intensity, though the features had little changed; only his furrowed brows seemed to have sunk lower.

'Magnin, I say ... to you!'

The hairy fingers at the end of the long ape-like arms were quivering convulsively. Magnin's eyebrows and moustache seemed to bristle up, his pupils grew curiously still.

'You'll leave tomorrow for France, all arrears paid. You will never again set foot in Spain. That's all.'

'I'll come back whenever I bloody well choose to, contract or no contract. You poor chump, you lousy son-of-a-bitch, think you can stop me? I was in the Legion once, don't you try taking me for a doormat.'

Scali, Attignies, and Gardet had taken their stand beside Magnin. Against the table stood Jaime, with his black glasses.

'I want a proper car,' Leclerc repeated, his hands twitching more and more convulsively. 'Get me?'

Magnin walked to the door, swift, indifferent, with his slight stoop. At the far end of the room the only sound now audible was that of forks plied in the kitchen. All eyes followed Magnin. He opened the door and said some words as if addressing the high wind sweeping across the plaza of Alcalá.

Six guards entered. They were armed.

'Forward, the crew!' Magnin shouted.

Determined to safeguard his precedence, Leclerc went out first.

*

Silence seemed hovering in the room, though now it echoed with the roar of the starting lorry, of grinding gears, and racing pistons; then gradually the noise died away, merged into the stridence of the wind. Magnin had been standing in the doorway, looking out. The moment he turned round, there was a sudden din of clinking glasses, clattering dishes, sneezes, exclamations – as at a theatre the audience relaxes when the curtain falls. Magnin sat down at the table and cut short the interval, rapping a glass with his knife to call for silence.

'Comrades,' he began, in a conversational tone, 'two or three miles from that door at which you have been looking, are the Moors. Only a mile from Madrid. One mile.

'With the fascists at Carabanchel, men who act as the men who have just left us acted, are playing the part of counter-revolutionaries.

'They will all be in France tomorrow.

'From today on, we are incorporated with the Spanish regular Air Force. Each one of you must procure a uniform for Monday. All contracts are cancelled as from today. Darras is appointed chief mechanic, Gardet chief machine-gunner, Attignies civil commissar. Those who do not accept this arrangement leave tomorrow.

'The business about the *Pelican* crew is definitely settled. And we must try to forget all but their previous good service. Let us drink to the *Pelican* crew.'

The tone in which he spoke made the toast seem a farewell, a peremptory dismissal of the subject.

'Officers and N.C.Os will kindly join me in my room,' he added, when the glasses had been put down.

*

Magnin explained his views on the reorganization of the squadron.

'But how are we going to find our crews and ground staff?' Darras asked.

'The International Brigade. I went to Albacete about that. Everything is fixed up with them. They have some fellows who served in the air force, and quite a few hands from aviation factories. All the men who have had anything at all to do with aviation will be transferred to us tomorrow. It's up to you to sort them out, and detail each man to the job that suits him. We shall have more than we need, I understand. As for discipline – at least 30 per cent of the men being sent are communists. There are two communists among you. It's for you to see to that amongst yourselves.'

Magnin remembered Enrique.

'How about pursuit planes?' Attignies asked.

'I hear we shall be given some.'

'Enough?'

'Quite.'

Obviously he was expecting to receive some Russian machines.

'Are you contemplating joining the Party?' Darras asked.

'No. I am not in complete agreement with the Party.'

'Can't you stop proselytizing for five minutes, Darras?' Gardet smiled.

There had been some trouble in persuading Gardet to take a commission. 'When the machine-gunners get balled up,' he had once remarked, 'I give them a hand. I like that, and they have confidence in me. But as for commanding them — that's not up my street.' 'And if the officers aren't just those men the comrades have confidence in, who the devil should they be?' Darras had said. And finally Gardet had given in.

'Did you come by way of Madrid?' Attignies asked.

'No. But I had a telephone call from there just now. Fighting is going on at the gates of the city.'

v

The Government had moved from Madrid to Valencia, and the Ministry of War was empty. On a gilded chair, in solitary state, sat a French officer who had come to offer his services and been told to wait. He was still waiting; it was 11 p.m. The white marble staircases and the florid carpets lining them were lit up only by the glimmer of candles planted on the steps and upheld by their filaments of tallow. Once the last wick had drowned itself in a little grease-pool, darkness unqualified would reign on the majestic staircase.

The only lamps lit were those in the attics, occupied by Miaja's staff and the Military Intelligence Department.

Scali sat down, while Garcia opened an untitled file of papers. The fascist advance, it seemed, was being held up at Carabanchel.

'You know Madrid well, Scali, don't you?'

'Pretty well.'

'You know the Plaza del Progreso?'

275

'Yes.'

'And, of course, you know the Calle de la Luna, the Plaza de la Puerta de Toledo, the Calle Fuencarral, and the Plaza del Callao?'

'I used to live on the Plaza del Callao.'

'And the Calle del Nuncio, the Calle de los Bordadores, and the Calle de Segovia?'

'Not the second street you named.'

'All right. I'm going to ask you a question; think it over before answering. Is it possible for an exceptionally skilful pilot to hit just those five places' – he repeated the names – 'which I've mentioned?'

'To hit them? What do you mean? To hit the houses along those streets?'

'No, to drop bombs on the streets and open places beside the houses, but without touching any of the roofs. Only the streets themselves. And always at crowded spots. A tram on the Plaza del Callao, for instance.'

'A tram? That would obviously be a matter of luck.'

'Quite so. And the other places?'

Scali ran his hand through his hair; behind the glasses his eyes looked thoughtful.

'How many bombs?'

'A dozen.'

'That would be extraordinary luck. What about his other bombs?'

'There aren't any others. Twelve bombs – and a direct hit with each. On women in front of the grocers' shops, children at the Puerta de Toledo.'

'I'm trying to find an answer. But my first reaction, let me tell you, is to say all that's beyond the bounds of possibility. Even if the plane flew very low.'

'Well, this particular plane was flying high – so high nobody heard it.'

The more fantastic Garcia's questions were, the more uncomfortable Scali grew; for he knew Garcia's scrupulous regard for accuracy.

'Look here – the whole idea's too grotesque for words.'

'You must allow for the possibility of the bomber being

highly proficient; a regular air force officer, for instance, who has won bombing contests.'

'He can be anybody you like. But it simply couldn't be done. Did anyone see the machine?'

'Now, they're claiming to have seen it. But on the first day not a word was said about it. And no one heard it.'

'It can't have been a plane. The fascists must have a gun with a longer range than those we've reckoned for. It's the "Big Bertha" stunt all over again.'

'But if it *was* a plane, how do you account for the accuracy of the bombing?'

'I don't account for it. Look here, why not issue orders and let's go up together tomorrow? I'll fly you over the Calle de la Luna at whatever height you wish. You'll find your theory hasn't a leg to stand on, or else that everyone below will see the machine as clearly as one sees a car bearing down on one. If there's a high wind, the pilot won't even be able to keep his course above the street.'

'Even if the pilot's Ramon Franco?'

'Even if it's Lindbergh!'

'Right. There's something else. Here's a plan of Madrid. You see those red rings; they show where the bombs landed. Don't take any note of those pencilmarks. Does this map suggest anything to you?'

'It bears out what I've just said. All those streets don't follow the same direction. So our hypothetical bomber must have had the wind at right-angles to his course now and then. And to expect to hit a given street from some height up under such conditions is –' Scali tapped his forehead, to convey: 'sheer lunacy.'

Meanwhile Garcia was thinking to himself: How, my dear Scali, could shells fired from a long-range gun and necessarily falling at a pretty steep angle land on streets running in different directions without touching a single wall?

'A final point,' he said aloud. 'Could a really first-class pilot fly over Madrid for some considerable time at a height of, say, sixty feet? In bad weather, let me add.'

'No.'

'The Spanish pilots, I may say, entirely share your view.'

The mention of Ramon Franco's name had made Scali suspect that Garcia was referring to the bombardment on 30th October ...

After Scali had gone, Garcia studied once more the photographs he had had taken of the various points where bombs had fallen. Artillery officers had told him these bombardments could not possibly have been the work of heavy guns; the angle of descent definitely ruled that out. Moreover, fragments of the missiles had been discovered; they were not shells but bombs. On the photographs were comments by different branches of the staff; Garcia, without explaining why he required the information, had asked the experts to give answers to his questions. One of the answers ran: 'This projectile was launched from a height not exceeding sixty feet.' It was noteworthy that the pavements had been little more than chipped.

Sad at heart, Garcia put the photographs back in his drawer. For him the problem was solved. No aeroplane, no field-gun was responsible; the so-called 'Fifth Column' had been at work. Twelve men operating at the same moment. He had contended, not without success, against the 'phantom cars' – the fascist cars that, armed with machine-guns, had roamed Madrid by night; against the shopkeepers who at dawn fired at the milicianos through their shutters; against all a civil war may stand for. But such things had only been what one expects of war; a blind man firing impersonally on his enemy. In these cases, however, each man before launching his bomb had looked down on the line of women queued up outside a grocery, had seen the old men and children in the square. The women had been slaughtered without a qualm – perhaps it was a woman who had thrown those bombs; a pity for women is a man's emotion. But what about the children? Garcia had seen photographs taken immediately after the explosion.

One of his colleagues, who had just come back from Russia, had talked to him of sabotage. 'Hatred of the machine is a new thing in emotions; but when all the enthusiasm and the hope of a people centres in *work*, that very fact is enough to inspire the enemies of the régime with bitter hatred for the work that is being done.' Nowadays, at Madrid, the fascists hated the people – whose very existence a year earlier they may well have questioned – and hated them so bitterly as to see in a group of

278

children playing in a city square no more than an embodiment of the people.

Very likely, he thought, at this moment the twelve killers were gloating over the impending victory; that afternoon the prisoners in the model jail had sung the fascist anthem.

And it was his duty to keep silence; no incitement must be given the brute that slumbers in the heart of man. And he knew that if torture is so prevalent in war a reason – *another* reason – is that it seems the only apt rejoinder to treachery and cruelty. Did he speak out, that tense, excited crowd whose distant rumour came to him on fitful gusts of the night wind, would take the first step towards sheer brutishness. Masses, like individuals, are apt to run amuck in their desire for vengeance on atrocities. And so, in the fine frenzy of its barricades, Madrid would go on believing in the exploits of Ramon Franco.

The Intelligence Service and Secret Police would deal with it themselves, as usual. A picture rose in Garcia's mind of the Gran Via as it used to be, in the gay light of an April morning; shop windows, restaurants, women who were not to be slaughtered, and on the café terraces sugar-sticks dissolving like hoar-frost in glasses of water, beside cups of cinnamon-flavoured chocolate. And now he sat alone in a deserted palace, confronting a polluted world, the very air of which was stifling. Whichever way this war ends, he mused, what sort of peace can possibly prevail after such bitter hatred? And what will the war make of me?

Moral problems! Yes, a man can never get away from them. He shook his head, picked up his pipe and, rising with an effort, started out for the Secret Police Bureau.

VI

A thin, bent figure, alone in the midst of the vast staircase, Guernico had come to the War Ministry to enlist official support for the ambulance corps he was trying to reorganize. As the tide of war drew nearer to Madrid, the ambulance corps he had built up in the Toledo days was losing its efficiency. On the ground floor of the Ministry was a display of armour, and in the gathering dusk the Catholic writer with the tall, spare form and the fair complexion we find in so many of Velasquez's portraits, looked as if he might have stepped out of one of those historic coats of mail, pledged to return to it before the break of day. Garcia, who had not met him for the last three weeks, was wont to describe Guernico as the only one of his friends in whom intelligence took the form of charity. And, for all the gulf that yawned between them, Guernico was perhaps the only man for whom Garcia had a real affection.

The two set out together for the Plaza Mayor.

Shadows glided along drawn shutters and bare walls, shadows parallel and bending forward, like haulers towing a boat upstream. Tawny smoke-clouds from the suburbs were rolling over the city. 'The general stampede,' Garcia thought – but then he saw that none of the passers-by carried bundles. All were walking very fast in the same direction.

'It has pluck,' he said, 'our city of Madrid.'

A blind man, his begging-bowl before him, was playing the 'International'. In their lightless houses, the fascists, a hundred thousand strong, were waiting for the next day's battle.

'There's not a sound,' Guernico said.

Only the sound of footsteps. The street was throbbing like a vein. The Moors were at the south and western gates, but the wind was blowing away from the city. Not a rifle-shot could be heard, not even the boom of cannon. Only the constant rustle of the moving crowd, like an army of moles digging their tunnels underground. And the accordion.

They walked towards the Puerta del Sol, in the same direction as the reddish smoke that drifted overhead and the unseen river bearing the crown on its futile way towards the Plaza – as though the Carabanchel barricades had been erected there.

'Supposing we stop them here . . .'

A woman plucked Guernico's sleeve and addressed him in French. 'Do you think I ought to leave?'

'She's a German comrade,' Guernico explained to Garcia, but did not answer her.

'He says I ought to go,' the woman went on. 'He says he can't fight properly when I'm near.'

'And I'm quite sure he's right,' Garcia said.

'But I just can't *live* if I know he's fighting here and I don't even hear what's happening.'

Another accordion playing the 'International' droned an

accompaniment to the words; a second blind man, begging-bowl on lap, was carrying on the tune from the point where the first had dropped it.

The women are all alike, Garcia mused. If that one goes, she'll take it hard at first, but she'll see it through; whereas, if she stays, he'll be killed. He could not see her features; she was much shorter than he and her face was screened by shadows of the passers-by.

'Why do you want to stay?' Guernico's voice was gentle.

'I don't mind dying, but food's the trouble; I got to eat my fill, and now that won't be possible. ... I'm in the family way.'

Garcia did not hear Guernico's reply. The woman drifted away on another stream of shadows.

'What can one do?' Guernico murmured.

Some milicianos in overalls caught them up and passed them. Paving-stones had been pulled up and phantom figures were building a barricade across the street.

'When are you leaving?' Garcia asked.

'I'm not leaving.'

Guernico would be among the first for the firing-squad when the fascists entered the city. Though Garcia did not turn to-wards his friend, he visualized him now, as he walked beside him, with his little fair moustache, his tousled hair and long, lean arms. The defencelessness of that body touched him in the way that children always stirred his pity, for it ruled out all ideas of fighting. No, Guernico would not fight; he would be killed.

Neither mentioned the Madrid ambulance section, for neither really believed it would materialize.

'So long as one can serve the revolution, it's up to us to do so. But getting oneself killed doesn't help in the least, my dear fellow. The Republic's not a matter of geography and its fate isn't sealed just because one town more or less gets captured.'

'I was at the Puerta del Sol on the day of the Montaña affair when the crowd was being fired on from every window. The people in the street lay flat; the whole square was a mass of prostrate bodies, on which the enemy were firing. On the next day but one, when I went to the Ministry I found a long queue of women outside it; they had come to offer their blood for transfusion. Twice I've *seen* the Spanish people. This war is the people's war, whatever the outcome; and I'll stand by it wherever it is. There are two hundred thousand workers here and *they* haven't any cars to take them to Valencia.'

Obviously nothing Garcia might say could have weighed with Guernico as the lives of his wife and children must have weighed with him. And Garcia could not bear the thought that if they were never to meet again their last conversation should have ended on a sort of wrangle.

Guernico made a spacious gesture with his long, slender hand. 'After all,' he said, 'perhaps I'll leave at the last moment.' But Garcia felt sure that he was lying.

A thud of heavy footsteps echoed down the street, seeming to precede the body of men who now emerged into the light. 'It's the navvies,' Garcia said. They were off to the front just behind Carabanchel for trench-digging and laying mines. In front, another company of shadows, dim in the mist, were building another barricade.

'They're staying right enough, you see,' Guernico said.

'At a pinch they've a retreat open by the Guadalajara road. But your rooms and the Association premises are positive death-traps.'

Guernico made the same gesture of uncertain fatalism. Another blind beggar; still the 'International'. The only tune blind men played just now. And more shadowy forms, building more barricades.

'Perhaps,' Guernico said, 'more duties are imposed on us, as Christian writers, than on other people.' They were passing the Alcalá church. Guernico pointed vaguely towards it. By his tone Garcia guessed that his lips were twisted in a bitter smile, as he continued. 'After a sermon by a fascist preacher in French Catalonia – the text was: "Be ye not unequally yoked together with unbelievers" – I saw Father Sarazola go up to the preacher. After the preacher had gone away Sarazola said to me: "Once to have known Christ leaves its mark. Of all the fascists I've seen here, he's the first to be ashamed of it."'

A lorry passed, laden with a serried mass of milicianos squatting on the floor, the muzzles of their obsolete machine-guns swaying above them. When Guernico spoke again his voice was lower.

'Only, you know, when I see the way they're behaving now it's I who feel ashamed.'

Garcia was about to reply when a little weasel-faced miliciano suddenly gripped his arm.

'They'll be right here tomorrow!' He said.

'Who's that fellow?' Guernico asked in an undertone.

'He used to work in Magnin's squadron, as a clerk.'

'This government – there's not a bloody thing to be done with it,' said the weasel-faced man. 'Why, ten days ago I brought them a plan, worked out in detail, mind you, for the large-scale culture of typhoid germs. Fifteen years' research, and I didn't ask a sou for it; just to down the fascists. They wouldn't do a thing about it. Turned it down, like they turned down my bomb. Well, the fascists will be in Madrid tomorrow.'

'Oh, shut your mouth, you!' Garcia exclaimed.

But already the little man had bobbed back like a jack-in-the-box into the stream of passing shadows: the 'International' had accompanied his appearance and eclipse.

'Come across many of his type?' Guernico inquired.

'At first, yes. ... The sort of volunteer we got at first was usually a bit of a lunatic or a bit of a hero. Sometimes both at once.'

On the Alcalá, as on all the narrow streets, brooded the feverish expectancy of nights when history is in the making. And here, too, there was no sound of guns, only the throbbing of accordions. Suddenly at the far end of the street a machine-gun loosed off a strip – a gunner opening fire on ghosts.

More barricades were being hastily thrown together. Garcia had no great faith in the utility of barricades; these ones, however, looked business-like enough. Everywhere in the dim light spectral forms were flitting to and fro, with here and there a stationary wraith that, after a brief gesture, resumed its immobility; the man directing operations. The mist was steadily thickening. Men and women carrying building materials sped through the gloom and workers from the various building unions were carrying out the tasks of supervision assigned them by their foremen. Experts from the Fifth Regiment had trained these foremen in two strenuous days. And in this insubstantial pageant the Old Madrid was passing away; for the first time, behind the incidence of private lives, of personal dreams and aspirations, beyond the lesser hopes and fears that urged these people on their diverse ways, a well commensurate with the collective soul of New Madrid was developing on the fog-bound dusk of the beleaguered city.

The lamps along the avenue were dwindling to dismal, ineffectual blurs of light under the prehistorically monstrous forms of the intricate skyscrapers. And Garcia recalled what his friend had said : 'More duties are imposed on us, as Christian writers, than on other people.'

'What the devil can you expect from those folk – things being as they are?' he asked, jerking his pipe in the direction of another church.

They were under a street-lamp. On Guernico's face was the pensive smile that so often gave him the look of an ailing child.

'Don't forget I'm one of those people who believe in an eternity.' He took Garcia's arm. 'I suspect that what's happening here just now – even the burnings of churches in Catalonia – may do far more for my church than the last hundred years of Spanish catholicism have done for it. For twenty years I've watched the priests officiating here and in Andalusia; well, in all those twenty years, I've never had a glimpse of a truly Catholic Spain. Only rites and ceremonies, and in the people's hearts as on the face of nature – a waste of land !'

At the Puerta del Sol all the doors of the State Building were open. Just before the rebellion an exhibition of sculpture was being held in the vestibule, and statues of all kinds – nudes, groups, and animals – were awaiting the coming of the Moors in the vast empty hall. Only the click of a distant typewriter fretted the silence; evidently the building was not completely abandoned.

And in all the streets radiating from the square, ubiquitous as the mist, similar wraiths were building similar barricades.

'Is it a fact that Caballero asked your advice about reopening the churches?'

'Yes.'

'What did you say?'

' "No", of course.'

'You told him not to open them?'

'Obviously. That may surprise you, but it doesn't surprise Catholics at all. If I'm shot tomorrow, I'll have the usual fears for myself, like any other man; but not one on that score. I'm neither a heretic nor a protestant; I'm a Spanish Catholic. If theology were in your line, I'd tell you I'm appealing to the soul of the Church against its body; but that's another story. Faith doesn't imply a lack of love. And hope doesn't imply a world that would justify itself by making people worship once again, like a fetish, that crucifix at Seville which they call "The Rich Man's Christ". (Simony, not heresy's the trouble with our Church.) Nor is it looking forward to a Spanish empire as the be-all and the end-all of the world; a régime in which no sound is heard because those who suffer must hide themselves to weep. "Order" – you find it in a convict prison, too. Even the best of the Fascists hasn't a single hope that isn't founded on pride. But what has Christ to do with such a world?'

Garcia tripped over a large dog and nearly fell. There were numbers of magnificent dogs – abandoned by owners who had fled – straying in Madrid. With the blind men they had taken possession of the city, pending the issue between Republicans and Moors.

'Those priests of Navarre,' Guernico continued, 'who permit men to be shot for the glory of the Holy Virgin, what have they to do with "charity"? No, it's the Basque priests who stand for charity; those priests, who till the fascists killed them, went on administering the benediction in the cellars of Irun, to the anarchists who'd burned their churches. I'm not anxious, Garcia, I recognize the Church of Spain, but – all the faith I've in me bears me out – I'm against it in the name of the three major virtues of out creed: Faith, Hope, and Charity.'

'Where will you find the Church that answers to your faith?'

Guernico stroked back his hair, which was falling on his forehead. Almost soundlessly the crowd was flowing to and fro between the arcades and hoardings which all but blocked the Plaza Mayor. The earthwork going on in the square had been held up, and it was littered with heaps of stone and paving-blocks; over these the moving stream of shadows skipped or glided, as in the movements of a melancholy ballet, against a background of haggard pinnacles resembling those of the Escorial. Madrid tonight seemed so thickly covered with barricades that in the whole city not one open space remained.

'Look!' Guernico exclaimed. 'In those squalid houses, and in the hospitals, there are priests at this very moment, dressed up in waistcoats like Parisian waiters, and collarless – and they're hearing confessions, giving extreme unction, perhaps baptizing children. I said to you that for twenty years I've not heard Christ's word in Spain. But those priests are being heard now. Yes, they're being listened to, and nobody, nobody will listen to the men who turn out tomorrow, in the cassocks they've fetched out of hiding, to bless Franco. How many priests are carrying on their ministry just now? Fifty, perhaps a hundred. Napoleon once walked under these arcades; in those days the Church of Spain shielded its flock, but since then I doubt that there's been a single night, till these last few nights, when Christ's words were *living* in our midst. Yes, tonight His Gospel is a living presence.'

His foot caught on a displaced paving-block and his hair sagged forward again.

'A living presence,' he repeated. 'There aren't many places in the world of which one can say: "His Word was present here." But soon it will be known that here, in Madrid, during these recent nights, His Word was amongst us all. In this land something is dawning for my Church, something which may well be its renaissance. I saw the last sacrament administered to a Belgian miliciano yesterday at San Carlos Hospital, do you know it?'

'Yes, when we were running that armoured train I had some casualties treated there.'

The enormous, musty rooms came back to Garcia's mind, the foliage sprouting through the narrow windows. How far away all that seemed!

'It was a ward for arm cases. When the priest said, *Requiem aeternam dona ei Domine*, several voices made the response: *Et lux perpetua luceat.* . . . Four or five voices, just behind me.'

'Do you remember Manuel's *Tantum Ergo*?'

Five months earlier several of Garcia's friends, including

Manuel and Guernico, had spent with him the last night before he started out on a journey; at daybreak they had all gone together to the hills overlooking Madrid. As the pale, mauve forms of the buildings loomed slowly forth against the shadows and the dark mass of the Escorial woods, Manuel had sung some Asturian folk-songs and the others joined in the refrains. Then he had said: 'Now, for Guernico's benefit, I'm going to sing the *Tantum Ergo*.' All had been educated by priests and all had joined in the last verse, singing the parts in Latin. As those half-forgotten Latin phrases had come back to his friend that morning, charged with a certain amiable irony, so to the wounded revolutionaries in the San Carlos Hospital had recurred the Latin of the death-bed.

'The priest said to me,' Guernico went on: ' "When I came in, they all took off their hats; they knew that I was bringing them consolation in the hour of death." He was wrong. They took off their hats because the priest who'd entered might have been their enemy, but was not.'

He stumbled against another loose stone; uprooted paving-stones lay everywhere as if the square had been through a bombardment. His voice was different when he spoke again.

'Oh, I know our "realists" are out to make us see all that from a new angle. The Son of God came down on earth merely to talk a lot of idle nonsense; His sufferings must have turned His head a little – considering the time He was hanging on the Cross, of course ...

'God alone knows the trials He is about to impose on the priesthood; but I think that the priest's vocation *should* become a hard task once again.' He paused for a moment, then added: 'As indeed every Christian life is hard.'

Garcia watched their twisted shadows gliding in front of them along the iron-shuttered shopfronts, and remembered the twelve bombs of the 30th October.

'What's hardest,' Guernico continued in a low tone, 'is the problem of the wives and children. Anyhow I've that much luck, my family's not here.'

Garcia turned to see his friend's face, but could make out little of his features. There was still no sign of battle; yet somehow, like a presence in a darkened room, the crescent of the fascist army made itself felt, closing in upon the city. Garcia recalled his last meeting with Caballero, and how the words 'eldest son' had cropped up in their conversation. He was aware that Caballero's eldest boy was held prisoner by the fascists at Segovia and would be shot. That had been in September; they had sat at the table facing each other; Caballero in dungarees, Garcia in a *mono*. Through a window open on the autumn sun a grasshopper had blundered in and fallen upside down on the table between them. Half-stunned, the insect tried to keep from moving, but its brittle legs were quivering and, as Garcia watched it, both men had kept silent.

VII

In the fog shadowy forms were drifting ceaselessly past the shopfronts, and the street was loud with unseen footfalls. In the huge dining-room at the Gran Via the waiters were serving three forlorn customers (whom they took to be the last guests of the Republic) with surly stupefaction. In the lobby of the hotel men of the Fifth Regiment were withdrawing their fists, bristling with bullets, from large sacks of ammunition and, filing out one by one, were falling in by companies along the pavement. At Tetuan and Cuatro Caminos women were carrying all the petrol they had been able to collect to the top floors of the houses. In the workers' districts the possibility of surrender or escape was not so much as mentioned. In lorries or on foot the Fifth Regiment was proceeding to Carabanchel, the Western Park, and University City ...

There was not much room in the car and a suit-case was the most that Jaime's father would be able to take with him.

The door opened and Scali saw a very tall, robust old man, with a sharply pointed beard that seemed wedged between his stooping shoulders. Once they were under the electric lamp in the hall, Scali noticed how curiously the hair modified the old face, much as a baroque copyist might modify an El Greco portrait: above the large keen eyes whose intensity seemed a little dulled by the heavy, puckered lids, the restless eyebrows tapered off, like the beard, into little comma-like wisps, and behind the smooth, bald crown was a fringe of scattered white hairs.

'You're Giovanni Scali, aren't you?' he asked with a friendly smile.

Scali was surprised to hear his first name used. 'Did your son talk to you about me?'

'Yes,' the old man answered. 'But I've read you, too; I know your work.'

Scali remembered Jaime telling him his father had been a professor of art-history.

They entered a room entirely lined with books, except for two high alcoves on each side of a divan. In one of the alcoves were some baroque, primitive statuettes, the work of Spanish-Mexican artists; in the other was a very fine Morales.

Holding his glasses to his eyes, Alvear looked down on Scali – he was a head taller than his guest – with the meticulous attention one gives to objects out of the common run.

'You seem surprised,' Scali remarked.

'Yes. To see a man with brains in that get-up always surprises me !'

Scali was in uniform. On a low table flanked by large leather chairs were some open books, a bottle of liqueur brandy, and a filled wine-glass. Alvear stamped heavily out of the room – his shoulders seemed too bulky for his legs – and came back with another glass.

'No thanks,' Scali said.

The shutters were closed, but he could hear a sound of hurrying footsteps and an accordion in the distance.

'You're wrong. Our Jerez liqueur brandy is extremely good, quite equal to the French. How about something else instead?'

'My car's waiting below,' Scali said. 'It's at your disposal. You can leave Madrid at once.'

Alvear sank into the nearest armchair. Huddled up in it, he looked like a sturdy old eagle in its eyrie, an old eagle shorn of its plumage, with a large but not unattractive beak, like Jaime's.

Raising his eyes, he stared at Scali. 'What for?'

'Jaime asked me to call for you on my way back from the Ministry. I'm going to Alcalá de Henares.'

Alvear's smile seemed even older than his body. 'When a man of my age travels, he takes his library with him.'

'I suppose you know it's quite on the cards the Moors will be here tomorrow.'

'Quite so. But what on earth can I do about it? Well, well, we've met, you and I, under most remarkable circumstances. I'm grateful to you for your offer of help; please thank Jaime for having asked you to make it. But what reason can there be for me to leave Madrid?'

'The fascists know your son is in the army. Do you realize that you stand a good chance of being shot?'

'Certainly.' A smile rippled down his thick eyelids and sagging cheeks. Then he pointed with his spectacles to the bottle. 'I've bought that brandy.'

The old man had the knobbly face, the lean hook-nose of Jaime, and the self-same eyes now that a shadow was casting two black disks, like smoked glasses, on his face.

'Do you mean,' Alvear went on, 'that the risk's enough to separate me from – ?' He pointed to the book-lined walls. 'Why? But why? It's curious. I've lived for art, immersed in art, for forty years, and how can you, an artist, wonder if I prefer to go on doing so? Listen to me, Monsieur Scali; I ran a picture-gallery for many, many years. I was the first to show people here the Mexican baroque art, Lopez's sculpture, Georges de Latour, our primitives. A woman would come to my gallery, look at a Greco, a Picasso, or an Aragonese primitive. "How much?" Usually she was an aristocrat, who came in her Hispano, with all her diamonds ... with all her miserliness. "Excuse me, Madame; why do you want to buy that picture?" Almost always she replied, "I don't know." "Then Madame, go home and think it over. When you know why, you can come back."'

Amongst all those with whom Scali came in contact and with whom he had been living since the war began, Garcia was the only man with any sense of mental discipline. And Scali felt all the more affected by the intellectual fellowship which was growing up between him and the old picture-dealer, because he had had a particularly trying day – and because, painfully conscious of his weakness as a leader, he was drawn to a world in which he felt at ease.

'They came back, those women?' he asked.

'They did their best to "know why" on the spot. "I want that picture because I like it ... because I think it's fine ... because Mrs So-and-So has one." Everyone knew that the finest Grecos in Spain were to be had at my place. Well, I wouldn't sell to her.'

'When did you consent to sell?'

Alvear raised a gnarled finger, matted with curly hair. 'When she said: "Because I *need* it." Then, if the woman was rich, I sold it to her – at a fabulous figure. But if it was somebody poor who "needed it", I sometimes gave it away.'

Two gun-shots rang out close to the house, followed by a clatter of footsteps scattering out fanwise.

'With these inside shutters,' Alvear remarked in a casual tone, 'it's impossible for people outside to see the light in here. ... Yes,' he continued, 'I sold according to the faith that's in me, Monsieur Scali. Sold my wares. I doubt if anyone could carry his faith further! Tonight it keeps me company. The Moors are coming? Well, why should I care?'

'So you'd let yourself be killed – out of sheer indifference?'

'Not indifference.' Alvear half rose, and his hands still resting on the chair-arms, gazed intently at Scali, as if to emphasize what he was saying. 'Not indifference. Disdain. Still – d'you see this book? It's *Don Quixote*. I was trying to read it just now. Couldn't manage it.'

'In the churches of the south where there'd been fighting, I sometimes saw great pools of blood in front of the pictures. And the pictures ... had lost their efficacy.'

'We've got to have new pictures, that's all,' Alvear said, slowly winding the tip of his beard round his forefinger; the tone of voice was that of a picture-dealer who suggests changing the pictures in a client's flat.

'I see,' Scali said. 'But surely it's rating works of art very high?'

'Not "works of art", but *art*. It isn't always the same works that give access to what is purest in ourselves; but it's always this work of art or that.'

At last Scali realized what had been worrying him ever since the beginning of the conversation. All the expression of that old face was concentrated in the eyes. And, with its usual fatuous malevolence, instinct was leading him, every time old Alvear took off his glasses, to expect to see a blind man's eyes.

'Tonight,' Alvear continued, 'neither philosopher nor novelist has any message. People who deal in life are unavailing in the face of death. Wisdom is more vulnerable than beauty; because wisdom's an impure art. But poetry and music hold good for life and for death. You should read *Numantia* again. Remember it? War is striding through the beleaguered city – with just that distant rumour of running feet. ...' He got up, looked for his collection of Cervantes's works, but failed to find it. 'Everything's topsy-turvy, what with this war ...'

Alvear had taken another book from one of the shelves and was reading aloud the last two lines of Quevedo's famous sonnet.

> ¿Qué pretende le temor desacordado
> De la que a rescatar piadosa viene
> Espiritu en miserias añudado?

The gnarled forefinger following the lines betrayed the pedagogue of old. His shoulders hunched against the chair-back, like a weary old eagle who had taken shelter in this shuttered room, in the armchair, in poetry, he read the lines slowly and with a feeling for their rhythm all the more impressive that his voice was toneless, senile as his smile. Muffled footsteps padding away into the distance, far-off explosions, and all the sounds heard from dawn to dusk that still were haunting Scali's memory seemed circling now like startled animals round that defunctive voice.

'Quite possibly the Arabs may kill me. For all I know, your people may do so in the end. Really it doesn't matter. ... Is it so hard, Monsieur Scali, to await death – that may or may not come, quietly sipping one's drink and reading excellent poetry? By the way, there's a very deep-seated feeling towards death which no one seems to have mentioned since Renaissance times ... And yet in my young days I was afraid of death,' he added parenthetically in a lower tone.

'What feeling?'

'Curiosity.'

He replaced the Quevedo on a shelf. Scali had not now any wish to leave.

'You don't feel any curiosity about death?' the old man asked. 'Any fixed opinion on the subject is, of course, ridiculous.'

'I used to think about it often.' Scali ran his finger through his curly hair. 'But since I've been on active service, I've ceased to do so. Death for me has lost all — what shall I call it? — metaphysical validity. I cracked up once. Well, between the moment when the nose of my plane struck earth and the moment I got wounded — very slightly, as it happened — I didn't think at all; I was just an animal at bay, watching desperately where and when to jump. I suppose it's always like that. A fight to the death with death. All the rest's just association of ideas. There's no need to take death seriously, but pain's another matter. And where there's suffering, art is pretty futile. No picture can stand up against a pool of blood — more's the pity!'

'Don't be so sure of it, my boy. When the French were besieging Saragossa the grenadiers took canvases of the great masters from convents and made tents of them. After a sortie, the camp was crowded with wounded men, amongst whom Polish hussars were to be seen kneeling, saying their prayers in front of Virgins painted by Murillo and serving now as tent-flaps. Yes, art, and not religion only, entered into it, for they never prayed thus before the "popular" effigies of the Virgin. You are deeply versed in art, Monsieur Scali, but you've much to learn about suffering. You're too young now but you'll discover later that suffering becomes less poignant once one realizes there's no changing it.'

A machine-gun began to stutter in short sharp bursts; a lonely, rancorous voice cutting across the little creaking sounds that filled the silence.

'You hear?' Alvear said in a listless voice. 'But the portion of himself which that man who's firing just now is bringing into play isn't, to my mind, the part of him that really matters. What's to prove that the benefits the "economic liberation" they prate about may bring will be greater than the losses entailed by the new order — threatened as it's sure to be on every side, and scared into acts of violence, repression, perhaps delation. I grant you economic servitude's a dreary state of affairs; but if, to do away with it, they're obliged to enforce a political, military, or religious servitude, why should I take sides?'

Alvear was bringing home to Scali a form of experience hitherto outside his range, and one which had a tragic aspect for the little curly-headed Italian. For Scali, what threatened the revolution was not the future but the present. From the day when Karlitch had so surprised him, he had been watching the physiological element of war getting a stronger and stronger hold of many of his comrades, and he had been deeply shocked by it. Moreover, the scene which he had recently witnessed had not been calculated to allay his fears. He was feeling baffled, perplexed.

'I like to be able,' the old man went on, 'to clarify my ideas.'

'That's all very well. But it may cramp one's life.'

'Perhaps.' Alvear's tone was pensive. 'But don't forget the least cramped life is that of lunatics. I like to consort with people for what they are, not for their ideas. I want true loyalty amongst friends, not the sort of loyalty that hangs on a political opinion. I want a man to feel responsible to himself — and that, you know, Monsieur Scali, whatever folk may say, is the hardest thing of all — not to any cause, even the cause of the underdog.'

Alvear lit a cigar. 'In South America' — a puff — 'every morning' — another puff — 'the monkeys always set up a terrific outcry. Once upon a time, the folk-tale tells us, God promised to change them into men at dawn. Morning after morning they hope for the best, are once again disappointed, and scream their grievances from tree to tree.'

'Hope "springs eternal" as they say, and it's a terrifying thing! A man who has been unjustly sentenced, or has run up against more than his share of ingratitude or baseness or stupidity — well, he's bound to stake his hope on some new order. Amongst other functions, the revolution plays the part that an "eternal life" used formerly to play; that explains many of its characteristics. If only each man would direct upon himself one-third of the efforts he devotes nowadays to politics, Spain would become quite a habitable country.'

'But he'd have to do that *alone*, unaided; there's the rub.'

'A man devotes to any line of action only a limited part of himself; and the more that line of action sets up to be "totalitarian", the smaller is the part of him involved. You know very well Monsieur Scali, how hard it is to be a *man*, far harder than the politicians think.' Alvear had risen from his chair. 'But good heavens!' he exclaimed. 'How can a man like you, the interpreter of Masaccio and Piero della Francesca – how can you endure the present state of things?'

Scali wondered whether the words conveyed Alvear's real thoughts, or his grief.

'So be it!' he replied after a short pause. 'Tell me, have you ever lived amongst uneducated men?'

It was Alvear's turn to muse before replying. 'I don't think so. . . . But I've a good imagination.'

'Do you know some of the famous sermons of the Middle Ages?'

Alvear nodded.

'Well,' Scali continued, 'those sermons were listened to by men still more ignorant than those who are fighting at my side. Do you think those sermons were understood?'

Alvear rolled the tip of his beard around his finger; his look implied: I can see what you're leading up to.

'Certainly,' was all he said.

'You spoke of hope just now. Well, men who are joined together in a common hope, a common quest, have, like men whom love unites, access to regions they could never reach left to themselves. And there's more nobility in the *ensemble* of my Flight than in almost any of the individuals composing it.'

Scali had taken off his glasses and Alvear's eyes were intent on the face that seemed lit up with beauty, now that he was expressing what he was meant to express: ideas. And there was a mysterious symmetry between the thick lips and the rather narrow eyes.

'I am sick and tired,' Scali continued, 'of many things in my present life, and yet I find it's just such circumstances bring out what is – how shall I put it? – most fundamental in man. "In the sweat of thy face shalt thou eat bread." And that's true for us, you know; truest of all when the sweat is icy cold.'

'Yes, of course, you're all of you hypnotized by what is "fundamental" in man!' Suddenly Alvear's voice grew earnest. 'The age of fundamentals is returning. And reason has to be rebuilt on a new basis.'

'Do you think Jaime was wrong to join up?'

Alvear's hunched shoulders quivered, his loose cheeks sagged a little lower. 'Let the world go fascist,' he said, 'but let my son get back his eyes.' Shrill with speed, a car sped past, receded. 'Do you think he'll get back his sight?'

'The doctors say it's possible.'

'So they say that to you! To you, as well! Of course they know you're his friend. And you're in uniform. Yes, they'd lie to any officer in these days; they're afraid of being taken for fascists, if they tell the truth, the wretched fools!'

'Why must what they tell me be necessarily untrue?'

'Do you think it's easy to believe even the truth, when it hangs on just one man's word, and when all one's happiness is staked on it?' He was silent for a moment, then continued listlessly, though in a firmer voice: 'The only hope that the New Spain has of keeping that for which you and Jaime and so many others are fighting, is that somehow the thing which we've been trying our best to inculcate year after year may be preserved ...'

He listened to something in the street, got up and walked to the window.

'Meaning – what?' Scali asked.

The old man turned. His voice was like a sigh of regret. 'The human element; the quality of man.'

He stood listening a little longer, then switched off the lights, and set the window ajar. Across a counterpoint of footfalls the 'International' drifted in. In the darkness his voice was more remote than ever, like a voice coming from a smaller body; a sadder, and still older voice.

'Well, if the Moors are here presently, the last song I'll have heard will be that hymn of hope played on a blind man's concertina.'

He spoke quite unemotionally, smiling perhaps a little to

himself. Scali heard the shutters closing, and for a moment the room was plunged in darkness. Alvear found the switch and turned on the light again.

'For it they need our world,' he said, 'in the hour of defeat, they'll need it too when the time comes for rejoicing.' He glanced at Scali who had just sat down on the sofa. 'Yes, Monsieur Scali, it wasn't the gods who created music, it was music created the gods.'

'Or perhaps what's happening outside there is what created music.'

'The age of fundamentals is returning.' Alvear said again.

He poured out a glass of brandy and drank it off. His face was expressionless. Scali was sitting just within the range of the lamp-light, which glinted on his forehead and crisp hair.

'That's where Jaime always sits when he comes to visit me. You, too, are wearing glasses. When he takes his off I can't bear to look at his face.'

For the first time a note of grief throbbed in the old, toneless voice, as Alvear murmured slowly to himself in French:

Que te sert, ô Priam, d'avoir vécu si vieux!

He raised his head, his brows puckered under the wisps of straggling hair, and looked Scali up and down; there was something at once childlike and haunted in his gaze.

'Nothing's more horrible than the mutilation of the *body* that one loves.'

'I'm his friend,' Scali said, in a low voice. 'And I'm used to wounded men.'

'It so happens,' Alvear said, 'that exactly in front of his eyes, on those shelves over there, are all my books on painting, with thousands and thousands of the photographs over which he used to pore. ... Still, do you know, when I turn on the gramophone – when there's music in the room – I can look at him, even if he isn't wearing his spectacles.'

VIII

Manuel, too, had found the Ministry of War made over to defunctive candles. Those vast, lugubrious halls where the last

Spanish Kings had staged their tawdry imitations of the spacious days of Charles the Fifth – Manuel had known them packed with milicianos sleeping on the sofas, each with a revolver on his chest, while the Premier listened in at a wireless set in a far corner; then, after that, he had seen them neat and orderly under the strict, rather pettifogging discipline of Caballero. Orderly they still were, but now the windows gaped upon a nerve-racked city, and when he switched on a lamp the arm-chairs had a positively startled air. The one exception was the War Minister's room where all the lights were on, and the French captain still was waiting by himself. On the staircases the candles had ceased to shed the theatrical illumination Garcia and Guernico had seen; now, on the point of guttering out, they shed no more than a dim religious glow. Here and there, along an arcaded inner corridor, hung little lanterns such as are lit by night on handcarts, or to mark blocked roads. Their rays seemed lost on the majestic staircase climbing into the darkness.

The room which General Miaja occupied and Manuel was approaching was high up under the roof. Here, too, the corridors were unlit, but lamplight showed under each door. The General himself was out, but half the staff-officers of the 'Junta of Defence' were sitting in the room, which looked like the lounge of a second-class hotel. The leader of the *dinamiteros*, the chief sapper, Miaja's personal staff and officers of the Vth Corps were there. None of the latter had been a soldier six months earlier; amongst them were a fashion designer, a contractor, a pilot, a factory manager, two members of joint committees of the various parties, steel-factory hands, a composer, an engineer and a garage-keeper. Enrique and Ramos, too, were present.

Manuel remembered the blind miliciano, with his legs paralysed by wounds, who had accosted Azaña.

'What do you want of me?' the President had asked.

'Nothing. Only to say to you: "Good luck and keep your chin up!"'

Then the blind man had hobbled away on his crutches.

It was not a council of war – but that night every gathering was a council of war. The destiny of all these men, formed in

298

active service, followed the same lines as that of Manuel and as that of Spain.

'There's one rifle for – how many men just now?' Enrique asked.

'One rifle between four men,' an officer replied. The officer was the ex-fashion artist and a friend of Manuel's. He was directing the mobilization of the civilians; on the previous day the Communist Party had asked for orders for a general mobilization of the syndicates.

'We've got to make arrangements to collect the rifles,' Enrique said. 'When the first men fall their rifles must be picked up and taken to the rear. The same procedure as the stretcher-bearers. Fix that up tonight, will you?'

The artist went away.

'It is absolutely impossible to unearth any more weapons at Madrid?'

Another voice replied: 'There's not a rifle left except at Police Headquarters. Even the sentries, escorts, and patrol-men have only kept their revolvers. No one's armed in Madrid tonight.'

'If we lose Madrid, we stand to lose the government offices – and, of course, all the leaders and ministers, if there are any left.'

'How are the fortifications coming along?' Miaja's second-in-command enquired.

'Twenty thousand men,' Ramos said, 'are working on them, hammer and tongs. All the members of the building syndicates are there, and with them plenty of volunteers. A man from the Vth Corps is directing operations at every barricade. As things are now the Moors will have a good half-mile and more of solid fortifications to fight their way through. And the day after tomorrow Madrid will be completely surrounded by barricades – not to mention the other defences.'

'The women's barricades are rotten,' an officer remarked. 'Much too small.'

'We've done away with them,' Ramos replied. 'The only ones we're keeping are those which are built on the lines I've just described, and the ones the Vth Corps boys have checked up on and passed as trustworthy. But you're wrong about the women's barricades. They're not too small; quite the contrary. There was no holding the women once they'd started!'

'What the women are doing – about the stocks of petrol in each house, I mean – is pretty futile,' another voice put in.

'Futile perhaps, but excellent for the morale.'

'Look here! Why couldn't all that have been done before?'

'Half our people here – more than that, nine-tenths of them – can't conceive of defending Madrid except inside Madrid. A fellow said to me only this morning, "If ever they reach Madrid, we'll teach them what's what!" "Look here," I told him, "you know where Carabanchel is – or don't you?" He only said: "Madrid's Madrid, and Carabanchel ain't Madrid."'

'Are they advancing on Carabanchel now?' Manuel asked.

'Yes, they're being held up there by the Fifth. But they're advancing from the South, and they'll be attacking on your side as well.'

Manuel had to leave that night for Guadarrama. He was now a Lieutenant-Colonel. His hair was cut short and, in the face that had grown darker, the greenish eyes shone paler than ever.

'I hear that Durruti's men have turned up. Is that so?'

'The railway's cut. We've sent lorries to Tarancon. They're on their way there now.'

'Are they still expecting the planes we've bought in Soviet Russia, for the day after tomorrow?'

No one answered. All knew the planes were being assembled. But how long would that take?

'Who'll they come up against in the South?'

'That depends on the time; just now the International Brigade is being brought up from Vallecas.'

More officers were entering the room.

The last candles on the huge staircase had burnt out. The French captain had left. Only a few decorative lanterns which formerly had hung beside the entrance-gates shed a funereal light, like the lamps in a death-chamber, at the far end of the long, lugubrious vistas. Empty as the last restaurants of Madrid, deserted as its streets, the old palace, like the city, was maturing its defence in silence and in gloom.

A blackbird's song rose through the air in seeming interrogation – and drew an answering whistle. It came again with a note of growing uneasiness; a furious protest followed, then a burst of laughter through the fog. 'You're right,' a voice said, 'we'll keep them out. Till the cows come home!'

The blackbirds were Siry and Kogan, of the first International Brigade. Kogan was a Bulgarian and knew no French. They were whistling to each other; question and response.

'Quiet.'

A dozen shells answered.

Germans, Poles, Flemings, and a few French stood waiting, listening to the explosions that were getting nearer. Suddenly they turned round; there was firing behind them.

'Explosive bullets,' the officers shouted. 'Nothing to worry about.'

The sound of the bullets cut through the mist so clearly that the ear could follow their actual flight. The battalion had been named after Edgar Andreas when they first started training. On the previous night the Germans had heard that Edgar Andreas's imprisonment under Hitler had been ended by the headsman's axe.

For months past, almost all the Germans had lived the wretched unselfconfident life of newcomers in a strange country. They were waiting. They had been waiting for three years. Now at last they were on the point of winning their spurs.

The Poles were tensely awaiting orders.

The Frenchmen were talking.

The shells were getting nearer. Half-consciously, many of the men were touching each other – a leg or a shoulder – as if the physical nearness of their companions were their sole defence against death.

Siry and Kogan were clinging to each other. They were too young to have been through the Great War, but old enough to have done their military service; fit for the front, therefore, after a fortnight's training. Siry was short and sturdy, with the gestures of a comedian and a broad, triangular face of pronounced swarthiness. Kogan looked like a tousled feather-duster, with his shock of hair always bolt upright.

They had shared the same blanket that night; all the troops had slept in pairs, for the November night had been cold. Kogan thought that he had never developed such a feeling of friendship for any man in so short a time. Whenever a shell fell near them, Siry gave vent to his birdlike whistles indicating approval, protest, or indifference. A '155' failed to explode, disappearing through the mud, into the bowels of the earth. Siry flapped imaginary wings, protesting frantically.

'The Moors!'

No: overstrained nerves. The mist was beginning to thin, but there was nobody in sight. Nothing but explosions and a deserted wood.

'Down!'

They flung themselves with one accord upon the scented moss, evocative of childhood. A batch of men hit in the face were falling back down the slope, with fingers already red with blood pressed to their wounds. Their comrades rose to salute with clenched fists, despite the bullets. But only one of the wounded saw them, disclosing, as he raised an answering fist, a face that might have been the incarnation of war. Branches were falling all round them, like so many men. 'If only there was a way down into this blasted ground!' Siry said.

'Forward!'

Bent double, they began to advance through the wood. They could hear the Moors advancing, too, but could see nothing except a tree or two which the mist assimilated with the spouts of earth thrown up by the bursting shells. There was no whistling now. Since they had started to move forward, since their legs had begun to carry them into action, they were thinking of nothing but the moment when the Moors would appear. And yet even the most ignorant of them felt also that events of incalculable significance depended upon their conduct on that misty morning.

The Fleming on Siry's right (Kogan was on his left) was hit in the leg, bent down to feel his calf, received two more bullets in his chest, and fell. The Moors had established a cross-fire.

Siry was amazed not only that so many bullets should be directed at him personally, but that there could be so many bullets in the whole world. But he was delighted to find that he had such control over himself. Fear was there, but not to the point of utter mental or physical inhibition. He was all right. 'We'll teach them a thing or two about Frenchmen!' Each member of the Brigade felt that in such a moment he was the custodian of the military prowess of his particular nation. An officer began to shout an order, and fell with a bullet in his mouth after the first two syllables. Siry felt a surge of anger; this assassination of his comrades was becoming something personal. A wounded captain was carried past by two soldiers. 'Stick it out,' he said. 'And above all don't throw your lives away needlessly.' Between the crashing shells Siry noticed the silence of the men. Only one phrase could still be heard, from several throats:

'They've got me!'

The Brigade were advancing through the haze. Were they ever going to get a sight of the Moors?

Heinrich was feverishly directing operations amid the telephones and hubbub of a field-headquarters. A civilian arrived. He had stiff grey hair and a moustache.

'What do you want?' Albert asked him. Albert was the general's adjutant; a sturdy, crisp-haired Hungarian Jew, ex-student, ex-dish washer.

'I hold the rank of captain in the French army. I have been a member of the World Anti-Fascist Committee since its formation. I've spent the whole day sitting on a chair at the War Ministry, surely I can do something better than that. Finally they sent me here. I am at your service.'

He handed Albert papers showing his army record and membership of the Committee.

'That's all right, sir,' Albert said to the general.

'A Polish company have just lost their second captain,' said the general.

'Very well.'

The captain turned to Albert.

'Where are the uniforms?'

'No time,' Heinrich grunted.

303

'Very well. Where are the men?'

'You'll be shown the way. I should warn you that the position is not ... a sinecure.'

'I served through the War, sir.'

'Good. Splendid.'

'I was born lucky. Bullets don't worry me.'

'Splendid.'

*

In between the trees in the West Park, so unsuggestive of war, beyond the motionless bodies of those who were taking no further interest in the fighting because they were dead, Siry at length had his first sight of turbans, moving behind the trunks like fat, furtive pigeons.

'Stick your bayonets in the ground!'

He had never seen the Moors. But a few nights before, detailed for liaison work, he had spent an hour within a hundred yards of their trenches. The November night had been thick and foggy. Though he could see nothing, during the whole of that time he distinctly heard the beat of their drums rising and falling beside their fires; and he awaited them now as he would have awaited the onslaught of a savage tribe. The Moors were supposed to be drunk when they attacked. Standing up, lying prone or dead, aiming and firing, all around him were his comrades from Ivry, and with them workers from Grenelle, Courneuve, and Billancourt, Polish emigrés, Flemings, exiles from Germany, men from the Budapest Commune, doctors from Antwerp, representatives of proletarian blood from half Europe. The turbans were dodging about behind the tree-trunks, as if taking part in some fantastic variation of 'puss-in-the-corner'.

Nearer and nearer they had been coming ever since Melilla.

Long blades of bayonets and sabres were moving through the mist; steel sharp and sheenless.

Where cold steel decides the issue, the Moors are among the finest troops in the world.

'Fix bayonets!'

The International Brigade were going into action for the first time.

They drew their bayonets. It was Siry's first battle. He was

304

not thinking that he would be killed, or that he would get through the day. He was thinking: 'Niggers just don't realize!' Would it be like the bayonet practice on the training ground? Or just a quick rip through the guts?

Between two shells, a distant voice could be heard behind the trees.

'For the Republic! Forward, Comp...!'

The end of the order was inaudible.

Every eye was fixed on the approaching Moors. Then another voice, much nearer, shouted across the mist words which each of them might have guessed in advance – words less important in themselves than in the vibrant fervour of their utterance – words which made each one of the crouching men stand needlessly erect.

'For the Revolution and for Liberty, Number Three Company – Forward!'

*

His shaven neck as furrowed as an anxious forehead, Heinrich was sitting with a telephone receiver to each ear. Company by company, the Brigade was launching bayonet attacks.

Albert put his receiver down.

'I can't make things out a bit, sir. Captain Mercery reports: "large quantities of booty; objective in our hands; at least two tons of soap captured!" '

Mercery was in command of a Spanish company on the right of the International units.

'Soap! What on earth does the damned fool mean?'

Albert picked up the receiver again.

'What? What factory? What factory, Christ Almighty?'

'He's explaining how useful the soap will be,' he said to Heinrich. The general was studying a map.

'What is the map-reading?'

Heinrich changed receivers.

'That's it,' he said. 'He got the wrong coordinate and he's captured a soap factory which was already ours! Ask the general in command of the Spanish troops to have that idiot relieved right away.'

*

The bayonets they were about to use were longer than they had thought. All that Siry could remember of the last quarter of an hour was a nightmarish chaos of bushes and large trees hurtling through the air, crashes of bursting shells drowning the noise of the explosive bullets, and the advance of the Moors, with their gaping mouths emitting unheard yells.

A detachment of Germans had just relieved Siry's company, which was retiring to form up again behind the line. The wood was strewn with Moors lying as thick as litter after a bank holiday. But while the battalion was charging, he had not noticed them. A Polish company was rumoured to have crossed the Manzanares.

*

'What about the captain with the Poles?'

'When he saw how things were, he said: "This position is untenable; you must abandon it. Those who reach our lines are to say that it was evacuated by my orders. You'd better leave by the back windows. You'll run into just as many shells that way, but not quite as many bullets. Carry on! And say that I did what had to be done." He put on the dead captain's tunic, went downstairs, and shot himself through the head. He fell right across the doorway.'

'How many got clear?'

'Three.'

Siry had lost touch with Kogan; neither of his new neighbours understood French (other than words of command), and they could not whistle. Siry knew that behind his battalion there were nothing but barbers carrying rifles; their reserve was known as 'The Figaro Battalion'. When the diabolical din slackened, he heard the firing of the Durruti column, which was steadily advancing.

And the 'Ironsides' were advancing, the socialists were advancing.

Behind the bloody confusion which reigned in the West Park, a line of attack was developing over a front extending the full length of the city. The Spaniards who, posted between the houses, had beaten off three attacks that morning, had just received the order to launch an attack. The houses captured by the Moors were being retaken with hand-grenades, dynamite was holding up the tanks, and the Moors driven back by the bayonets of the International Brigade were meeting the anarchists pushing the Republican field-guns through the streets towards the front line.

Behind them the mobilized syndicates were waiting to take over the rifles of the first casualties.

The fascists had been gaining ground ever since they left Morocco, but now that they had reached West Park they were yielding it.

Now that the line of the Moors had been broken, the decimated detachments of the International Brigade were retiring, and, after forming up in new companies, returning to the attack. The Moors were in full retreat. The Durruti anarchists, the units representing the various Catalan parties, the socialists, the bourgeois 'Ironsides' – all were pressing their advantage.

'Hallo!'

It was Albert who held the receiver now.

'The enemy are counter-attacking again, sir.' The general was beside him.

'More tanks?'

Albert repeated the question over the line.

'No, no new tanks.'

'Any planes?'

Again Albert put the question.

'Usual number.'

He did not hang up the receiver, but sat staring at his foot, which was shaking. On the table the receiver quivered.

'That's the stuff, sir! They're falling right back to the Manzanares. And they're going to re-cross the Manzanares, sir!'

*

Company after company was streaming past Siry's detachment with fixed bayonets, and the ground which he and his comrades now were occupying yard by yard was strewn with men with haggard, war-worn faces. Company after company charged past them, nation after nation, stooping, rifle in hand, advancing at the double through a mist that was clotted with the smoke of battle. It was like a battle-scene in a film – and yet how different! Each of these men Siry knew for one of his kind, a brother. And some were coming back with fists pressed against their faces or clutching their bellies with both hands — if they came back at all. They had accepted that; and so had he. And he still accepted it. Behind them lay Madrid, loud with the incessant roar of distant rifles.

Another forward surge brought them to a narrow river.

Men were shouting: 'The Manzanares!'

A blackbird broke into ecstatic song. Somewhere in the mist, his life-blood gushing out on to the fallen leaves from a bayonet wound in the thigh, Kogan made answer for the wounded, for the dead.

TWO

Comrades' Blood

I

INTO the profound silence crept an even deeper note, till presently it seemed to Guernico that the whole sky was full of it. It was not like the crisp hum of a racing car – which reveals the presence of a single plane – but a very massive throbbing that grew deeper and deeper, sustained like a ground bass. Whenever he had heard planes before, the sound had been irregular, rising and falling. But this time the engines were so numerous that everything was merged into a single implacable, robot progress.

The city was practically without searchlights. How could the Government fighters, such as were left, hope to find the fascists in that blind darkness? The deep, full drone which permeated sky and town and night alike set the nerves tingling at the roots of Guernico's hair in the long moment of sickening suspense before the bombs fell.

At last a muffled explosion rumbled through the ground like a distant mine; then one by one, he heard three very violent detonations. Another dull explosion; then nothing more. Another; somewhere above Guernico the windows of a big flat opened all together.

He refrained from using his electric torch; the milicianos were all too ready to imagine that a light was a signal. The drone of the engines went on, but the bombs had ceased. In the pitch darkness, the fascists were quite invisible from below and the city was almost invisible from above.

Guernico tried to run, but stumbled at every step over heaped-up paving-stones. And the utter darkness made it impossible to follow the pavement. A car dashed past, with its headlights tinted blue. Five more explosions, some rifle-shots, a desultory burst of machine-gun fire.

The concussions still seemed to be taking place somewhere

below the ground, and the bursts about ten yards up in the air. Not a glimmer of light; more windows were flying open, impelled by some mysterious agency. Following an explosion nearer at hand, shattered panes of glass fell from a great height on to the roadway. By the sound Guernico realized that he could only see up as far as the first storey. Like an echo from the broken glass, his ears caught the clatter of a bell. It came nearer, passed in front of him, and was lost in the darkness; the first of his ambulances. Finally he arrived at the headquarters of the first aid service. The street was filling up in the darkness.

Doctors, nurses, surgeons, and those with organizing jobs were all, like him, reporting for duty. At last his ambulances were in being. The responsibility for the purely medical side lay with a doctor. Guernico looked after the organization of the relief units.

'We're all right at present,' the doctor said, 'but we soon won't be, if things go on like this. We are having to send out the ambulances in relays, what with the swine bombing San Geronimo Hospice, San Carlos Hospital, and so on ...' An institution for old men, and a hospital. Suddenly Guernico pictured the wounded stumbling through the wards at San Carlos – in the dark.

'Have the ambulances all got the right number of torches?' he asked calmly.

'Look at that blaze. The fascists must be using thermite bombs.'

The doctor opened the inside shutters.

'Look !'

On all sides, gleams of rosy light were flickering behind the dark houses. Guernico wondered whether a Great Fire of Madrid was now beginning. He repeated the question with patient insistence.

'The torches are in the ambulances all right, aren't they?'

'I don't expect so. But I assure you, we won't need them.'

Guernico organized things with a calmness that astonished the surgeons; he was impervious to life's comedies and tragedies. He gave orders for the torches to be placed in each ambulance; in that impenetrable darkness, light was the first essential for the work of rescue.

Another explosion; the windows shuddered. While one of the nurses was closing the shutters again they heard the bells of two ambulances go clanging through the night.

Another detonation. It seemed as though the bombs, light ones no doubt, were being thrown with the savage accuracy of grenades rather than dropped from planes. Guernico had sat down and begun examining the telephone messages which were being handed to him on slips of paper.

'They're all round the Palace,' he said.

'One thousand wounded,' said the doctor. 'And so it goes on.'

The hospital and the Soviet embassy were in close proximity.

'Calle San Augustin,' said Guernico. 'Calle de Leon. Plaza de Las Cortes.'

'Anyhow they're hitting able-bodied men and women now, not wounded,' a doctor remarked.

An assistant half-opened the windows from which the doctor had flung back the shutters; dominating all other sounds — words of command, buzzing telephones, the tramp of marching feet (almost indecently unflurried), and the continual clanging of ambulance-bells — the even drone of the fascist air-fleet came flooding into the room.

A sudden draught sent some papers whirling into the air; one of the nurses who had accompanied the ambulance sent to the old men's hospice, was coming in.

'Well, this is a nice business! Guernico, my dear, they'll need at least two more ambulances at the Institution!'

'Shut the door, Mercedes,' the doctor shouted, chasing his papers like so many butterflies.

'What brutes they are!' she said, as if she had been speaking of the engines upon whose drone the window had been closed once more. 'Things are in a shocking mess over there. Those poor old men are trampling each other down on the stairs. They're in a panic, naturally.'

'How many casualties?' Guernico asked.

'Oh, the first ambulance will take all the casualties. The problem is, how to evacuate the others.'

'The ambulances are intended for casualties; and we shall have quite enough of them. Are the old men in the cellars anyhow?'

'I should say so!'

'And the cellars – are they pretty solid?'

'Rather! They're like catacombs.'

'Good.'

He ordered one of the assistants to warn the Junta.

'You know, Guernico,' Mercedes said in a low voice – she had suddenly grown calm – 'some of them are going crazy.'

'What sort of bombs are they? Incendiary?' the doctor asked.

'The people who seem to know about that sort of thing call them calcium bombs. Green they are, like absinthe. Horrible things, you know; it's impossible to put them out. And those poor chaps running down the corridors, groping in the darkness like blind men! And others hobbling on crutches! It's ghastly!'

'Where did the bomb fall?'

'In a passage between the wards.'

Was one of the windows badly shut? The persistent drone of the planes was echoing inside the room now, punctuated by bursts of fire from a Republican machine-gun – an attempt to raise morale, no doubt. But from below, as though it were coming up from the foundations of the building, a long, incessant rumble like the roll of muffled drums was rising and falling on the air; along the Manzanares, the International Brigade was launching a new attack against the Moors.

'Where's the fighting taking place?' Guernico asked.

Mercedes answered him. 'Everywhere.'

'At the Casa del Campo and the University City,' the doctor said.

An explosion in their immediate neighbourhood made the pens jump on the table. There was a noise of tiles falling on distant roofs, the scurrying footsteps of a crowd running for shelter. Then, after a moment's silence, a scream, sudden and intolerably shrill, rose through the darkness. Then silence fell once more.

'An incendiary bomb on the French Embassy,' Guernico said; he had taken up the telephone receiver again. 'Another present from non-intervention.' He turned to an assistant. 'The motor-cyclists are at their posts, aren't they? ... Two bombs have fallen near the Plaza de Las Cortes ... Send six dispatch-riders to Cuatro Caminos at once.'

Another assistant whispered something into his ear.

'Send another ambulance to San Carlos,' he continued. 'There are a number of casualties there. And tell Ramos to go and have a general look round, please.'

Since the beginning of the siege, Ramos had been given the task of directing the help of the Communist Party to the points where it would be most efficacious. Though he had rendered useful service to the medical staff, which was short of anaesthetics and X-ray plates, he had not so far played an active part in ambulance work. But, as from tonight, first aid was to be one of the principal functions of the Junta at Madrid . . .

II

Ramos was travelling as fast as his blue-screened headlights would permit.

He stopped the car at the first big fire. The darkness was loud with muffled cries, echoes of racing feet, explosions, calls for help, and the long-drawn crashes of falling buildings, sounding above the never-ending din of battle. A convent was collapsing in a cataract of toppling masonry, over which sleek scarlet flames were scurrying, like hungry beast of prey, through the red rolling smoke. The building had been evacuated and pickets of milicianos, Assault Guards, and first-aid parties were watching the scene, fascinated by the exultant havoc of the flames, their irrepressible vitality. A grey cat sitting on the kerb raised its eyes to watch.

Was the air-raid over, all were wondering.

A faint glow kindled on the left. In a sudden lull a tramp of heavy boots and a sound of shouting in the distance jarred the silence.

The faint glow grew into an incandescence shaped like the head of a tremendous artichoke, then sank again, and presently a vast glare began to light up the sky and houses. Though the bombers had flown back – their landing-grounds were near, and November nights are long – under the roofs innumerable fires were surreptitiously alive, creeping from floor to floor; to the left four more houses were ablaze, not with the blue-green flare of calcium, but vomiting great bursts of tawny flame. When Ramos passed, the big conflagrations had dwindled to a horde of little restless wisps of fire, battening on the houses like a plague of insects. There was a general exodus in progress; hand-carts, piled high with mattresses and chairs, lumbered past him, followed by old women, the last to leave. Ambulance sections were speeding up. Doing their work well, too. Ramos counted ten of them.

At San Carlos, where the houses acted as a screen, it was pitch dark in nearly all the streets around the Plaza. Ramos ran into a stretcher; the bearers cursed him roundly. Like a cloud of fiery confetti, a flurry of sparks swept across the bodies of the wounded, laid out in rows; and for a second their limbs glimmered faintly in the darkness. Three yards further on Ramos collided with another stretcher; this time it was the wounded man who cursed him. On an islet of roof, at a street corner, the black forms of a group of firemen swayed above the huge flames they were fighting with their preposterous little hoses. At last Ramos reached the Plaza.

The gusts of smoke were coming faster and the glow was increasing. Everything was becoming visible; the cats in the street, the lint bandages round the heads of the wounded. And, like an accompaniment to the roaring of the flames, once more the dim sky throbbed with a deep drone of engines.

So desperately anxious was Ramos that these wounded men should have some peace – they were being gradually evacuated in ambulances – that he almost persuaded himself the sound was only that of heavy cars coming towards him. But then a slithering avalanche of rafters stifled for a moment the fury of the flames and a great cloud of sparks whirled up across the sudden silence – and in the lull there was no mistaking the drone of aeroplanes deploying overhead. Two batches of four bombs each, eight crashes, were followed by a confused, startled din of voices, as if the whole city had wakened in alarm.

A peasant miliciano, whose dressing had come undone, was standing beside Ramos, watching the blood trickle down his bare arm and splash drop by drop upon the mud. In the sombre flamelight his skin looked red, and the blood, pale brown as it ran down his arm, turned in falling to a bright diaphanous yellow, like the tip of Ramos' cigarette. He had the man evacuated at once. Other wounded men with arms that seemed to be in splints were drifting past in measured cadence, like the mimes in a dance of death, showing at first as flat black silhouettes till as they crossed the square and came into the dark glow of the fires, their light-coloured pyjamas grew a bright and brighter red. All the casualties were soldiers; they showed no signs of panic, but observed a self-imposed discipline of weariness and helplessness, of rage and resolution. Two more bombs fell and the long line of wounded men rippled like a wave ...

There was a telephone-box a hundred yards off, up a dark side-street. As Ramos switched on his torch, he stumbled over a body; the man uttered a cry, his mouth wide open. One of the stretcher-bearers felt his hand.

'He's dead.'

'No,' Ramos said, 'he cried out.'

They could hardly hear each other speak across the roar of aeroplanes, the shrilling of far-off sirens, boom of guns, crashes of bombs. But the man was really dead, his mouth wide open, as if in the act of crying out; perhaps he had cried out. Ramos walked on. More stretchers, more shouting, and then a sudden glare scattered the darkness into a multitude of crouching forms ...

Manuel rang up, asking for ambulances and lorries; a good many of the wounded could be evacuated in lorries. Evacuated where? he wondered, as he said it. One after the other, the hospitals were going up in flames. Guernico had told him to go to Cuatro Caminos. It was one of the poorer quarters and had been a favourite target since the siege began. (Franco, rumour said, had announced that he would spare the fashionable quarter, Salamanca.) Ramos got into his car again.

In the glare from the conflagrations, through the spectral sheen of misted street-lamps, and along streets of total darkness, one of the great migrations history reiterates was silently afoot. Many peasants from the Tagus had taken shelter with relations here, each family had brought its donkey. With their quilts, alarm-clocks, canary cages, and pet cats in their arms, all were streaming out – why they knew not – towards the richer quarters, unflurried, stolid as poor folk are stolid. Bombs were falling, falling to teach the under-dog to 'keep his place'.

Driving past some gutted houses, Ramos saw in the weak

glow of his blued headlights some twenty bodies laid out parallel on the road; of all shapes and sizes, they looked alike beside the havoc of their homes. He stopped his car and whistled for an ambulance, thinking how effectively the interminable thunder of those planes far overhead had ranged all sorts together – anarchists, communists, socialists, and republicans – in that ultimate fraternity of death.

In the darkness sirens wailed, nearing, meeting, crossing each other, with long hootings that died out on the clammy air like the hooting of liners putting out to sea. One car halted and its call, motionless amidst the moving patterns of shrill sound, rose forlorn as the baying of a lost dog. In a reek of burning wood and scorched masonry, under flurries of bright sparks that raced along the streets like mad patrols, the vicious detonations of the bombs seemed to be hunting down the jangle of the ambulances, spraying them with showers of flying steel, whence they emerged, as from a tunnel, clanging their way between the frenzied sirens. The slums of Cuatro Caminos were as full of poultry as any country village, and with the crashes of the first bombs cocks had started crowing by the thousand; now the ferocious racket of the aerial torpedos had sent them crazy. And, furiously, frantically, all crowing all together, they blared in a shrill chorus, brazen with rage, the battle hymn of poverty, towards the menace of the sky.

Restless as an insect's feeler, the slender beam of Ramos' torch probed the darkness; it lit on another body lying at a lower level than the bodies aligned along the wall. The man was wounded in the side and was groaning. An ambulance-bell was clanging somewhere near by. Ramos whistled. 'It's coming for you,' he said. The man made no reply, but went on groaning. Directed from above, the beam of the torch cast on his face a tracery of shadows from the tall grass growing between the paving-blocks. With the frenzied stridence of the cocks still ringing in his ears, Ramos looked down compassionately at the man's quivering cheek fretted with a delicate pattern of waving grasses, dainty as the line-work of a Japanese print.

On the corner of his mouth fell the first drop of rain.

The first big fires that Madrid had known were glowing behind the trenches of the German section of the International Brigade. The volunteers could not see the planes; but the silence of that crowded night – so different from the hush of a nightbound countryside – mysteriously charged with the undertones of war, was throbbing, like a train changing tracks. The Germans were all together; some had been exiled for being Marxists, some for being romantic and fancying themselves revolutionaries, some for being Jews. And there were some, too, who were not by nature revolutionaries but had become so and accordingly found themselves there. Since the assault on the West Park, they were beating off two attacks a day; the fascists were trying in vain to break through at the University City. The volunteers watched the ruddy glow spreading up the lowering rain-clouds; as with electric signs, an aura of prodigious size is given off by big conflagrations on a misty night, and the whole city seemed to be ablaze. None of the volunteers had yet seen Madrid.

For over an hour a wounded Republican had been crying out.

The Moors were only about half a mile away. They must surely know where the wounded man lay; no doubt they were waiting for some of his comrades to come and fetch him; already one volunteer who had left the trench had been killed.

The volunteers were quite ready to play this stool-pigeon game; what they were afraid of, on this pitch dark night where the only light came from the flame-lit clouds, was that they would not be able to find their way back to their own trenches.

At last three Germans got permission to go and look for the man whose cries came to them through the black mist. One after the other they crossed the parapet and were engulfed in the murk; in the trench the silence could be felt despite the explosions.

The cries were coming from at least four hundred yards away. It would be a long job; they all knew by now that a man does not crawl very fast. And then there was the load to bring back. Provided they did not stand up and provided the dawn did not break too soon.

Silence and battle. The Republicans trying to effect a junction behind the fascist lines; the Moors trying to break through by the University City. Somewhere in the night, enemy machine-guns were firing from the Clinic; Madrid was in flames. The three Germans were creeping along on their bellies.

The cries from the wounded man came every two or three minutes. If a flare were to go up the volunteers would never get back. They must be fifty yards away from the trench by now; the others could smell the stale odour of the mud outside, not quite the same as that inside the trench, as if they had gone with them. It seemed an eternity since the wounded man last called. If they could only keep their sense of direction, if they could at least keep heading straight towards him.

Flat on their stomachs, the three men waited for a cry to guide them through the flame-gashed haze. The voice was silent. That wounded man would never call again.

White-faced, they raised themselves up on their elbows. Madrid was still burning, the German trench still holding out; and to the dull boom of artillery, the Moors were still trying to force the University City under cover of the fog.

IV

Slade stopped before the first gutted house. The rain was no longer falling, but he felt it brooding in the air. Black-shawled women had formed a chain behind milicianos from the salvage corps who were dragging from the ruins a gramophone horn, a bundle, a little chest . . .

From the third storey, cut in section like a stage set, a bed hung down, one leg still caught in a wrecked floor; the contents of this room had tumbled out into the gutter, almost at Slade's feet: pictures, toys, cooking utensils. The ground floor, though ripped open, was still intact, as peaceful as in times of normal life, its inmates having been taken away *in extremis* by an ambulance. On the first floor, above a blood-spattered bed, an alarm-clock was ringing; a small, shrill sound forlorn in the grey desolation of the morning.

The rescue corps were passing their finds from hand to hand. The last miliciano passed a bundle to the first woman. She did not take it by the middle with her hands, as it was offered to her, but held it in her arms; a head fell backwards, for the child was dead. The woman glanced back along the line, found what she was looking for, and began to weep; perhaps she had seen the mother. Slade moved on. Mingling with the damp morning haze, a smell of burning was filling the city with the brisk, cheerful smell of wood burning in autumn forests.

At the next house there were no victims; the occupants, small employees of some kind, were silently watching their shattered house burn down. It was Slade's business to be on the look-out for picturesque and tragic details, but his job revolted him; the picturesque was grotesquely out of place in the circumstances, but tragedy in plenty was to be found in this banal scene, in these thousands of human lives one like another, in these grief-stricken, sleep-starved faces.

'You are a foreigner, sir?' The speaker was a man watching beside him.

The face was refined and old, with vertical furrows – the face of an intellectual. He pointed towards the house, without speaking.

'War revolts me,' Slade said, tugging at his little tie.

'You're getting plenty of it.' And then, more quietly, 'If you can call this war.'

'The electric-lamp factory is on fire over by the Alcalá road, my friend. San Carlo and San Geronimo are alight. So are all the houses round the French Embassy; many of the houses round the Plaza de Las Cortes and the Palace. And the Library.' He did not look at Slade as he spoke; his eyes were fixed on the sky. 'I, too, find war horrible. But less horrible than assassination.'

'Nothing's so bad as war,' Slade said stubbornly.

'Even the giving of power to those who use it as these men are using it?' He was still watching the sky. 'No, I can't accept war, either. Yet how is one to accept this. What am I to do?'

'Can I help you?' Slade asked.

The speaker smiled as he pointed to the burning house, from which pale flames were rising through the grey morning, under a gloomy pall of smoke.

'Every paper I possessed, my friend. I am a biologist.'

A hundred yards in front of them a heavy shell burst in a square. The last remaining windows clattered down, and in the midst of the broken panes a donkey, without making any attempt to run away, brayed dismally as the rain began to fall again.

By the time Slade reached the institution which housed the old men, many of them had emerged from the cellars. The fire was no longer burning, but among those meek, defenceless old people, with their infirmities and their palsied movements, the ravage of the bombing struck a note of supreme incongruity.

'How did you manage?' he asked one of the old men.

'Oh, sir. We're no age to go running about. Running away like that. Especially the ones on crutches . . .'

He took hold of Slade by the sleeve.

'What's going to happen to us, sir? I used to be a barber, with my own special class of customer. All my gentlemen counted on me for their death-bed shave, haircut, everything . . .'

Slade had to listen hard to hear him, for a stream of lorries was passing, shaking intact and fallen walls alike.

'The Popular Front put us here, sir. Very nice and comfortable, it was. But what good has it been? Too good to last, it was! Well, I suppose it will have an end sometime. But so shall I!'

On the first floor the more robust of the old men were working away at something or other which Slade did not quite understand. There were a dozen of them, all with the traditional gravity of aged Spaniards. They worked as if they had been condemned to silence, straining to catch every sound, watching the sky. On the floor above, half deafened by the gongs of the ambulances which were scouring the city in all directions and the ceaseless noise of the lorries, were some milicianos who had been specially detailed to try to drag some of the old men forcibly from under their beds where they had taken refuge in their panic during the bombing; clinging to the iron legs, they refused to be dislodged. Suddenly, like a sinister echo of the ambulances, the warning sirens shrilled through the city. Abandoning the beds, the old men rushed to the doorway of the stairs leading to the cellar, carrying their bedding on their backs; one of them took his whole bed with him, tortoise-like.

Within ten seconds, the first explosion pulverized the fragments of glass that lay on the tables and under the windows shattered by last night's bombs. And as if all Madrid were replying with a punctual tocsin, above the roll of the guns in the University City, one after another, the clocks began striking nine.

'There they are!' one of the milicianos cried.

Slade went under cover of the hospital gateway to watch. First his long pipe, then his nose peered round the corner. Broad-bellied like the German commercial planes he had so often used since he came to Europe, the Junkers came into view from behind a gable; black with their long prows bulging in front of them, flying very low beneath the rain-clouds. They crossed slowly over the street and disappeared behind the roof opposite, followed by their fighters. Chance alone directed the incendiary bombs. They burst right and left, in bunches. Some pigeons took to the air; above their flapping circles the rigid flight of the bombers swept back, inexorable as fate. The utter haphazardness of this death dropped from the sky filled Slade with horror. Hadn't the Government enough pursuit planes left to bring a single machine back from the front? The lorries were still churning past the door, their covers streaming wet; it was raining near by.

'There's a cellar,' a voice said behind him.

He stayed beneath the gateway, though he knew it was but poor protection. Shadowy forms were passing along the walls, stopping for a few moments in front of every gate, then moving on. He had often visited the front, but he had never had this feeling before. War was war, but this was something other than war. What he wanted to see the end of was not so much the aerial torpedos themselves as the particular slaughter-house shambles which they were causing here. The bombs went on falling; no one knew where they would fall next. Slade thought of his interviews and his notes, of the tables laid for dinner in houses that had been sliced open, of the shattered glass of a picture with a little trail of blood beneath it, of a travelling coat hanging above a suitcase – packed for the journey to another world; of a donkey of which the hoofs alone remained, of the long trails of blood left on pavements and walls by the men wounded at the Palace, like the tracks of hunted beasts; of the empty stretchers with a blood-stain where each wound had touched. How much blood there was for this rain to wash away! There were shells intersecting the falling bombs now. After each explosion Slade waited for the rattle of falling tiles. In spite of the rain, the smell of fire began to pervade the streets. And still the lorries streamed past incessantly.

'Where are they going?' Slade asked, tugging at the ends of his little bow-tie.

'Reinforcements for Guadarrama. "They" are trying to break through up there.'

v

Manuel's brigade was advancing from the Sierra de Guadarrama through blinding sheets of driven rain, across a land of shattered church-towers; a 1917 landscape. Slowly they crept down the slopes − clumsy dark forms ploughing their way across the mud. Long lines of ancient furrows streamed down to a deep valley that climbed again toward a draggled horizon, grey in the wan morning light that looked like nightfall. That skyline seemed to end the world, but behind it lay the vast Segovia plain, like sea beyond a cliff-wall, stretching out to infinity. And throughout that unseen world, drenched in lethargic rain, the guns were thundering. Behind it lay Madrid.

The men moved steadily on, floundering deeper and deeper in the deepening mud. Now and then amongst the shell-bursts came another sound, the long-drawn swoo-oosh of a dud diving into the slush.

Manuel's headquarters were quite near the lines. Some other regiments had been attached to his and he was now commanding a brigade. His right wing and centre were doing well; but the left was wavering. In the last engagement 60 per cent of the officers and commissars had been wounded. 'Be so good as to stay at your posts,' he had told the latter an hour before, 'and don't go into battle in front of your men, singing the "International".' The counter-attack was working out well − except for the left wing.

The men on that wing were not those who had fought at Aranjuez, not the Vth Corps which had reinforced them, nor the new troops attached to them; the latter were fighting in the right wing and centre. The left wing consisted of companies from the Valencia area, so-called 'anarchist' companies, though actually the men had never belonged to any syndicate before the war. And since the last day but one, not one of the veteran sergeants was left amongst them; all were dead or in hospital.

Manuel's tanks were advancing in front of the left wing. With the mechanical stolidity, that air of merely taking part in field manoeuvres, peculiar to tanks, they were driving through an artillery barrage of the same volume as that directed on the infantry behind them. But it was not so much the shells that seemed to trouble them as the state of the ground, which looked as if it had been blown to pieces by land-mines. One tank vanished, as though dissolved into the rain; it had fallen into an anti-tank ditch. A column of mud and pebbles shot into the air, and alongside it another tank started to topple slowly, very slowly, over. The rest forged placidly ahead, through showers of heavy clods that, soaring briskly up, floundered to earth between the downward-flashing shells in limp parabolas, forlorn as the interminable cadence of the rain.

For months Manuel had been watching tanks advancing just like this; only, for months, they had been enemy tanks. One day the Aranjuez brigade had built a wooden tank — by way of sympathetic magic, to conjure up real ones. But today those were his own tanks forging ahead, as far as eye could reach — far ahead on the right, and on the left more slowly, followed by the infantry. The Republican heavy guns were pounding the enemy lines; the enemy were retaliating, but failing to hold up the counter-attack. In the grey immensity little specks of a darker grey were advancing behind the tanks: the *dinamiteros*. And the machine-gun sections were occupying small, cramped islets of semi-solid ground, won foot by arduous foot from the all-encroaching mud.

Were more tanks being sent in support of the troops on the extreme left wing? Manuel wondered. And was it because the advance was not progressing at that point? Viewed from end to end, the line of tanks was gradually taking the form of a crescent. It seemed to Manuel that the tanks on the left had actually turned back; those he could see were moving towards him, not against the fascists. Then he understood; those were not reinforcements, they were enemy tanks.

If now the left wing faltered, the whole brigade was as good as wiped out, and through the gap the enemy might sweep down on Madrid. But if the left held, none of the enemy tanks would get back to the fascist lines.

His reserves were in readiness beside the lorries. He could throw them bodily into the battle, as another contingent of reserves was on its way up from Madrid.

The left-wing liaison car pulled up in front of him; the yellow upholstery made it recognizable at once. The commanding officer was sitting in the back of the car, an arm crooked over the folded hood and his head resting on it. He seemed to be snoring.

'What's up?' Manuel asked, flicking his boot with the pine-branch he had in his hand.

The major had ordered him, the chauffeur said, to drive to headquarters. And what Manuel heard was not snoring, but the death-rattle.

'Where's he hit?' Manuel asked the chauffeur. There was no sign of a wound.

'Back of the neck.'

For an officer in action to be wounded in the back is rare; presumably this one had turned.

'Put him down here,' Manuel said, 'then drive back and bring Gartner.'

Manuel had already telephoned orders to get in touch with the civil commissar and send him over.

The car lumbered off, vanished into the deluge. Manuel took up his field-glasses. On the extreme left of his sector he could see men running towards the fascist tanks, which were, apparently, not firing, for no one fell. Manuel turned the screw of his field-glasses, blurring the landscape, then focussed it anew behind the rain. The men were holding up their hands. Going over to the enemy.

They could not be seen by the company behind, as there was some rising ground between.

Behind the small dark specks running with their arms above their heads, like insects waving their antennae, the ground sloped. Sloped all the way down to Madrid. It crossed Manuel's mind that, since the arrival of the new recruits, Falangist inscriptions had sometimes been found in the billets.

The other companies in the rear were firing now. Thinking that the first line was advancing, they were moving ahead, towards certain death. Manuel was puzzled. Couldn't their captain recognize Italian tanks?

Just then he saw the captain being carried up, on a blanket — the dressing-station was just behind Manuel's headquarters. Dead, too. A bullet in the back.

He had been one of the best officers of the brigade, and had formerly led the Aranjuez delegation. Now he lay curled up on his blanket, his grey moustache clotted with raindrops.

There were Falangists amongst the recruits; and the officers were being shot from behind.

The right wing was still advancing.

'The Commissar has just bumped off a fellow,' the chauffeur said.

Manuel told another officer to carry on and, with all his reserves, made haste to the left.

Gartner, the civil commissar with the brigade, scrupulously obeying Manuel's orders 'not to go singing the "International" at the head of the troops', had taken up his position in a pinewood at the beginning of the nearest valley – on which the enemy tanks were now advancing.

A soldier had come running up to him. It was Ramón, one of the old-timers, one of the fifty men from Aranjuez with whom Manuel had 'salted' the recruits.

'Look here, skipper, there's half a dozen swine amongst the rockies, who want to bump off the colonel. Six of 'em. Want to go over to the other side. I pretended to be in with them. They said: "Let's wait for the others." Then they said: "We got the captain laid out, we got the major, now we'll have a shot at the chap in the white tunic." About the captain – that was O.K., you know. The dirty bastards!'

'Yes, I know . . .'

'They want to go over to the enemy. Maybe it ain't them that's going to do in the colonel, but some of the others. Anyhow, when they said that, I said, "Wait a bit, some of my mates want to go over, too." "All right," they said. So I've come to you.'

'How can you get in touch with them again? Now that the whole line's moving up.'

'That don't matter. They won't budge, not they. They're waiting for the enemy tanks to show up. Some dirty trick they've planned. Oh, and then there's another gang of the boys that's raising hell, they say we ought to beat it, we can't hold out against the tanks. The way they yell – there's something up. It don't sound natural to me. So the mates sent me to let you know.'

'What about your regimental commissar?'

'Killed.'

Gartner had ten Aranjuez men with him.

'Boys,' he said, 'there are traitors in the line. They've shot the captain. They're out to kill the colonel and go over to the fascists.'

He exchanged clothes with one of the soldiers who stayed behind. Gartner's angular, clean-shaven face which always looked rather vacant in repose, looked even more so when he took care not to betray emotion. Most vacant of all just now when, taking off his service cap, he set a faded *képi* on his mop of hair, which in a few minutes was sopping with rain. Handing over the post to a regimental commissar he went off with his men.

All the paths in the rolling landscape seemed to converge either on Manuel's headquarters and the casualty-clearing station, or else on the road to which Ramón now was taking Gartner.

As they passed a little clump of pine trees, dripping with rain, two infantrymen came running down a slope towards them, shouting: 'Come on, boys, they're beating it!'

'Them's the ones,' said Ramón to the commissar.

'Two of the six, you mean?'

'No, not them, but the chaps who've got cold feet, the belly-achers. They've all got to pass this way.'

'Where are you going?' Gartner shouted. 'Are you crazy?'

It was unlikely the recruits had ever set eyes on him; their regimental commissar was the only one they knew. Probably they had often seen Gartner before, but just now their thoughts were far from him; and they had no suspicion.

'They're hopping it, I tell you! Not a dog's chance up there. The tanks are coming up! In a half-hour we'll be cut off. They'll mow us down!'

'Madrid's there, at the rear.'

'What the hell do I care?' said the other, a good-looking youth, who now seemed dazed with fright. 'If the officers knew their bloody jobs, we wouldn't have to beat it. Come on, boys! Let's save our skins while we can!'

'Know what they're doing, the men who're bolting now? They're letting the enemy turn our flank. They're letting down their mates who're holding on in the centre! You'll hear about it, tonight. Now, up you go, lads! Up the hill again!'

He barked out the harangue rather than spoke it, across the downpour. Gartner was facing one of the soldiers, his mouth looking grotesquely small in the enormous face. The soldier brought his rifle to the ready.

'Say, you big cod-face, are you trying to win a stripe? If you're that keen on getting yourself smashed up by the tanks, go to it! I ain't stopping you. But if you think you're going to get the rest of us done in you have another think coming!'

Ramón's fist crashed on the man's ribs, sent him sprawling in the mud. The fugitives were disarmed and, escorted by four of Gartner's men, led off to the rear, Gartner pushed forward, at a run. The khaki greatcoats of his men showed grey through the rain.

The six men Ramón had described to Gartner were waiting, crouching in a twenty-foot shell crater, thickly smeared with mud. But they were not standing to for an attack.

'Here's the mates,' Ramón said to them, as if to introduce Gartner and the others.

'Everything set to go?' Gartner asked.

'Hold on!' said the man who seemed to be in command. 'The others are up there.'

'Who?' Gartner asked, with his best dazed air.

'You want to know too much, mate!'

'I don't give a damn. What I want to know is whether they're to be trusted or not. You see, I've got some guns. But not to hand out to the first bloody fool I meet. How many can you do with?'

'Us? Six.'

'Me and my mates, we can have ten machine-guns right now.'

'Nope. Six will do us. No more.'

'Mind, these are the goods. Big 'uns – with the large chargers.'

The man merely patted his rifle, shrugging his shoulders.

'Not that we need them,' said another one of the six. 'But all the same, they might come in handy. We could do with the lot.'

The man who had spoken first nodded acquiescence, as if taking an order. The last speaker had delicate hands. 'That's a Falangist,' the commissar thought.

'Can't you see, men,' Gartner went on, addressing the first speaker, 'it's in a different class from that popgun of yours? This ain't no pocket-pistol. See here. You shove in the charger like this. Got it? Now it's loaded. Fifty rounds. There's six of you ... That makes eight rounds – and two to spare – for each of your dirty mugs. Hands up!'

The one who had talked first had barely time to stretch his hand an inch towards his rifle, when he collapsed into a puddle, a bullet through his head. The blood oozed out through the water, black in the grey light. The enemy tanks were still coming on.

Gartner's men had covered the others with their guns, and were escorting them towards the rear. On their way to the farm, they met Manuel and his lorries. Gartner jumped into Manuel's car and told him what had happened. Manuel had already despatched the anti-tank section of his reserves to the left wing.

The fascist tanks would reach the sector in a few minutes. If the centre held, the reserves could take over the left wing, and if the right kept on advancing, all would go well. This was a critical moment.

The centre was made up of the men from Aranjuez, together with all those who had joined the same unit, experienced troops who had fought at Madrid, Toledo, the Tagus, even in the Sierra; workmen from the villages, *junteros*, farm labourers, small shopkeepers, metal-workers, barbers, textile-workers, bakers. They were fighting over ground criss-crossed with low dry-stone walls, running parallel like the curving lines on military maps. From where they were now they could not help seeing that if the enemy tanks advanced another mile – a matter of five or ten minutes – not one of them would come out of it alive. Manuel had given them the order to hold on; and they held on, hugging their bits of wall, lying flat in folds of the ground, or taking what cover they could behind tree-trunks slenderer than themselves. The enemy trench-mortars were in front and behind, machine-guns were cross-firing, heavy shells coming over through the curtain of rain, searching the whole position. Manuel had first made a tour of inspection of the centre, and there he had seen his men falling one after another, engulfed at once in the mud thrown up by the next batch of shells.

Across the paroxysms of the riven earth roaring up to the streaming clouds, vomiting across the downpour great cascades of clods and stones and blood, Manuel could see a wave of enemy troops advancing, with fixed bayonets. They had no sheen, for the rain melted to liquid slime all that was hurtling up into it from the sodden plain, yet Manuel could feel those bayonets as if they were jabbing at his own flesh. Something was happening amongst those preposterous low walls, in the dim chaos of the deluge. And the enemy – they were not Moors this time – were surging back, as though repulsed not by the old milicianos, but by the never-ending rain, which was already beating their dead into the earth, sweeping away towards their unseen trenches the attacking waves, in a seething spate of dissolution, across the welter of a cloudburst shuddering with explosions countless as the raindrops.

Four times the fascists launched a bayonet charge, four times it melted away into the blinding rain.

The line held. But, pressing Manuel's left, the tanks of the fascist right wing were now engaging his anti-tank section.

*

Pepe was in command of the section. All the old *dinamiteros* who had survived the August fighting and shown the least gift for leadership now held commissions. Pepe was grousing. It was damned bad luck, he said, that his mate Gonzales was not there with him, to see the stunt he was going to try out. But Gonzales was fighting at the University City. All the same, Pepe was jubilant. 'I'll learn 'em a thing or two, this time!' Followed at some distance by the infantry, the fascist tanks were advancing at full speed towards the first valley, where they would be under shelter from the Republican gunfire. There is a track or road of some kind through every valley of the Sierras; the lorries had brought up Pepe and his men in good time.

On each side of the road the country was fairly open, with occasional clumps of pines that showed black against the rain. Pepe's men took up their positions, lying flat on the sodden pine-needles, amid an earthy odour of mushrooms.

The first tank started to traverse the valley, on the right of the road. It was a German tank, very swift and mobile. The *dinamiteros* all had the feeling that the works must be going rusty in that never-ending rain. Fleeing before it was one of the packs of dogs that had gone wild and taken to the Sierras.

The other tanks were coming into view. From his hiding-place Pepe could not see across the undergrowth the ground between him and the tanks which, from where he was, seemed to be advancing along the road, dipping their turrets and jerking them up like restive horses' heads. They had already opened fire, and it seemed as if their caterpillar bands were emitting, not a light mechanical patter of turning links fretting the hiss of the rain, but the hoarse roar of large machine-guns. Pepe was used to machine-guns, and he was used to tanks.

He waited.

Then, his teeth bared in an unamiable grin, he opened fire.

Even a machine can seem startled on occasion. The moment they heard the machine-guns, the tanks charged. Four of them – three in the first line, one in the second – tilted up simultaneously, with an air of puzzlement: 'What on earth is happening to us now?' – and stayed there, rageful, rearing forms, looming across the nightmare rain. Two swung round, one toppled over, the fourth came to a halt, standing on end, against a lofty pine.

It was their first brush with anti-tank machine-guns.

The second wave of tanks had seen nothing of all this – a tank is practically blind. They came on at full speed. The second line of machine-gunners, also lying flat, began firing over the heads of the front line. The tanks were all knocked out – all but four, which got past Pepe and bore down on the second line.

But Manuel had reckoned with this possibility, and given the necessary orders to his men. The second line of machine-gunners slewed round two of their guns, while the others and the men in the front rank continued firing on the main body of tanks which was scattering through the black pine-woods in drunken zig-zags. Pepe, too, swung round. Those four tanks might prove more dangerous than all the rest, if driven by determined men. The brigade, on which they would presently bear down, would think that other tanks were coming after them.

Three had already crashed against three separate pines. Runaways; their drivers had been killed.

The last tank was still advancing under the fire of the two guns. Suddenly it swung on to the empty road and roared away along it, the clatter of its caterpillar bands jangling across the din of the machine-guns. Its own guns silent, it was making a good forty miles an hour along the road, absurdly small and futile between the steepening slopes, a lonely fugitive on the rain-drenched asphalt that gleamed with broken lights reflected from the livid sky. At last it came to a bend, crashed against a cliff, and stayed propped up against it, like a child's toy.

The unhit tanks had taken the same direction as the Republican tanks, and were charging down on their own lines, which were beginning to break up in panic. In front, among the pine trees, grouped round the tank which, standing up on end, looked like some prehistoric effigy of war, other tanks sprawled in every attitude of havoc. They were gradually being coated with broken twigs, pine-needles, and cones that had been ripped off by flying bullets, and seemed already succumbing to rain and rust, as though they had been lying derelict for many months. Manuel, who had just come up, could see, beyond the lurching turrets of the last enemy tanks, the fascist right wing breaking up. The Republican heavy artillery was beginning to shell the line of their retreat.

Manuel went at once towards the centre of his front.

The retreat of the enemy right wing before its own tanks was turning into a rout. The men of Pepe's section who were not manning machine-guns, together with the *dinamiteros* and Manuel's reserves, were now following on the tracks of the fleeing tanks as though they had been their own. The enemy right centre was also beginning to give way. Manuel's troops, reinforced by detachments from the contingent which had been rushed up in lorries from Madrid (the remainder staying in reserve) emerged from the stone walls behind which they had been sheltering, and dashed impetuously forward.

These were the men who, on the day of the fight for the Montaña barracks, had lain flat in the surrounding squares while snipers were shooting at them from every window. And these were the men who had fought in units which had only one machine-gun to the half-mile and had had to lend it round wherever it might be needed; and these the men who, armed with shotguns, had attacked the Alcázar. There were some, too, who had done nothing yet, some who had run away at the sight of a plane, and whimpered at the hospital that their comrades had 'let them down'. And there were men who had fled before the tanks; and others who had faced the tanks with dynamite. All were men who knew that *señoritas* judge the poor man's worth by his servility; they were the innumerable, predestined victims of the firing-squad, impersonal as the drumfire thundering against them along the line.

Guadarrama would not be taken by the fascists today.

His pine-branch to his nose, Manuel stood watching the brilliant advance of the men of Aranjuez and Pepe's company; watching his first victory in progress, marching on through the viscous mud, through the steady, slanting curtain of the rain.

By two o'clock all the fascist positions had been captured; but there a halt had to be called. There was no question of driving on to Segovia. All the reserves of the centre were already in the front line and the fascists were strongly entrenched ahead.

VI

At the 'Granja' the tables along the boulevard were empty, but the back of the restaurant was crowded. The rainstorms from the Sierra, which had been deluging Madrid, had passed. There was a new sound in the explosions; less loud than bombs, they seemed to be taking place some fifty feet above the ground.

'Have our anti-aircraft guns arrived?' Moreno asked.

No one answered.

All the men drinking in the café were more or less acquainted with each other. Glasses shivered in rhythm with the incessant gunfire from the University City. It was the early afternoon and the lamps had not been lit; the only light in the café came from outside, a cavernous half-light filling the long room from end to end.

An officer entered by the swing-doors, flashing the silver facets of a lark-mirror on the grey November air.

'Fires are breaking out again everywhere,' he said. 'And coming our way.'

'We'll put 'em out,' a voice replied.

'Easier said than done. They've started on the Calle San Margos and the Calle Martino de Los Hijos.'

'On the Avenida Urquijo, too.'

'The San Geronimo Hospice, San Carlos Hospital, and the buildings round the Palace are on fire.'

More officers entered. The swing-doors whirled into the café a smell of red-hot stone.

'The Red Cross Hospital.'

'San Miguel Market.'

'Some of those fires have been extinguished. At San Carlos and San Geronimo they're out.'

'What's that noise? Is it our "archies"?'

'Waiter, an absinthe.' The speaker was a man with ragged, unkempt hair, sitting beside Moreno.

'I can't say. But I doubt it.'

'That's shrapnel,' said the officer who had just entered. 'It's coming down in bucketsful on the Plaza d'España. But they're not getting through at Guadarrama.'

He took a chair beside Moreno, who also was in uniform. Moreno looked quite young now that he had shaved and had his hair cut.

'How's the man in the street taking it?' Moreno asked.

'They're only just starting to crowd into the shelters. Somehow they all seem rooted to the spot, especially the women.

Others drop on the ground, others just start screaming. Of course, there's some who want to see the show. And others who go tearing all over the town. The women with children keep on the move.'

'All the morning,' Moreno said, 'I've felt as if an earthquake were taking place.' He meant that it was not so much fear of the fascists that gripped the crowd as the sort of terror a cataclysm inspires; the idea of 'giving in' never entered their heads – one doesn't talk of giving in to an earthquake.

To a jangle of bells an ambulance sped past.

A black crash and the glasses on the tables sprang up like toy rabbits into the air and landed tinkling back amongst saucers, spilt liquor and V-shaped splinters from the windows. The panes had caved in like drum-heads as the bomb exploded on the boulevard outside. A waiter's tray toppled over, bounded on the floor with a thin clash of cymbals, muted by the silence. Half the people in the room rushed for the stairs leading down to the cellars, in a clatter of falling teaspoons others stood their ground in blank suspense ... waiting for the second bomb. None came and, as usual, cigarettes were extracted from dozens of pockets, and dozens of matches flared across the smoke-clouds swirling round the room. Once the smoke had ebbed away through the two large saw-edged gaps of what had once been mirrors, a dead man was seen leaning on the bar of the swing-door between the splintered panels.

'They're aiming at us,' said Moreno's companion.

'Oh, cut it out!'

'You're all a pack of fools – can't you realize how things are? You'll all be killed like rats in a trap. I tell you, they've got us taped.'

'The hell they have!' Moreno growled.

'Sorry, old fellow. I've done my share of fighting, that you can't deny. A straight fight – I've nothing against it. But, as for getting wiped out by an air-raid, nothing doing. I've been working all my life till now, and all the things I've dreamt of lie ahead of me.'

'Then what the hell are you doing here? Why aren't you down in the cellar?'

'Yes, like a bloody fool, I'm staying upstairs. I wonder why?'

' "Watch how I act, don't listen to what I tell you," as the philosopher said.'

Shells were bursting on all sides and wan gleams of wintry sunlight, caught on the scraps of broken glass that littered floor and tables, kept flickering imperceptibly amid little quaking pools of vermouth, absinthe, and manzanilla. The waiters began coming up again from the cellar.

'They say Unamuno's died at Salamanca.'

A civilian came from the telephone box.

'A bomb has just fallen,' he announced, 'on the Puerta del Sol metro station. There's a thirty-foot hole.'

'Let's go and see.' Two voices.

'Were there people sheltering in the metro?'

'Can't say.'

'Over two hundred killed and five hundred wounded; that's what the ambulance corps reported at noon.'

'And that's only a beginning.'

'They say there's been a battle at Guadarrama.'

The man who had just been at the telephone seated himself before the wreckage of a vermouth.

'I've had my bellyful of it,' grumbled the long-haired man at Moreno's side. 'I tell you once again, they're aiming at us. What the hell are we after here – staying in the heart of the city? It's ridiculous.'

'Hop it, then.'

'Yes, to China or the South Seas, any old place that isn't here!'

'Look! The Del Carmen market's ablaze,' someone began shouting in the street. The clangour of another ambulance cut across the voice.

'To the South Sea Islands? And what'll you do there, I'd like to know! Make necklaces of sea-shells? Organize the savage tribes?'

'What'ld I do? I'd get a boat and go out fishing goldfish! I'd do anything, any darned thing, to get away from all this.'

'Why, man, you hate so much the thought of breaking with the rest of us that you can't even bring yourself to go down to the cellar. But I'm used to that sort of stuff, I used to talk like that myself, in the old days. To Hernandez, poor chap.'

Suddenly he cast an apprehensive glance at the man beside him. Then it had been Hernandez; 'Hernandez is dead,' Moreno thought; 'very likely it's my turn next!' But then the superstitious dread passed from his mind, like the smoke-clouds ebbing from the room.

'I'd meant to cross the frontier to France, then I hesitated, then I was caught up by all the old associations, by life. When I'm under fire I don't believe in "thinking things out" or the "eternal verities", or anything at all. I believe only in fear. Real fear, not the sort that makes one talk, but the fear that sets one running. If you've decided to bolt, there's an end of it; but as in point of fact you're staying here with us, that settles it, and you'd do better to keep silent. See?

'When I was in jail I saw all sorts of things – men playing pitch-and-toss with their lives, for instance, and I looked forward to each Sunday, as no one was shot on a Sunday. I saw men playing games of *pelota* against a wall spattered with human brains and tufts of hair. There were over fifty men under sentence of death whom I used to hear playing pitch-and-toss in their cells. Oh, I'm not making it up; I was there. Right on the spot. Only, old chap, there's something else to it, and don't you forget it. I fought through the Moroccan war; there, too, it was a sort of magnified duel – with an even chance of survival. But here in the front line it's a very different story. After the first ten days you're an automaton, a sleep-walker. You see too many men die, there's too much of the machine in what's against you: tanks, artillery, planes. Fate takes charge, and you're only sure of one thing – that you haven't a dog's chance. You're like a man who's drunk a poison that kills after a certain number of hours, or like a chap who's taken the monastic vow. Your life is over.

'Then the whole world's changed. You get a new line on the truth, and it's all the others who are off their heads.'

' "A new line on the truth!" That's you all over!'

'Yes, that's how it is, one pushes ahead into the barrage; nothing, not even one's own life, makes the least difference. Hundreds of shells are falling, hundreds of men going forward. You're just another case of suicide, yet at that moment you're sharing in all that's best in all of them. You're sharing in ... in something that's rather like the ecstasy of the crowd at Carnival. I wonder if you see what I mean ... I've a pal who calls that the moment when the dead start singing. Yes, for a month now, I've known dead men can sing.'

'Like hell they do !'

'And there's something else which even I, the first Marxist officer in the army, never dreamt of. There's a fraternity which is only to be found – beyond the grave.'

'There's fellows who guessed they'd had enough of it when they had to fight planes with rifles. And there's others as had enough of it when they'd to fight tanks with rifles. Me, I've had enough of it, right now !'

'My nerves used to go all on edge, like yours, but I've got over that !'

'Well, they'll be quieter when you're a stiff.'

'Yes. But now I don't give a damn about it.' Moreno's smile disclosed his white, beautifully formed teeth.

All the ornamental bottles above the bar dived off the shelf together with a clatter of empty glass. The table seemed to stiffen at the impact of the explosion; a vermouth poster fell on Moreno's back, ending his smile as if a hand had sealed his lips. The noses peeping from the cellar stairs hastily retreated.

A wounded man, bearded, in civilian clothes, flung himself on the café entrance, trying to get in; the door swung round violently, hit the dead man's chest, and jammed half-way round. A dull thud jarred the silence following the explosion. The wounded man pressed on the frayed glass panels, battered and banged them with his fists, then suddenly collapsed.

All around, the din of explosions broke out again.

VII

Heavy shells were dropping between the Central Telephone Building and the Calle de Alcalá. One was a dud, and two milicianos carted it off, one in front, the other behind. The late afternoon sky lay colourless and clear over Madrid. The city was full of driven sparks and tiny tongues of flame. The smell of dust and explosives was mingled with the more sinister odour which Lopez remembered having already smelt at Toledo; it was, he supposed, the smell of burnt flesh.

337

Two Grecos and three small Goyas from a palace abandoned by its owner had been expected that morning by the Commission for the Protection of Works of Art to which Lopez had been appointed; but they had not yet turned up. He wanted to be present when they were being sent away. Little good at fighting, Lopez had turned out quite brilliant at the job of rescuing works of art. Thanks to him, not a single Greco had been destroyed in the Toledo debâcle. Eminent old masters had been dug up by the dozen out of the dust where they had lain mouldering in convent attics.

At some distance ahead, in front of a church, a small shell exploded. No sooner had the pigeons flown away than they came back, interested, to examine the latest dents in the stonework of their cornice. Through the windows of a gutted house, now gaping to the winds of heaven, one could see the high tower of the telephone building, with its baroque escutcheon, gaunt in the thickening November dusk.

That the little skyscraper which towers above Madrid as does the Church of the Sacré Cœur over Paris, had not yet been blown to smithereens was nothing short of a miracle. Only one corner was chipped off. But all the window-panes had gone. Behind the tower rose the smoke of a shellburst. 'Gosh,' Lopez thought, 'sooner or later they'll be plonking one on my Grecos?'

A panic-stricken crowd, in flight from perils known to the unknown, seethed in the streets. Others, indifferent, curious or excited, moved along, peering skywards. A second shell fell near by. Some children, accompanied by women, or old men, fled in panic. Other children, unaccompanied by any parents or relatives, discussed the shot like experts.

'What bloody fools them fascists are! Can't shoot for nuts, not they! Pooping off at the soldiers in the Casa del Campo – and just see where they land their stuff!'

One morning, in the nursery-school of the Plaza del Progreso, three kids were playing at soldiers, looking skywards like the people Lopez now saw before him. 'A bomb!' cried one. 'Get down!' And all three fell flat, like well-disciplined soldiers. It was a real bomb. The other children, who were not playing soldiers, remained standing, and were killed, or wounded ...

A shell dropped somewhere to the left. Some dogs trotted past across the road in single file. Another small pack issued from a neighbouring street, running in the opposite direction. And the stray dogs, turning in the mazes of a hopeless quest, seemed to portend the coming plight of human beings. Lopez watched them, as he would have done formerly, with the eye of a sculptor and lover of animals. But other animals were awaiting his attention . . .

The house to which Lopez was going was, like most of the requisitioned palaces, such as the Casa d'Alba, lavishly adorned with stuffed animals. Many of the Spanish aristocrats preferred their blood sports to paintings. And, if they preserved their Goyas, they were very apt to mingle them with their hunting trophies. The inventories of the houses of the great who had fled – and only the houses of proprietors who had fled were requisitioned – often included a dozen masterpieces (when these had not been sent abroad the week before the uprising) and a surprising number of elephant-tusks, rhinoceros horns, stuffed bears, and divers other animals.

When Lopez, heralded by a shell-burst a hundred yards away, entered the gardens of the house, a miliciano ran out to meet him.

'Well, you owl,' Lopez bellowed, slapping him on the back, 'what about my Grecos, damn it?'

'What? The pictures? We hadn't no transport for them. They make good fat packages, you know, now that your fellows have packed them in cotton-wool like eggs. But your lorry came for them.'

'When?'

'About a half-hour ago. But it wouldn't take these here cattle of ours.'

Planted out amongst the trees, and around a neat pile of elephant-tusks under the portico, the bears, stuffed in realistically lifelike poses, seemed indeed to be alive. The ground was slightly shaken by the shell-bursts, and the derelict bears, their paws flapping in the twilight, seemed to proffer threats or benedictions.

'They, anyhow, aren't fragile,' Lopez said complacently. He refused to regard these natural-history specimens as the concern

339

of his department. It was the business of another section of the Works of Art Commission to collect and store them.

'Yes, but see here, comrade,' said the miliciano, 'if the shells are bad for pictures, they can't do much good to elephant-tusks. What the hell am I supposed to do with all this stuff? And it's sure to rain again!'

A shell exploded quite near. The whole menagerie leapt into the air and tottered, while a canary in a cage which had been left behind in the gilded halls of the West Indies Company, burst into frantic song.

'Right. I'll phone for someone to shift your bears.'

Lopez lit a cigarette and went away, carrying the canary cage. At each explosion the canary sang more shrilly, then quietened down again. A building was burning from top to bottom, a moving-picture conflagration. Behind an elaborately ornamental façade, as yet intact, the gaping, shattered windows on every floor were lurid with the flames within, as if the house were inhabited by elemental fire. Further along, at a street corner, a motor bus stood waiting. Suddenly Lopez stopped, breathless for the first time since he had come out. He started frantically gesticulating – the bird-cage flew out of his hand – he shouted. 'Get down!' The people in the bus stared at him as though he had been any one of the hundreds of crazy people exhibiting their antics in a hundred other streets. Lopez dropped flat on the ground. There was an explosion. The bus went up in flame.

When Lopez got to his feet again blood was streaming down the walls. Among the dead stripped by the explosion, a whiskered gentleman, naked but unhurt, picked himself up, screaming. The shelling, still pounding the vicinity of the telephone building, grew more intense.

VIII

Slade was at the Central Exchange. It was the hour for sending off his article. Shells were falling on the whole quarter; but here, in the telephone building, each was convinced they had him personally 'taped'.

There had been a direct hit on the building at five-thirty. Shells were dropping now, one after another, all round it. After the direct hit the enemy had lost the range. Now they were feeling out for it again. Operators, employees, journalists, messengers, milicianos, all felt as if they were in the front line. Shells followed each other in quick succession, like the interminable echoes of a clap of thunder. Perhaps the bombing planes were taking a hand in it again. Darkness was falling, the clouds hung low. But amid all the noises in the exchange no drone of aeroplane engines could be heard.

A miliciano came for Slade. Major Garcia requested the presence of all the newspaper-men in an office of the Central building. All correspondents of any importance were there, waiting. 'Why just now?' Slade wondered. But Garcia was in the habit, when he had any dealings with the Press, of summoning the journalists to places where they imagined they were most exposed to danger.

In one of the old board-rooms of the Central – all leather, wood, and nickel – Garcia had the duplicate copies of all articles sent out from Madrid brought to him. They were brought in two files, labelled respectively 'Political' and 'Descriptive'. While waiting for the correspondents to arrive, he glanced through the second file. It made one feel weary of belonging to the human race. Every article was overflowing with atrocities. Garcia read:

'For PARIS-SOIR. On my way to the telephone exchange, I was the witness of a moving scene of horror. Last night a three-year-old child was picked up near the Puerta del Sol, where it had been wandering in the darkness, crying. There happened to be a woman in one of the bomb-proof shelters of the Gran Via who had lost her child, a little boy of the same age as the child found at the Puerta del Sol and fair like him. Upon being informed of the finding of this child, she ran to the house in the Calle Montera where it was being cared for. There, in the gloom of a shuttered little shop, the child was munching a piece of chocolate. I happened to be there when the mother arrived. Holding out her arms, she approached him. Then her eyes widened and settled into a look of horrible, insane fixity. It was not her child.

'For several long minutes she stood there, motionless. Then the lost child smiled at her, and the woman sprang towards him, gathered him up into her arms, and carried him away ... thinking, most likely, of her own child that had not been found ...'

'They won't pass that,' Garcia reflected. He read on:

'For REUTER: A woman was carrying a child, a little girl scarcely two years old, whose lower-jaw was missing. But she was still alive, and the wide-open wonder-struck eyes seemed to ask who had done this to her. Another woman crossed the street; the child in her arms was headless.'

Garcia had seen, time and again, that terrifying gesture of a mother shielding in her arms what remained of her child. How many similar gestures could be seen in the streets today!

Three shells burst at a distance with a muffled sound like the three hammer-strokes in a French theatre before the curtain rises.

The door opened and the correspondents entered. On a low table, some artificial flowers in glass, as yet unbroken, shivered with each explosion. Through the broken panes of the two windows came the smell and smoke of the burning city.

'Whenever a line happens to be free,' said Garcia, 'the person who has asked for it will be advised here immediately. As you know, I only summon you here to convey to you the contents of documents. Before communicating to you the document which is the reason for our present meeting, I'd like to draw your attention to this fact: According to the fascist despatches we have since the beginning of the war, destroyed enemy planes on nine flying-fields. It is, of course, easier to bomb Seville than it is to bomb the Seville aerodrome. Now, if it has happened that some of our bombs have missed their military objectives and wounded civilians, at least we can assert that never has a Spanish town been systematically bombed by us.

'Here, then, is the document. I am going to read it to you. Each of you is requested to examine the original. Which we shall take steps, in any case, to make known in London and Paris, I assure you. It is simply a little circular addressed to senior officers in the rebel army. This copy was found on 28th July in the possession of an officer, Manuel Carrache, taken prisoner on the Guadalajara front.' Garcia spread out the document and read:

One of the conditions essential to victory is that the morale of the enemy troops shall be shaken. The opponent has at his disposal neither sufficient troops nor sufficient arms to resist us; nevertheless, it is indispensable that you adhere strictly to the following instructions:

To secure our occupation of the hinterland, it is essential to inspire a certain salutary dread in the population.

It must therefore be made a rule that all measures adopted shall be impressive and spectacular.

All points situated in the line of the enemy's retreat and, in a general way, all points to the rear of the enemy front, must be considered as zones of attack.

Whether or not these localities harbour enemy troops makes no difference. Panic prevailing among the civilian population along the line of the enemy's retreat has a lowering effect on the morale of his troops.

Experiences during the World War showed that damage unintentionally inflicted on enemy ambulances and hospital trains greatly contributes to the demoralization of the troops.

Following our entry into Madrid, heads of all units must immediately install, on the roofs of buildings commanding the more dangerous areas – on public edifices and in church-towers as well – nests of machine-guns capable of commanding all adjacent streets.

In the event of any attempt on the part of the population to resist, it will immediately be fired upon. Considering the large number of women fighting on the opposite side, the sex of the combatant need not be taken into account. The more uncompromising our attitude and the more ruthless our elimination of all resistance on the part of the population, the sooner will our triumph bring about the renovation of Spain.

'May I add,' Garcia continued, 'that *from the fascist point of view* I find these instructions logical. It is my personal opinion that terrorization is one of the means expertly and systematically employed by the rebels since the first day of the war, and that you are here and now witnessing a drama of which Badajoz was only the rehearsal. But enough of personal opinions!'

As the journalists went out he added:

'You will also receive the Franco interview of the 16th August, the one beginning "I shall never bombard Madrid. ... Innocent people are there ..."'

Shells were still dropping, but a good distance away. At the Central no one any longer paid any attention to them.

A secretary entered.

'Has Colonel Magnin telephoned?' Garcia asked.

'No, sir. The Internationals are fighting in Getafe.'

'Lieutenant Scali hasn't come?'

'They telephoned from Alcalá. He will be here at about six o'clock. I came to tell you Dr Neubourg is here, sir.'

Neubourg, head of one of the Red Cross units, had come over from Salamanca. He and Garcia had previously met at two Geneva conferences. Garcia was aware that Neubourg could have seen but little in Salamanca; he knew, however, that the doctor had spent some time with Miguel de Unamuno.

Unamuno, the greatest contemporary Spanish writer, had just been deprived by Franco of his rectorship at the University. And Garcia realized how dangerously the menace of fascism was weighing on this man who had been its eminent defender.

IX

'For the last six weeks,' said Dr Neubourg, 'he has been staying in his small bedroom, lying in bed, reading. After he had been removed from the University staff he said, "I shall leave here only as a condemned man, or a corpse." He went to bed, and is staying there. Two days after his dismissal, the University was handed over to the Order of the Sacred Heart.'

Neubourg glanced as he passed at his own face reflected in the only mirror in the room; his thin clean-shaven face which aspired to look alert and shrewd, but succeeded only in being the ruined reminder of his youth.

At the beginning of the conversation, Garcia had taken a letter out of his pocket-case. 'When I heard that you were coming,' he said, 'I went through our correspondence of the old days, and I found this letter which he wrote ten years ago, in exile. There's a passage I'd like to read to you.

Truth alone is justice; there is no other justice. And truth, as Sophocles said, is mightier than intellect. As life is mightier than pleasure or pain. Truth and Life then shall be my motto; not Intellect and Pleasure. To live in Truth, even though it means to suffer, rather than to exercise intelligence in pleasure or take pleasure in intelligence.

Garcia placed the letter before him on the polished desk which reflected the red sky.

'That,' said the doctor, 'is the gist of the speech which caused his dismissal. He said, "Politics may lay certain demands on us, into which it is needless to enter. ... As for the University, it must serve Truth." Miguel de Unamuno could not remain where lies ruled. There's something else he said. "As to the Red atrocities of which we constantly hear, there can be no doubt that the least of the woman combatants, even were she, as we are told, no better than a prostitute, is less contemptible to the reasoning mind, when she fights, rifle in hand, and risks her life for her beliefs, than are the women who have never been able to dispense with flowers and fine linen, those bare-armed women whom I saw leaving our banquet the other night to go and see the Marxists being executed." '

Neubourg had a well-known gift for mimicry.

'And as a physician I may say,' he went on in his natural voice, 'that there is something pathological in Unamuno's horror of the death penalty. Also, he was doubtless rather flustered at having to reply to the general who was the founder of the "Tercio". When he defended the cultural unity of Spain the heckling began.'

'What sort of heckling?'

' "Death to Unamuno!" "Death to the Intellectuals!" '

'Who were the interrupters?'

'Silly young undergraduates. So then, General Millay Astray stood up and shouted: "Death to intelligence, long live death!" '

'What do you think he meant?'

'Of course he meant, quite simply: "Go to the devil!" As to "Long live death!" – perhaps he was alluding to Unamuno's protests against the executions by the firing squads?'

'In Spain that cry comes from pretty deep down. The anarchists went in for it once.'

A shell dropped in the Gran Via. Proud of his courage, Neubourg continued to pace Garcia's office, his bald head shining in the light that poured down from the lurid sky. On each side of his skull there stood out tufts of black curly hair. During twenty years Dr Neubourg, though distinguished enough in his own domain, had rather prided himself on looking like an eighteenth-century ecclesiastic, and he still retained some vestige of that resemblance.

'It was at that point,' the doctor went on, 'that Unamuno made his famous reply: "A Spain without Biscaya and Catalonia would be a country lacking both an arm and an eye – as you do, General Astray." Which, coming as it did after his well-known remark to Mola, "To conquer and to convince are two different matters," could not be dismissed as a mere witticism.

'That evening he went to the Casino, where he was openly insulted. Whereupon he returned to his room and announced that he would never leave it . . .'

Garcia, while listening attentively, had his eyes fixed on Unamuno's old letter which lay on his desk. He picked it up again:

Will the crusaders of revenge abandon the idea of imposing upon the Rif Tribesmen the *guardia civil* that is of decivilizing them? When shall we give up that hangman's notion of 'honour'?
I don't wish to hear anything of what is going on over there or in Spain. I am even less interested in what is called 'Greater Spain' by the other people who shout so that they may not hear. For my part, I take refuge in that other Spain, my little Spain. I wish I had the strength of will never to read a Spanish paper. Our papers are appalling. Not even the snapping of a broken heart-string can be heard as one reads them. Only the creaking of the strings and pulleys by which puppets are moved. Our giants are only windmills . . .

A vague murmur was coming up from the Gran Via. The glow from the conflagrations flickered on the walls of the room, as the reflection of a sunlit river trembles on a bedroom ceiling.

'"Not even the snapping of a broken heart-string,"' Garcia repeated, tapping the bowl of his pipe against his thumb-nail.

'What I should like to know is what he is *thinking*. I can picture him, with his lordly airs, his goggle eyes and wise old owl-like stare, telling off Millay Astray. But that's only a picturesque incident. There's more to it than that.

'We talked a lot, in private, afterwards. He did the talking, I only put in a word or two. He can't bear Azaña. To him the Republic, and only the Republic, is still the one means of achieving Spanish federal unity. He is against an absolute federalism, but he is also against forcible centralization. And he now sees, in fascism, that very centralization he dislikes.'

An incongruous scent of *eau de Cologne* was mingling with the reek of smoke and fire that poured into the office through the broken windows. A perfumer's shop was on fire.

'He wanted to shake hands with fascism, you see, doctor, but he forgot that fascism has feet as well. That he still has his desires for federal unity explains more or less his inconsistencies.'

'He is sure Franco will win, and when interviewed by the journalists, says to them, "Write that, whatever happens, I'll never be on the side of the conqueror." '

'Which they are careful not to write. What did he say to you about his sons?'

'Nothing. Why?'

Garcia looked at the red sky, musingly. 'All his sons are here, two as combatants. .... I can't believe he doesn't think of them. And he hasn't so many chances of seeing someone who knows about both sides.'

'After the speech he went out once. They say that, in reprisal for his remarks about the women, he was summoned to a room from which he had a view of men being executed by firing-squads ...'

'I have already heard that – and don't much believe it. Have you exact information on the subject?'

'He said nothing to me about it – which is quite natural. And I certainly did not mention the matter to him. But, by the way, his uneasiness has much increased of late, what with the country's eternal recourse to violence and irrationality.'

Garcia dismissed the phrase with a vague gesture of his pipe.

'But really, my dear Garcia, it strikes me that what we are saying is, after all, a little beside the point. Unamuno's opposition is purely ethical. Our conversations bore on that aspect only indirectly, but pretty constantly.'

'Evidently, the question of firing-squads has nothing to do with centralization.'

'When I left him there in that bed, a sad and embittered man surrounded by his books, I felt as if I were leaving behind me the nineteenth century.'

Rising to show Neubourg out of the room, Garcia pointed

with the end of his pipe to the last lines of the letter which he
held in his hand.

When I turn my mind's eye towards my last twelve troubled
years, ever since I tore myself away from that little study in Salamanca, where I had dreamed my sheltered dreams – ah, how I used
to dream there! – it all seems to me like the shadow of a dream. ...
You ask if I read. Not much, except about the sea, with which each
day I grow a closer friend.

'Written ten years ago,' Garcia said.

X

At the moment when, having got Paris, Slade was called into
the telephone room, a shell dropped quite near. Then two others,
nearer still. Almost all the occupants of the room rushed to the
wall farthest from the window. Despite the electric lights, all in
the room were conscious of the fierce red glare in the street; it
seemed as if it were the fires outside that were bombarding the
Central, with its thirteen stories of windows, at none of which
was the last shadow of a human form. Finally an old journalist
with a big moustache ventured away from the wall. One by
one the others followed suit. But they kept glancing back at the
wall, as though looking to see if they had left their traces there.
    More shells were falling. Scarcely farther away than the first
ones. Yet now they had regained their places no one moved
again. They say that wherever people meet together, every
twenty minutes an angel of silence passes. Here an angel of
indifference passed.
    Soon Slade was able to begin dictating. As he went on des-
cribing his experiences of the morning, the shells came nearer.
At each explosion, all the pencil-points leapt up at the same
instant from the writing-pads. When there was a pause in the
firing the tension increased. Were the guns, over there, correcting their range? Everyone was waiting, waiting, waiting. Slade
went on speaking. Paris relayed to New York.

'This morning, comma, I saw bombs falling all round a hospital
where lay a thousand wounded, full stop. On the sidewalk, comma,
on the walls, comma, were spoors of blood, comma, such as are left
by wounded animals ...'

348

The shell dropped less than twenty yards away. This time there was a general rush to the basement. In the almost empty room there remained only the operators and the correspondents on the wire. The operators listened to the messages, but their eyes seemed watching for the coming of the shells. The journalists who were dictating went on doing so; once cut, the communication would not have been made again in time for the morning edition. Slade dictated what he had seen at the 'Palace'.

'This afternoon I arrived a few minutes after a shell had exploded in front of a butchershop; there, where women had been standing in line, waiting their turn, were stains; the blood of the slain butcher ran down the counter between the sides of beef and carcasses of mutton hanging from iron hooks, and dripped on to the floor where it was washed away by the water from a burst pipe.

'And, mind you, all this serves no purpose. None whatever. The inhabitants are far more shaken with horror than with fear. For instance, while bombs were falling all round us, an old man said to me: "I have never meddled in politics. I have always regarded them as beneath contempt. But we can't let power fall into the hands of people who use power this way – power which is not even theirs by right as yet – can we?" I stood a whole hour in a line-up in front of a bakery. In the queue were only a few men, but about a hundred women. And everyone, remember, feels it is more dangerous to stay for an hour in the same spot than it is to walk about. Five yards away from the bakery, on the other side of the street, the dead collected from a demolished building were being put into their coffins. (The same thing is being done at this very moment in all the shattered houses of Madrid.) There was no noise of guns or of airplanes, and the hammering echoed in the silence. At my side a man said to a woman, "Juanita's arm has been torn off; do you think her young man will marry her in that state?" They were all talking about their own personal affairs. Suddenly a woman shouted out, "It's horrible to be obliged to eat as we do!" Another woman, answered gravely, with something of the manner they have all picked up more or less from La Passionaria: "You haven't got much to eat, none of us has got much to eat; but in the old days we hadn't much to eat either. Well, anyhow, our children are better fed nowadays than they have been for at least two hundred years." To the general approbation of the others in the queue.

'All these people who are being disembowelled, maimed, beheaded are being martyred in vain. Every shell that falls only confirms the people of Madrid, more deeply in their faith. In the bomb-proof shelters 50,000 people can take refuge. And there are a million people in Madrid. In the sections of the city that are being most constantly bombarded, there is not one objective of military value. But the bombardment will go on.

'As I write this, shells are bursting every minute in the poorer quarters of the city. In the uncertain light, at this moment, the glare of the conflagrations is such that the night into which the daylight is fading is wine-red. The curtain, a smoke curtain, is rising on Fate's dress rehearsal for the coming war. Fellow Americans, I say to you : Down with Europe!

'Let us find out what it is we want. When a communist addresses an international conference, he puts his fist down on the table. When a fascist addresses an international conference, he puts his feet on the table. A Democrat – be he American, English, or French – when he addresses an international conference, scratches his head, and asks questions.

'The fascists have come to the aid of fascists, communists have come to the aid of communists; have even assisted the Spanish democracy. But democracies do not come to the aid of democracies.

'We, the democratic people of the world, believe in everything except ourselves. If a fascist state or a communist state disposed of the combined strength of the United States, the British Empire, and France, we should be struck with terror. But since it is *our* strength, we don't believe in it.

'Let us find out what it is we want. Either let us say to the fascists – or to the communists, if need be – "Get out of here! If not, you will have to deal with us!"'

'Or let us say, once and for all: "Down with Europe!"'

'The Europe I see from this window no longer has anything to teach us, neither strength, which it has lost, nor faith, which it now manifests by decorating Moorish mercenaries with Sacred Hearts. Fellow Americans, all you who desire peace, who hate those who blot out ballots with the blood of shopkeepers murdered on their counters, turn your eyes away from this continent! We're through with this Old Europe who has gone out of his mind, yet, with his passions of a savage, his shell-shocked face, presumes to still come and read lessons to us!'

When he had done dictating, Slade went up to the top storey, the best observation-post in Madrid. Four other correspondents were already there. They seemed relatively calm, for in the open air nerves are never so strung up as in a confined space; and also because the little *mirador* of the Central, being smaller than the tower itself, seemed less vulnerable. That evening had no sunset, and nothing seemed alive except the dancing flames; it was as though the city of Madrid were stranded on the face of some dead planet, and the nightfall had made it over to elemental chaos. All trace of human life seemed buried in the dank November mist, blotched with angry red.

A huge burst of flames shot through a roof so small that Slade wondered how a house so tiny could have contained it. Instead of spreading upwards, the flames slithered along the house-front downwards to the street. There they fixed on another house and went soaring up it, to the roof. Then, as at the close of some spectacular display of fireworks, the conflagration ended in a whirl of brilliant sparks across the mist. A shower of red-hot cinders compelled the journalists to duck for a moment. As the fire approached the buildings which were already gutted, it lit them up from behind. They showed as gaunt, phantasmagoric skeletons, against the flames that prowled behind the ruins like beasts of prey loath to leave their kill. The ghastly twilight seemed ushering in another Age of Fire. The three largest hospitals were burning. The Savoy Hotel was burning. Churches and museums were burning, the Biblioteca National was burning, the Ministry of the Interior was burning, a market was burning, all its little wooden stalls were blazing, houses were crumbling, collapsing in volleys of sparks, two entire quarters were glowing fiery red, scored with long black walls like gridirons placed upon a coal fire. With impressive slowness, but with grim persistence, the fire advanced, by way of Atocha and the Calle León, in the direction of the centre, towards the Puerta del Sol, which was also buring.

'The birth-pangs of a world,' Slade murmured.

The bunches of shells were now dropping further over to the left. And from the depths of the Gran Via, immediately beneath Slade and almost invisible to him, there rose a sound, audible at times even above the clanging of the ambulance bells, a sound as of barbaric litanies. Slade strained his ears to catch the sound which seemed to come from some far-off prehistoric age, congruous with this world of fire. After a phrase rhythmically recurring, it seemed that everyone in the street was uttering a response which imitated the clang of funeral gongs: *Ding-ding-a-dong*.

At last Slade guessed what it was, though he could not catch the words. He had heard the same rhythmic chant a month previously. In response to words he could not hear, that human gong was beating out: '*No pasarán.*' Slade had seen La Passionaria, dark, austere, widow of all the slain Asturians, had seen her leading a fierce and solemn procession marching beneath red banners inscribed with her famous phrase, *Better be a hero's widow than a coward's wife*, had heard twenty thousand women chanting, in answer to another long, incomprehensible phrase, this same refrain: '*No pasarán.*' He had been less moved by them than by this smaller, but unseen, crowd, whose desperate courage rose towards him through the smoke-clouds of the burning city.

XI

Still holding his pine-branch, Manuel left the town hall where the court-martial (its members were elected by the soldiers) had been held. The death penalty had been pronounced on both murderers and fugitives. It was the genuine anarchists who had shown themselves most obdurate regarding those who had run away. 'The whole proletariat is responsible,' they had said. 'Even if these men were fooled by the Falangist spies, that's no excuse.'

A motor-car went by, the bright flails of its headlights pitted by the rain.

'They can bomb Madrid at their ease, now,' Manuel thought. One couldn't see a thing.

As he passed the little side-door of the town hall, marked only by the light that issued from the corridor, he felt someone seize him by the leg. Gartner and the others who were close behind him turned on their electric torches and, in the rain-drenched light, they saw two soldiers of their own brigade. They were kneeling in the deep mud, clinging to Manuel's legs. He could not see their faces.

'They've no call to shoot us!' one of the men was shouting. 'We're volunteers! You got to tell them!'

The gunfire had ceased. The face of the man who was shouting was not raised, but bent towards the mud, and his cries were deadened by the hiss of the downpour. Manuel said nothing.

'They can't do it! They can't do it!' the other began to shout. 'They can't, sir!'

His voice sounded very young. Still, Manuel could not see their faces. Around their forage caps, pressed against his hips, in the blurred radiance of the electric torches, droplets which seemed rising from the ground danced across the lines of driven rain. Suddenly, as Manuel still did not reply, one of the condemned men raised his head and gazed up at him. He was kneeling, his arms dangling, his shoulders thrown back the better to see Manuel's face above him, and against the timeless background of the rain-swept night the man looked the very symbol of defeat – the eternal scapegoat, he who pays. He had been rubbing his cheeks frantically against Manuel's muddy top-boots. His forehead and cheek-bones were thickly smeared with mud, and on the darkness of the face only the eye-sockets showed, blobs of cadaverous white.

Manuel felt inclined to say: 'The court-martial's nothing to do with me.' But he was ashamed of such a disavowal. He could think of nothing to say, and he knew he could only shake off the second condemned man by pushing him away with his foot. And the idea of that revolted him. He could only stand there motionless looking down at the frantic eyes of the suppliant, whose breast was heaving and down whose cheeks the rain was streaming as though all his face were dissolved in tears.

A picture rose in Manuel's mind of his men at Aranjuez and those of the Vth Corps crouching in rain like this behind their little parapets. He had not lightly come to his decision that a court-martial must be held; but now he did not know what to do, caught between two alternatives, one odious and the other hypocritical. To shoot men down was bad enough, he thought, without adding moral sermons.

'You got to tell them!' the man who was looking at Marcell wailed. 'You got to tell them!'

Manuel wondered what he could say to them. The argument for their defence was something inexpressible in words; it was

353

in that streaming face, that open mouth, which had made Manuel aware that here was the everlasting visage of the man who pays. Never had he realized so keenly the necessity of choosing between victory and compassion. Stooping, he tried to push aside the man who was still clinging to his leg. The man clung desperately, his head still bowed, as if in the whole world nothing but that leg could save his life. Manuel all but fell, then thrust more heavily against the man's shoulders; it struck him that several men would be required to dislodge his grasp. Suddenly the man let his arms fall, and he, too, looked up at Manuel, slowly raising his eyes till they met Manuel's. He was young, though not so young as Manuel had imagined. He had passed beyond resignation or despair, as though at last it all were clear to him – not for now only, but for ever and ever. And with the forlorn detachment of men who are speaking almost from beyond the grave, he said:

'So that's it? You've no voice now, as far as we're concerned?'

Manuel realized that he had not spoken a word.

He took a few steps; the men were left behind him.

The elemental fragrance of the rain on leaves and branches was drowning the odour of the wool and leather of wet uniforms. Manuel did not look back, but he still felt the presence of the men behind him, kneeling unmoving in the mud; felt their eyes haunting his receding steps.

XII

Suddenly there was a blinding flash that left the lighted room in twilight for a moment. For Garcia and Scali to have noticed it in spite of the electric light, it must have been caused by a terrific burst of flame. They both crossed over to a window. The air was cold now, and a light mist was rising from the ground and mingling with the smoke from hundreds of houses smouldering in the darkness. No alarm-whistles could be heard, but there were fire-engines and ambulances everywhere.

'This is the hour when the Valkyries come down to glean the dead,' Scali remarked.

'I seem to hear Madrid speaking to Miguel de Unamuno to-night, saying with its tongues of fire: "What good to me are all those thoughts of yours, if you can't give my tragedy a thought?" Let's make a move. We'll go to the other office.'

Garcia had been describing to Scali his conversation with Dr Neubourg. Of all the men he was to see during that day and night, Scali was the only one who would feel as he had felt about it.

'When an intellectual who was a revolutionary once,' Scali said, 'attacks the revolution, it always comes to this: he is judging the political methods of that revolution by his own moral standards. But seriously, Garcia, would you rather such criticisms were left unsaid?'

'How could I wish such a thing? ... Intellectuals are always rather inclined to think that a party means a collection of people rallied round an idea. A party is really much more like a living, acting personality than an abstraction. Take the purely psychological side; a party is surely more than anything else a means of organizing for common action an aggregate of feelings that are often incompatible. In this case they include poverty – humiliation – Apocalyptic vision – and hope. For the communists: love of action, organization, intensive production and the like. Yes, my dear fellow, to draw conclusions about a man's own character from the programme of the party he belongs to would be much the same as if I'd set out to deduce the psychology of my Peruvians from their religious myths.'

He picked up his cap and revolver and switched off the light. The glow of flames outside, invisible so long as the lamps were on, now suffused the room, which was filling with smoke clouds that rasped their throats with the acrid fumes of burning wood, as the fires advanced slowly, resistlessly, towards the Puerta del Sol. The fiery sky seemed lowering in the darkened room. Clouds were piling up in dark-red masses that seemed almost solid to the touch, above the Telephone Building and the Gran Via. Coughing and sneezing, though the smoke was no thicker, only more visible, than before, Scali went back to the window. Had the paving-blocks caught fire? No, they were only reflections, those little gashes of flame gleaming red on the smooth surface of the asphalt. A pack of stray dogs began howling, grotesquely, senselessly, aggressively, as though the world of men had passed away and they were rulers of its desolation.

The lift was still working.

They walked as far as the Prado through the black streets beneath the angry sky. Here in the utter darkness they were still surrounded by the sounds they had heard from the windows of the Telephone Building; Madrid was licking its wounds. As they advanced another sound came to their ears, a sound of countless tiny footfalls drumming on the asphalt.

'Unamuno will have made a fine mess of his death,' Scali said. 'Here, in Madrid, fate had prepared for him the funeral of his dreams.'

Garcia's thoughts harked back to the room at Salamanca.

'Here he'd have found another tragedy,' he said, 'and I'm not so sure he would have understood it. The great intellectual is a man of subtleties, of fine shades, of evaluations; he's interested in absolute truth and in the complexity of things. He is — how shall I put it? — "antimanichean" by definition, by nature. But all forms of action are manichean, because all action pays a tribute to the devil; that manichean element is most intense when the masses are involved. Every true revolutionary is a born manichean. The same is true of politics, all politics.'

Just then he felt a pressure on his legs, a moving mass hemming them in. He groped round with his hands. Was it a pack of dogs? But where could that dusty smell of country fields have come from?

The pressure increased; there was no getting through. The patter of feet on the pavement was too sharp, too rapid for a pack of dogs.

'What on earth's happening?' Scali shouted; the moving mass had carried him a good five yards away, 'Can it be sheep?'

He was answered by a bleat close by. Half-suffocated, Garcia managed to get out his torch and the thin ray rippled along the surface of a fleecy mass scarcely denser than the smoke-clouds overhead. Up to the limit of the light a flock of sheep was surging around. There seemed no end to it; they could hear bleat after bleat far into the distance. And not a trace of a shepherd.

'Bear to the right,' Garcia shouted.

Fleeing from the battlefields, the flocks were passing through Madrid on their way down to Valencia. Somewhere behind, or coming down the side-streets parallel to the boulevard, there was doubtless a band of shepherds armed as they all were nowadays. But in the meantime, the nightbound flocks, masters of the Prado as they might be hereafter when men had passed away, were pressing forward between the smouldering houses in a warm, compact mass, their stolid silence broken now and again by a plaintive bleat.

'Let's go and fish out our car,' Garcia said. 'That's about the best thing we can do.'

They made their way back towards the middle of the town.

'Go on with what you were saying, Garcia.'

'Remember this, Scali: In all countries, in all parties, the intellectuals are always at loggerheads. Adler against Freud, Sorel against Marx. But in politics a dissenter is an outlaw. The intelligentsia always has a tremendous sympathy for the outlaw; out of generosity, or because they appreciate his cleverness. But they forget that what a party wants is to make good, not to find good reasons for its programme.'

'I grant you that those who, on humane or intellectual grounds, may feel inclined to pick holes in revolutionary politics, know nothing of the stuff of which a revolution's made. And the men with practical experience of revolutions never have the talent of Unamuno; often they are incapable of expressing themselves at all.'

'If, for instance, as we are always being told, there are too many pictures of Stalin in Russia, it's not because that ogre Stalin, squatting in a corner of the Kremlin, has decreed it should be so. Why, look at the craze for signs and badges right here in Madrid, and, heaven knows, the Government doesn't care a damn one way or the other! It would be interesting to analyse the reasons for all those portraits. The trouble is, to talk about love to a lover, you've got to have been in love yourself; it's not enough just to have dissected love in the laboratory. It isn't by approving something or resenting it that a thinker proves his worth, but by his power of exposition. Let the intellectual first explain why and how things are as they are; then he can lodge his protests if he thinks fit – only, by then, it'll be a waste of breath. ... Analysis is a great force, Scali. I don't believe in ethical systems which exclude psychology.'

Not a sound from the fires. Streaked with clouds of dense smoke hanging in tattered shreds, the glowing sky was mottled with great blotches of glowing red, like red-hot iron cooling on the anvil; one would have thought the whole of Madrid was ablaze. Now and again a rustle of small sounds – absurdly out of keeping with the tragic sky – fretted the silence; the patter of thousands of small hoofs trotting up from the Prado.

'All the same,' Scali said after a moment, 'soon men will have to be taught again the art of living.' A memory of Alvear crossed his mind. 'To be a man, in my view, one needn't necessarily be a good communist. For Christians, to be a man used to mean being a good Christian. Well, I mistrust that sort of thing.'

'The question is far from being a trivial one, my friend; it raises the whole problem of civilization. For quite a while, the philosopher – let's call him that – was more or less explicitly regarded as the highest type of European man. The intellectuals were the clerics of a world in which the politicians represented the nobility, for better or for worse. Their claim to act as spiritual advisers was uncontested. It was they, the intellectuals – Miguel de Unamuno and not Alfonso XIII; indeed, for that matter Miguel and not the bishops – who were responsible for teaching men how to live. But nowadays the new political leaders claim to rule our minds as well; Miguel against Franco (against *us*, till the other day), Thomas Mann versus Hitler, Gide versus Stalin, Ferrero versus Mussolini; it's a conflict of prerogatives.'

The street began to turn and above them now a lurid glow was filling the sky, reflected from the flaming masses of the Savoy, invisible behind the houses.

'Or Borghese rather than Ferrero.' Scali raised a pointing finger in the darkness. 'The whole business, to my thinking, turns on the famous and preposterous notion of "totality" as they call it. It's a sort of mania with our intellectuals; in the twentieth century such a phrase as 'totalitarian civilization" is meaningless. It's as absurd as if one said the army constitutes a totalitarian civilization. And, as for the truth about things in general, the only man who aims at a "totalitarian reality" is, precisely, the intellectual.'

'Perhaps, my dear fellow, he's the only one who needs it. The close of the nineteenth century was an entirely passive epoch, whereas activity seems to be the keynote of the new era. Which indicates a pretty drastic contrast between the two periods.'

'From that point of view, the political leader cannot but be regarded by the intellectual as an impostor, since he preaches a solution of life's problems, without telling us what those problems really are.'

They were in the shadow of the house. The pink glow of Garcia's pipe described a semicircle as if implying: That would lead us too far afield. From the moment they had left that day, Scali had been conscious that Garcia was feeling worried – an unusual state of mind for the robust officer with the pointed ears.

'Tell me, Major, how can one make the best of one's life, in your opinion?'

An ambulance bell, shrilling like a danger-signal, sped past them and receded. Garcia was pondering.

'By converting as wide a range of experience as possible into conscious thought, my friend.'

They were passing a picture house that occupied the angle of two streets. An aerial torpedo had ripped it open, peeling off the entire wall giving on the narrower street. A rescue party with electric torches was burrowing about amongst the ruins, searching for victims, most likely. And, as if summoning men to watch this search for the dead or dying, as it had once called them in to while away an empty hour, the cinema bell was buzzing away behind an almost intact façade, in the winter night.

Garcia was thinking of Hernandez. And, as he watched the flames rising above Madrid, he realized with a rush of agony how similar are all the tragedies of man's estate, each circling his sad small orbit of despair like a madman turning in his cell.

'The business of the revolution is to solve its own problems, not ours. Ours depend on ourselves alone. If fewer Russian writers had cut and run along with the flood of émigrés, very likely the relations between writers and the Soviet government wouldn't be what they are today. Miguel made the most of his life – I mean, he lived as nobly as possible – in monarchial Spain, which he loathed. And he'd have also made the most of it in a less rotten social order. It might still have been difficult, perhaps. No state, no social structure can create nobility of character, nor intellectual qualities; the most we can expect of it is favourable conditions. And that's a good deal.'

'You know, of course, that communists claim to do so.'

'What a party claims in such respects only goes to demonstrate either the intelligence or the stupidity of its propagandists. What interests me is what a party *does*. What are *you* doing here?'

Scali stopped, amazed to find that he could give no definite answer, and pushed back the tip of his nose as he always did when thinking hard.

'Personally,' Garcia continued, without waiting for his reply. 'I'm not in this uniform because I expect the Popular Front to put the noblest into power, but because I wish to see a change for the better in the lot of our Spanish peasantry.'

A remark of Alvear's crossed Scali's mind.

'And if to give them economic freedom,' he suggested, 'you've got to have a system which will enslave them politically?'

'In that case, as no one can be perfectly sure of the purity of his ideals in the future, there's nothing for it but to let the fascists have their way. But once we're agreed on the vital point – that we've *got* to put up a resistance, we've taken up a line of action which commits us once for all. To a programme, with all its inevitable consequences. In certain cases, the choice is a tragic one; for the intellectual, it's almost always so, above all for the artist. Yet, even so, wasn't it up to him to resist?'

'For a thinker, the revolution's a tragedy. But for such a man, life, too, is tragic. And if he is counting on the revolution to abolish his private tragedy, he's making a mistake – that's all. I've heard almost all your problems stated already by a man you may have known, Captain Hernandez. As a matter of fact, they led him to his death. There aren't umpteen ways to fight, there's only one and that's to fight to win. One doesn't engage in a war or revolution just to please oneself.

'Some writer – I don't remember who – once said: "I am as thronged with corpses as an old graveyard!" For four months all of us have been "thronged with corpses", Scali. The path that leads from moral standards to political activity is strewn with our dead selves. Always there is a conflict between the man who acts and the conditions of his action – the line of action he must follow to win, not that which he must take to lose all that we want to save. The whole thing's not a matter for debate but a matter of hard facts, and, in a way, of personal talent. Yes, it's a conflict, almost a rough-and-tumble!'

A rough-and-tumble! Scali remembered the struggle between Marcelino's plane and its own flames.

'There are just wars,' Garcia went on, 'such as the one we're waging now – but there's no such thing as a just army. And that an intellectual, a man who's business it is to think, should go and say like Miguel: "I'm leaving you because you are not just" – well, it strikes me, my friend, as downright immoral. Yes, one can have a policy that's just, but there's no such thing as a just party.'

'That point of view opens the door to every kind of racket.'

'Every door's open to those who are set on forcing it. The quality of one's life is like the quality of one's mind. The only guarantee that an enlightened policy will be followed by a popular government isn't our theories but our presence, now and here. The moral standard of our government depends on our efforts and on our steadfastness. Enlightenment in Spain will not be the mysterious outcome of some vague aspiration, it'll be exactly what we make it.'

A fresh fire broke out close by.

'Anyhow, my good friend,' said Garcia with a touch of irony, 'it's the workers themselves who'll bring about their own emancipation.'

XIII

Motionless as marksmen taking aim, the firemen stood on their ladders, between the flames of the Savoy and the cascades of their fire-hoses. Suddenly they gave a start, and the long nozzles shook like anglers' lines when fish are biting. For a moment even the flames seemed to stand still, quelled by a terrific crash like the noise of an exploding mine. An aerial torpedo had just landed somewhere in the rear.

Mercery was watching the scene with professional interest.

'They're quicker at lighting fires than we are at putting them out.'

Once he had fancied he might serve the Republic best as an

adviser, maybe as a strategist. But after that regrettable incident of the soap factory, he had gone back to his old post of captain in the Fire Brigade. And never before had he been so useful, or so popular. Never, at the front, had he faced the enemy as he had been doing here during the last twenty hours.

'Fire's a tricky beast to handle,' he would say, giving a dexterous twist to his moustache; 'you've got to know the ropes, of course . . .' And so forth.

He stood on the pavement in his fire-fighting kit watching each nest of flames as if it were an enemy advance-guard he were fighting. The smouldering furnace was constantly flaring up again. The calcium flares seemed inextinguishable. On the left, where the fire seemed to have died out, bursts of dense white smoke were rising, frayed into long level streamers by the wind from the Sierra, and reddened by the flames below.

There were only four hoses to fight three separate fires, but these were now only a few yards away from the nearest building. The fire on the left blazed up again. The conflagration might be prevented from spreading if it were mastered where it was fiercest, on its extreme right, before the fire on the left got out of hand.

Again the nozzles gave a sudden jerk, and the flames seemed to stand still. A second torpedo had dropped, just in front, this time.

Mercery tried to distinguish the various sounds he heard. Despite the darkness, numerous fascist planes were about. The blazing fires in Madrid made perfect landmarks for them. Ten minutes previously four incendiary bombs had been dropped. Heavy shells were still coming over in the workers' districts and in the centre of the town. And, further away, the firing of the field-guns could be heard, mingled with the sounds of battle. Now and then they were drowned by the long shrieks of sirens and the clang of ambulance bells, the crash of buildings toppling over amid geysers of sparks. But Mercery listened in vain for the sound of fire-engine horns announcing the arrival of the sorely-needed extra hoses.

A third bomb dropped, in line with the others. When Mercery was fighting fire a dozen bombing planes could not have made him budge an inch.

The central patch of flames spread out suddenly, but as quickly writhed and flattened down. 'After the war,' Mercery thought, 'I'll turn gambler!' The fires on the extreme left remained stationary. If only those reinforcements would hurry up! Mercery felt quite Napoleonic. He tugged his moustache cheerfully.

The fireman on the extreme right suddenly dropped his hose, hung for a moment on the ladder by one foot, then fell into the fire. The others hurried down their ladders, rung by rung, in parallel lines.

Mercery ran up to the first man who reached the ground.

'They're firing at us!' the man said.

Mercery looked round. None of the neighbouring houses was high enough for anyone to be firing from the windows. But someone might be shooting at them from a distance: there were plenty of fascists in Madrid.

'If ever I lay hands on the bastard!' a fireman exclaimed.

'If you ask me, it's a machine-gun,' another man put in.

'Say, are you off your head?'

'We'll soon see,' Mercery said. 'Come on, lads. Up the ladders again! The fire is picking up. Come on, lads! For the People, and for Liberty!'

'Immortal Liberty!' He murmured, as he turned to grasp the ladder. He took the place of the fireman who had fallen into the blazing furnace.

From the top of the ladder he looked round. No one was shooting at them; there was no place from which anyone could shoot. A machine-gun can be camouflaged easily enough, but the sound would have given the alarm to the patrols. He aimed the nozzle of the hose. The seething mass of flames on which he played it was the fiercest of all. It was an enemy with more life in it than any man, more life than anything else in the world. Combating this enemy of a myriad writhing tentacles, like a fantastic octopus, Mercery felt himself terribly inert, as though made of lead. But, for all its tentacles, he would best the monster. Behind him avalanches of smoke were billowing, black and garnet-red. Through all the noises of the conflagration he could hear people coughing in the street, scores and scores of them. He seemed floundering in a dry, dazzling sea of incandescence. The patch of fire died down. The last smoke-wisp lifted, and Mercery could see Madrid below him in a lightless pit. All lights had been extinguished and the town was outlined only by the distant fires, flapping, like bull-fighters, their scarlet capes across the darkness. He had given up all, even Madame Mercery, to help to make a better world. He pictured himself stopping with a gesture those little children's hearses, white and quaintly decorated like wedding-cakes. For him each explosion he heard, each fire he saw, meant those poor, heart-breaking little hearses. Carefully he aimed the jet of water from his hose on the next patch of fire. Suddenly he felt as though a racing car had gone by at full speed. As if he had been blown from his foothold by a gust of wind, another fireman dropped off his ladder. This time, Mercery understood. They were being machine-gunned by a plane.

There were two of them.

Mercery saw them coming back, flying very low – not more than ten yards above the fire. They were not shooting. The pilots, who could see the firemen only when their forms showed up against the glow of the flames, had to wait till they flew behind them. Mercery had his revolver under his fireman's suit. He knew it was useless; and anyhow he could not get at it. But he felt a mad desire to shoot. The planes came back, and two firemen dropped, one in the flames, the other on the pavement. Mercery was filled with such passionate disgust that, for the first time, he felt completely calm as he saw the planes swooping towards him across the glowing sky. They struck him with the rushing tempest of their wings as they passed, before the return journey that would enable them to 'spot' him. Mercery climbed down three rungs and faced them, erect on his upright ladder. As the first plane bore down upon him like a hissing shell, he turned his fire-hose on the cockpit of the machine, drenching it from end to end. Then he fell back against the ladder, with four bullets in his body. Living or dead, he still clung to the nozzle of his hose which was notched between two rungs.

Below, the spectators had taken shelter in doorways from the machine-guns that now were flaying the streets.

At last, slowly, Mercery's hands began to open. His body

364

rebounded twice against the ladder, crashed upon the empty street.

XIV

In the main room of an old suburban house, the walls of which were completely covered with maps, the officers were waiting for Manuel, who had been called to the telephone.

'One of the falangists has killed himself,' a captain observed.

'But another has given away the entire organization,' Gartner replied.

'Isn't it amazing? Of course, to take on a job like that, a man has to be a scoundrel – but he must have pluck as well.'

'We've still a lot to learn about human nature, old man. You saw the state they were in. When the morale is at a low ebb as the colonel puts it, there's always someone ready to turn traitor.'

'Have you seen the German tanks?' another voice put in. So far they had seen only the dim outlines in the rain.

'I went into one, it was open. One of the fellows had got away, the other was dead. Dead at his post, in the turret, and his pockets turned inside out. And the rain coming down outside I shan't forget it in a hurry!'

The rain was still streaming down the window-panes, interminably.

'Had his mates rifled his pockets, do you think?'

'Yes – so that no papers might fall into our hands. But they hadn't time to tuck back the lining of his pockets.'

'That's natural enough, damn it! Taking things out is one thing – they might come in handy. But tucking back the lining, after – that's another matter.'

'Have those chaps been executed?'

'Not yet, I believe.'

'What are they saying at the base?'

'The comrades are very firm. Especially the ones from Toledo. The men who ran away when they had neither officers nor ammunition can't forgive these men who bolted when they had everything.'

'Yes, I got the same impression; they're much more down on them than the others.'

'Well, you see, these particular fellows remind them of

365

the one thing in the world they're most anxious to forget.'

'Yes, it's like they'd been building up something with the hell of a lot of trouble and then these fellows barge along and lay it flat!'

'They've had a tough deal – like a lot of us, for that matter. But don't forget that the story of the bastards who killed their captain won't do the others any good.'

Manuel came in. His lips were drooping. In his hand was a fresh pine-branch.

On the wall, amongst the maps, hung a case of mounted butterflies. A shell burst near the villa; the bombardment had begun again. Another shell. A butterfly came loose and fell, pin upwards, to the bottom of the case.

'Comrades,' said Manuel, 'Madrid is burning –'

He was so hoarse that his voice was almost inaudible. He had been shouting all day; but that alone could not account for his voicelessness. He went on speaking in the same low tone to Gartner, who repeated his words more loudly.

'The fascists are attacking all along the south-east sector. The International Brigade is holding out. The bombardment is now being carried on by artillery and planes cooperating.'

'And they're holding out?' a voice inquired.

Manuel raised his pine-branch. Holding out? That went without saying.

'The executions will take place,' he went on. 'A detachment of the Civil Guard is being sent to us.'

Gartner repeated. By now, Manuel had lost his voice altogether.

More shells exploded. No one paid any heed to them. But at each explosion, one or two more butterflies broke loose and fell.

Manuel scribbled a phrase on the margin of one of the staff maps lying on the table.

Gartner glanced at it, then looked at each of his comrades. His small mouth pursed in his flat face, he swallowed hard, then said at last, in the tone of one announcing a definitive event: victory or defeat or peace – 'Comrades, the Russian aeroplanes have arrived.'

XV

The enemy were retreating on Segovia. The loyalists had too few adequately armed troops to harry their retreat, nor did they wish to deplete the Madrid defences. Manuel's regiment, and the troops attached to it, were 'resting'. Now they were marching off by companies for drill.

The rain had stopped, but in the drab morning sky the tattered clouds were drifting low, skimming the flat roofs of the Castilian houses and turning their stones and tiles a dirty grey. Standing on the steps of the town hall, Manuel watched the arrival of these men, for whom he was responsible.

In front, a huge half-ruined castle, of the kind to be seen in every village of the region, seemed dissolving into the soft, crumbling rock on which it stood. To the right was a steep street, up which the troops were marching to parade on the plaza between the town hall and the ruined castle. Manuel had not seen his men since the executions of the previous night.

The first company, in formation as correct as that of regulars, the heavy boots of the men keeping punctual step on the sharp cobbles, came up to the saluting point. And as they passed the town hall steps, the captain rapped out an order.

'Eyes – Left!'

All heads turned smartly towards Manuel. It was the first time the command had been given in the regiment; it was perhaps the first time it had been given on the entire Madrid front. The order for the salute which bound the volunteers more closely to their commander had been given by the revolutionary officers; and Manuel felt it was not unconnected with the events of the night.

When the second company marched past, the same order was given, and so on for each successive company. Manuel watched these troops pass in fighting order, as efficient now as their opponents. They were the defenders of the people of Spain; he would be their defender. He would protect them from everyone, even from themselves. And yet he could not forget the mud-smeared faces he had seen gazing up at him; he could not forget the words: 'So you've no voice, now, as far as we're concerned?' Still, the eyes which now met him, as the men marched past, were not indifferent or expressionless; they were full of the events of the night, full of a tragic fraternity.

The castle looked much like the one on the Tagus front, near which Ximenes had advised him never to court his men's affection. Well, there was now no longer any question of courting the affection of his troops. It had been necessary to kill – not enemies, but men of his own, and volunteers. And he had done it because he was responsible to each of the men who now were passing before him. Responsible for their lives. Each man pays in the coin of his responsibilities, and, from now on, Manuel would have to pay in lives ...

With ever-growing sadness, with ever stronger resolve, Manuel's eyes encountered his men's eyes, rank by rank, and their gaze told him that today they were pledging themselves to him in a blood-bond.

*

After the regiment had passed, Manuel was left alone on the empty plaza, with only some stray dogs and the sound of distant gunfire to keep him company. Gartner was away with the brigade. Never had Manuel felt so much alone.

He had three hours to while away. The castle made him think once more of Ximenes, who was also in a rest camp six or seven miles away. Manuel got him on the telephone. Yes, 'Old Quack-Quack' was there. Manuel gave some instructions and got into his car.

The village in which the Ximenes brigade was quartered lay behind the village Manuel had left. Peasants were still fleeing along the road, and Manuel reached the colonel's headquarters through lines of donkeys and carts, herds of cattle of every sort.

They walked out together. The damp air made Ximenes's slight deafness worse. Enemy batteries were in action at some distance to the right and the gunfire at Madrid was audible. The Segovia plain showed through gaps in the Sierra.

'I believe that yesterday I lived through the most important day of my life,' said Manuel.

'How's that, my boy?'

Manuel told him what had happened. They walked in silence for a while.

The change in Manuel's appearance, his cropped head, his air of authority, had immediately struck Ximenes. All that remained of the young man he had known was the rain-drenched pine-branch in his hand.

According to report, there were big fires in the direction of the Escurial; and dark clouds were hanging on the slopes of the Sierra. Further off, towards Segovia, a village was burning. Through his field-glasses, Manuel could see peasants and donkeys hastening away.

'I knew what had to be done, and I did it. I'm determined to serve my party, and I'm not going to let myself be deterred by any personal psychological reactions. I don't believe in regrets. But there's something else. You said to me once: "It takes more nobility to be a leader of men than just to be oneself. Because it's harder." Well, I'm becoming less and less "myself". Music, for instance. . . . All that's over, so far as I'm concerned. Look here. Last week I slept with a woman whom I'd loved in vain . . . for years. Well, after two wretched shots at it, I found myself wanting to get away. No, I haven't any regrets on that score. But if I give up all that, it must be for some good reason. To command is to serve, nothing more and nothing less. I take upon myself the responsibility for those executions. They were necessary to save the lives of others . . . our men's. But there's something else; every step I've taken towards greater efficiency, towards becoming a better officer, has estranged me more and more from my fellow-men. Every day I'm getting a little less human. But I expect you've been up against the same thing?'

'All I could tell you, my boy, would be things you wouldn't understand. You'd like to lead men and yet remain their comrade; well, in my opinion, no man's big enough for that.'

He was thinking that fraternity of that kind was only to be found in fellowship in Christ.

'Still, I imagine, our humanity takes care of itself better than we think. All that estranges you from your fellow-men is bound to link you up more closely with your Party . . .'

Manuel had thought so too, and sometimes with dismay.

'To be linked more closely with the Party is worthless, if one's to be estranged from the very men for whom the Party's working. Whatever the Party is aiming at, that aim exists only as the aim of each and every one of us. One of those condemned men said to me: "Ah, so you've no voice, now, so far as we're concerned!"'

He did not mention that as it so happened he had, at that moment, lost his voice. Ximenes linked his arm with Manuel's, but did not reply. From the height where they were standing, the activities of the men below seemed dwarfed to insignificance by the stately pageant of the rolling clouds and the slow sheets of fire streaming across them. As though, in the gods' eyes, mankind were nothing but so much combustible material.

'And what did you expect, my boy? That you could sentence men to death without a qualm?'

Ximenes looked at Manuel affectionately. His eyes seemed dark with perplexing, perhaps bitter memories.

'But you'll get used even to that!' he added.

As a sick man seeks the company of a fellow-invalid to discuss death, so Manuel was drawn to speak of a moral conflict with a man to whom such conflicts were familiar. But it was much more for the warm humanity of his remarks than for their meaning. As a communist, Manuel did not question the rightness of his decision; he had done what he had done, so be it! Any problem of that kind should, he held, be settled either by modifying his conduct (and there could be no question of doing that) or else by simply refusing to consider it. And words, as he knew, tend merely to wear down the edge of insoluble problems.

'The real struggle,' Ximenes said, 'begins when you have to contend against a part of your own self. Up to that point, it's all plain sailing. Yet it's only from such inner conflicts that a real man emerges. Yes, we've always got to fear the world within ourselves, there's no escaping it.'

'I remember something you once said to me. Something like this: "The first duty of a leader is to make himself beloved without courting love. To be loved without 'playing up' to any one – even to oneself."'

Through a great rent in the rocks of the Sierra the further slopes had just come into view. From Madrid, scarcely visible across the grey expanse, pillars of dense black smoke were slowly, mournfully spreading up the sky. Manuel knew only too well what that smoke meant. The city was veiled in the shroud of its conflagration as warships are veiled in swirling banks of battle-smoke. The smoke was rising from buildings whence no glow of fire was visible, towering in columns that frayed out across the murky sky. And all the clouds seemed to have welled up from one unseen furnace, progressing like an army on the march in the direction of their drift. Above the thin white line of the beleaguered city, nestling in its woods, brooded an infinite distress, a holocaust of agony, filling the whole immensity of heaven. And to Manuel it seemed that even the memory of the night was being borne away by the slow, stagnant breeze, that brought to him the reek of the smouldering fires of Cuatro Caminos and the Gran Via.

One of Ximenes's officers came up in a car.

'Lieutenant-Colonel Manuel is being asked for on the telephone. By General Headquarters.'

They hurried back, Manuel feeling vaguely uneasy. He rang up G.H.Q.

'Hullo? You asked for me, I believe?'

'The general staff wishes to congratulate you on the way you handled your men yesterday.'

'At your service.'

'You may have heard that some of the militiamen who ran away the other day have asked to re-enlist.'

'Yes?'

'The general staff has decided to form a brigade composed of these units. They will be quite the most difficult troops to handle of any we have now.'

'Yes?'

'The chief-of-staff believes you have the qualities required for the command of such a brigade.'

'Ah, yes.'

'Your Party is also of that opinion.'

'Yes.'

'General Miaja thinks likewise. You will be immediately put in command of this brigade . . .'

'But what about my regiment? My own regiment!'

'I believe it will be incorporated with another division.'

'But I know each man in it! Who else could . . . ?'

'General Miaja thinks that you are qualified for this command.'

*

Coming back from the telephone, he found Heinrich waiting for him. The Internationals were planning a counter-attack on Segovia, and Heinrich was going in the direction of Guadarrama. They went away together.

The car was coming down the slopes of the Sierra. Manuel had fancied he understood Heinrich, because he knew his qualities as a commander. But as he recapitulated to him the events of the day and of the previous night, and repeated his conversation with Ximenes, it became obvious that the only human contact he had with the general was the strange affinity which always springs up between an interpreter and the person he interprets.

Heinrich's head was bent forwards; his shaven neck was smooth, and his lips, reflectively pursed up, gave a childish look to his grizzled old face.

'We are, both of us, engaged in changing the conditions of this war,' Heinrich said. 'Surely you don't believe you can change things without being changed yourself? From the day you take a commission in the army of the proletariat, your soul is no longer your own.'

'What about that brandy?'

Manuel had seen Heinrich handing out bottles of brandy to all the drunkards of his brigade; the labels on the bottles had been replaced by others reading, *Presented by General Heinrich. To be drunk when off duty; not a drop on duty.*

'You can keep your heart: that's another matter. But you must lose your soul. You've already lost your long hair – and the sound of your voice has changed.'

Heinrich's vocabulary was almost the same as Ximenes's. But the tone was Heinrich's hard tone, and his lashless eyes were set as they had been at Toledo.

'What do you, as a Marxist, mean by "lose your soul?"' Manuel asked, a little stiffly.

Heinrich watched the pine-trees scudding by in the melancholy light.

'All victims involve losses,' he said; 'and not only on the battlefield.'

He gripped Manuel's arm, and added in a voice which might have been bitter, or merely practical and firm – Manuel could not guess which: 'And now, you must never again waste pity on a hopeless case.'

XVI

Madrid, 2nd December

Two corpses were lying in front of the window. A wounded man had been dragged back to cover, by the feet. Five of the Internationals were holding the staircase, with their dumps of hand-grenades beside them. There were some thirty members of the International Brigade occupying the fourth floor of the house painted pink.

An enormous loud-speaker, one of those which the Republicans drove round in propaganda lorries more than half-filled by the huge funnels, was bellowing through the failing light of the winter afternoon:

Comrades! Comrades! Hold on to your positions. The fascists will be out of munitions by this evening. The Uribarri column blew up thirty-two of their lorries this morning. Comrades! Comrades! Hold on!

The loud-speaker, knowing there was no answering it, reiterated ...

The fascists would be out of munitions by the evening, but for the time being they had plenty; they had counter-attacked, and were holding the first two storeys of the building. The third floor was a no-man's-land. The Internationals occupied the fourth.

'Dirty swine!' a voice yelled up the chimney, in French. 'You'll soon see whether or not we have enough munitions to lay you out!'

That was one of the Tercios, down below. Chimneys make good speaking-tubes.

'Dirty ten-francs-a-day hirelings!' Maringaud yelled back, getting down on all fours. Heads were in the line of fire, even at the back of the room. Formerly Maringaud had believed all the usual romantic stuff about the Foreign Legion. Rebels, tough fellows, those boys! Well, there they were, just below, the Spanish foreign legionnaires, come here to defend they knew not what, full of vanity, and crazy to fight. Maringaud had been in a bayonet charge against them a month before, in the Western Park. What price the Tercios then? That pack of trained bloodhounds, servile to their unknown masters, now utterly disgusted him. The International Brigade, likewise a foreign legion, hates above all that other Foreign Legion.

The Republican six-inch guns continued to fire on the hospital at regular intervals.

The flat in which Maringaud and his mates were looking for good sniping posts had formerly been a dentist's. One of the rooms was locked. He decided to break open the door. Squat to the point of tubbiness, Maringaud had black eyebrows and a short nose set in a round, genial face, bringing to mind the 'bonny baby' of advertisement. Under his weight the door burst open, and the dentist's operating-room appeared. There, sprawling in the dentist's chair, was a dead Moor. The Republicans had been occupying the two lower floors of the building only the day before. The window in this room was wider and lower than the others. The enemy's bullets had broken the dentist's glassware only above a height of three yards from the floor. It would be possible to look out of the window and shoot from there.

Maringaud was not a commissioned officer as yet – he had not done his military service – but he was not without authority in his company. Everyone knew that he had been secretary of the Workers' Union in one of the largest munitions factories, and what he had done there. The Italians had given the firm an order for 2,000 machine-guns to be delivered for Franco. The factory manager was a fire-arms enthusiast, and would not let the packers box the arms for shipping until they were 'up to the dot'. So each night, when the day's work was over, lights burned until late in a portion of the factory where the old boss was working by himself indefatigably in a brightly lit work-room, tinkering with a bolt on a minute piece of mechanism, putting the last touch to an all-important gadget which would make those machine-guns 'top-notch, I'm telling you!' And at four in the morning, the militant workers, following Maringaud's instructions, would come, one after another, to the factory and, with a few strokes of a file, put out of gear the piece to which such patient industry had gone. So it went on for six weeks. For almost forty nights the dogged struggle persisted in the munitions factory between the workers' solidarity and the technical zeal of Maringaud's employer. (He was not a fascist, but his sons were.)

All the men knew – they now had reason to know! – that this work had not been in vain.

In the pink house, Maringaud's mates had at last installed themselves below the line of fire.

That house, in which fighting had been going on now for six days, with attacks and counter-attacks, was impregnable, except by the staircase, where five Internationals with hand-grenades kept constant guard. The space round the house would not permit of training a gun. Rifle-bullets took no effect on it. There remained the possibility of the place being mined. But so long as the Tercio held the lower floors, it was certain that the mine would not be set off.

The six-inch guns of the Republicans went on firing.

The street was empty. In a dozen houses insults were being bandied up and down the chimneys.

Now and then an attacking party from one side or the other made an effort to rush the street, failed, and fell back. Behind the windows the look-out men, bored even by death, waited idly. Had a misguided journalist come along to survey the situation, he would at once have had a load of lead in his body.

There was a machine-gun or a rifle behind every window. The loud-speaker drowned with its hoarse blare the insults bowled up the chimneys, and the street was empty, seemingly for ever.

But to the right stood the hospital, the best fascist position on the Madrid front. A thick-set skyscraper, standing apart in wooded ground, it overlooked the whole suburban quarter. From their fourth floor, Maringaud's mates could see the Republicans in every street near by, crouching in the mud; had the hospital not been visible, its proximity might have been inferred from the way the men kept below the line of fire from its windows.

375

The Hospital looked deserted, as did the neighbouring houses. But from all its windows machine-guns spat unceasingly. There it stood, stolid and ox-like, a gloomy, murderous sky-scraper, a ruined Babylonian tower, amid the bursting shells that scoured it with flying debris.

One of the Internationals, after searching all the cupboards, had found a pair of opera-glasses.

Some grenades exploded suddenly in the stairs. Maringaud went out on the landing.

'It's nothing,' one of the International guards informed him, above the roar of bursting shells.

Nothing, only the Tercios trying again to come up the stairs. Maringaud took the opera-glasses. In nearness, the Hospital changed colour, grew red. Its clean-cut outline was seen to be due merely to its bulk. That it was undamaged was an illusion. The glasses showed that under the pounding of the six-inch guns it was being hollowed out, dented, flattened, like red-hot iron under hammer-blows. A close-up view of the windows gave it the look of an abandoned beehive. Yet even at a con-siderable distance from that ruined fortress, men crept warily along the rain-drenched pavements and rusting tram-lines.

Suddenly Maringaud began waving frantically his fat arms. 'Oh boys, look! Look! It's begun! Our fellows are attacking!'

The men crowded up between the window and the dead Moor on the dentist's chair. Dynamiters and bombers could be seen, dark specks rising from the ground round the Hospital. They raised their arms, sank into the mud again, then re-appeared where, five minutes before, their dynamite cartridges and hand-grenades had made a ring of red beads.

Maringaud rushed to the chimney, and bellowed to the Tercios:

'Just have a look what's happening to your hospital, you bloody fools!'

Then he ran back to his place at the window. The dynamiters were closing in. From the smashed beehive a swarm of insects was pouring out towards the fascist lines, swept by their own machine-guns.

No reply had come from the chimney. One of the fellows, a Czech, suddenly crouched lower than his comrades and, bringing up his rifle, started banging away. From the houses on the opposite side of the street, some other besieged Internationals were also firing. Hugging the wall, the Tercios were filing out of the pink house. It was mined, and now that the Tercios had left, the mine would be set off.

*

Cautiously the Negus crept along the counter-mine. For a whole month he had ceased believing in the revolution. The Apocalypse was over. There remained the struggle against fascism; and the Negus's respect for the defenders of Madrid. There were anarchist members of the Government; other anarchists, in Barcelona, were fiercely defending their doctrine and their status. Durruti was dead. But the fight against the bourgeoisie had been, for such a long time, the breath of life to the Negus that he found it easy to go on living for the fight against fascism. He had always fought for negative emotions. Yet things were not going well with him. He listened to the men of his clan making their radio appeals for 'discipline', and he envied the young communists who spoke after them. *Their* lives had not gone topsy-turvy in the last six months! With the Negus now was Gonzalez, the fat man with whom Pepe had attacked the Italian tanks advancing on Toledo. Gonzalez belonged to the C.N.T. But that made no difference to the Negus. The fascists must be mopped up first, he guessed; plenty of time to argue afterwards. 'You know,' the Negus once remarked, 'the communists are good workers. I can work with them. But as to liking – no! I done my bloody best, but I can't get to like 'em!' Gonzalez had been an Asturian miner; the Negus had been a dockhand in Barcelona.

Since his exploit with the flame-thrower at the Alcazar, the Negus had taken to mine-laying. He liked that underground warfare in which nearly all the fighters are foredoomed and know it; in which, for the most part, each plays a lone hand. When up against insoluble problems, the Negus always fell back on violence or self-sacrifice; best of all, on both together.

Now he was creeping forward, a thin figure, followed by fat Gonzalez, along the gallery which was believed to extend a little beyond the pink house. The ground sounded more and

377

more hollow. That meant either that the enemy sap was very near (but he could hear no thud of spades), or – ?

He set the detonator of a hand-grenade.

The last blow of the pick landed on emptiness, and his momentum carried the miner through the hole into a sort of chasm in front.

Groping round with his electric torch like a blind man with his hands, the Negus took stock of the cavern below. Earthenware jars were everywhere, jars the height of a man. Obviously, a cellar. The Negus switched off his light and jumped. In front of him shone another electric torch, groping about. The man who held it could not have seen the Negus's lamp, put out a moment before. A fascist. The Negus hesitated. Should he fire? No, he could not see the man. The pink house must be almost directly above them. Gonzalez was still in the sap. The Negus threw his grenade.

When the smoke-clouds, swirling across the ray of Gonzalez' torch, had lifted, two fascists came into view sprawling in a slimy pool of oil or wine, from which their heads emerged. Fragments of the enormous jars stood up like cliffs from the pool which, slowly deepening, rose to the dead men's shoulders, then to their mouths, then above their eyes.

*

The Republican counter-attack was over. Maringaud and his mates were rescued, Gonzalez and his men returned to brigade headquarters. They had to cross a district of Madrid to get there.

The city had acquired the routine of bombardment. As soon as pedestrians heard an explosion, they ran for shelter to the nearest doorway; then, when the danger was past, they went on their way. Here and there, smoke-streamers trailed in a languid breeze, recalling in the midst of tragedy the peaceful smoke of cottage chimneys when supper-time approaches. A dead man had fallen in the street. He was still holding a lawyer's brief-case, which no one had dared to touch. The cafés were open. A draggled crowd, like the denizens of some ill-famed doss-house, was streaming from each metro exit. Others were swarming down the entrances, with mattresses, towels, baby-carriages, hand-carts heaped with kitchen pots and pans, tables, family portraits, and children clasping cardboard bulls. A peasant was trying to push a stubborn donkey into one of the entrances. Since the twenty-first, the fascists had been shelling the city every day. Round the Salamanca quarter, queer negotiations were in progress to bespeak the tenancy of 'cushy' doorways. Sometimes a mass of wreckage in the street would begin moving, and a hand, with its fingers fantastically splayed, emerge. But in the bombarded areas, amongst the horror-stricken faces of the fugitives, children could be seen playing at 'pursuit planes'. Stories, worthy of the *Arabian Nights*, were going round of women who had come back to their homes in Madrid packed up in baskets or tucked inside mattresses. ... A tram-driver joined the soldiers who were returning to head-quarters, and began talking to Gonzalez.

'I ain't grumbling at the life, nohow, but it's a rum go nowadays, this job of mine. I start off, I do my run, I reach the terminus – with half my fares alive! The others have been knocked out on the way. No. What I say is, I don't cotton to the job, not like it is now!'

Suddenly the tram-driver stopped. Gonzalez and Maringaud stopped. All the people in the street stopped, or ran for doorways. Five Junkers, escorted by fourteen Heinkels, were approaching overhead.

'Keep your pecker up!' a voice said. 'You'll get used to it!'

And then, before Gonzalez or Maringaud had noticed anything in the grey evening sky, a huge crowd of people came pouring out of shelters, cellars, doorways, houses, underground railway-stations – with cigarettes in their mouths, kitchen-ware or newspapers in their hands – variously clad in overalls, jackets, blankets, and pyjamas.

'Them's our planes!' someone, a civilian, was shouting.

'How the hell do *you* know?' Gonzalez asked.

'Can't you hear? The sound of the motors. It's louder, clearer.'

From the other side of Madrid, for the first time, thirty-six Republican pursuit planes were approaching; the planes sold by the U.S.S.R. after the Soviet Union's denouncement of non-intervention, had at last been assembled. Some had already fought over Getafe, and the patched-up machines of the International Flight had flown over Madrid, dropping pamphlets announcing the reorganization of the Republican air force. But these four squadrons of nine planes each, in V formation, with Sembrano in command, were being used that day for the first time for the protection of Madrid.

The leading Junker swerved to the right, swerved to the left, hesitated. The Republican squadron swooped all out upon the bombing planes. Men's hands gripped excitedly the shoulders of their women. In every street, on all the house-tops, at each cellar opening, at all the underground entrances, the people who for eighteen days had gone their ways in terror of the bombs raised their eyes, looked up in wonder and delight.

And then – they saw the enemy squadron turn tail towards Getafe; the roar of half a million voices, a wild, inhuman, exultant paean, rose to the dim sky, loud with the thunder of the people's planes.

*

In the gathering darkness, Heinrich watched from his window a crowd of soldiers in the street below; they had been cut off from their units and had come there to join up again. Before him lay a map on which he noted the movement reports which Albert, tethered as usual to the telephone, was transmitting to him. On all sides it was being confirmed that, cut off from their supply train by the Uribarri column, the fascists had run out of ammunition.

'The attack on Pozzuelo-Aravaca has been repulsed, sir,' Albert said.

Heinrich marked the new positions on the map. The creases at the back of his fat white neck puckered like a smile.

'The attack on Las Rosas has been repulsed,' another staff officer reported.

Again, the telephone.

'Good. Good. Thank you,' Albert murmured. Then he turned to Heinrich. 'The attack at La Moncloa has been repulsed.'

Everyone in the room felt like celebrating.

'Brandy all round at the next good news!' said Heinrich.

The War Office was transmitting the new positions, serially, through Albert's receiver, brigade headquarters were calling up at the other telephone.

'Hand out the brandy, sir,' said Albert. 'We are advancing towards Ferrol, and the Coruna road is now open.'

'Villaverde has been retaken.'

'We are advancing on Quemada and Garalito.'

PART THREE

THE PEASANTS

8th February

MAGNIN ran into Vargas in the Air Ministry at Valencia – much the same as he had found him at Madrid on the night after Medellin. The Ministers were new, those on active service were wearing uniform, Franco had come near to taking Madrid, the people's army was beginning to take shape. But the war was still the same war, and however many others had found either death or salvation in it, neither Vargas nor Magnin had changed much. As at Madrid, Vargas had just called for a whisky and cigarettes; as at Madrid, both their faces wore expressions of deep gloom.

'Malaga has fallen, Magnin,' Vargas said.

Magnin was not surprised: he had not imagined that the Republicans would be able to hold their smashed centre line against the Italians and Germans. A week ago Garcia had said to him:

'I expect everything from the centre and nothing from the minor fronts: Malaga has been a second Toledo.'

'The number of refugees is extraordinary, Magnin.'

'Yes, more than a hundred thousand in flight! Terrible.'

Above them, in the centre of that great room in which a rich merchant had lived, was a stuffed eagle supporting a chandelier.

'With Italian planes chasing them, and lorries. If the lorries can be stopped, they'll get to Almeria.'

Eyes and moustache registering equal despondency, Magnin made a movement which seemed to say: When do we start?

'Madrid is the place for our best planes, Magnin, I know.' (The fascists had launched a big offensive on the Jarama front.)

'We need two big bombers for the Malaga road. We've got practically no pursuit planes here.'

'But we've got to find someone for Teruel too. Nobody in the

385

column knows Teruel as well as you. I want you ...' He went on in Spanish. 'Not to choose the most risky, but the most useful work. You for Teruel, Sembrano for Malaga. He's here.

'You know,' he added, 'Teruel hasn't any pursuit planes either.'

For two months now, the International air force had been fighting on the Mediterranean front: the Balearics, Andalusia, Teruel. The suicidal flights of the 'Pelican period' were a thing of the past. In the air twice a day, and spending a substantial proportion of their time in hospital, the squadron had supported the International Brigade all through the battle of Teruel; fighting, doing repairs, photographing the results of their bombing while they fought.

The airmen lived in an abandoned château surrounded by orange-groves, near a secret landing-ground. During one engagement they had scored hits on Teruel station and the enemy headquarters despite the anti-aircraft batteries, and an enlarged photo of the explosion was pinned on the wall of their mess-room. Magnin and his pilots knew every inch of that front by instinct now.

'At dawn?' Magnin asked.

They began to study maps.

Jaime and Scali, Gardet and Pol, Attignies, Saïdi, the mechanic from one of the International contingents, and Karlitch were drinking *manzanilla* in the town.

Behind them, on the other side of the café windows was a miniature fair, complete with lottery-wheels, sweetstalls, and shooting-galleries. They could hear the music from inside. It was the children's gala-day. The shooting-galleries had attracted the machine-gunners, who were breaking pipes and knocking down pasteboard pigs to their hearts' content; that was where they had found Karlitch, surrounded by admirers. It was the children rather than the shooting-galleries that had brought Gardet and Saïdi there. They had spent all their money handing out cakes. Gardet loved children much as Slade loved animals, to offset his own dourness; in Saïdi they evoked his own childishness, and his Moslem compassion.

'The Americans are fine,' Pol said.

The first American volunteer pilots had just arrived.

'What I like,' said Gardet, 'is that they don't think that they are saving democracy every time they leave the ground.'

'And they've shown the other money-grubbers where they get off,' said Attignies.

He loathed all mercenaries instinctively.

'But as for the new commandant,' Pol went on, 'he's just the local brand of bloody fool.'

It was the first time that the Spanish commandant appointed to share the command of the aerodrome with Magnin had been difficult to work under.

'Cut it out!' Attignies said. 'Nobody expects a bed of roses. It'll come right in time. Sembrano is coming back. Let's do our jobs, that's all that matters. The Bréguets have got a fine Spanish captain, anyway.'

'Fighting modern planes week after week, handicapped like that, needs a bit of putting up with!'

'It's a curious thing,' Scali said. 'There's no other country with a sense of dignity and "style" like this one. Take a peasant, or a journalist, or an intellectual and give him a job. He may do it well or badly, but he'll nearly always do it with a "style" which could give points to any other country in Europe. This commandant hasn't any style. And when a Spaniard loses that, he's lost everything.'

'I saw what you mean at the Alhambra last night,' said Karlitch. 'A dancer came on the stage pretty much in the nude. Right close. Could almost touch her. And a drunk miliciano ran up on to the stage and gave her a bunny-hug. The audience roared with laughter. Then the miliciano turned round with his eyes closed and his hands clenched tight. As if she had given him her beauty when he had her in his arms, and it was there in his hands still. And he turned to the audience and threw her beauty in their faces. Contemptuously. Marvellously done. And only possible here.'

His French had got much worse. Leader of an irregular unit, always dapper, he seemed to have just left a bathroom where the eau-de-Cologne had been replaced by camphor. He removed his peaked captain's cap, and Scali saw the familiar crest of stiff, black hair.

'What I like about this show is that I'm learning something,'

Pol said. 'Seriously! But the commandant's a swine all right.'

'That's no way to talk of a commandant,' Karlitch burst out.

He had let his moustache grow; his face was less childish, harder, and Scali could see something of the ex-Wrangel cadet coming to the fore again.

Pol shrugged his shoulders. Then, with raised finger emphasizing the words:

'A dud. The *local* brand of bloody fool, he is.'

This looks like leading to trouble, Attignies thought. 'What made you join?' he asked Saïdi.

The latter raised an absurdly youthful finger as he answered: 'When I heard that the Moors were fighting for Franco, I told my socialist section: "We must do something. Otherwise what will our fellow-workers think of the Arabs?"'

'I can see lights,' Jaime said, fiddling with a piece of wire. He made aeroplanes out of wire, with controls that worked. And the airmen pulled them to bits, playing with them.

He had been 'seeing lights' every day for a month now. At first his friends used to look in the direction to which he pointed; but always found, not lights, but only another disappointment. Scali and Jaime were sitting next to each other with the others opposite.

'Well,' said Karlitch, 'we've taken Albarracin. There was one of the big-noise fascists there. Quite young: perhaps twenty. He was hiding. When we first went there, all we could find was two old women. That boy had denounced maybe fifty of us. And others who weren't even anything to do with us. All shot.'

'Nothing worse than those young pups,' Scali said.

'One of the old women says to us: "No, there's nobody else, only my other nephew." They were his aunts. Then, the next thing that happens, a boy comes out wearing socks and a hat.' Karlitch made a circular gesture round his head to indicate a sailor-hat. '. . . and a sailor-suit, and kid's shorts. "You see," said the old hags, "there he is!" It was the little bastard we were after. They had dressed him up in the kid's clothes to make us . . .'

'The lights are going round,' Jaime said; he had taken off his black spectacles.

Karlitch laughed, the same laugh which had got on Scali's nerves before, in August.

'We shot him.'

They all knew that Karlitch had twice rescued wounded comrades under fire. And that he'd be killed sooner or later. His passion was to serve others, and it was a quality which he expected to find also in those who served under him. The first time he had found some of his wounded tortured by the Moors he had himself given their officers the *coup de grâce*. His contradictory character worried Scali and Attignies. The others thought Karlitch a little mad, Scali was not so sure about it.

Scali remembered Karlitch's arrival. He was wearing magnificent riding-boots, and had started to have them cleaned by the first shoe-black he came to. But polishing a pair of Cossack top-boots is by no means the same thing as polishing a pair of shoes, and the thirty fellow-officers in the *char-a-banc* they were sharing, had had to wait for half an hour while Karlitch fumed and fretted, drumming his fingers on the table, waiting for the final gloss to be given to the second boot.

'The lights are stopping,' Jaime said.

This continual renewal of hope provoked an atmosphere of intolerable strain each time that it occurred. The fact that Jaime was half-ashamed of being blind, and his consequent attempts at facetiousness, made it worse. One day he had promised them oysters, which he imagined he had got on the track of by means of some crazy plan. Not a bit of it. And the first ones to arrive (Scali and he were the last) had found a note for them at the café: *On second thoughts we shan't be coming — 'The Oysters!'*

'Do you like this life?' Attignies asked Karlitch.

'When my father died (I've got three brothers) I was doing my military service, but even then my father said: "I want three of them to be happy; number four has got to fight his way through life." '

Scali was once more coming up against the thing that had been worrying him for the past two months: what those who cared to analyse people's motives for fighting referred to as 'the warlike spirit'. Scali liked natural fighters, mistrusted professional ones and loathed 'warriors'. Karlitch was a comparatively amiable specimen, but what of the others? And there were thousands of that kind on Franco's side.

'I'm hoping to get into the tank corps,' the machine-gunner went on.

Tank corps, air force, machine-guns — were German mercenaries of the sixteenth century going to reappear in Europe?

'What is the most frightening war-experience you can remember, Karlitch?'

He wanted to ask what had aroused his horror and pity, as well; but it was no good being too subtle.

'Most frightening? All of it, at first.'

'And afterwards?'

'I don't know.'

'Do you see the lights?' Jaime asked.

'Wait!' Karlitch went on. 'There's one thing that I'm really scared of. Men who have been hanged. How about you?'

'I've never seen any.'

'You're lucky. There's something terrifying about it. When a thing like that happens, you see, it's natural enough if there's blood. But men who have been hanged aren't natural. When there's no blood, it's not natural. And it's when things aren't natural that you get scared.'

For twenty years now Scali had been hearing talk about 'the human ideal' and had puzzled over it. Metaphysics! Now they were up against the spectacle of men engaged in a life-and-death struggle, a fine show it was making! Scali was completely unable to sort out his ideas. There was courage, generosity — and there was the physiological side. There were the revolutionaries — and there were the masses. There was politics — and ethics. 'I like to know which of them I'm talking about,' Alvear had said.

'The lights have started to move again,' Jaime said.

Scali sat up straight, with his mouth open and both fists on the table, pushing the wire aeroplane yards away from him. Gardet had taken Jaime by the shoulders, and they were both looking out through the café window at the big electric bulbs on the wooden horses which had just begun to revolve once more.

*

Gone completely crazy, whistling like linnets, Jaime and his friends, with Magnin in another car, were on their way up to the aerodrome to report for duty – for Malaga. An enemy squadron was shelling the harbour from four miles out at sea. Valencia was obscured beneath a fine drizzle which dripped gently off the oranges. For the children's fête-day the syndicates had decided to organize a procession of record dimensions. The children's delegations, when consulted, had asked if their favourite characters from the animated cartoons could be represented. The syndicates had accordingly constructed enormous cardboard models of Mickey Mouse, Felix the Cat, Donald Duck (preceded, nevertheless, by a Don Quixote and a Sancho Panza). Of the thousands of children who had come in from all over the province for the fête, which was in aid of the refugee-children from Madrid, many were without shelter. Their course completed, the triumphal chariots stood abandoned on the outer boulevard. Over a mile and a half and more the headlights of the motor cars revealed the talking-animal denizens of the modern fairyland, the world in which those who are killed all come back to life. Small children with nowhere to go for shelter had taken refuge on the bases of the cardboard puppets, between the legs of the mice and cats. The enemy squadron went on shelling the port; and in time with the explosions, while Don Quixote kept his nocturnal vigil over them, trembling in the rain, the animals bobbed their heads above the sleeping children.

*

Attignies was Sembrano's bomber. The crews of the two planes had been mixed up: in his machine were Pol, the mechanic, and Attignies. Sembrano had brought his second pilot with him, a Basque named Reyes. At their southernmost aerodrome they had found some bombs that they had had to change, and a degree of confusion worthy of Toledo; nearing Malaga, the refugees one hundred and fifty thousand strong, streaming along the coast road; then, beyond, the fascist cruisers trailing their smoke-clouds through the brilliant morning light as they made for Almeria; finally, the first of the combined Italian and Spanish motorized columns. Seen from the planes, it looked as if it must catch up the exodus within a few hours. Attignies and Sembrano had exchanged glances and come down as low as possible. Nothing more could be seen of the column.

To speed his return, Sembrano opened out his engine and turned out to sea.

When Attignies looked round, the mechanic was rubbing his hands, which were covered with oil from the bomb-releasing controls. Attignies looked at the sky in front again, full of round clusters of cumulus-cloud reminding him of the animated cartoons; eighteen enemy pursuit planes – overdue – were approaching in two groups. And still more behind, probably.

Their bullets began whizzing through the front gun-turret.

Sembrano felt a ferocious cudgel-blow on his right arm, which went limp. He turned to the second pilot: 'Catch hold of the stick!' Reyes was holding not the joystick but his stomach, with both hands. But for the belt which held him up, he would have fallen on top of Attignies, who lay prone behind his seat, with one foot a mass of blood. Now that the enemy fighter was behind their plane, it would probably fire on them from above; there was no possible protection; faced with that number of enemies, the five Republican fighters had to cover the escape of the other heavy bomber, which was in a better position to put up a fight. The holes in the fuselage were like shell-holes: the Italians were using big quick-firers. Was the tail gunner wounded?

As Sembrano turned to look, the starboard engine caught his eye; it was alight. Sembrano cut it out; all his machine-gunners had stopped firing now. The plane was losing height every second. Attignies was bending over Reyes, who was down off his seat and calling repeatedly for something to drink. 'A stomach-wound,' thought Sembrano. A new enemy onslaught swept over the plane, only hitting the right wing. Sembrano was piloting with his feet and his left arm. Blood was trickling gently down his cheek; he had probably been hit in the head, too, but he felt no pain. The plane sank lower and lower. Behind, Malaga; beneath, the sea. Just the other side of a strip of sand ten yards wide, a reef of rocks.

Parachutes were out of the question. The enemy fighter was following, and their machine was already too low. To climb was impossible; the elevator, probably torn by the explosive bullets, scarcely answered the controls. The water was so near now that the lower gunner drew in his projecting turret and lay flat in the cockpit; his legs, too, were covered with blood. Reyes had closed his eyes and was talking Basque. The wounded men were no longer watching the enemy fighter, from which only a few final bullets were reaching them now; they were watching the sea. Several of them could not swim – if swimming were possible with an explosive bullet in one's foot, arm, or stomach. They were more than half a mile from the shore, and a hundred feet above the sea; beneath them, twelve or fourteen feet of water. The enemy fighter returned, opening fire with every gun again; the bullets wove a pattern of red streaks like a spider's web around their plane. Beneath Sembrano the clear calm morning waves threw back the sunlight placidly; the best thing was to shut one's eyes and let the plane drop slowly down, until. ... Suddenly he noticed Pol's face, alarmed, blood-stained, but still to all appearances jubilant. Spurts of red flame flashed round the blood-soaked cockpit, in which Attignies was now bending over Reyes, who was down off his seat and seemed to be *in extremis*. Pol's face, the only one of which Sembrano could get a full view, was also streaming wet; but in the smooth cheeks of the fat, vivacious Jew burned such a desire for life that the pilot made a last effort to use his right arm. The arm had disappeared. With all the strength of his legs and left arm he pulled the plane's nose up.

Pol, who had lowered the wheels, now began to take them in again. The body of the plane glided along the surface of the water like a flying-boat; for a moment it slowed up, then plunged deeper into the waves and capsized. They struggled against the water which came flooding into the plane, like so many drowned cats. It stopped short of what was now the roof of the body. Pol threw himself against the door, tried to open it in the normal way, downwards; failed, realized that now that they were upside down he ought to look for the handle at the top, but the door had been jammed by an explosive bullet. Sembrano, having righted himself in the overturned plane after seeing the pilot's cabin tilt over in front of him, was groping for his arm in the water like a dog chasing its tail; the blood from his wound was leaving bright red stains in the water, already pink, that filled the cockpit, but his arm was where it should be. The lower gunner had forced a way through one of the main panels of his turret, which had come open during the somersault. Sembrano, Attignies, Pol, and he succeeded in getting out and at last found themselves facing the endless stream of fugitives, with the upper halves of their bodies in the open air and their legs in the water.

Attignies was shouting as he propped himself against the mechanic. But the waves drowned his voice. Maybe the peasants saw him beckoning to them as they fled, but that was all. And Attignies knew that each member of a crowd believes that an appeal for help is meant for his neighbour. A peasant was walking along the beach. Attignies crawled as far as the sand : 'Come and help them !' he shouted as soon as he was within earshot. 'Can't swim,' the other answered. 'It's not deep.' The peasant stood there. When he saw Attignies close beside him, out of the water, he said at last : 'I've got a family.' And moved away. It may have been true, and what help was to be expected from a man who would leave that headlong flight to wait patiently for the fascists? Perhaps he was suspicious; Attignies's fair and strongly moulded head looked too much like the Malaga peasant's conception of a German pilot. In the east, the Republican planes were just disappearing over the tops of the mountains. 'Let's hope that they'll send a car for us,' Attignies muttered.

Pol and Sembrano had got all the wounded out, and had carried them to the beach.

A group of milicianos broke off from the surging mass of fugitives. Poised on the roadside embankment, and as a result much taller than the crowd, they seemed more in keeping with the rocks and heavy banks of cloud than with living things; as though nothing which did not join in the stampede could be alive. Their eyes fixed on the plane, which was burning itself out and sending short flames out of the waves that hid the colour of the wing-bands, they dominated the rush of jutting shoulders and upraised hands like keepers of some legendary vigil. Between their legs, wide splayed to resist the sea-wind, the heads seemed fluttering past like dead leaves. At last they began moving down towards Attignies. 'Help the wounded!' They waded out to the plane, step by step, impeded by the water. The last man stopped and took Attignies's arm on his shoulder.

'D'you know where there's a telephone?' Attignies asked him.

'Yes.'

The miliciano belonged to the village trainband; without artillery and without machine-guns, they were going to attempt to defend their homes of rubble against the Italian mechanized columns. On the road, in tacit sympathy with them, one hundred and fifty thousand unarmed citizens out of the two hundred thousand inhabitants of Malaga were flying till their last breath from 'the liberator of Spain'.

They stopped half-way up the bank. 'People who say bullet-wounds don't hurt can have this one!' thought Attignies; and the sea-water did not improve matters. Above the embankment, the bent figures were still retreating eastwards; some walking, some running. In front of many mouths a fist held up an ill-defined object, as if all were playing on some silent bugle; they were eating. Some short, thick, vegetable; celery, perhaps.

'There's a field of them,' said the miliciano. An old woman trotted down the bank, shrieking; went up to Attignies and held out a bottle. 'The poor things poor little lads!' She saw the others below, withdrew her bottle before Attignies had taken it, and hurried down as quickly as she could, shouting the same words again and again.

Attignies trudged up the slope, leaning on the miliciano. Women went running past, stopped, started to scream when they saw the wounded airmen and still smouldering plane, and ran on.

'The Sunday promenade,' reflected Attignies bitterly, as he reached the road. Against the background of the noises of the flight, punctuated by the pulsing of the sea, another sound, and one which Attignies recognized, was growing more insistent every second: an enemy pursuit plane. The crowd scattered; they had already been bombed and machine-gunned.

It was making straight for the big bomber, where the last flames were dying into the sea. The milicianos were already carrying the wounded away; they would reach the road before the enemy plane arrived. They did their best to make the crowd lie down but nobody heard them. On Sembrano's instructions the milicianos laid the wounded at the foot of the little wall. The plane came down very low, circling over the multi-seater, which with its undercarriage sticking into the air and the glowing sparks coursing over it looked like a chicken on a spit. A photograph was no doubt taken, and the plane flew away again. 'Don't you forget your lorries' feet are sticking in the air as well!' Attignies grinned.

A cart was passing. Attignies stopped it, and took his arm off the miliciano's shoulder. A peasant girl gave up her place for him, and went and squatted between an old woman's legs. The cart started off again. There were five peasants in it. Nobody had asked any questions, and Attignies had not said a word; the whole world, just then, was moving in the same direction.

The miliciano walked beside the cart. About half a mile farther on the road swerved away from the sea. Fires had been lighted in the fields; fires from which, as from those who sat or lay motionless around them, emanated the same sense of hideous suffering as from the flight itself. Between the fields the unresisting mass of homeless humanity continued its forlorn migration to Almeria. The various vehicles began to get into a hopeless jam. The cart stuck.

'Is it far now?' Attignies asked.

'Nearly two miles,' replied the miliciano.

A peasant passed them on a donkey; leaving the road all the time and slipping through gaps, the donkeys were getting along much faster.

'Lend me your donkey. I'll give him back at the post-office in the village. It's for a wounded airman.'

The peasant dismounted without a word, and took Attignies' place in the cart.

A young man and a girl, students no doubt – they were almost smartly dressed – without baggage, passed the donkey. They were holding hands. Attignies realized that until then he had seen no one except poor people in the crowd; a few artisans, but mostly peasants. And all with Mexican blankets on their backs. No talking: shouts, or silence.

The road entered a tunnel.

Attignies looked for his electric torch. No good taking it out of that soaking wet pocket. Countless little lights – lamps of all kinds, matches, torches, flares, were flashing into life and dying out, yellow or reddish; others remained alight, throwing out a halo, on both sides of the stream of humanity, beasts, and carts. Protected against aeroplanes, a huge *caravanserai* of nomads had come into subterranean existence there, between the two far-away blue disks of daylight. A rout of shadows capered here and there around the torches and hurricane-lamps, their heads and shoulders momentarily silhouetted, legs veiled in darkness. And the rumbling of carts through the rock was like an underground river, flowing through a silence so profound that it had imposed itself even on the animals.

Attignies felt half-stifled in the tunnel. Did the heat come from the closely-packed crowd or from the fever growing in his blood? He must get to the telephone; yes, he must get to the telephone. But perhaps he had died on the way there, perhaps the cart and donkey were phantasms of an unexpectedly gentle dissolution? A moment ago he had been in the water; now he was drifting into a close and airless world in the bowels of the earth. More cogent than the consciousness of life in living men, that sense of death beginning in the blood-drenched plane was with him now in the airless, soundless tunnel; all that his life had meant was dissolving like an idle dream into a vast, desolating torpor; the points of lights became so many deep-sea fishes in the hot darkness, and the political commissar was wafted, motionless and imponderable, far beyond the confines of death, across a mighty river of sleep.

The daylight was getting nearer; flashing out suddenly as the road turned a corner, it vivified his body as if its rays had been ice-cold. He was amazed to find everything still there, the telephone obsession, his throbbing foot, the donkey between his legs. Now that he had survived both the battle in the air and the crash he felt the world of shadows giving place once more to the mystery of life. One more the tawny soil of Spain rose up around the flood of fugitives, as far as the Mediterranean, with black goats standing on the rocks.

Its cohesion sorely tried, the crowd surged around the first village, leaving innumerable evidences of its passage round the first houses, as an ebb-tide reveals a bench littered with pebbles and debris. A motley of costumes, with weapons jutting out here and there, was penned between the walls like a herd within a corral. The exodus was becoming less like an irresistible avalanche: it was just a mob, now.

Thanks to the miliciano, Attignies, still on his donkey, managed to reach the telephone. The wires had been cut.

*

Once the wounded had been laid out in a row beneath the wall, Pol had asked the miliciano where he could find lorries. 'At the farms; but there's no petrol!' He had run to the nearest farm, and found a lorry with an empty tank. Coming back with a bucket, still at a run, he had managed to drain off some of the petrol which remained in the plane's undamaged tank. He had made his way back to the farm, keeping the bucket level, compelled to make slow progress on the fringe of the incessant stream of peasants, and expecting every moment the arrival of the lorries which were certainly following those which he had destroyed that morning. He tried to start the engine; the magneto had been put out of action.

He ran to the second farm. Imagining that Attignies would be hampered by the prevailing confusion, Sembrano was counting on their happening on a lorry rather than on one being sent. In that country-house-like farm, bare of furniture, where the earthenware, in a mixed Spanish and Moorish style, and the pseudo-romantic frescoes with their parrots seemed to await impending incineration, the muffled murmur of the fleeing mob became still more ominously suggestive of the enemy's arrival. This time Sembrano came with him, using his left arm to support the right arm which had been ligatured by a Spanish machine-gunner. When they found the lorry, Sembrano at once lifted the bonnet; the petrol feed had been cut. The lorries had been systematically put out of action in order to prevent their being used by the fascists. Sembrano drew back from the bonnet, squaring his shoulders, with his mouth wide open and eyes half-closed, like a picture of Voltaire stunned. Then he staggered on like a groggy boxer towards the next farm, mouth still gaping.

*

In the middle of a field, he heard someone shout his name; the Spanish machine-gunner, plump and rotund as a rosy-cheeked apple, still smeared with blood was coming leaping and hopping over the ground. Attignies had brought back a lorry. Republican pursuit planes had notified the hospital. Sembrano and Pol put the wounded on the floor and the seat at the back; the machine-gunner stayed with them.

A doctor, the chief of the Canadian blood-transfusion service, had come also.

Since their plane crashed, not one of the airmen had mentioned the arrival of the fascists; and no doubt each of them, like Attignies, had constantly before him that picture of the mechanized column bombed outside Malaga.

Overloaded in front, the car seemed empty behind; every half-mile it was stopped by milicianos who wanted to put women on board, but saw the wounded as they stepped on the running-board, and got off again. At first the crowd had fancied that the Committees were in flight; after seeing the wounded men piled inside each seemingly empty car, they had begun to watch them passing with looks of sad solicitude. Reyes' breath was rattling in his throat. 'We'll try transfusions,' the doctor said to Attignies, 'but I haven't much hope.' So many men lay stretched beside the road that it was impossible to distinguish the wounded from those who were asleep. A number of women lay across the road itself; the doctor got out and spoke to them; they stood up, let the car pass without a word, and lay down to wait for the next one.

An old man, all nerves and sinews, with the strongly gnarled features peculiar to aged peasants, was calling for help; he carried a child only a few months old in the crook of his left arm. There were plenty of equally pitiful cases along that road. But perhaps a young child appeals to human sympathy more poignantly than anything else. The doctor had the car stopped, despite the desperate condition of Reyes. It was impossible to take the peasant inside. He settled himself down on a wing, still with the child in his left arm; but he found nothing to hold on to. From his place on the other wing Pol was able to clutch the door handle with his right hand; his left hand he stretched across to the peasant, who gripped it firmly. The driver was obliged to sit bolt upright in his seat, as the two hands met in front of the windscreen.

Attignies and the doctor could not take their eyes off them. In theatre or cinema, love-scenes invariably made the doctor feel like an eavesdropper. And it was the same here; there was something about this working man from another land gripping the wrist of the old Andalusian peasant while a whole populace in flight surged around them, which made him ill at ease. He made an effort not to look at them. Yet something fundamental in him remained linked to those hands – that same part of him which had caused the driver to stop the car a moment before, that which recognized maternity, childhood, and death even under the most incongruous aspects.

'Halt!' shouted a miliciano. The driver did not slow down. The miliciano aimed his rifle at the car. 'Wounded airmen!' the driver shouted. The man sprang on to the running-board.

'Stop, blast you!'

'I tell you they're wounded airmen, you bloody fool! Haven't you any eyes?'

Some more amenities, missed by those inside, were exchanged between the men. The miliciano fired; the driver toppled forward over the wheel. The car all but crashed into a tree. The miliciano jammed on the brake, jumped down, and made off along the road.

An anarchist soldier with a red-and-black cap and a sword at his side jumped on to the lorry. 'Why did that damn' fool stop you?'

'I haven't any idea,' Attignies answered.

The anarchist jumped to the ground and ran after the miliciano. Both of them disappeared behind the trees, dark forms against the sunlight. The car was stranded. None of the wounded could drive. Suddenly the anarchist reappeared, like an actor entering abruptly from the wings; his sword was red. He walked up to the lorry, laid the dead driver by the roadside, took his seat and drove off without a word. Ten minutes later he turned round, showing the blood-stained sword.

'Swine. Enemy of the people. No more trouble from him!'

Sembrano shrugged his shoulders, he was utterly weary of death. Offended, the anarchist turned away.

Thereafter he ostentatiously refrained from looking at the men in the car, driving with elaborate care, even to the point of trying to minimize the jolting.

'Nice guy, ain't he?' Pol said in French, his face only a few inches away from the red-and-black *képi*. 'You got to come to Spain to find that sort. When he's finished sulking, I suppose he'll tell us all about it.'

Attignies glanced at the anarchist's face, set and scowling, behind the hands linked across the windscreen.

At last they reached the hospital.

An empty hospital, but still littered with surgical instruments and bandages – vestiges of the suffering it had harboured. The empty hollows in the unmade, often blood-stained, beds were such a vivid reminder of the sentient beings who had occupied them only a short while before, that it seemed as if not living or dying men had been lying in them but disembodied wounds – blood doing duty for an arm, a head, a leg. The steady unwinking glare of the electric lights seemed to weigh on the room, giving it an air of unreality; the white expanse of beds and walls might almost have been the figment of a dream, but for the brutal realism of the blood-stains and, here and there, a body. Three cases too serious to be moved lay waiting for the fascists, their revolvers beside them.

There was nothing for those men to do but wait for death; whether from their own hands or from their enemies', unless the relieving aeroplanes turned up in time. They silently studied the new arrivals: Pol with the fuzzy hair, Sembrano with the projecting underlip, and the others in such agony that all personal traits were blotted out. And the wards seemed to grow vibrant with the fellowship that links the victims of a great disaster.

Forty thousand Italians in completely mechanized units, with tanks and aeroplanes, had broken through the Republican front at Villaviciosa. Their plan of campaign was to work down the valleys of the Ingria and the Tajuna, take Guadalajara, and Alcalá de Henares, and link up with Franco's southern army checked at Aranda, thus completely encircling Madrid.

Flushed with their victory at Malaga, the Italians had found less than five thousand men in front of them. But at Malaga the milicianos had fought no better than at Toledo; here they were fighting as they had fought at Madrid. On the 11th the Spaniards, the Poles, the Germans, the Franco-Belgians, and the Garibaldi contingent from the 1st Brigade – one against eight – checked the flood of Italians from both sides of the Saragossa and Brihuega roads.

As the first pale rays of daylight slid under the heavy snow-clouds, shells began to smash into the copses and the open woodland from which the German Edgar-Andreas battalion and the new volunteers hastily sent forward were operating. Uprooted by a single shell, entire olive-trees were flung into the air, zooming up to the snow-laden clouds and coming down like rockets on the surrounding branches, with a noise of rustling paper.

The first wave of Italians arrived. 'Comrades,' said a political commissar, 'in ten minutes the fate of the Republic will be decided.' Every man in the heavy machine-gun section stood to his gun, withdrawing its breech-bolt just before he died. The Republicans managed to construct a line of defence despite the fire, and to protect their flanks.

Sometimes the fascist shells failed to explode.

The commissar appointed to the new company stood up: 'Hurrah for the munition workers shot at Milan for sabotage!'

They all stood up, the munition workers among them a little sceptically; they knew that in any case shells do not always explode.

Then came the fascist tanks.

*

But the International Column and the dynamite-squads had got used to tanks at the battle of the Jarama. When the tanks reached a stretch of open country, the Germans fell back among the trees and refused to budge. The tanks had machine-guns, but so had they; vainly the tanks prowled up and down in front of the serried wall of trees, like monstrous dogs. Now and again a small oak was projected violently skywards.

From the battered wood, the machine-guns of the Flemish contingent mowed down the lines of advancing fascists. 'As long as we've the stuff to go on pumping out like this, we're all right,' bawled the corps commander amid the thunder of artillery and the rifle-fire, the intense drumming of machine-guns, the detonations of explosive bullets, the high-pitched screeching of shells from the tanks and the sinister drone of the aeroplanes which found the clouds were hanging too low to allow them to emerge.

In the evening the Italians attacked with flame-throwers, which met with no more success than the tanks.

On the 12th, the Italian shock-troops attacked again, meeting the brigades of the Vth corps; Manuel's, and the French and Germans. When the day ended, the Italians were concentrated on a narrow strip of ground, with their communications blocked. Their heavy artillery and their rations were no longer reaching the front, and snow was beginning to fall. The road was still in danger; but the Italian army not less so.

On the 13th, the snow ceased and men died from the cold.

During the night the Spanish brigade from Madrid arrived as reinforcements, together with a fresh draft from the International Column and the Ximenes carabineers. The Republicans were only outnumbered by two to one, now. The International units came into the firing-line equipped, if not well armed; but meanwhile, Manuel's men and the Lister Brigade were moving up on the other side of the road, wearing light canvas shoes. Never during their three months at the front together had Siry and Maringaud (now in the Franco-Belgian battalion) felt so close to the Spaniards as on that freezing March night when the people's army marched steadily towards the shell-shaken horizon, advancing through the darkness in their torn, tattered foot-gear. When, at times, one gun quickened its rate of fire, a dozen others took up the challenge, like the dogs on the Guadalajara farms in other days. The louder the noise of the guns grew, the closer the men huddled against each other.

On the 14th, Manuel and the Vth Corps attacked and captured Trijueque. The enemy's other flank was protected by the Ibarra palace where there were submachine-guns behind every window; it was being attacked since two o'clock in the afternoon, by the Franco-Belgians and the Garibaldi contingent.

Sixty per cent of the Garibaldi contingent were more than forty-five years of age.

From the wood they could see nothing of the low flat palace now except the bright spurts of flame gashing the dusk, and the snow which had begun again. The firing was slackening, and they could now distinguish separate shots. And a mighty voice, transcending the human voice as artillery predominates over rifle-fire, began to boom out in Italian:

'Comrades, workers and peasants from Italy, why are you fighting against us? The noise that will cut off this loud-speaker from your ears, means death. Will you die to prevent the workers and peasants of Spain from living a life of freedom? You have been misled. We . . .'

The voice of the Republican loud-speaker was drowned by a crash of guns and grenades. Four-cornered, like a petrol-container lying flat, larger than the lorry which carried it, it stood by itself behind a screen of trees; inert, yet alive because it spoke. With a range of more than a mile and speaking very slowly so that the words came clear, the stentorian voice blared out like the last trump through the empty, darkening forest, the bullet-shattered branches, and the interminable snow.

'Comrades, those of you who are prisoners with us will tell you that the "Red scum" welcomed them with open arms, arms still bleeding from the wounds which *you* have inflicted . . .'

A fascist patrol was advancing through the snow in the part of the wood dominated by the loud-speaker. Yet another burst of firing; one of the fascists fell.

'Drop your rifles, you !' came a shout in Italian, during a second of silence.

'Cease fire, you blithering idiots,' the officer shouted back.
'Friends!'

'Drop your guns!'

'I tell you it's us!'

'We know all about that. Drop your guns!'

'Drop yours!'

'We shall count three, then fire.'

The patrol was beginning to realize that the Italians who were answering them were on the enemy side.

'One. Surrender.'

'Never.'

'Two. Surrender.'

The patrol threw down their arms.

*

The Garibaldi contingent were attacking the Palace from one side, the Franco-Belgians from the other. A rocket soared above the wood, showing up black branches against the driving snow. A tree with low, serried branches seemed to jump into the air. As it fell to earth far away with a noise of snapping wood, Siry saw five of his comrades run, four of them fall, the head of the man on his right disappear, and bullets ploughing the ground on all sides; the outstretched hand of a man who was pointing at something was bleeding as he drew it back. Even before he realized that, now that the tree had disappeared, he was under fire from one of the windows of the Ibarra Palace, Siry was off at top speed, contracting his back muscles to stop the bullets from penetrating. Common sense suddenly returning, he flung himself flat on his stomach in front of a lieutenant who raised himself from his prone position and immediately fell back with a surprised groan: 'A – ah!' 'What is the matter with him?' said Siry, half to himself. 'Wounded?' 'Dead,' a voice answered.

Siry and the others had got as far as the wall of the Palace; but the considerable gap made by the demolition of the tree was drawing the fire from twenty windows, each furnished with a submachine-gun. The soldiers began to retire, crawling back, pressed to the ground, as if they had all been hit in the stomach.

Squirming like a wounded cockchafer, a man was dragging a comrade behind him, moving back slowly, with a look of terror on his face, but refusing to abandon his friend. His head pillowed on his left arm, Siry could hear through the incessant detonations of artillery, rifles, machine-guns and explosive bullets, the almost imperceptible ticking of his watch; as long as he heard that sound he was still alive. He had a confused feeling of something discreditable to be hidden, reminiscent of his fear of the keepers, in former days, when he was filching pears. At last he reached cover, at the same time as the wounded man and his rescuer.

Maringaud was within ten yards of the wall protecting the palace: one could throw hand-grenades from there. In the darkness and the snow the enemy shots, coming from the ground level and from every window, crackled like flames above the crest of the wall. Firing, firing away at the red flashes and the detonations, Maringaud felt more at ease. Someone bent forward behind him; it was the captain. 'Don't make such a row: it gives away your position.' One of the Internationals was hanging with both hands from the palace wall, dead no doubt. Maringaud went on firing; on his right some of the others were advancing, through the din of submachine-guns, grenades, the shouting and the shells. Another rocket soared through the trees, lighting up the grenades bursting convulsively, branches, and a bodiless arm with outstretched fingers. Maringaud's rifle was burning hot. He laid it on the snow and began to throw the grenades which a wounded comrade handed to him. Another man was opening and shutting his mouth like a suffocating fish. Three more were firing. Two yards to go; he was close up to the wall now, with his grenades; between his lips a cigarette which he imagined he was smoking.

'What in hell are they playing at on the left?' a voice shouted imperiously through the snow. 'Quicken your fire!'

'They're dead,' another voice answered.

The bravest of the fascists were trying to defend the wall, and it seemed to their crack shots that their eye was out, for the Garibaldi contingent and the Franco-Belgians, maddened alike by battle lust and the snow, hurled themselves frenziedly against the wall and kept standing there for several seconds after they had been hit. Gusts of shrill, eerie shouting burst suddenly from the palace and the wood, but there was a momentary silence when, in the light of a rocket, the fascists and the riff-raff gathered from the remotest corners of Sicily saw the grey-moustached veterans of the Garibaldi contingent charging down upon them through the blue-lit snow. Then the racket began again. Once more – whether it was that the attackers had reached the wall, or that that brief, inexplicable hush which sometimes falls on public gatherings or crowded cafés, occurs in war as well – the furious din of the explosions seemed suddenly to be borne aloft with the whirling snowflakes which a fierce wind was flinging back into the black sky. And then (the loud-speaker had been waiting for this lull) the fascists, the Garibaldi unit, and the Franco-Belgians heard a stentorian voice.

Listen, comrades! It's not true, what we were told. It's Angelo speaking. For one thing they've got tanks, I've seen them. And guns! And generals! A general questioned us. They don't shoot you, not a bit of it! It's Angelo, your mate Angelo, speaking. We've been had; we're being used as cannon-fodder, all of us! Come over, boys, this is the side for us!

Siry was back at the wall, listening. The Garibaldi contingent were listening. Maringaud and the Franco-Belgians were guessing what was meant. Every fascist submachine-gun in the palace replied. The wind had slackened and the snow was falling again, heavily, impartially.

From the corner of the wall where he was standing Siry could see under the trees in the distance some little houses. Those on the right were held by the Republicans, those on the left by the fascists. And sounding faint after the loud-speaker, like the wails of wounded men, the voices of some of last night's prisoners, who had joined the Garibaldi unit, came to him through the snowflakes.

'Carlo, Carlo, don't play the bloody fool, don't stay with them. It's me, Guido. You needn't be afraid, I'll fix everything.'

'Bloody bastards, dirty traitors !'

An order, a ripple of fire from the submachine-guns.

'Bruno, they're our mates, don't fire !'

The tumult rose and fell as though the tide of battle flowed and ebbed with the great wind churning up the flurries of the blizzard. Maringaud flung his last hand-grenade and picked up his rifle. It was instantly wrenched from his hand, and simultaneously his three companions were swept away in a sheet of flame. He ran to the wall, pressed himself against it, and picked up the rifle of a soldier who was clinging with both hands to the stones.

It stopped snowing.

There was a sudden silence again, as if the elements were stronger than the war, as if the peace which fell from the winter sky, no longer muffled by the snowflakes, had imposed itself upon the battle.

The moon had just appeared through a great rift in the clouds and for a time the snow, blue till now in the glare of the rockets, showed up white. To the rear of the foremost International units, across a maze of little dividing walls at different levels, the Poles were attacking with cold steel. Not in a body, but split up into small groups, protected by the low walls half buried in the snow. The Franco-Belgians and the Garibaldi contingent could hardly see them. But when the bayonet attack was over they could distinctly hear their fire coming nearer, as the almost invisible ranks whose firing line was stubbornly progressing, amid the wild clangour of detonations and explosions, as an underground attack might have advanced, through a huge, soft veil of tiny snowflakes poised in the moonlight, scaled the towering slopes of snow like some strange cavalcade of super-human warriors sent by the gods to earth.

In the distance, Siry heard the unintelligible staccato utterances of a Spanish loud-speaker through which old Barca, Manuel and Garcia's friend, was talking.

Suddenly Siry and Maringaud, and the Franco-Belgians, and the Garibaldi unit fighting next to them, wondered if they were going mad; from the palace a song that they knew well came floating down. The Column was attacking from three sides, and other units might have reached the interior of the palace while they had been checked at the wall; but they all remembered the singing of the 'International' at the battle of Jarama by the fascists who later assailed their trenches. 'Throw down your arms first!' they shouted. There was no reply: the bombardment was still going on, the intensity of the firing was diminishing, the snow was streaming down more heavily again. Yet just visible across the blizzard the windows of the palace were empty of red flashes; and the singing was going on. In French or Italian? Impossible to distinguish a single word. They were no longer being fired at. And the loud-speaker shouted through the lopped trees, in Spanish: 'Cease fire. The Ibarra Palace has been captured.'

III

The next evening,
Levant Front

The aerodrome telephone had been fixed up in a sentry-box. Holding the receiver to his ear, Magnin was watching the *Canard* land, outlined by the dust-laden rays of the setting sun.

'Headquarters speaking. Have you got two machines ready to go up?'

'Yes.'

In use every day against Teruel, repaired with bad spare parts, the machines had become as unreliable as at Talavera. The breakdown squad were constantly busy with the carburettors.

'Commandante Garcia is sending you a peasant from up north of Albaracin who came through the fascist lines last night. It seems that there's a landing-ground for planes next to his village. And lots of them there. No underground shelters.'

'I don't believe in their underground shelters. Any more than in our own. I said so in my report yesterday. Our bombing of the aerodrome on the Saragossa road was a failure simply because the planes were hidden in fields used as secret landing-grounds; not because they were in underground shelters.'

'We are sending you the peasant. Decide whether the scheme is feasible, and ring us back.'

'Hullo !'

'Hullo?'

'Has the peasant got anybody to vouch for him?'

'The commandant. And his syndicate, I believe.'

Half an hour later the peasant arrived, escorted by an N.C.O. from headquarters. Magnin took his arm and began pacing the field with him. The planes were finishing their test-flights in the fading light.

Dusk was descending on the sea and the flying-ground, a wide, open expanse stretching as far as the hills, bathed in the peace of evening. Where had Magnin seen that face before? Everywhere; every Spanish dwarf had it. But this man was strongly built, and taller than he.

'You crossed the lines to warn us. We must all thank you for that.'

The peasant smiled, a gentle, hunchback's smile.

'Where are the planes?'

'They're in the wood.' The peasant raised his forefinger. 'Under the trees.' He looked at the wide glades between the olive-trees where the Republican planes were hidden. 'In glades like that, just the same. But much deeper hidden, because it's a real wood.'

'What's the flying-ground like?'

'Where they fly up into the air?'

'Yes.'

The peasant looked around him.

'Not like this.'

Magnin took out his notebook. The peasant drew a picture of the field.

'Very narrow?'

'Not wide. But the soldiers are working hard on it. They are going to make it larger.'

'Which way does it face?'

The peasant shut his eyes and turned from side to side.

'It faces to the east wind.'

'H'm ... I see. Then the wood is on the west side of the field? You're certain?'

'Certain sure.'

Magnin glanced at the wind-cone above the olive-trees. The wind was coming from the west. On a small aerodrome, however, aeroplanes take off into the wind. If the wind was blowing from the same direction at Teruel, the planes there would have to take off with the wind behind them, if attacked.

'Do you remember where the wind was yesterday?'

'North-west. It looked like rain was coming.'

So the planes were certain to be still there. If the wind stayed the same, everything would be just right.

'How many planes?'

The peasant had a spur-like 'quiff' in the middle of his fore-head; he reminded Magnin of a macaw. Now he raised his fore-finger again.

'I counted six little 'uns. That's all I saw. But some of the others managed to make a count, too. They don't all say the same; they say there are at least as many big ones. At least. Perhaps more.'

Magnin thought for a minute. He took out his map, but, as he expected, the peasant could not read it.

'It ain't in my line nohow, but take me up in your contrap-tion, and I'll show you. I'll lead you straight there.'

Magnin understood why Garcia had vouched for the peasant.

'Have you ever been up before?'

'No.'

'You won't get the wind up?'

He did not understand.

'I mean, you won't be afraid?'

He thought it over.

'No.'

'You'll recognize the field all right?'

'I've lived twenty-eight year in the village. And I've worked in towns, too. You find me the Saragossa road and I'll find you the field. Without any trouble at all.'

Magnin sent the peasant to the *château* and phoned head-quarters again.

'It seems that there are about ten enemy machines, or there-abouts ...'

'It would obviously be best to attack at dawn; but tomorrow morning I shall have two transport machines and no fighters; all the fighters are at Guadalajara. I know the district pretty well, and the stake is a considerable one. There are nearly always clouds over there just now. ... My idea therefore is to call Sarion for a weather report at five in the morning, and if the sky is at all overcast, make a start.'

'Colonel Vargas leaves you to decide. If you should go, he would place Captain Moro's plane at your disposal. Don't for-get that there may be pursuit planes at Sarion.'

'Good. Thanks. ... Ah! another thing. Starting at night is

all very well, but there are no ground-lights. Have you any beacons?'

'No.'

'You are sure?'

'I'm being asked for them all day long.'

'What about the Ministry?'

'Same thing.'

'Oh! Lorries, then?'

'All in use.'

'Right. I'll see what I can fix up myself.'

He telephoned to the War Ministry; the same answer.

So he would have to take off at night from a small unlighted landing-ground. With headlamps on three sides, it might be all right. But the lorries had still to be found.

Magnin took his own car and started off, in the dark now, for the nearest village committee.

Requisitioned objects of all kinds were piled up on the floor: sewing-machines, pictures, hanging-lamps, beds, and a mass of harness amongst which the projecting handles of tools caught the light of the lamps standing on a table at the far end of the room. Magnin was reminded of the organized chaos of an auction room. The peasants filed one by one past the table. Some-one in charge approached Magnin.

'I need some lorries,' said the latter, giving him his hand.

The peasant delegate raised his arms discouragingly, but said nothing. Magnin knew these village delegates well; seldom young, earnest, shrewd (half their time was spent in defending the committee against uninvited assistance), and almost always efficient.

'It's like this,' Magnin said. 'We have made a new aerodrome. There are no beacons yet, I mean no lights for take-offs and landings at night. There's only one thing to do; mark out a small area with motor headlights. The Ministry haven't any lorries. Staff headquarters haven't any lorries. You have. You must lend them to me for tonight.'

'I ought to have a dozen, and I've got five, three of which are only light ones. How do you expect me to lend them? If it was a question of one, perhaps . . .'

'One's no good. If our aeroplanes get to Teruel they'll stop the

412

fascists. If not, it's the fascists who will get there and the militia who will be wiped out. You understand. That's why lorries are wanted, light ones or heavy ones. It is a question of life or death for our comrades up there. Listen now, what are they used for?'

'Nothing so important as that! Only, you see, we aren't allowed to lend them without drivers, and the drivers have done a fifteen-hour day and . . .'

'If they want to sleep in them, I don't mind. I can have them driven by mechanics from the aerodrome. I'll talk to them if you want me to, and I'm sure they'll agree; and they'll agree if you explain to them yourself what is at stake.'

'What time do you want them?'

'Four o'clock tomorrow morning.'

The delegate discussed the situation with two others behind the table with the paraffin lamps, then came back.

'We'll do what we can. I promise you three, more if possible.'

Magnin went on through the darkness from one village to another, from rooms littered with every kind of object to large whitewashed ones where delegates and peasants in black blouses cast a tracery of shadows on the walls: through squares coloured like stage sets, more and more deserted, where the café lights and the few gas jets still burning threw large iridescent reflections on to the violet domes of the secularized churches. The villages possessed twenty-three vehicles of various kinds. He had been promised nine of them.

It was half-past two in the morning when he passed through the first village again on his return. In the half-light which outlined the frontage of the house occupied by the Committee there were men carrying sacks, one behind the other, as if they were coaling a ship; they were crossing the road to enter the civic hall, and Magnin's chauffeur had to stop. One of them passed close in front of the bonnet, bending under the weight of a side of beef.

'What are they?' Magnin asked a peasant sitting at his doorstep.

'The volunteers.'

'What volunteers?'

'The food volunteers. Transport volunteers have been called for. Our lorries have gone to the flying-ground, to help Madrid.'

413

When Magnin got back to the aerodrome, the first cars were arriving. By half-past four, twelve large and six light lorries were there with drivers. Several had brought hurricane lamps on the off chance.

'Isn't there any other job we could do?'

One of the volunteers was muttering vituperations, without anybody quite knowing why.

He allotted them places, and gave them instructions not to switch on their headlights until they heard the engines of the planes, and returned to the *château*.

Vargas was waiting for him.

'Magnin, Garcia says that there are more than fifteen machines in that field.'

'All the better.'

'No; because in that case they are for Madrid. You know an attack on Guadalajara started the day before yesterday. They broke through at Billaviciosa; we're holding them round Brihuega. They're trying to take Arganda.'

'Who are "they"?'

'Four Italian mechanized divisions, with tanks, planes, and all the fixings.'

From the sixth to the twentieth of the previous month, in the bloodiest battle of the war, the German high command had attempted to capture Arganda from the south.

'I'll start at dawn,' Vargas said.

'See you soon,' Magnin replied, touching the wooden butt of his revolver.

*

It was five o'clock, and the chill which precedes dawn was in the air. Magnin wanted coffee. In front of the lime-washed *château*, blue in the darkness, his car was lighting up one of the orchards where the vague forms of his airmen, already up and about, could be seen roaming amongst the trees, picking the dew-drenched oranges that glimmered pale as hoar-frost. At the end of the field the lorries waited in the gloom.

During the fall-in, Magnin explained their objective to the commanders of the planes, who would give the orders when the machines were in flight. He made sure that all the machine-gunners had their gloves. Behind the lorry which had lit up the oranges and was deputed to keep the planes in touch with each other until the last possible moment, the crews were crossing the field still fragrant with the scents of night; they seemed straining against their flying-kit, like young dogs on the leash.

Slender wings barely perceptible against the sky, the aeroplanes waited. Dazzled by the unaccustomed lights, discouraged rather than roused by the wind which flung back in their faces the icy water with which they had sprinkled themselves, the men trudged along in silence. In the cold with which night flights begin, each man knows that he is taking his life in his hands.

With pocket torches to help them, the mechanics had begun their work. The engines of the first plane were warming up. At the far end of the field, two headlights cut suddenly through the wall of darkness.

Two more: the lorries had heard the engines of the planes. Magnin could just make out the hills in the distance, and high above him, the nose of a large machine; then the wing of another plane, above the bluish sheen of a revolving propeller. Two more lights came on from the lorries marking one of the boundaries of the field. Behind were the tangerine-woods; and in the same direction, Teruel. In the distance, near the cemetery and among the frozen mountain torrents, an International Brigade supported by the anarchists, whose cloaks made them look like Mexicans, was standing to in anticipation of an attack.

Fires were being kindled with dried oranges. Their sputtering red flames were drowned by the blaze from the headlights, but the wind wafted their bitter smell across the field, in intermittent smoke-like gusts. One by one, the lights were coming on. Magnin remembered the peasant with a skinned side of beef on his back, and the volunteers provisioning the depot as if it were a ship. The lights were flashing out now on all three sides at once, linked by the orange-fires, with the cloaks moving to and fro around them. For a moment, the planes were silent and the engines of the eighteen lorries from the villages, could be heard roaring on all sides. In the vast central mass of darkness unpenetrated by the beams of light, the hidden planes, whose engines suddenly all began to roar at once, seemed to represent the contribution of the collective peasantry of Spain that night to the protection of Guadalajara.

Magnin was the last to leave. The three planes from Teruel circled over the field, looking for each other's navigation lights before getting into formation. Beneath them, the oddly shaped flying-ground, quite small now, was dwindling away into the monotonous expanse of the dim countryside which to Magnin seemed converging on the humble orange fires. The three multi-seaters were veering round. Magnin switched on his pocket-torch and checked the peasant's sketch against a map. A biting draught was sweeping in through the opening in the turret underneath the body. 'In five minutes I shall have to put on my gloves; no good trying to use a pencil.' The three planes were in formation. Magnin headed for Teruel. With the wind still carrying the smell of the burning oranges from the field, and the interior of the plane still in darkness, the rising sun showed up the merry, ruddy features of the gunner in the lower turret.

'Hullo, chief!'

Magnin could not take his eyes off the laughter-widened mouth, with the broken teeth, so oddly pink in the first rays of the rising sun. It was getting lighter in the plane. Down on the ground it was still dark. The planes were approaching the first barrier of mountains through the uncertain light; below, blurred contours, like the shadings on roughly made maps, were becoming visible. 'Unless their machines are in the air, we're arriving absolutely at the right moment.' Magnin could just distinguish some farm roofs now; day was breaking on the earth below.

Magnin had done so much fighting on this Teruel front, that jutted southwards in a narrow strip like the Malay peninsula, that he knew it all by heart and kept his bearings unconsciously.

Machine-gunners and mechanics, strung up as usual before going into action, had finished looking at Teruel and began furtively to eye the peasant. Their covert glances saw a macaw-like tuft of hair kept obstinately lowered among the flying-helmets or, for a moment, a terrified face with the teeth gnawing the lips.

The enemy batteries were not firing; the planes were sheltered by the clouds. Down on the ground, it was probably quite light. On the right Magnin could see the *Canard Déchaîné* commanded by Gardet; on the left Captain Moros's Spanish bombing plane; both were slightly behind him, linked to the *Marat* like the two arms of a body, keeping their formation in the vast peaceful spread of sky, between the sun and the sea of clouds. Every time a flight of birds passed beneath the machine, the peasant pointed to them with his finger. The curved black humps of the mountains round Teruel loomed on all sides; and on their right, sparkling white beneath the winter sun, brighter than the duskier white of the clouds beneath, was the huge mass which the airmen called the 'snow mountain'. Magnin had grown used now to the primordial peace of that high world, so aloof from man's restless strivings; but just now the world of men still imposed itself even up there. The impassivity of the sea of clouds could not dominate those aeroplanes flying wing to wing together against their common enemy, united in their present comradeship and in the face of the perils ambushed all around them in the peaceful sky, no less united; it could not overshadow those men ready, one and all, to die for something higher than themselves, comrades whose compasses were set upon the same fateful course. Teruel would no doubt be visible beneath the clouds. But Magnin preferred to keep above them, in order not to give the alarm. 'We'll be crossing that wood in a minute,' he shouted in the peasant's ear, conscious that the latter was wondering how he was to guide them when he could see nothing.

Up to the slim, dazzling crest-line of the Pyrenees the earth below showed only in dark rectangular patches, like night-blue lakes in snowfields, gliding towards them. Once more, they could only wait.

The planes began to turn, with the patient malevolence of war-machines. Now they were over the enemy lines.

At last a grey stain seemed to spread through the clouds. Roofs appeared through it, now on one edge of the stain and now on the other, like goldfish motionless against a moving background; then veins became paths, but still only two-dimensional. More roofs and an enormous pale circle: the bull-ring. And immediately, yellow and tawny red in the leaden light, a cluster of roofs like the scales of some huge fish filled the hole in the clouds. Magnin gripped the peasant by the shoulder.

'Teruel.'

He failed to understand.

'That's Teruel!' Magnin bawled in his ear.

The town was looming bigger through the grey hole, isolated among the clouds which billowed away to the horizon, set in the midst of its countryside, river, and railway lines, and growing clearer every minute.

'Is *that* Teruel? Is *that* Teruel?'

Shaking his mane of hair, the peasant was staring at the confused, scarred map-like expanse beneath him.

Pale in the early light, the Saragossa road stood out from the darker background of the fields, to the north of the cemetery which the Republican army was attacking. Sure of his position, Magnin mounted above the clouds again immediately.

Keeping a straight course, the planes followed the Saragossa road, invisible below them. The peasant's village was twenty-five miles away, a little to the right. The other aerodrome, unsuccessfully bombarded on the previous day, was half as far. They were probably flying over it now. Magnin was calculating the distance they had to go by seconds. Unless they found the second field very quickly the alarm might be given and they would have on top of them not only the enemy chasers from both Saragossa and Calamocita and the hidden aerodrome, but those from this one too, if there were any there, barring their return. The clouds were their only protection. Twenty miles from Teruel, twenty-two, twenty-four, twenty five; the plane dived.

The battle seemed already to have begun with their entry into the white cloud-mist. Magnin had his eye on the altimeter. There were no more hills now on that part of the front. But were there pursuit planes waiting beneath the cloudbank? The peasant had his nose glued to the window. The dark line of the road began to appear, painted on a pale background of mist; then the red houses of the village, staining the cloudwrack like dried blood-stains on a bandage. No pursuit planes or anti-aircraft batteries yet. But to the east of the village were several long fields, all bordered on the same side by small woods.

No time to turn. They were all craning forward, peering. The plane flew over the church. They were taking a line parallel to the main street. Magnin gripped the peasant by the shoulder again and pointed out the roofs flashing by beneath them, bunched together like a herd of cattle. His mouth half-open, and tears zigzagging down his cheeks, one after the other, the peasant was straining every nerve to see where they were. He could recognize nothing. 'The church!' Magnin shouted. 'The main street! The Saragossa road!'

The peasant recognized them when Magnin pointed them out, but could not get his bearings. His chin was quivering convulsively beneath his stolid, tear-stained cheeks.

There was only one thing to do: to approach at an angle from which things would look familiar to him.

The earth rushed violently up towards the plane, swaying from right to left as if it had lost its balance, sweeping from its path a flight of panicked birds. Magnin was down to within a hundred feet of the ground.

The *Canard* and the Spanish plane followed in line.

The ground was flat. Magnin had nothing serious to fear from the ground defences; as for the small-calibre quick-firers, if there was an anti-aircraft battery protecting the aerodrome, it would be unable to fire so low. He nearly ordered the machine-gunners to open fire, but was afraid of unnerving the peasant. Skimming the ground, their angle of vision was that of a racing motor car as they approached the woods. A herd of cattle scattered frantically beneath them. The peasant peered in all directions as if his life depended on it. He seized Magnin by the middle of his flying-suit and pointed at something.

'What? Where?'

Magnin tore off his flying-helmet.

'There!'

'What, for Christ's sake?'

The peasant was pushing him to the left with all his strength, as if Magnin were the plane, and pointing at a black and yellow hoarding advertising vermouth, dabbing at the mica window first in one place then in another.

'Which one?'

Six hundred yards ahead were four patches of trees. The peasant was still pushing him to the left. The clump of trees farthest to the left.

'Is that it?'

Magnin stared wildly. Eyelids fluttering, the peasant was uttering wordless cries.

'Is that it?'

The peasant jerked down head and shoulders in assent, without moving his outstretched arm. At that very moment a bright circle of light sprang to life at the edge of the wood, showing up against the dark background of leaves. It was a revolving propeller. An enemy chaser was coming out into the open.

The bomber turned round. He had seen it, too. Too late to drop bombs, and they were too low. The forward machine-gunner, who might have fired, had seen nothing.

'Open fire on the wood!' Magnin bellowed to the man in the lower turret, just as he caught sight of a big bomber out in the open near the wood.

The gunner worked his pedals to swing the 'dust-bin' round, and fired. The enemy machine was already hidden from their field of vision by the trees.

Gardet had realized that these unrehearsed tactics would require a maximum of vigilance if they were to come off. He had taken charge of the forward gun of the *Canard* some minutes before, and was keeping his eyes glued to the *Marat*. He caught sight of the gleaming propeller against the dark green background of the wood almost immediately he saw the firing from the *Marat*'s lower gun; muttered: 'Steady, now!' and opened fire.

His tracer bullets showed the whereabouts of the Fiat to Scali, who was handling the *Canard*'s lower gun. He had given up bombing for machine-gunning as a concession to the urgency of the problems which now confronted him; passivity was no longer endurable. In the rear turret, Mireaux was prevented from firing by the tail. But Moros's plane was able to bring all three guns to bear.

*

Rising and banking, Magnin saw the propeller of the enemy plane cease turning as he passed over it again. A group of men were pushing the bomber under the trees. At that very minute, from somewhere inside the wood, the fascists would be telephoning to the other aerodromes. The *Marat* was rising in spirals, in order to drop its bombs from a height sufficient to prevent the risk of itself being brought down by them. But the spiral would have to be wider if the bomber was to have time to aim, and Darras time to make sure of passing right over the wood. Once must be enough, thought Magnin. The wood made a very good target. And if that was where the petrol drump was, as was probable, the whole lot would go up. He went over to the bomber, wishing it were Attignies there.

'Let all the bombs go!'

The plane banked twice to give a clear view of the objective. At twelve hundred feet it ceased climbing and came straight over the wood at full speed, machine-guns firing. The bombers would have time to base their aims on the height. Huddled up near the mechanic, the peasant was trying not to get in the way. The mechanic, with both hands on the releasing-controls, was watching for a signal from the bomber's uplifted hand, as the latter saw the wood move into focus in his sighting gear.

All three hands fell together.

Magnin had to bank at right-angles to see the result. The other two machines followed suit, until there seemed to be a whole chain of tilted planes. A heavy black smoke that they all recognized, was beginning to billow from the wood: petrol. It rose in abrupt, intermittent swirls, as though subterranean reservoirs had been ignited beneath that peaceful little wood, to all appearances no different from any other in the grey light of early morning. A group of about a dozen men ran out from the trees – then, a few seconds later, a body of about a hundred; both at the same panic-stricken scamper as the herd of cattle they had just stampeded. Driven back over the fields by the wind, the smoke was beginning to spread out into the majestic mushroom shape which petrol fires assume. The enemy pursuit planes were certainly in the air by now. The bomber was taking photographs, peering through the view-finder as he had peered through the sights a moment earlier; the mechanic was wiping his hands, oily from the releasing-controls; the peasant was drumming the soles of his feet against the side of the cabin-wall, half to express his joy, half on account of the cold. His big nose was crimson from being pressed against the mica.

The plane re-entered the clouds and made for Valencia.

As soon as Magnin came out above them again and could see farther ahead he realized that things were going badly for them.

The clouds were breaking up. Beyond Teruel an immense rift revealed thirty miles of earth and sky.

To get back without leaving the clouds would have meant a wide detour over the fascist lines – and there, too, the clouds might break up very quickly.

Their sole remaining hope lay in the Sarion chasers arriving before the enemy.

Delighted with their success and particularly anxious to survive that day, Magnin was counting the minutes. If nothing appeared before he counted up to twenty . . .

They were going out into open sky without a cloud in it.

One after another, one, two, three, four, five, six, seven enemy planes came out of the clouds. The Republican pursuit planes were single-seaters with low wings which could not be mistaken for Heinkels. Alertly, Magnin lowered his glasses and had his three planes close in on each other. 'If we had decent guns we might take on even that lot,' he thought. But he still had the old Lewis models, uncoupled. '800 rounds a minute by 3 guns makes 2,400. Each Heinkel, 1,800 rounds by 4, makes 7,200.' He knew that well enough, but it gave him a curious satisfaction to repeat it to himself.

The fascists were bearing down on the three bombing planes: they were keeping to the left, planning to begin by attacking one bomber alone. Not a Republican pursuit plane in the sky.

Beneath the wings the quails were passing on their annual migration.

Gardet's plane was on the left.

*

Pujol, piloting Gardet's plane, had just had chewing-gum handed round by Saïdi by way of celebration. Pujol lived up to to the best Leclerc tradition. Shaved on one side of his face only (the result of a romantic vow), his gardener's straw hat trimmed with scarlet feathers on his head again, now that the bombing was over, twenty-four years old, beak-nosed, and wearing an F.A.I. scarf (though he was not a member of the Party), he fitted in perfectly with the standard fascist conception of a 'Red bandit'. But for one or two socks wrapped round flying-helmets, and Gardet's little rifle, the appearance of the others was quite normal. While maintaining with discreet but firm authority the order indispensable to military efficiency, Gardet welcomed any picturesque touches such as his own wooden rifle; even Magnin was willing to countenance eccentricities which did not handicap the men in action, particularly when he felt that there was a fetish element involved.

Gardet understood the Germans' plan, too. He saw that Magnin was having the other two planes come down below him, so as to combine the fire of all the guns when the *Canard* was attacked. He glanced round at his own guns, took charge of the forward turret himself, thought once more how miserably inadequate a Lewis was, and turned his turret to face the Heinkels which were looming above the sights.

One or two bullets whizzed past.

'Don't get rattled!' Gardet shouted. 'There'll be plenty more!'

Pujol's flight was twisting, S-shaped. This was his first experience of a frontal attack by a chaser, at full speed; and he felt the natural bitterness of a pilot flying a slow, heavy machine attacked by fast planes. The Pelicans knew that the best of their own fighters would have brought the enemy down without difficulty. As always before an engagement, there was not a man who could quite forget the void beneath him.

Getting ready to fire, Scali suddenly saw on his left one of their large bombs; it had stuck while the others were released.

'There they come!'

Magnin had judged his distances well: the Heinkels were unable to surround the *Canard*. Two above, two below, three on one side, they grew so large that the pilots' flying-helmets could be seen.

The *Canard* shook all over as its three guns opened fire together. For ten seconds there was an unholy din, with the noise of wood snapping as the enemy bullets struck it, and a shrill network of tracer bullets.

Gardet saw one of the Heinkels attacking from underneath drop headlong. Either Scali or the guns of the other two planes had made a hit. He was conscious of the void again. Mireaux was leaving the rear turret, his mouth half-open; one of his arms hung limply, and from it blood was pouring into the cockpit like water from the nozzle of a watering can. Scali came up out of his under-turret and lay down. One of his shoes seemed to have split open.

'Make a ligature!' Gardet bawled. He threw the first-aid outfit to Mireaux as if it were a match-box, and sprang down into the lower turret. Saïdi had taken over his own gun and the bomber had replaced Mireaux. The pilots did not seem to have been touched.

The Heinkels were coming back.

None underneath this time. Those which tried to attack zooming up from below were caught by the fire from the *Canard's* under-turret gun and all six guns of the *Marat* and Moros's plane, whose criss-crossing tracers formed a network of smoke-trails beneath the *Canard*. The companion of the Heinkel which had been shot down had soared above them. Pujol was travelling all out, each corkscrew twist flatter than the last.

Once again came the tracer bullets, the rattle, the sound of splintering wood. Silently, Saïdi left the rear turret. Propped on his elbows, he lay face downwards above Scali, beside whom Mireaux was lying. 'If they have the nerve just to stick on to our tail and follow instead of passing us ...' thought Gardet. The holes made by the enemy bullets shone like little flames where the bright light came through from outside into the half-light within. The port engine stalled. The *Marat* and the Spanish plane closed in round the *Canard*. Pujol thrust his blood-stained head out of his cabin, still wearing the feather-decked gardener's hat.

'They're beating it!'

The Heinkels were withdrawing. Gardet reached for his fieldglasses; the Republican pursuit planes were arriving from the south.

He sprang out of his turret, opened the first-aid box, untouched by the others, and put tourniquets on Mireaux and Scali. Mireaux had three bullets in the left arm and one in the shoulder (simultaneous hits), and Scali an explosive bullet in the foot. Saïdi had a bullet in his right thigh, but was not in great pain.

Gardet went over to the pilot's cabin. The plane was flying

424

tilted at an angle of thirty degrees, kept in the air by the one engine only. Langlois, the second pilot, pointed to the revolution counter: 1,450 instead of 1,800. Soon the plane would only have its height to rely on. And the snow-covered mountain was close in front of them. From a house below smoke was rising placidly, straight into the air.

Bleeding, but not badly hit, Pujol could feel the contact of the stick, welded to his body, identified with it, as the others felt their wounds. The counter dropped from 1,200 to 1,100. The plane was losing height, a yard a second.

Underneath them lay the spurs of the snow mountain. Landing there meant plunging headlong into the ravines, like a drunk wasp dashing itself to pieces against a wall. A broad undulating expanse of snow lay beyond. And what underneath?

They went into a cloud, a zone of snowy whiteness; the floor of the cockpit was patterned with red footprints. Pujol was trying to rise above the cloud. Actually their unchecked fall brought them out below it. They were only 60 yards from the mountain. The earth was rushing towards them; how would these soft curves treat them … ? They wanted desperately to come through alive, now that they had brought off the bombing successfully and escaped the machine-guns.

'The bomb!' Gardet shouted.

If it failed to dislodge itself this time, they would all be blown sky high. Saïdi wrenched at both handles of the releasing mechanism, tugging them frantically downwards. The bomb fell, and the snow engulfed them as though the earth had been flung up against the plane by its fall.

*

Pujol sprang from his seat, suddenly open to the sky. Deaf? No, it must be the silence of the mountains after the noise of the crash, for he could hear a crow cawing, and shouts. Blood was trickling gently down his face and punching red holes in the snow in front of his shoes. His cheeks felt warm. He had nothing but his hands with which to wipe away the blood that was blinding him – through which he had a confused view of a black heap of metal loud with cries; the fantastic, inextricably fused tangle, characteristic of wrecked aeroplanes.

Magnin and Moros had been able to get back. Headquarters had telephoned to the aerodrome to say that the wounded had been taken to a little hospital in Mora. The planes would have to be overhauled and would not fly again till the following day. Magnin had already left, after giving the necessary orders. An ambulance would follow.

'One killed, two badly wounded, all the others slightly wounded,' the officer on duty had said over the phone.

He did not know the names of the wounded or the dead man. He had not yet heard the result of the bombing.

Magnin's car was speeding along between interminable orange-groves. Ringed here and there with cypress trees, the orange-groves went on mile after mile, with the ruined fortresses of Sagunto in the background, Christian fortifications built upon Roman ones, Roman fortifications upon Carthaginian – avatars of war. Above them the snows on the Teruel mountains shimmered, poised in the cloudless air.

Oaks replaced the orange-trees, as the road entered a mountainous tract. Magnin phoned headquarters again. There had been sixteen planes at the peasant's aerodrome. They had all been burnt.

The hospital at Mora was in a school. No sign of any airmen. There was another hospital in the village hall: no sign there either. The local Popular Front Committee advised Magnin to phone to Linares. A call for a doctor had come from there, for some wounded. Magnin set off for the telephone with one of the Popular Front delegates, through streets of blue, pink, and green houses with wooden balconies; past bridges with pointed arches dwarfed into insignificance beneath the beetling ruins of a castle straight from the ballads of chivalry.

The postmaster was an old militant socialist. His little boy was sitting on the telegraph-counter.

'He wants to be an airman, too!'

There were bullet-marks on the walls.

'The man before me here belonged to the C.N.T.,' said the postmaster. 'The day the rebellion started, he was telegraphing to Madrid all the time. The fascists didn't know that, but they killed him just the same; those are the bullets.'

At last Linares answered. No, the airmen were not there.

They had come down near a little hamlet called Valdelinares. High up, in the snow.

What village would he have to call now? 'Higher up, in the snow!' But the friendly tone in which the answers were given made Magnin feel more than ever that this was the real Spain which surrounded him, as though in each hospital, in each committee, in each post office a peasant were waiting with comradely greetings. At last there was a ring. The postmaster lifted the receiver; Valdelinares was answering. He listened, then turned round.

'One of the airmen can walk. He has gone to fetch him.'

The little boy no longer dared to move. A cat's shadow flitted across the window.

The postmaster handed Magnin the antiquated receiver, from which came a muffled voice.

'Hullo! Who is that?'

'Magnin speaking. That's Pujol, isn't it?'

'Yes.'

'Who has been killed?'

'Saïdi.'

'And the wounded?'

Gardet, nastily: eyes in danger. Taillefer, left leg broken in three places; Mireaux, four bullets in the arm. Scali, an explosive bullet in the foot. Langlois and I will be all right.'

'Can anyone walk?'

'All the way down?'

'Yes.'

'No, nobody.'

'Or ride down on mules?'

'Langlois and I. Perhaps Scali, with help; but I'm not sure.'

'How are you being looked after?'

'The sooner we get down, the better. They're doing all they can, but ...'

'Are there any stretchers?'

'Not here. Wait, the doctor's saying something.'

He could hear the doctor's voice.

'Hullo!' Magnin said. 'Can all the wounded be moved?'

'Yes – if you have stretchers.'

Magnin questioned the postmaster. He didn't know. Perhaps

there were stretchers at the hospital. But certainly not six. Magnin picked up the receiver again.

'Can you fix up litters with branches, straps, and mattresses?'

'Well . . . I think so.'

'I'm bringing what I can in the way of stretchers. Get them on to making the litters right away, and start down. I am waiting here for an ambulance. It will come up as far as it can.'

'What about the body?'

'Bring everybody down. Hullo! Hullo! And you might tell the men that sixteen enemy planes were destroyed. Don't forget.'

The journey through the streets began again; past the brightly coloured houses, the square and its fountains, the steeply pitched bridges and the sharp cobbles, still shining after the showers which had fallen that morning from the low clouds. There were two stretchers in all, and they were tied on to the roof of the car.

'Sure that won't be too high to go through the gate?'

At last, Magnin set out for Linares.

From now on, he was in contact with the very soul of Spain. Passing through a village of houses with open balustrade-fronted lofts, the car came to a gorge where the spreading horns of a fighting bull showed dimly outlined on the grey sky. A dark, primitive hostility seemed rising from the soil, on which these un-European villages had left their scar; a hostility intensified for Magnin by the way the rocks continually reminded him, in between glances at his watch, of their ruthlessness towards the wounded airmen. Nowhere to land; nothing but rocks, trees, and fields terraced like steps. Every time the car ran down a slope Magnin imagined the plane sinking down towards this land of ruin and despair.

Linares has a wall round it. Children were sitting on the ramparts, on either side of the gate. At the inn, where the ground floor was jammed full of carts with their shafts sticking up in the air, there were mules waiting. At the committee-room he found a doctor, who had come up from the valley, and fifteen or twenty young men. They stared curiously at the tall stranger with the drooping moustache who wore the uniform of the Spanish air force.

'We don't need all those bearers,' said Magnin.

'They all insist on coming,' said the delegate.

'Right. What about the ambulance?'

The delegate phoned Mora; it hadn't arrived yet. Their carts drawn up in a semicircle around them, the mule-drivers were sitting in the courtyard eating from the communal pot, in this case an enormous inverted bell. It was full of bubbling olive-oil, and covered with soot, which hid the inscription on it. Above the doorway was engraved: 1614.

At last the rescue party got under way.

'How long will it take to get up there?'

'Four hours. You'll meet them coming down.'

Magnin was walking two hundred yards ahead, his burly silhouette – uniform cap and leather coat – clear-cut against the mountain-side. There was hardly any mud, only stones to impede progress. Behind him came the doctor on a mule; further behind, the stretcher-bearers wearing jerseys and Basque berets (the local costumes were kept for fête days and old age); in the distance, mules and stretchers.

Soon there were no more bulls or fields; nothing but rocks, the rocks of Spain, that sparkle red and yellow in the sun, but now were pale beneath the overcast sky, with shadows lurking in the huge clefts. They fell away in two or three precipitous tiers from the snow on the skyline right down to the bottom of the valley. Pebbles fell over the edge of the path as they walked, clattering down from rock to rock until the silence of the gorge engulfed them as it seemed to be engulfing the noise of the mountain stream they were now leaving behind them. After more than an hour the valley down which Linares could still be seen came to an end. The moment they rounded the spur of the mountain which separated them from it Magnin could no longer hear the noise of the water. The track went behind a sheer wall of rock, which overhung it in places. At the point where it changed direction was an apple tree, outlined against the sky, in the centre of a minute field, recalling a Japanese landscape. Its apples had not been picked. Strewn on the ground, they formed a dense ring round it, which merged gradually into grass again. This apple tree was the only living thing among the rocks, living with the mute ageless indifference of endlessly reincarnated plant-life.

Magnin could feel the fatigue growing steadily in his shoulders and leg-muscles as he climbed. Gradually the feeling of effort invaded his whole body, driving everything else from his mind. By now the litters would be making their way down these same precipitous paths, with their load of shattered arms and broken legs. His eyes wandered from the short stretch of path visible in front to the snowy peaks fretting the white clouds, and each new effort brought home to him with vivid intensity the comradeship that binds a leader to his men.

The Linares peasants, who had not seen any of the wounded yet, followed him in silence, keeping him stern and dignified company. He was thinking about the lorries that were to come from the villages.

He had been climbing for at least two hours when the path which they had been following round the face of a spur of the mountain came to an end. The track now led through snow, up a new gorge, towards the higher and much less rugged part of the mountains that the aeroplanes had seen rising beside the other when they left for Teruel. From here on, the mountain streams were frozen. Where the path changed direction again, a Saracen warrior was waiting, like the apple tree lower down – black against the background of sky, and foreshortened like a statue on a high pedestal seen from below. The horse was a mule, and the Saracen was Pujol, complete with flying-helmet. He turned round, his profile thrown into relief like a carving, and shattered the intense silence with a shout. 'There's Magnin!'

*

Two long legs hanging straight and stiff on either side of a tiny donkey, and a tuft of hair sticking up out of a bandage, like a badger's crest, came over the sky-line: the second pilot, Langlois. As Magnin clasped Pujol's hand he saw that his leather coat was so coated with congealed blood below the belt that it looked almost like crocodile skin. What could have stained the leather with blood like that? There was a whole network of trickles across the chest, down which the blood had spurted so copiously that it could still be smelt.

'It's Gardet's coat,' Pujol said. Craning his neck, he was looking round for Gardet; as there were no stirrups he could not rise

430

from the saddle. But the stretchers had not yet come into view over the sky-line.

Magnin was still staring at the leather coat. Pujol had already started to tell his story.

*

Langlois, slightly wounded in the head, had been able to drag himself clear, limping on one foot; the other was sprained. Saïdi and Scali were lying among the splintered ruins of the tapering box which had been the cockpit. Beneath the dome of the over-turned lower turret was Mireaux, his limbs sticking out from under the boss, the top of which was grinding into his broken shoulder as in an engraving of some ancient torture scene; right in among the wreckage, was the bomber, lying flat. Obsessed by the ever-present danger of fire, all who had strength to do so were shouting for help, their cries echoing through the mountain stillness.

Pujol and Langlois had freed Scali and Saïdi. Then Pujol had begun to extricate the bomber, while Langlois tried to lift the turret which was crushing Mireaux. At last he managed to tip it over, with a fresh crash of steel and mica which startled the wounded lying in the snow, then died away.

Gardet had seen a hut and went off towards it, shoring up his broken jaw with the butt of his revolver. (He did not dare to use his hand, and blood was still pouring from his chin.) A peasant who had seen him in the distance had taken to his heels. The hut was nearly a mile away, empty except for a horse; it eyed him, hesitated, and began to whinny. 'My face must be a god-awful mess,' Gardet thought. 'Still, a living, unrequisitioned horse must mean that we're in Republican territory ...' The hut was warm after the snow outside, and he felt a desire to lie down and sleep. Nobody came. Gardet picked up a shovel that was in a corner, with his free hand; it would help to get Saïdi out when he got back to the plane, and it would help him to walk. He was finding it difficult to see clearly, except just at his feet. His upper eyelids were swelling. He found his way back by following the trail of blood in the snow, and his footprints, blurred and elongated at the spots where he had fallen.

As he walked he remembered how a third of the *Canard* had

been built of old parts from another machine, paid for out of a joint international proletarian subscription, which had been brought down on the Sierra : the *Commune de Paris*.

Just as he reached the plane, a little boy approached Pujol. 'If we're among fascists, we're done for,' the pilot was thinking. Where were the revolvers? Machine-guns don't lend themselves to suicide.

'Which are you, here?' Pujol asked. 'Reds or Franco?'

The boy — an inauspiciously sly-seeming brat with ears that stuck out and a parting right on the top of his head — looked at him without answering. Pujol began to realize how extra-ordinary he must look. He had put on his red-feathered hat again, unconsciously, and was still wearing it; his face was only shaved on one side, and the blood was trickling down over his white overalls.

'Which is it, tell me !'

He moved towards the boy, who backed away from him. Threats would do no good. And there was no chewing-gum left.

'Republicans or fascists?'

They could hear the noise of water in the distance, and the cawing of rooks in flight above them.

'There's all sorts here,' the boy answered, looking at the plane. 'Republicans and fascists.'

'What about the syndicate?' Gardet shouted.

Pujol had an inspiration.

'Which is the most important? the U.G.T? The C.N.T. Or the Catholics?'

Gardet was walking towards Mireaux, on the boy's right, and the boy could only see his back with the little wooden rifle slung across it.

'The U.G.T.,' the child said at last, with a smile.

Gardet turned round. His face was still supported by the revolver-butt; it had been slashed wide open from ear to ear. The lower part of the nose was hanging down, and the blood, which was now flowing quietly after its first violent uprush, was con-gealing on the leather flying-coat which Gardet wore outside his overalls. The lad gave a shriek and fled, scuttling sideways like a cat.

Gardet helped Mireaux to gather his spread-eagled limbs together and got him into a kneeling position. When he leant forward his face began to burn, and he tried to keep his head erect as he helped him up.

'We are on our own ground!' Pujol said.

'I must be looking the hell of a sight!' Gardet said. 'Did you see how that kid beat it?'

'You're crazy!'

'Ain't surprising after that slosh on the napper!'

'Look! There's people coming.'

Some peasants were making for them now at last, led by the one who had run away when he saw Gardet. Now that he was no longer alone he had found the courage to return. The explosion of the bomb had brought out the whole village, and the boldest of them were approaching.

'Frente Popular!' Pujol shouted, hurling his red-feathered hat into the middle of the heap of twisted steel.

The peasants started to run. They seemed to have guessed that the crashed plane was one of theirs, for they were practically unarmed; perhaps one of them had caught sight of the red wing-bands while the plane was still in the air. Gardet saw the reflecting-mirror hanging still in place amid the jumble of joists and wire, in front of Pujol's seat. 'If I look at my mug now, I'll kill myself,' he thought.

When the peasants were near enough to see the pile of frayed and twisted steel, the battered engines, the propeller bent double like an arm and the bodies lying in the snow, they stopped. Gardet went towards them. They stood waiting in a bunch, absolutely still, as if they were awaiting some catastrophe. The women were wearing black scarves round their heads. 'Look out!' said the peasant leading them; he had noticed that Gardet's broken jaw was supported by a revolver. Reverting instinctively to their former habits at the sight of the blood, the women began to cross themselves. Then, looking towards the bodies in the snow rather than at Gardet and Pujol, who had also started to walk towards them, one of the peasants raised his clenched fist; and one after another, all saluted with their fists the wrecked plane and the bodies which they imagined to be those of dead men.

'There's no need for all that,' Gardet muttered. Then, in Spanish: 'Give us a hand.'

They returned to the other wounded. Directly the peasants realized that only one of the bodies in the snow was dead, they began to bustle round them with clumsy affection.

'Wait a bit!'

Gardet began to organize things. Pujol was showing great activity, but nobody was obeying him. Gardet was in command, not because he was the actual commander but in virtue of his face-wound. 'If Death in person were to arrive on the scene, he'd have everybody at his beck and call!' he thought. Somebody must go for a doctor. A long way; but it couldn't be helped. Moving Scali, Mireaux, and the bomber looked like being difficult; but, he reflected, they're used to broken legs in the mountains. Pujol and Langlois could walk. Himself too, if it came to the worst.

They started the journey down to the village, a little group of men and women dwarfed by the snow. Before losing consciousness Gardet glanced once more at the mirror. It had been smashed to pieces when the plane crashed; there had never been a mirror in the wreckage.

*

Magnin could see the first improvised stretcher coming into view. Four peasants were shouldering it. Four others followed close behind. They were carrying the bomber.

He looked more like a case of long-standing tuberculosis than a man with a broken leg. The deep-cut furrows in his face increased the tensity of expression in the eyes to the maximum, and the bullet-head with the small moustache had now an air of high romantic dignity.

Mireaux came next. He had changed, too, but in another way. In his case pain had brought back the look of childhood.

'It was snowing when we started down!' he said when Magnin shook his hand. 'A damn' queer show!' He smiled, and closed his eyes again.

Magnin went on, with the bearers from Linares following. It must be Gardet in the next litter; a dressing covered almost the entire face. Only the eyelids could be seen – swollen to bursting

434

point, pale mauve in colour, and so distended that they almost met – between the flying-helmet and a flat bandage. The nose underneath seemed to have disappeared. Seeing that Magnin wanted to say something, the front two bearers lowered their end to the ground before the others, and for a moment the airman's body lay aslant, like a tragic bas-relief Armageddon.

Direct contact was impossible. Both Gardet's hands were under the blanket. Between the lids of the left eye, Magnin fancied he could distinguish a faint line.

'Can you see?'

'Not too well. Just about see you, old chap!'

Magnin felt an impulse to take him in his arms and hug him.

'Anything we can do?'

'Tell the old woman to bloody well stop fussing round with that soup! And listen, when do we reach the hospital?'

'You'll get to the ambulance in an hour and a half. Hospital this evening.'

The stretcher got under way again, with half Valdelinares behind it. As Scali's stretcher went past Magnin, an old woman with a black handkerchief over her hair approached with a cup and gave him some soup. She was carrying a basket containing a thermos flask and a Japanese cup, her most treasured possessions, very likely. Magnin pictured the rim of the cup slipped beneath the turned-up bandage on Gardet's face.

'Better not to give any to the man who's wounded in the face,' he said to her.

'It was the only chicken in the village,' she answered gravely.

'Even so!'

'You see my boy is at the front, too –'

Magnin watched the rest of the peasants and stretchers go past, with the coffin bringing up the rear. It had taken less time to make than the stretchers: a matter of habit. . . . The peasants had tied one of the buckled machine-guns from the plane on to the lid.

The bearers changed over every twenty-five minutes, but without putting the stretchers down. Magnin was amazed at the contrast between the women's appearance of extreme poverty and the thermos flasks that several were carrying in their baskets. One of them approached him, pointing at Mireaux.

435

'How old is he?'

'Twenty-seven.'

She had been following the stretcher for some minutes with a confused idea of being helpful, and there was a precise and gentle tenderness in her movements, a way of propping up the shoulders of the wounded man whenever the bearers had to choose their footing carefully over a steep stretch, in which Magnin recognized the changeless maternal instinct.

The valley was taking them steadily down. On one side the expanse of snow rose until it met the grey, disconsolate waste of sky; on the other, dreary-looking clouds were sailing past the peaks.

The men were maintaining an unbroken silence. Once more a woman approached Magnin.

'What are they, the foreigners?'

'One Belgian. One Italian. The rest are French.'

'Are they the International Brigade?'

'No, but they're the same thing.'

'The one who is . . .'

She pointed vaguely towards his face.

'French,' Magnin said.

'Is the dead one French, too?'

'No, Arab.'

'An Arab? Who'd have thought of it! An Arab – my word!'

She went off to spread the news.

Magnin moved up from the rear of the procession to Scali's stretcher; he was the only one who could do anything except lie flat. In front of him, the path led down in even zigzags to a small frozen stream where Langlois was waiting. Pujol had moved back to the rear. On the far side of the water the path turned at right-angles. The stretchers were about two hundred yards apart. Langlois, their outlandish advance-guard with the bristling mane of hair, was more than half a mile away; a ghost-like figure on his donkey, blurred by the mist which was beginning to rise from the valley. Behind Scali and Magnin there was only the coffin. The stretchers were crossing the stream one by one; seen from the side, the cortege looked like a long, moving fresco painted on the cliff-wall.

'Do you know,' Scali began, 'I used to . . .'

Magnin cut him short:

'Look at that: what a picture!'

Scali did not pursue his story. No doubt it would have got on Magnin's nerves as much as his comparison of the scene before them with a picture got on Scali's.

In the days of the first Republic a Spaniard courting his sister, who neither encouraged nor discouraged his advances had taken her once to his country house in Murcia. The house was a fantastic product of the end of the eighteenth century, with cream-coloured columns against a background of orange walls, stucco decorations freaked with tulips, and box hedges in the garden tracing a palm-like motif beneath the garnet-red roses. One of its former owners had built a miniature shadow theatre, holding thirty people; the magic lantern was already working when they entered, and the silhouettes were visible on the tiny screen. The Spaniard had been successful; she had slept with him that night. Scali had been jealous of that supremely fanciful tribute.

As he approached the mountain stream below, he thought of the four loggias, gold and salmon-pink, which he had never seen. A house full of floral designs, with plaster busts between the dark leaves of the orange-trees. His stretcher crossed the stream and turned the corner. The bulls came into view again opposite. The Spain of his youth — love, make-believe, and misery! Now Spain was that twisted machine-gun on an Arab's coffin and birds numbed with cold crying in the ravines.

*

The mules in front were vanishing round another corner, following the original direction again. The new line of descent led straight to Linares; Magnin recognized the apple tree.

What forest was that on which the rain was beating down, on the far side of the rock, where the path turned? Magnin coaxed his mule to a trot, went past all the others, and arrived at the turning. No rain; it was the sound of the streams which the cliff wall had screened from him as a rock-wall hides a landscape, and which could not be heard from the other slope. The sound was rising from Linares, as though the ambulances and the new lease of life which lay before them were sending up this insistent rustling, as of a high wind on leaves, from the far depths of the valley. Night had not fallen yet, but the light was failing. Like an equestrian statue, Magnin was sitting askew on his saddleless mule, gazing at the little apple tree surrounded by its dead fruit. Langlois's bristling crest of blood-stained hair came into view in front of the branches. In the silence suddenly grown murmurous with the sound of rippling water, the ring of decaying fruit seemed to typify the passage from life to death that not only was the doom of men but was an immutable law of the universe. Magnin's eyes wandered from the tree to the ageless ravines. One after another, the stretchers were going past. Branches reached forward on either side over the swaying stretchers, as above Langlois's head; above the corpse-like smile of Taillefer, the childlike face of Mireaux, Gardet's flat bandage, and Scali's lacerated lips; above each blood-stained body gently borne along by comrades' hands. The coffin went by, with its machine-gun twisted like the branch of a tree. Magnin moved on again.

Without his quite knowing why, the deep gorges into which they now were plunging, as if into the bowels of the earth, seemed imbued with the same agelessness as the trees. He thought of the quarries in which prisoners were left to die in former days. But that shattered leg which the muscles barely held together, that sagging arm, that obliterated face, that machine-gun on a coffin, all these were the results of risks voluntarily accepted, sought after. The solemn, elemental progress of that line of stretchers had something as compelling about it as the pale rocks that merged into the lowering sky, something as fundamental as the apples scattered on the ground. Birds of prey were crying again, close beneath the clouds. How many years had he to live, still? Twenty?

'What made that Arab airman join in?'

One of the women was approaching him again, accompanied by two others.

Up above the birds were wheeling through the air with rigid wings, like so many aeroplanes.

'Can they really give people new noses now?'

The path widened steadily as the valley approached Linares; the peasants were walking beside the stretchers now. The black-clothed women, scarves on their heads and baskets on their arms, were still bustling around the wounded, moving from one to another. The men were keeping pace with the stretchers, without ever getting in front of them; walking abreast of each other, holding themselves with the stiff erectness of those who have been carrying a weight on their shoulders. At each change-over, the new bearers abandoned their stiff walk as they took up the shafts with affectionate care, moving off again to the accompaniment of the grunts which tell of physical strain, as if anxious to mask the betrayal of their emotions which their solicitude conveyed. Their attention concentrated on the stones which obstructed the path, thinking only of the necessity not to jolt the stretchers, they moved steadily forward, slowing up a little on the steeper inclines. And the steady rhythm of their tread over the long pain-fraught journey seemed to fill the vast ravine down which the last cries still come floating from the birds above, with a solemn beat like a funeral drum. But it was not death which haunted the mountains at that moment; it was triumphant human will.

They were beginning to be able to make out Linares at the bottom of the valley, and the stretchers were drawing closer together; the coffin was level with Scali. The machine-gun had been tied on where a wreath would normally have been laid; the whole procession recalled a funeral as precisely as that twisted machine-gun recalled the wreath which it replaced. Near the Saragossa road down below, around the fascist planes, the trees in the dark forest were still burning in the fading light. Well, those planes would never reach Guadalajara now. And all that long line of black-clothed peasants, the women with their hair hidden beneath the scarves which they had worn from time immemorial, seemed to have more of the character of an austere triumphal progress than a rescue party bringing home wounded men.

The gradient was easy now. Leaving the path, the stretchers spread out across the grass, and the hillmen scattered out fanwise. Children were running up from Linares; a hundred yards from the stretchers they moved aside, to let them pass, and followed on behind. The road followed the fortifications up to the gate; its cobbles, set edgewise, were more slippery than the mountain path.

The whole town was massed behind the battlements. Night had not yet fallen, but there was little daylight left. Though there had been no rain, the cobbles were moist and shining, and the bearers picked their way carefully. In the houses which projected above the battlements lamps were glimmering.

The bomber still headed the line. The women on the battlements looked at him gravely, but without surprise; only the face of the wounded man appeared above the blanket, and it showed no sign of injury. Scali and Mireaux likewise. Langlois gave them a shock; with a bleeding bandage round his head, and toes sticking into the air (he had removed the shoe from his sprained foot), he looked like Don Quixote. Was this how war in the air ended, war in its most romantic form? The atmosphere grew tenser when Pujol went past; there was still light enough for observant eyes to see the large blood-stains on his leather coat. When Gardet arrived a hush so profound fell upon the crowd that the noise of the distant mountain torrents suddenly became audible.

All the other wounded could see; and all, even the bomber, had made an effort to smile when they saw the crowd. Gardet did not look at them; he was alive, but that was all. From the battlements the crowd could make out the bulky coffin behind him. Covered with a blanket up to his chin, and with the bandage under his flying-helmet lying so flat that it was impossible that there could be any nose beneath it, this stretcher was the visible incarnation of the peasants' immemorial conception of war. And nobody had forced him to fight. For a moment they hesitated; not knowing what to do, but determined to make some gesture. Then, as at Valdelinares, they silently raised their clenched fists.

It had begun to drizzle. The last stretchers, the peasants from the mountains, and the last mules were advancing between the vast background of rocky landscape over which dark rain-clouds were massing, and the hundreds of peasants standing motionless with raised fists. The women were weeping quietly, and the procession seemed to be fleeing from the eerie silence of the mountains, its noise of clattering hoofs and clogs linking the everlasting clamour of the vultures with the muffled sound of sobbing.

*

The ambulance set out.

Through the driver's communicating-window Scali could see square patches of the nightbound countryside. Here and there a section of the ramparts of Sagunto showed up, and cypresses, black and massive in the misty moonlight (that self-same mist which favoured night-bombing raids); ghostly white houses, emblematic of peace; sheen of oranges in their dark groves. Shakespearian orchards, Italian cypresses. ... 'On such a night as this, Jessica. ...' Yes, there still was happiness in the world. On the stretcher above him the bomber was groaning at every jolt.

There was no room for thoughts in Mireaux' brain. He was in a high fever, fancied himself struggling to keep afloat in scalding water.

The bomber was thinking of his leg.

Gardet thinking of his face. Gardet had been a great lover.

Magnin was listening to Vargas over the telephone.

'It's the decisive battle, Magnin. Bring everything you can, as best you can.'

'The controls of the *Marat*'s rudder are pretty well smashed.'

'Do what you can.'

IV

Guadalajara, 18th March

The Italians were counter-attacking towards Brihuega; if they broke through there they would take the Republican forces in the rear. It would mean Guadalajara being threatened again, the centre army cut off from Madrid, the town left more or less defenceless, the Dmitroff, Thaelmann, Garibaldi, André-Marty, and '6th February' battalions deprived of their line of retreat. The advantages of the capture of Trijueque and Ibarra would be wiped out.

The Thaelmann and Edgar Andreas battalions threw themselves into the fray again.

The Dmitroff battalion (Croats, Bulgars, Roumanians, Serbs, with representatives from all the Balkan States, and Yugoslav students from Paris) felt when facing the fascists that they were facing the murderers of their own people. They had spent twenty-four hours screaming curses at the Italian tanks from under cover of their woods, as they had done on the Jarama front; had captured half a mile of ground, and had been forced to give it up, in a furious rage, for the sake of keeping the line straight; had slept huddled together like flies in groups of four or five as a protection against the cold: such was the battalion that was attacking now under the bursting shrapnel. One of the section leaders, a Montenegrin, was running towards the rear shrieking: 'Look after the line and don't bother about me, you bastards!' He was supporting his broken left arm with his right, when an explosive bullet sent his head whirling into a flurry of snow.

It had started to snow again, and all along the front the advancing men, with their heads held low and their stomach muscles steeled in expectation of wounds, felt the shrapnel flying around them as thickly as the falling snowflakes.

In the Thaelmann battalion only two remarks were heard just now: 'Where's the grub!' and, 'You can't expect to have a war without casualties, old chap.'

The political delegate from the machine-gun corps, delirious from a stomach-wound, kept crying out: 'Send us our tanks! Send us our tanks!'

The battalion had just repulsed its eleventh attack since the beginning of the battle. The trees still had trunks, but no more branches.

'This isn't war!' yelled Siry to the Franco-Belgians, 'it's just a dose of clap that's going on for ever!' And he would start to imitate the spluttering rat-tat-tat of the machine-guns.

The rifles were starting to burn their hands.

In Manuel's command, Pepe's men had 750 rounds left for a machine-gun which fired 600 a minute. Half of it was distributed to the best shots. At sight of the obsolete rifles the recruits wept with exasperation and dismay. 'Bring the machine-gun here,' the section-leader shouted. When the smoke of the first shell had drifted away he lay dead at the very spot he had just pointed to. But presently some ammunition arrived, together with a few extra rifles.

At last a shout rolled down from the woods and plains above Brihuega, audible despite the bombardment which had just started again; it was taken up in the olive-groves and the low walls along which the Republicans seemed embedded like insects, and in the devastated farms and fields. The horizon seemed to be expanding under the shattering detonations from all the fascist batteries; the Republican tanks were coming into action.

They were attacking along the whole front, more than fifty abreast, from one end to the other of the horizon, which was blotted out at intervals as blizzards swept across it.

The men who had been snatching a few moments of uneasy sleep under the frozen olive-trees, and those who had been plunged in the coma of utter exhaustion and had woken up stiff as boards, started to run behind the last tanks, of which they lost sight now and then in flurries of snow.

In the Vth Corps the commander of No. 1 Company was the first to be killed.

A few moments later one of the Republican tanks went up in flames, lighting with an uncanny blue effulgence the white-swathed battlefield and the snowflakes hanging in the air above it.

Caught by a cross-fire from enemy machine-guns, pressed flat to the ground behind the tree-stumps, the men began scooping up the snow with their cartridge-clips and peaked caps – had they used their bayonets they would have had to expose themselves – and settled down into the cavities, standing up for a moment to launch their bombs, and ducking down again as the machine-guns swept their line. Of six volunteers who were trying to carry back the wounded captain, four fell. The International companies on either flank could only hear the explosive bullets bursting behind them and now and then a voice shouting, 'Getting on all right, boys?' and others answering, 'Not so bad. What about you?' – and meanwhile, less loudly, all over the battlefield a pitiful chorus of cries for help.

At three o'clock, however, through sheer fatigue the men were getting drowsy, and they were dreading the prospect of a night out in the snow. Hot coffee was handed round again. Under the heavy cowls their heads were full of memories of the Madrid trenches where they had used to loose off a casual shot or two during meals, where the brighter spirits had tamed mice and, as they waited for the shells to land, the married men had gazed in silence at the photographs of their children. Those were the 'cushy' days! And they remembered, too, the Jarama front, where they had joined in an attack behind the fascist tanks when these had run out of ammunition, and men had come up shouting wildly for urine to cool the barrels of the machine-guns.

'No tank without bullets, no bullet without a tank,' Pepe shouted, pleased with his slogan, to his men as they advanced. On his right, the Vth Corps, too, was steadily advancing across a hail of bullets. The Internationals were shouting, 'If they get me, there's a pack of American cigarettes in my right-hand pocket!' or, 'I'll have to miss the semi-finals this year, damn it, thanks to those ruddy fascists!' as they advanced behind a barrage of artillery fire brilliantly directed by a Spanish officer. Even the pacifists from the first-aid units, with bombs in their hands and no armlets, were attacking the tanks so as to be able to carry away their wounded.

A few voices started the 'International', drowned at once by a furious roar from the Spaniards and a short, shrill yell from the International Brigade: 'Forward!'

*

'The fascists are not being supported by their planes,' one of the officers from the Air General Staff remarked.

The clouds were only two hundred feet up, and more snow was threatening.

'They're on the far side of the Sierra,' Sembrano replied. 'It's most unlikely that they'll get across it today.'

His arm was in a sling and he could not fly his plane. The Italian troops were between the Republicans and the Sierra.

Vargas made no comment.

'Obviously,' one of the officers observed, 'if we go up, we risk losing every machine we've got; it needs this wind to freshen to a gale. No military authority would take the risk of such a catastrophe.'

Vargas called for the orderly officer.

'Those machines they have at Teruel could get round the Sierra even in this weather,' Sembrano said.

'I doubt if there are any left,' Vargas replied.

444

The orderly officer went to the telephone. 'Hullo, Alcalá! Send us at once every plane you can muster to Aerodrome 17 at Guadalajara. Hullo, Aerodrome 21? Send us every plane you have to Aerodrome 17 at Guadalajara. Hullo, Sarion? Send us every plane you have to Aerodrome 17 at Guadalajara.'

'If we lose this battle,' Vargas said, 'we lose everything. After all, we are only accountable to the Spanish people for our air force. For the fascists, it's not so simple. ... Anyhow, let's risk it !'

For the first time in many months he put on his flying-helmet again.

*

The recruits were attacking. The recruits' battalion, composed of men who had not yet been attached to any of the International companies, consisted chiefly of volunteers from distant countries, recently arrived: Greeks, Jews, Syrians, North Americas, Cubans, Canadians, Irishmen, South Americans, Mexicans, and a few Chinamen. They had started by blazing away without any system; men who do not feel the need to make a noise in their first battle are rare. At the first shock of encounter many had imagined that they were wounded, because they had been told that just at first wounds did not hurt. Some had diagnosed the swish of the first bullets as the noise of 'Spanish birds'. Hampered by their helmets, the peaks and neck-flaps of which jogged them each time they fired; unnerved by the grisly aspect of the dead; dumbfounded by the sight of the first casualties, they had awaited the order to advance with the same forced smile on every face. Then they had heard a muffled clamour indicating that the Edgar Andreas battalion on their right was coming out on to open ground; and they had rushed forward behind the tanks with their hand-grenades.

On the extreme left, an extraordinarily mobile machine-gun attack had left Manuel's battalions numb with surprise, until the Moorish cavalry, armed with Lewis guns, had charged down on their trenches. Those who were having their first experience of such methods of attack were on the point of running away. But Manuel had surrounded his recruits with Pepe's *dinamiteros,* who knew very well that cavalry in motion are unable to take proper aim, and that they themselves were under cover. They met the first charge with hand-grenades.

Then, entrenching themselves close behind a barricade of dead horses, and aided now by the recruits – who had understood what was expected of them and were firing at the cavalry as they tried to rally – they started to crawl under the horses so as to pick up the fallen Lewis guns. Only the peasant recruits remained behind, eager enough to fight the men, but hating to kill such fine horses. Standing behind a tank, Gartner was urging them on by word and gesture, taking care, however, not to spread his gestures beyond the shelter of the turret.

All along the front the stretcher-bearers' hands were turning red.

Then, as if miraculously it had squeezed through between the white snow on the ground and the dingy snowclouds overhead, the first Republican plane appeared.

And after it, one by one, quaint and ungainly, like wounded soldiers, came the old planes which had not seen service since the first month of the war, the little machines of the 'Señoritos', the transport planes, the mail planes, the Contact Patrol machines, Leclerc's old 'Orion' and the practice planes; and the Spanish troops greeted them with half-hearted smiles – such as their feelings at the moment may well have inspired.

Emissaries of an aerial Apocalypse, they bore down on the Italian machine-guns, skimming the snow; and at that moment the battalions of the people's army which had been waiting to advance received the order.

Despite the lowering sky and the menace of the snow, they came on, three by three at first, then flight by flight, bumping against the clouds like birds beating their wings against a ceiling, and swooping down again; filling all the far-flung field of battle raging from horizon to horizon with a roar that ruffled the snowdrifts on the ground and the thin shrouds of snow above the dead; spanning the bleak desolation of the steppes drearier even than the forest's gloom – on they came, eighty Republican planes in battle formation, like an invading host.

*

Below, the Republican troops were advancing, wrapped in greatcoats and wearing on their heads peaked cowls like the Moors'. Across the battlewrack, between the broken lines in headlong flight before the planes, Magnin had a brief glimpse of a vibrating road which gradually resolved itself into an Italian mechanized column. As the wind was blowing from the Republican lines Magnin could not make out, from the *'Orion'*, whether the column was fleeing from the cowls, from the tanks scattered across the trackless plain, or whether it was being driven before the wind, like the endless ranks of clouds, borne on the endless flux of things below.

And yet he had never felt so keyed up in a battle; it was as if the clouds and columns had been the expression of one and the same mysterious will, as if guns and gale and fascism were all attacking him together; as if the grey, lightless world around him were conspiring to cut him off from victory. A huge cloud, so thick that it gave the pilots the impression they were going blind, plunged on to the light planes, the wings of which were getting tipped with snow and beginning to shudder under the furious impact of the flakes that poured upon them. It hid the earth and sky from them, penning them in on every side, making the planes, creaking and grinding in their struggle against the elements, seem motionless in a moving world. Taking his bearings from a dark grey patch, Magnin saw the *'Orion'* turning at almost 180°. The compass jammed, the instruments showing the horizontal were smashed. Cold though it was, Darras took off his helmet and bent over the altimeter, which too had smashed, his hair as white as everything around the plane – perhaps they were diving earthwards at a hundred and fifty miles an hour, and they were less than 1,200 feet up!

No, they were emerging from the top of the cloud.

Between the layer of ragged clouds dissolving on to the earth and the second layer of clouds stretched out above like some frozen Arctic sea, all the Republican air force was dancing in line.

Darras tried to shake his wings to get rid of the snow.

'The bombs! For God's sake be careful!'

But there was little carefulness in the way he dived again.

'A fight in the snow – that'll be exciting!' Magnin murmured to himself. With his planes scattered to all the winds of Spain,

447

and his comrades scattered – but how worthfully! – in all its graveyards, all that he lived for now was this incredible *'Orion'*, furiously buffeted by the blizzard, and the ramshackle planes beside it tossing like dead leaves upon the gale.

Those clean-cut ranks of hooded figures below the seething cloudwrack were recovering not only the Italian positions of the previous day but the spirit of a bygone epoch. Magnin knew well what he was watching now as, like a crazy lift, the *'Orion'* jerked him up and down: it was the birth-pangs of war.

Campesino was issuing from his forest, the Garibaldi and Franco-Belgian units were streaming down behind the Dombrovsky battalion, the *carabinieri* surging up along the Tajuma. From one end of the front to the other, machine-gunners changing the barrels of their guns and standing up, stung by the heated metal, were being mowed down. Tanks were advancing all along the line; first-aid parties running backwards and forwards behind them, gathering endless harvests of wounded in their blankets. One Republican tank, with half its caterpillar-wheels hanging over a gully, stood gaunt and derelict against the low grey sky. Karlitch, at last a section-leader in the Tank Corps, was advancing, firing ceaselessly on the enemy anti-tank units – mere shadows of eyeless, crouching men armed with hand-grenades.

Passing over Teruel, Magnin had had a glimpse of the walls of huge estates, with their bulls, lethargic or unruly, scattered among the mountains which the war had claimed. And here, too, he had a glimpse, half blurred by the snowflakes, of the little stone walls which the Internationals and Madrid Brigades were attacking below him, and they brought to his mind the new-built squat stone walls which he had seen at Teruel and in the south, still insecure amongst the giant relics of the past. And he remembered the fallow land which the goitrous agricultural labourers were not allowed to cultivate. Those infuriated peasants fighting beneath him were struggling to raise those little walls, the first condition of their dignity. And Magnin now discerned, across the chaos of the dreams that had obsessed him during the last few months, something beyond the range of town-dwellers' preoccupations, something simple, clear and fundamental as childbirth, joy and pain and death: the age-old struggle of the tillers of the soil against their hereditary land-lords.

When for the fifth time the 'Orion' and its draggled squadron swept across the battlefield, the Republican machines had come down below the clouds and were attacking in front of the line of cowls. Hardly any fascist planes had put in an appearance. The Republican tanks, in a formation as orderly as a parade in the Red Square, were attacking, forming up, and attacking again and again. An evening mist, red with the flashes of bursting bombs, was creeping up, and already the convents and churches of Brihuega, down in a hollow, were all but swallowed up in it. The horseshoe curve of the Republican army closing in on the town was etched against the mist in a red glare of explosions. At each end of the horseshoe gushes of flame were pouring from the batteries, like bonfires kindled to counteract the snow which had set in again. Once the two ends met it would mean an Italian retreat along the whole Guadalajara front.

Ahead of the empty space between them, strip-signals were being laid out on the ground. But the mist was swallowing up everything now; it was impossible to make out a uniform. If darkness saved the Italians, they would counter-attack on Trijueque.

The 'Orion' lurched drunkenly through the air – all its bombs had been released and it was taking no further part in the fight – but it still held its course above the battlefield, buffeted, struggling against the darkness closing in upon the destinies of Spain, just as night had fallen – how long ago that seemed! – on Marcelino's homing flight. The long, dense line of the regular army planes was veering at less than two hundred yards distance from the battle. They, too, could see nothing, and they, too, were loth to leave the sky above the battlefield. And still the mist rose brimming over from the Tajuma valley.

In the dusk the desperate struggle of the volunteers went on, the ordeal that was to make or mar the fortunes of the Republican army. And the planes which perhaps had won the battle were hovering near, not on the lookout for an opening for attack, but watching and waiting for the Spanish victory. Spellbound in the gathering dusk, they had forgotten the perils of return to lightless aerodromes.

Flying over the gap between the tips of the horseshoe, Magnin saw beneath him one of the Horca roads, which widened at that point and was lined with abandoned lorries. He dived and skimmed the ground as he had done with the peasant on the Teruel aerodrome; and while the Republican troops, mistaking his identity, were riddling his wings with bullets, he recognized the strip-signals laid out there; they were those of Mera, the anarchist, of Campesino and the *carabinieri*.

v

Last spasmodic bursts of gunfire were rumbling in the distance. His lines established, Manuel, followed by his dog, was going round the village to get hold of some lorries. He had adopted a magnificent – ex-fascist – Alsatian dog, and it had been wounded four times. The more he felt cut off from men, the more he loved animals: bulls, army horses, large dogs and fighting cocks. The Italians had abandoned a number of lorries, and while waiting for their official distribution, each commander of a unit tried to get hold of as many as he could (shrewdly maintaining that if they waited until Campesino arrived there would not be one left). The lorries were garaged for the time being in whatever building were large enough to house them: churches, village halls, or barns. In the village occupied by the *carabinieri* they were in the church. But Manuel had been warned that Ximenes was there with the same intentions as himself.

The church was a lofty red-stone building, its stucco palms badly chipped by bullets. The slanted shafts of daylight which came through the cathedral-like vaulting fell on the debris of chairs smashed to matchwood, and the lorries lined up in order in the centre of the nave.

A miliciano guarding the church accompanied Manuel and Gartner.

'Have you seen the Colonel?' Gartner asked.

'He's over there, behind the lorries.'

'That's bad, he'll have already pinched them.'

Manuel's eyes were not yet used to the darkness; vaguely he seemed to see a mass of tangled gold quivering in the shadows above the porch like a bouquet of flames pinned to the wall. A band of angels, a medley of projecting wings and feet, was massed around the pipes of an oddly shaped organ. Manuel noticed a spiral staircase and went up it, anxious for a clearer view.

The miliciano followed him. Gartner remained below, as if to guard the lorries, with the dog at his heel.

'How is it this has remained intact?' Manuel asked the miliciano.

'It's the Revolutionary Artistic Committee, as they call it. Some fellows came along and told the local committee: "That organ and the choir, they've got to be preserved." Quite right, they were; a lot of work went to it. So they took the necessary steps.'

'What about the Italians?'

'There hasn't been much fighting here.'

Just recently an anarchist had used the torch with which he was about to set fire to a chapel to trace a huge black arrow above Cervantes' tomb, pointing to the crucifix which had been left intact; and had written on it: 'Cervantes has saived ye.'

'How do *you* feel about that?' Manuel asked.

'Well, the man who made those sculptures loved his job. I've never been one for destroying things. Priests, of course, I don't hold with. But I've nothing against churches. My idea is that they should be turned into theatres; they're nice to look at and you can hear well.'

Manuel remembered the miliciano he had questioned with Ximenes on the Tagus front. He scanned the nave closely, and finally discerned, beside a pillar, a shaved, downy pate like a duckling's head, shining in the gloom. Manuel knew that Ximenes appreciated music. He looked at the old man's white hale with affection, smiled as if he were meditating a practical joke, and seated himself at the keyboard.

He began to play the first piece of sacred music which came into his head – the Palestrina *Kyrie*.

Essentially the music of devotion, the notes echoed down the empty nave, stiff and severe as Gothic draperies; quite out of keeping with war, but all too much in tune with death. Despite the chairs smashed to atoms, and the lorries, and the war, the voice of the next world was claiming the church for its own again. And Manuel was moved, not by the melody but by his

451

memories. The miliciano was gaping in amazement at the lieutenant-colonel who had taken to playing 'hymns'.

'Well, that's all right, the old contraption's still O.K.,' he said when Manuel had ceased playing.

Manuel climbed down from the stool and began stroking his dog, which had tactfully refrained from barking. He went on stroking it: he had nothing in his right hand now. Gartner was waiting for him at the bottom of the staircase. Near the lorries, big black stains covered the flagstones. Manuel had long since stopped wondering what liquid accounted for such stains.

'That *Kyrie* is a marvellous thing,' he said with emotion, 'but I was thinking of something else while I was playing it. I'm through with music. . . . You saw that there was a whole pile of Chopin on the piano in our quarters last week – all the best things. I looked over them, but all that seemed to belong to another life.'

'Perhaps it was too late – or too early.'

'Perhaps . . . but I don't think so. I think a new life started for me with the war – as definitely as the first time I slept with a woman. War purifies you.'

'There's a lot could be said about that.'

At last they found the colonel, who was supervising the testing of the engines.

'So it's you, my son, who've been playing the music of heaven for me? Thank you. You did it with that in mind, I think?'

'It gave me pleasure to do it.'

Ximenes was looking at him.

'You'll be a general before you're thirty-five, Manuel.'

'I am a Spaniard of the sixteenth century,' Manuel said, with the grave smile which drew down the corners of his mouth.

'But, tell me, you aren't a professional musician – how the devil did you learn to play the organ?'

'It was the result of a piece of blackmail. The padre who was supposed to teach me Latin used to confine his efforts to the first hour out of every two, the second being free for me to do whatever I liked. But at first what I liked became what *he* liked. He used to stick an ivory needle (a great luxury in those days) into an old-fashioned, second-hand gramophone he had picked up, with a horn like a convolvulus, and play Verdi. I got to know *L'Africaine* by heart. Later on, I insisted on having lessons in tactics. (You hear that, colonel!) He pointed out that he was neither competent nor disposed to teach such a subject. But he brought me an old shoe-box full of soldiers cut out in cardboard.'

There were soldiers going past them now, on stretchers, rolled in blankets, living and dead.

'Then the Palestrina records appeared. He was a shrewd old chap. To escape being pestered about tactics, he used to ply the ivory needle on poor old Palestrina. It was a great success. I gave up tactics and clamoured for organ lessons. I was a good pianist already.'

'Well, my son, it seems there are some priests who aren't such bad lots,' the old man said ironically.

Manuel skilfully switched the conversation to his lorries, but he had hardly started when Ximenes cut him short.

'It's no good trying to wangle things. Until definite orders arrive, those lorries are sacred.'

'So it seems. We found them in a church. But your *carabinieri* have got all the light lorries they need.'

Ximenes chuckled, closing one eye in the old way.

'Nothing doing! You may be a general by the time you're thirty, but you won't get my lorries. I haven't got enough, anyway. Let's go and hunt for some more.'

'In the Sierra I told a militia girl she had lovely hair – and I asked her to give me one, and she sent me packing. You're as mean as she was!'

'Help yourself to a screw-spanner, and – let's drop the subject.'

They set off; before they had got to Brihuega they had already found three lorries each. The drivers brought by Gartner and Ximenes' men climbed into the drivers' seats and followed on after them.

'This is a nice little jaunt,' Manuel said. 'Quite an Andalusian wedding-party.'

'Kilometre 88!' a messenger shouted to them.

Victory was in the air.

In the square at Brihuega, in front of the military headquarters, which all the senior officers were expected to visit in the course of the mornings, Garcia and Magnin were listening to a talkative old windbag wearing an elaborate cravat, who had not shaved for days, and whose general appearance suggested that he had just emerged from a cellar.

'When they decided to kick us out,' he was saying, 'they tidied up the place. But they forgot to take down the wires we'd used to hang our trousers on. And the new guides hadn't a notion what to say about those wires. All except one. One of the lads he was; an artist chap . . .'

He made as who should comb out long, 'artistic' hair.

'He used to do sketches, write poetry, and so on. Yes he was a real artist. That's what he used to tell the tourists from the Toledo Alcazar: "Ladies and gentlemen, that famous warrior, the Cid, was naturally a very busy man. But when he had finished all his work, giving orders and writing and making expeditions, he used to come to this room. All alone. And then what do you suppose he used to do, by way of taking a rest? Hang on to this wire and swing!"'

'He used to be a guide at the Guadalajara Palace, that comrade,' Garcia said to Manuel and Ximenes; 'and before that at Toledo.'

He was an old man with side-whiskers like a rabbit's paws and the face and mannerisms of a professional actor, the sort that can only exist in a world of make-believe. 'I was one for queer things too,' he continued, 'before I lost my first wife. I've travelled all over the world; used to be with a circus. Whenever there was something worth seeing, that was what I made for. But all this business here . . .'

He extended a thumb in the direction of Guadalajara, whither the wind was carrying, under the lowering clouds, the reek of a charnel-house, and the Italian prisoners were being marched.

'Yes, all this business here, and all those cardinals, even the Grecos, and the tourists, and the whole caboodle, when one's had twenty-five years of them – and this war too, after six months of it . . . !'

There was superb indifference in his gesture as he waved his hand towards the south-west – to Guadalajara, and Madrid, and Toledo – like a man brushing away a swarm of flies.

An officer came and spoke to Manuel, who gave the dog a re-

sounding smack on the back and shouted: 'We're at Kilometre
90! They're abandoning all their material.'

'Do you wish to hear, Monsieur?' the guide went on.

He shrugged his shoulders and continued, as though sum-
ming up the experiences of a lifetime.

'Stones ... old stones, that's all. Now if you go further south
you'll find things that are worth while, Roman remains! More
than thirty years before Christ! Thirty years B.C. – that's talking, eh? Sagunto is a fine place. Or give me the new districts of
Barcelona. But all these old buildings! Just stones, if you ask
me, like war.'

Some Moors were being led past, with the Italian prisoners.

'The longer you fight, the nearer you get to the real heart of
Spain,' Garcia said. 'But in my case the harder I work, the further away I get. I spent the morning questioning Moorish
prisoners. There were only a few here, but still there were some.
There are some everywhere. Magnin, do you remember Vargas
saying to me: "There are only twelve thousand Moors!" Right.
Well, as a matter of fact, there are a considerable number of
Moors from French territory here. At the present moment the
real Islam, Islam considered as a spiritual unity, is more or less
in Mussolini's hands. The French and English still nominally
govern North Africa but Italy controls the religious side. And
the immediate result is that here in Brihuega we are capturing
Moorish and Italian prisoners. There's unrest in French
Morocco and Libya, unrest in Palestine, Egypt, promises from
Franco to restore the Cordoba mosque to the followers of
Mahomet ...'

Garcia loved talking; and the others liked listening to him.
They read nothing, except well-censored papers, and Garcia had
good sources of information. But both Manuel and Ximenes
remembered that they had their lorries to think of.

From the doorway of the house where he had taken refuge
during the Italian occupation a woman was calling to the guide.

'We are waiting for Azaña to tackle the job now,' he was
saying to Garcia. 'What will he do? That's something we just
don't know.' Pointing up at the low clouds he suddenly dropped
the mysterious tone which he had till now assumed and said with
complete indifference, 'Nothing. He will do nothing. There's

455

nothing can be done. Franco's a holy terror, of course. But apart from him, it doesn't matter if it is Azaña or Caballero, the U.G.T. or the C.N.T., or you; now that I've come out of my cellar I shall serve customers and guide fools, and I shall die in Guadalajara serving customers and guiding fools.'

The woman called to him again and he left them.

'He's a quaint bird, all right, Magnin said.

'In the most ferocious civil war there are always plenty of people who take no interest in it,' Garcia replied.

'Do you know, Magnin,' he continued, 'after eight months of war there's something still remains a bit of a mystery to me — the exact moment when a man decides to pick up a rifle.'

'Our friend Barca used to do some hard thinking on that point,' Manuel said.

The Alsatian barked approvingly.

'On people's fundamental reasons for fighting, yes. But what interests me is the actual spark that sets them off. It seems as if fighting, the Apocalypse, and hope, are baits used by war to catch men. After all, syphilis starts with love. Pugnacity forms part of the play-acting which almost every man indulges in, and it leads men into war just as almost every sort of play-acting leads us right into life. Yes, the real war is only starting now.'

The same thought had occurred to Magnin in the *'Orion'*, and probably to many others too. This conversation reminded him of his talk with Garcia and Vargas on the night after Medellin; and he felt once again that the International Air Force was dead.

'We're going to have Japan in the picture very soon,' Garcia said. 'An empire almost as big as the British Empire is being built up over there.'

'Think of what Europe was when we were twenty, and look at it now,' Magnin said.

Manuel, Gartner, and Ximenes started off again in quest of lorries; Garcia took Magnin's arm.

'What about Scali?' he asked.

'Explosive bullet in the foot at Teruel. He'll lose his foot.'

'What were his politics?'

'H'm, well — more and more anarchist, more and more Sorelian, almost anti-communist.'

456

'It's not communism that he is opposed to, it's the Communist Party.'

'Tell me, Major, what do *you* think of communists?'

So that's not finished yet, Garcia thought.

'My friend Guernico,' he answered, 'says: "They have all the virtues of action, but no others." But action is what matters just at present.'

His voice went lower, as always when he was recounting an unpleasant experience.

'I went to see the Italian prisoners this morning. There was one of them, an oldish man, blubbering like a baby. I asked him what was the matter, but he just cried and cried. At last he said, "I've got seven children – what's going to happen to them?" In the end I realized that he was convinced that we intended shooting the prisoners. I explained that we had no such intention, and at last he brought himself to believe me. Then suddenly he went frantic, jumped on to the bench and started yelling out a speech – just a few phrases like: "We have been tricked in Italy," and so on. Then he yelled: "Down with Mussolini!" Didn't cause any great stir. He began again. And the other prisoners took it up: "To hell with him!" but like a chorus singing with closed lips, and looking with scared eyes towards the doors. And yet they were safe with us.

'It wasn't fear of the police which was weighing on them, Magnin: nor even personal fear of Mussolini. It was the fascist Party. And it has been the same with us. At the beginning of the war loyal Falangists died shouting, "Long live Spain!" But later it was "Long live the Falangists!" Are you sure that among your airmen the type of communist who at first died shouting "Long live the Proletariat!" or "Long live Communism!" doesn't shout today, in the same circumstances: "Long live the Party!" '

'They won't have much more shouting to do, anyway, for they are nearly all either in hospital or under the ground. Perhaps it's all a matter of personal feelings. Attignies would probably shout: "Long live the Party!" the others, something else.'

'The word "Party" is misleading, in any case. It is most difficult to group together under one label a mass of people united

457

because they voted the same way, and parties whose ultimate roots strike down into the deep, irrational bedrock of human nature. The age of Parties is beginning, my friend.'

All the same, Magnin was thinking, Garcia was positive that the U.S.S.R. would never intervene. He is interesting, but not infallible. The Major was tightening his grasp on his arm, which he still held.

'Don't let us exaggerate our victory. This battle is no Battle of the Marne. But it's a victory, all the same. There were more unemployed here than Blackshirts, that's why I arranged for the propaganda by loudspeakers, which you will remember. Still, we were fighting actual fascist units. We should regard this patch of ground with due deference, my friend, for it is our Valmy. The two real parties have come up against each other here for the first time.'

Some officers were coming out of their headquarters, clapping each other on the back.

'Kilometre 92!' they went shouting down the street.

'Have you been through Ibarra?' Magnin asked Garcia.

'Yes, but only during the fighting.'

'The whole place is full of bowls of rice. *Riz au lait*, it seems; which the Garibaldi units kept on asking for – they hate Spanish oil – and which they at last managed to have made for them. Then the rice in the bowls got covered with snow. So did their first casualties. When the bodies were dug out of the snow, for burial, every one of those dead faces looked happy, with smiles on their lips, the smiles of satisfied stomachs.'

'Life's a damn' queer business,' Garcia said.

Magnin was thinking of the peasants. He was by no means as much at home with abstract thinking as was Garcia. But his flying experience had given his mind a purely physical flexibility which at times made up for lack of depth. The peasants obsessed him: the one Garcia had sent him, those whom he had asked for lorries in the villages, the ones who had accompanied the wounded down from the mountains, and those whom he had seen fighting below him the day before.

'What about the peasants?' was all he said.

'Before leaving Guadalajara, I had a coffee and *anis* (still without sugar). The inn-keeper was having the paper read to him by

458

his little daughter – she knew how to read. Either Franco will do what we are doing, wherever he wins, or he'll embark on an endless guerrilla war. Christ's triumph was only won through Constantine; Napoleon was completely crushed at Waterloo, but the essential points of French liberty defied suppression. One of the things that worries me most is seeing how in every war each side adopts the characteristics of the enemy, whether they wish it or not.'

The guide was behind Garcia, who had not heard him return. He raised his forefinger and screwed up his eyes, and an enigmatic look gave his face an air of refinement, despite the drunkard's nose.

'The deadliest enemy of man, gentlemen, is the forest. It is stronger than we are, stronger than the Republic, stronger than the revolution, stronger than the war. ... If man ceased to struggle against it, Europe would be covered with forests in less than sixty years. It would be here in the street, in the devastated houses, branches growing out of the windows – pianos tangled up with the roots. Yes, gentlemen, that's a fact !'

Some soldiers had entered the gutted houses and were picking out tunes on the pianos with one finger.

'Kilometre 93 !' a voice shouted from a window.

More prisoners were crossing the square.

'The bunch of bastards !' said the guide. 'Why couldn't they stay at home !'

He lowered his eyes, and caught sight of his new shoes.

'Still, I've got them to thank for these shoes, you know. My word, haven't they just left some stuff behind them ! But some of them are quite good scouts, though. Hey you, sing us something !' He waved his arms at the men who were passing. One of the prisoners shouted something that he could not understand.

'What did he say?'

'Sad folk don't sing,' Garcia translated.

'Then sing about your troubles, you fool,' the guide replied in Spanish.

The prisoners were getting further away; he followed them with his eyes.

'Cheer up, old boy, it'll all come out in the wash !'

In the distance, the sound of an accordion was coming from the Garibaldi battalion.

'Yes, how little it all matters! At Guadalajara I look after a garden. The lizards come. ... When I was out East with the circus I learnt an Indian tune. I whistle it, and the lizards run on to my face. You've only got to close your eyes – and know the tune. And now, what? War, prisoners, and death. And when it's all over, I shall stretch myself out as usual on the bench and whistle, and the lizards will crawl over my face.'

'I shall look forward to seeing that,' Magnin said, tugging at his moustache.

The guide looked at him, raised his finger again, and said:

'Nobody understands that, Monsieur, nobody.' Then, pointing at the door from which he had been summoned: 'Not even my second wife.'

'Kilometre 94!' shouted a second messenger.

VI

As soon as the requisition order for the Italian lorries came in from headquarters, Manuel had left Ximenes. He walked back to the place where his brigade was quartered, with the Alsatian trotting composedly beside him, while Gartner busied himself returning the lorries that had been 'scrounged' before the battle.

The soldiers were wandering about Brihuega, empty-handed and unwontedly at a loose end. The main street with its pink and yellow houses, austere churches, and huge convents, was so full of rubbish, so many shattered houses had disgorged their furniture into the roadway, and the whole street was so closely linked up with the war that, now there was a cessation of hostilities, it seemed unreal, preposterous as the tombs and temples of an extinct race, and the soldiers roaming it now without their rifles had the 'lost' look of civilian unemployed.

Some streets, however, seemed unscathed by war. Garcia had told Manuel how at Jaipur in India all the house-fronts are painted in sham perspective and how each house wears in front of it, like a mask, its pink facade. Many of the Brihuega streets brought to mind a city not of mud but of the dead; death was lurking behind the windows that stood half-open on the cheerless sky and the gay house-fronts that recalled siesta and the holiday season.

It seemed to Manuel that he heard the plash of fountains everywhere. A thaw had set in. Water was gushing from the stone corbels and along the gutters, fraying into little rivulets between the pointed cobblestones so typical of old Spain, and tumbling over them with the sound of miniature mountain torrents, amid the pictures, scraps of furniture, pots and pans, and miscellaneous wreckage in the street. Not an animal had stayed in Brihuega; but now, like homeless cats, the milicianos were to be seen prowling from one street to another, in the desolation murmurous with running water.

As Manuel approached the centre of the town another sound mingled with that of rippling water, in a counterpoint of limpid harmonies – the tinkle of a piano. The front wall of a house he was passing had collapsed into the street, leaving all the dwelling-rooms open to the sky; in one of them a miliciano was picking out the notes of a popular song with one finger. Manuel listened attentively; now across the water-music of the street he made out the sounds of three pianos. Nothing like the 'International'; the tunes were those of sentimental refrains, but played so slowly that they might have been in homage to the infinite pathos of the slopes, strewn with derelict lorries, that rose from Brihuega towards the livid sky.

Manuel had told Gartner that he had given up music, but he suddenly realized that what he needed most at this moment – alone in the street of a conquered town – was to hear some music. He had no desire to play, himself, and he wanted to remain alone. There were two gramophones in the Brigade messroom. He had discarded the records which he had carried about with him in the early days of the war, but the big gramophone cabinet was well stocked. Gartner was a German.

He found some Beethoven symphonies and the *Adieux*. He was no more than a half-hearted admirer of Beethoven, but that made no difference. Taking the smaller gramophone into his room, he set it going. Now that the tension of his will relaxed, the past came into its own. He remembered his exact gesture when he had handed over his revolver to Alba. Perhaps, as Ximenes said, he had found the life he was meant for. He was

461

born to war, born to the responsibility of death. Like the sleep-walker who wakes up suddenly on the edge of a roof, he felt the dying cadence of the music bringing home to him the terrible precariousness of his mental foothold; any false step might land him in ... a shambles! Another memory crossed his mind – of a blind beggar he had seen in Madrid on the night of Carabanchel. Manuel had been with the Chief of Police, in his car, when suddenly the headlights had lit up a blind man's out-stretched fingers, magnifying their form against the steep upward slope of the Gran Via to a prodigious size, showing them humped and gnarled against the cobbles, criss-crossed by the pavements, and momentarily effaced by the few cars which the war had not driven from the streets – long, groping hands, long as the hands of Fate.

'Kilometre 95! Kilometre 95!' men were shouting in all parts of the town, always with the same intonation.

He felt the seething life around him charged with portents, as though some blind destiny lay in wait for him behind those lowering cloudbanks which the guns no longer racked. The Alsatian was listening, lying full length like the dogs in bas-reliefs. Some day there would be peace. And he, Manuel, would become another man, someone he could not visualize as yet; just as the soldier he had become could no more visualize the Manuel who once had bought a little 'bus' to go ski-ing in the Sierra.

Most likely it was the same with all those others moving through the streets, and the same with the men he could hear strumming their favourite tunes on pianos open to the public gaze – the men whose heavy pointed cowls had led the battle yesterday. Once it had been deliberate contemplation that had taught Manuel about himself; now it fell to chance to snatch him from the activities of the moment and force his mind upon his past. And, like himself, like all those others, drained of her blood, Spain, too, was growing conscious of herself – as in the hour of death, suddenly, a man takes stock of all his life. ... But war may be discovered only once in a lifetime; life, many times.

As the strands of melody took form, interwoven with his past, they conveyed to him the self-same message that the dim sky, those ageless fields, and that town which had stopped the Moors might, too, have given him. For the first time Manuel was hearing the voice of that which is more awe-inspiring even than the blood of men, more enigmatic even than their presence on the earth – the infinite possibilities of their destiny. And he felt that this new consciousness within him was linked up with the sounds of running water in the street and the footfalls of the prisoners, profound and permanent as the beating of his heart.